LIBERATOR

Other books by Bryan Davis

Dragons of Starlight series

Starlighter

Warrior

Diviner

Echoes from the Edge series

Beyond the Reflection's Edge

Eternity's Edge

Nightmare's Edge

Dragons in Our Midst series

Raising Dragons

The Candlestone

Circles of Seven

Tears of a Dragon

Oracles of Fire series

Eye of the Oracle

Enoch's Ghost

Last of the Nephilim

The Bones of Makaidos

DrAgons
OF STARLIGHT

LIBERATOR

BRYAN DAVIS

ZONDERVAN®

ZONDERVAN.com/
AUTHORTRACKER
follow your favorite authors

ZONDERVAN

Liberator
Copyright © 2012 by Bryan Davis

This title is also available as a Zondervan ebook.
Visit www.zondervan.com/ebooks.

Requests for information should be addressed to:
Zondervan, *Grand Rapids, Michigan 49530*

Library of Congress Cataloging-in-Publication Data

CIP applied for: 978-0-310-71839-0

Cover design: Mike Heath/Magnus Creative
Interior design: Carlos Eluterio Estrada
Interior composition: Greg Johnson, Textbook Perfect

Printed in the United States of America

13 14 15 16 17 18 /DCI/ 19 18 17 16 15 14 13 12 11 10 9 8 7 6 5 4 3 2

LIBERATOR

one

$\mathcal{J}$ason steadied himself on the stone-movers' raft and scanned the sky from horizon to horizon. Still within the confines of the Southlands, he dipped his steering pole into the river as quietly as possible. Elyssa had said dragons lurked in the area, and her Diviner's gift of detecting a presence in the air or hidden in the shadows seemed as sharp as ever. At least one fire-breather was out there ... somewhere.

As he, Elyssa, and Koren floated northward on the river's slow current, clouds hovered low to the east over the Zodiac's spires, drifting closer on a freshening breeze. The western view revealed a forest beyond the river-bank — peaceful and quiet. Now late in the day, Solarus had already settled near the treetops. They would have to make camp soon, but definitely not until the dragons' village lay well behind them. Although no scaly-winged beasts sailed or shuffled anywhere in sight, sleep would come more easily if they could put some distance between the dragons' abode and their intended camping spot.

Jason allowed his gaze to settle on the forest once more. Somewhere in that area Randall and Tibalt marched in search of Wallace and the cattle-camp children, meaning the lack of a dragon patrol was good news. Maybe they would find the refugees in time to warn them about the deadly disease spreading through Starlight, a hard-enough task even without dragon interference. Since the disease was so contagious, and since Randall and Tibalt had both been exposed, providing a warning while staying at a safe distance would require more than a little ingenuity.

Turning to the front of the raft, Jason looked straight ahead. The first obstacle to their journey stood due north: the great barrier wall separating the Southlands region from the rest of Starlight, the same barrier that imprisoned hundreds of slaves and kept them from escaping the dragon kingdom. Now he and his friends had to break out and travel beyond the forbidden boundary.

Less than an hour earlier, the dragon Arxad had assured them that the wall was clear of guardian dragons when he passed by. He had escorted his daughter, Xenith, part of the way to the Northlands as she ferried Cassabrie's finger to Uriel Blackstone, who they hoped could use the girl's genetic material to find a cure for the disease the punctured Exodus star had unleashed on the world.

Arxad then returned to the dragon village to care for his injured mate, Fellina. He offered the humans no direct transport, only a brief message describing how to get past the wall—vague advice based on what he had been told by those who constructed that section centuries ago. Still, if his advice proved reliable, easy passage would help them avoid a delay they couldn't afford.

With the army from Jason's home planet of Major Four marching southward from the Northlands, and Taushin, the new dragon king, planning to send a diseased human into their ranks in order to infect the soldiers, someone had to warn the troops to stay away from the contagion. Since Elyssa was immune to the disease, she was the only one who could deliver the warning safely, making her transport vital.

Jason glanced down at his chest. Although Cassabrie's finger embedded under his skin seemed to provide immunity for him as well, no one knew how long the protection would last. Though if danger cropped up, he would go in Elyssa's place.

He settled to a sitting position and laid the steering pole next to his sword near the raft's left edge. Built for moving stones from the mining pits to the barrier wall, the raft seemed quite steady, easily carrying its three riders—he and Elyssa near the front, and Koren closer to the back—as well as two gunny sacks filled with food and extra clothing.

Still aching from cuts, scrapes, and bruises he suffered in his battle with a dragon named Hyborn, Jason let his muscles relax. The Southland's warm weather drew sweat from his pores, but the long-sleeved tunic and cloak would feel much more comfortable when they reached the frozen Northlands.

Elyssa and Koren were also recovering from wounds, though a gap in Elyssa's hair was now the most noticeable result of their recent battles. Her glow from consuming a stardrop had faded, but it seemed that the manna pendant dangling from a chain around her neck still carried a slight radiance, the remnant glow from a recent healing.

During the first part of their journey, Elyssa had been chatty, providing updates on sensations she felt as they procured the raft and provisions. Lately, however, she had grown quiet and somber.

Koren, sitting cross-legged with her cloak's hood pulled over her head, had hardly uttered a word — just a thank you whenever Jason helped her move from place to place. With the Exodus disease ravaging her body, she seemed to be getting feebler by the hour. Her face had turned pale, a stark contrast to the physical traits of a Starlighter — red hair poking out around the edges of her hood and sparkling green eyes.

Less than a quarter mile away now, the wall loomed. The uneven stones, cobbled together with pebbly mortar, seemed to rise before them as the raft drifted closer on the placid current. They would arrive in a few moments.

Leaning close to Elyssa, Jason whispered, "Do you sense anything?"

"I still sense a dragon, if that's what you mean, but I can't tell how close it is. I don't detect anger or a heightened sense of alertness." She rubbed her thumb and finger together. Her eyes, not quite as green as Koren's, gleamed in the sunlight. "I sense a change, the way the air feels after a bolt of lightning strikes nearby."

Jason searched the sky again. Though the clouds to the east seemed benign, it was wise to heed Elyssa's gifts of perception. Hers may be subtler talents than Koren's vivid abilities, just as her auburn hair seemed a shadow of Koren's more striking red, yet the two girls were equally remarkable. "I don't see any storms," he said. "What else could be causing what you're feeling?"

Koren spoke up, her voice wispy. "The history of Starlight holds many mysteries. It's obvious that humans lived here long before we slaves arrived, and they were far more advanced than humans today, either on Starlight or on Darksphere. I didn't really understand Arxad's description of how we're supposed to get past the wall, but when we try, I think we might learn a lot about what the earliest humans here were able to do—and what is signaling Elyssa."

Jason nodded. Arxad's instructions were puzzling, something about an opening at the river's surface and a lever near that spot. As one of the oldest dragons, the high priest of the land, he was privy to many ancient secrets, and now one of those secrets was about to come to light.

After another minute, the raft's front end bumped against the wall, and the current turned it until the side abutted a mortared gap between two vertically stacked rough stones. The slight collision made Jason's sword clink against the steering pole.

Jason pressed his palms against the stone, pushed the raft back a few inches, and looked at the line where the water met the wall. According to Arxad, a spillway had been cut into the stones somewhere, but since the water level fluctuated seasonally, he wasn't sure if the opening would be exposed.

"This is where the Diviner comes in," Jason said. "Can you probe for a hole and a lever?"

Elyssa rose to her knees and laid a hand on the wall. "It's too dense to probe through, but I'll look for a hole of some kind." Closing her eyes, she rubbed her fingers along the imperfections, as if tickling the nooks and knobs. Tiny twitches and flinches danced across her face, as if her skin had taken on the dips and divots her mind searched through. Finally, her brow arched. "I think I see something. Move us a little to the left."

Pushing against the wall, Jason shifted the raft, first a few inches, then a couple of feet.

"Wait!" Elyssa called, her eyes still closed. "Keep it right there!"

He held the raft in place. "What do you see?"

"A gap of some kind." She opened her eyes and pointed at the river. "Down there. Just below the surface."

Jason reached into the water and felt the wall. About six inches down, the stone gave way to a hole. A wooden grating covered the opening, allowing water to pass through. "Found it."

"Do you feel a lever?" she asked.

"No. Do you see one?"

Elyssa drew in the air with a finger. "I think there's a cave behind the wall, and I sense a protrusion jutting into it."

"Into it?" Jason pushed the grating, but it wouldn't give way. "If the lever's on the inside, I can't reach it from here."

"Jason!" Elyssa hissed. "A dragon! Straight up!"

Above, a dragon perched atop the wall's parapet and looked straight down at them, its wings extended as if ready to swoop. Webbed spikes fanned out behind its head, and fangs appeared over its scaly lips. Beginning with a growl, it shouted, "How dare you humans approach the wall!"

Jason inched his hand toward his sword. "We are here at Arxad's bidding."

"Arxad has no authority to grant such permission." The dragon reared back its head. "Now you will die!"

Koren lifted a hand. "Wait!"

The dragon looked at her, blinking. "Why should I?"

"Because I said so." Koren slid her hood back, revealing her scarlet locks. "I am a Starlighter. You must listen to me. I am no danger to you."

"No danger," the dragon repeated, its eyes becoming glazed. When it glanced at Jason, they began clarifying again. "He has a weapon."

"Ignore the other humans!" Gasping for breath as more color drained from her cheeks, Koren kept her gaze on the dragon. "You must pay heed only to me."

The dragon's head swayed from side to side, its eyes locked on Koren as she rocked with the gentle waves. "Only to you."

"While you're talking," Elyssa whispered as she slid into the river, "I'll find the lever."

"Elyssa!" Jason lunged, but she submerged before he could catch her hand. The sudden shift tipped the raft, sending him over the side. He popped to the surface and slung water from his hair. She was nowhere in sight.

Koren clutched the side of the raft, steadying herself. Her stare still fixed on the dragon, she waved at Jason. "Find her! I'm all right!"

Jason dove. His eyes open in the clear water, he probed the area. The wooden slats covering the hole were broken at the center, creating an opening big enough to fit into. With a quick stroke, he glided through the breach and into darker water, too dark to see beyond a few feet.

He swam straight ahead until a second wall blocked his progress. A narrower, cruder hole had been cut into the stone, leading down and away. It seemed big enough for a slender person to fit into, but Elyssa, who had once again skipped steps, was far too smart to venture into a death trap like that.

He pushed to the surface and looked around. A few feet above the water, Elyssa clutched a wooden rod protruding from the wall, her knees pushing against the stone as she struggled for leverage. Water dripped from her hair and clothes. "I can't get it to move," she grunted.

"Are you sure we want it to? Maybe it's not the right—"

"Augh!" The lever jerked downward. Elyssa slipped away and splashed into the river. Jason pulled her to the surface and held her trousers waistband to keep her steady.

"Thanks." Water sprayed from her lips. "The river tastes different under here, sort of acidic."

"I didn't notice." Jason glanced around the dim cave. The two walls blocked movement upstream and downstream, but it was too dark to see how far the water extended to the sides. "Any other sensations?"

A loud clunk sounded, then a buzzing hum.

Elyssa lifted her hand and felt the air. "Heavy static. Something big is happening."

A creaking sound echoed. As pebbles drizzled into the water, twin vertical gaps appeared in the downstream wall about ten feet apart, and a horizontal line joined the two gaps at the top. Above, the humming sound heightened. Sparks arced across the ceiling from wall to wall, like miniature lightning bolts, revealing a set of wheels connected by a long belt. The wheels spun furiously, driving the belt and a notched wheel on one side. The mechanism appeared to be sitting on a shelf-like protrusion from the downstream wall, but the intermittent sparks provided only brief glimpses.

The newly formed wall section pushed outward, and water rushed toward the opening, dragging Jason and Elyssa with the flow. Still holding Elyssa's trousers, Jason lunged for the lever and hung on with one hand. With his legs dangling in the current and with Elyssa half submerged, the current pounded against them, making his grip slide down the rod. Since the exit was now much bigger than the hole they had entered, the river's surface descended. With support from the water lessening, their weight seemed to increase with every passing second.

Another clunk reverberated through the cave. More rocks fell. Two vertical gaps appeared on the upstream wall. As if copying the downstream wall, the section began to push inward, bringing in a fresh rush of water. The surge slapped them from the lever, wrenched Elyssa from Jason's grip, and sent them hurtling downstream.

Jason tumbled in multiple somersaults, making it impossible to tell up from down. Water ran up his nose, and gritty silt stung his eyes. After several seconds, the current slowed. Still disoriented, he focused on a light and swam toward it, glancing in every direction in search of Elyssa.

When he broke the surface, he gasped for air. No sign of her, either in the water or on the banks. After taking a deep breath, he dove again. No longer dizzy, he searched the depths, now becoming clearer as the turbulence settled. Grass grew here and there in tufts, and bristly heather covered most of the terrain.

A dark, humanlike shape appeared at the bottom. Jason thrust his arms and kicked, whipping his body into a fast glide. As he neared the shape, Elyssa's form clarified. Her foot appeared to be wedged under a log, anchored in place by a boulder. Her limp arms undulated with the current, and her face and closed eyelids stayed slack.

Jason surged toward the log, shoved his hands under it, and heaved it away. He grabbed Elyssa around the waist and kicked toward the riverbank. When he reached shallow water, he trudged up toward a grassy shore, dragging her limp body, but with the river still spreading out over the flat meadow, it seemed that dry ground and a place to lay her retreated as quickly as he could walk.

"Jason! I'm coming!" Koren drove the raft toward him, standing as she thrust the pole into the river, her cloak fanning out behind her. By the time she reached him, he stood in thigh-deep water.

His heart racing, he rolled Elyssa onto the logs. Her lips were blue and her limbs slack. He pressed his ear against her chest. No heartbeat. No breathing. Nothing at all.

Heat surged through his skin. Bile spilled into his throat, burning as he tried to speak. "She's ... she's gone!"

"Maybe not yet! Exodus is showing me something." Koren dropped to her knees, slid her hands over Elyssa's chest, and began thrusting down with rhythmic repetition, making the raft bob wildly.

Jason swallowed down the bile and grabbed the edge of the raft. Her green eyes flashing, Koren nodded at Elyssa's head. "You have to help! Blow into her mouth! You'll have to pinch her nose and seal her mouth with your lips so the air goes into her lungs."

While Koren eased away, Jason pinched Elyssa's nose, set his lips around hers, and blew. Her chest expanded, but when he pulled back, nothing happened. She remained blue and motionless.

Koren returned to her task, her body rocking with the raft as she continued thrusting. "Oh, Jason!" Her voice weakened, and her face again grew pale. "I don't know if I'm doing this right. The images are so blurry!"

"Should I blow air into her again?"

Tears now streaming, Koren nodded and pulled back, giving him room.

Jason took a breath and blew into Elyssa's mouth. Her chest rose, then sank. She lay motionless, limp, and silent.

Koren set her hands on Elyssa's chest. Her thrusts punctuated her words. "Keep … doing … it…. Don't … stop…. Both at … the same time."

With the raft shifting and tilting, Jason's lips kept sliding away from Elyssa's. He lifted her head and held it still as he blew again and again. *This has to work! Koren's vision has to be true!*

Out of the corner of his eye, light flashed. A fireball slammed into the edge of the raft, and flames splattered across the surface. As the sloshing water doused the fire around her knees, Koren continued shoving down on Elyssa's chest.

The guardian dragon dove at them. Jason and Koren ducked under its surging claws. Jason reached for the sword, but Koren batted his hand away. "Keep breathing into her! Get on the raft while I talk to the dragon! The farther we get from the wall, the better!"

Jason pushed off the riverbed and thrust the raft into the current, sliding onto the logs in the same motion. He knelt next to Elyssa and again pressed his lips over hers. As he breathed into her lungs, sucking in a breath after each blow, Koren kept thrusting against Elyssa's chest while shouting toward the sky. "Pay heed to me again ... guardian of the wall! ... If you wish to ... protect your domain ... leave us be! ... We are fleeing ... your protective flames ... and have no desire to ... pass the barrier!"

As they rode the current downstream, the dragon flew toward them from behind, its toothy maw spitting sizzling wads of fire. "I will ensure that you make haste!" With its forelegs extended, it grabbed the back edge of the raft with its claws. Beating its wings, it propelled them forward, faster and faster.

While Jason continued breathing into Elyssa's mouth, the sound of rushing water reached his ears. As the rush became a roar, the current grew swifter. A rising spray appeared in the distance. He glanced at the steering pole lying on the raft. He couldn't stop breathing into Elyssa to battle the dragon or try to halt their momentum. She would die. Only one option remained—ride it out.

Jason hugged Elyssa close, still breathing into her. The raft hurtled toward the falls. The front tipped over the precipice and stopped. Below, the water cascaded down a steep slope of grass and rocks, including boulders partially hidden by violent splashes.

"Leave us be!" Koren shouted, her voice failing. "You must ... pay heed to me!"

"As you wish." The dragon lifted off, calling as it ascended, "Pay heed to yourself, Starlighter. You are weaker than you realize."

TWO

As water gushed from behind, the raft teetered in place. Spray cascaded all around. Koren pointed at the sky. "Look!" A different dragon flew northward, carrying a human in its claws. "He's taking Yeager to your army."

Jason pushed another breath into Elyssa. Her chest lifted, then settled again to a motionless state. "We have to warn them!" His arms trembling, he grabbed the steering pole, lurched to the front, and jammed it against the rock. Pulling against the pole with his full weight, he battled the jamming stone and the pounding current.

Finally, the raft broke free and surged backwards several feet. With water splashing and sloshing over her body, Koren snatched the supply bags and held them in her lap. Jason threw the pole down, hooked elbows with Koren, and scooped Elyssa into his arms.

As the raft again reached the precipice, this time missing the stone, Jason leaned backwards. "Here we go!"

The raft slid onto the slope and streaked down the rushing current. Bumping and bouncing, Koren clutched a side while Jason tightened his grip on her arm and Elyssa's body. Water crashed over the front and splashed into their faces, veiling the path ahead and the sky above. As the raft rattled, the logs shook against the binding vines, as if ready to fly apart at any moment.

A boulder protruded straight ahead, only seconds away. Still clutching both girls, Jason lunged over the edge of the raft and slammed against a flat stone just inches below the river's surface. The force ripped Koren from his grasp. With Elyssa clutched tightly in his arms, he tumbled down the slope, turning somersaults in the shallow water and bouncing against the riverbed again and again.

Finally, he slid to a stop on his bottom, Elyssa in his lap, and the water beating against his lower back. While thrusting on her chest with one hand, he pinched her nose with the other and blew into her mouth, once ... twice ... three times. *Come on! Breathe!*

Still carrying the supply bags, Koren sloshed toward him from downstream. With every step, she teetered back and forth, and water dripped from her hair and her sagging cloak.

Jason pressed his lips over Elyssa's once again and blew hard. She coughed, sending a stream of water into his mouth. He pulled back a few inches. A strand of saliva still connected their lips. She spat, breaking the connection, then heaved in a constricted breath, making a wheezing noise as precious air squeezed into her lungs.

Koren splashed to a stop at his side. "Give her room! Let her sit up!"

Jason slid Elyssa from his lap and helped her sit in the water. While blocking the current with his body, he slapped her on the back. She drew in breath after breath, each one easier than the last, and each exhale finishing with another cough. Wet, stringy hair covered her eyes. Her head continued swaying as if she were bouncing on a stormy sea. "I think—" She coughed again. "I think we made it."

Jason swallowed a hard lump. His heart pounded, and his own breathing rattled. "I guess you could say that."

He rose to his feet and helped her stand in the calf-deep water. Pieces of the raft floated by—broken logs, some with torn vines still attached. Her clothes clung to her body, outlining her rail-thin frame, the result of weeks in the dungeon. "Good thing I found that lever," Elyssa said as she pushed her hair out of her face.

"Right." Koren, her voice weak, arched her brow at Jason. "Good thing."

Elyssa glanced at Jason and Koren in turn. "You two look awfully worried about something."

Koren narrowed her eyes. "You act like dying happens to you all the time."

"Dying?" Elyssa blinked rapidly. "What do you mean? I just swallowed some water the wrong way."

Koren shook her head. "Your heart stopped for a long time. You weren't breathing."

Elyssa's skin paled. "Did you revive me?"

"Jason did." Koren nodded at him. "I helped, but he did most of it."

"Not really," Jason said. "Koren showed me how."

Elyssa stared at Jason, tears trickling down her cheeks and blending with the river water. She threw her arms around him and held him close. Her body trembling, she whispered into his ear. "Thank you."

"You're welcome." He returned the embrace. With wet clothes pressing against his skin, the contact raised a chill.

Jason pulled back and brushed a wet strand of hair from Elyssa's eyes. "Are you sure you're all right?"

"I'm okay." Offering a weak smile, she grabbed a fistful of hair and began wringing it out. "I mean, I nearly died. Give a girl a break."

After tossing her wet hair over her shoulder, Elyssa took one of the supply bags from Koren. Water streamed from the bottom. "I guess the food will be all right. Just soaked."

"Probably." Jason looked at his boots through the river's clear water. "While you two get to dry land, I'll look for my sword."

He slogged upstream to the boulder where the raft met its demise. Near the upstream side, the blade lay in the bending grass, gleaming in the sunlight. He snatched it up by the hilt and hustled back to the girls, who now stood at the river's edge, squeezing out the edges of their clothes.

He propped the sword against his shoulder and surveyed the river upstream and downstream. They had tumbled into a meadow and now stood in a field of grass and flowers. The river curved toward the west where it spilled into its original north-flowing channel and proceeded on its way at a pedestrian pace. To the south of that spillway, the old channel carried only a small stream that originated from a rocky slope. From that section of the slope, lying to the west of their wild ride, water trickled from several holes, giving evidence that the river once exited from those springs, the river's escape route when the wall blocked the flow. "It looks pretty calm downstream."

Koren gazed at the sky, her face paler than ever. "And no sign of either dragon. Maybe things will get easier for a while."

Elyssa squinted. "Either dragon?"

"We saw a dragon carrying Yeager while you were napping." Jason winked. "Let's get going. Maybe Koren will tell the tale, and you can see what happened."

After taking the second bag of supplies from Koren, he followed the edge of the river, Koren to his left and Elyssa to his right. Their wet clothes swept through calf-high grass and flowers, raising a sweet fragrance from the red and yellow four-leaf-clover-shaped blossoms.

When they reached the river's original channel, Jason stopped and scanned the forest beyond the opposite bank, his sword hilt tight in his grip. Maybe the dragon carrying Yeager hid within, waiting for the army from Major Four to arrive. If the dragon took notice of the three escaping humans, would it try to stop them? Taushin had said in the other dragons' presence that Koren would likely overhear their plans, so if a hidden dragon recognized her, it might realize that they were on a mission to warn the soldiers.

Elyssa and Koren joined Jason, one on each side. Elyssa slid her arm around his and leaned her head against his shoulder. "What are you thinking?"

He cocked his head to look at her, but her face stayed out of view. He whispered in reply. "The dragon that carried Yeager. We have to watch for him."

She pulled away. Narrowing her eyes, she stared into the forest. "I sense a presence, something smaller than a dragon. Not human."

"I know there are wolves around," Koren said. "I was dragged through this area by the leader of a pack."

Jason looked down at the muddy riverbank in front of his boots. Paw prints drew a line parallel to the river, pointing northward. If the wolves were smart enough to walk single file, there could be dozens. "It looks like we might have company."

"Someone else has been here." Elyssa pointed across the river. "I see markings in that tree, the big one closest to the bank."

Jason set the supplies bag down and waded across the river, trudging through waist-deep water and soft sand at the bottom. When he arrived at the tree, he set the point of the sword on the mark. Someone had carved a large letter *M* in the trunk at about chest level. A line radiated from the center of the top of the *M* and pointed to the left at an angle of less than ten degrees. "It's Adrian's mark," he called. "He was here early in the morning, just after sunrise."

"Today?" Koren asked from the opposite side.

Jason shifted the point to the base of the *M*. Tiny spheres rested within the notch. He dug them out with a finger and laid them in his palm, five brown kernels no bigger than grass seeds. He pivoted and looked across the river where Elyssa and Koren stood next to the supply bags, both watching with tired stares. Still wet, their shoulders slumped under the weight of their clothes. "What number day is this since we got here?" he asked.

Elyssa looked at her hand, raising a finger every few seconds until she had extended all four and a thumb. "This is day number five."

Jason dropped the seeds to the ground. "He was here this morning."

"Can you tell if he's heading north?"

He looked again. A line protruded from the bottom-right leg of the *M*, pointing to the right. "He is."

"Alone?" Elyssa asked.

Laughing under his breath, he looked across the river again. "How much do you think I can tell from a mark in a tree?"

Elyssa wrinkled her nose. "I thought you Masters boys might have a whole language made out of tree carvings."

"He was not alone." Koren raised her wet hood over her head. Her green eyes sparkled brightly. "He is accompanied by friends."

Adrian appeared, carving the bark with the point of a sword. Semitransparent and completely white, he looked like the ghostly girls who lived in the Northlands. Wallace stood nearby, gripping the handles of a cart that held someone inside. A girl stood next to Wallace, and a bald child, perhaps another girl, sat on the ground in front of the cart.

Adrian blew into the carving, scattering dust. He and Wallace spoke to each other, but no sound came from their lips. Adrian poured seeds from his palm into the carving and kept his fingertip over them until they stayed in place. He studied his mark for a moment, then marched northward. Wallace pushed the cart behind Adrian, and the two girls shuffled along at each side, their heads and shoulders low.

As the cart passed, Jason looked inside. Partially covered by an animal skin, Marcelle lay curled on a bed of straw. Her eyes were open in an unblinking stare. A few seconds later, the entire company faded and vanished from sight.

Jason turned slowly toward the girls. Koren knelt at the edge of the river, shivering. Elyssa crouched next to her and hugged her from the side. With the Exodus disease ravaging Koren's body, the effort to tell a tale had likely sapped her reserves.

Sword still in hand, he hurried across the river and laid an arm over Koren's shoulders, linking arms with Elyssa. "Do you have the strength to go on?"

She nodded, her face locked in a grimace. "I don't think I have a choice."

"True, but we're still a long way from the Northlands." Jason looked at the river. Pieces of the broken raft drifted by, some still bound together. If only the raft had survived, they could ride the current at least as far as the waterfall.

"I sense something new." Elyssa closed her eyes. "In the forest. I think it's a dragon. He's perplexed. Uncertain as to what to do."

"How close is he?" Jason asked.

"It's hard to tell. I normally can't sense a living presence outside of hearing range, so it's probably pretty close, but since a dragon is so big, maybe it's farther than I think."

Jason combed the forest with his gaze. Maybe the dragon carrying Yeager could be persuaded to carry Koren instead, but could she summon the energy to hypnotize it? How far might it be willing to take her?

Cupping a hand around his mouth, Jason shouted, "Dragon! If you can hear me, come forth. I want to speak to you."

"Jason! What are you doing?"

"Skipping steps." He tossed his sword to the side. "I am now unarmed. I know you are contemplating your next move. Come to the riverbank. Maybe we can help each other."

A rustle disturbed the silence, then a rumbling growl penetrated the trees from deep within the forest. "How do you know what I am contemplating?"

"You are carrying Yeager, the diseased human, in an attempt to infect the approaching army. Yet you have stopped here in the forest, and you're wondering what to do next. My guess is that Yeager has died, and you're unsure if he is contagious any longer."

"You are perceptive ... for a vermin." The rustling continued. A human flew out from between two trees and landed on the opposite bank. When he flopped over face-up, his diseased arm slapped the water. Yeager was barely recognizable. Sores covered his face, and most of his hair had fallen out, revealing ulcers on his scalp and a missing ear.

Elyssa gasped. Koren swallowed but said nothing.

The dragon pushed himself between two trees and shuffled closer. His head swayed at the end of his curled neck, and his wings fluttered, half-extended. When he stopped, he grabbed Yeager's torn shirt with a foreclaw and lifted him a few inches. "He died only moments ago. The disease is hungry. It is merciless."

Jason glanced at Koren. She had pulled her hood low over her eyes, making her expression difficult to read. So far, she had stayed silent. He would have to persuade the dragon himself.

"The disease kills quickly," Jason said, "so you need another victim, someone who is still alive."

The dragon's brow slanted. "Why would a human suggest a living victim to be used to infect other humans?"

Jason touched the top of Koren's head. "We hope to find a cure in the Northlands. She will die soon if we don't get help."

"Yours is a believable answer." The dragon dropped Yeager back to the ground. "Now tell me why I should help you spoil our best defense against the human army that seeks to invade our domain?"

"Unless you deliver a living victim of the disease, you can't be sure of fulfilling your mission, and returning to Taushin without that assurance might be fatal to you. While you hope for infection, we hope for a cure. If we are successful, which is far from guaranteed, that won't be your fault. You will have accomplished your task."

"How do you hope to find a cure? If I deposit her in the path of an advancing army south of the Northlands, she will not reach the destination you desire."

"Wherever you wish to leave her, we will take her the rest of the way, even if it means exposing the army to the disease. So we need you to carry all three of us on your back and—"

"No."

"No?" Jason drew his head back. "Then how will you deliver an infected human if you don't take her?"

"I will take her. Alone." The dragon beat his wings and lunged toward them, his foreclaws extended. He dug them into Koren's shoulders and zoomed upward.

Koren cried out. Jason leaped and swiped a hand at her foot but missed. Within seconds the dragon ascended above the treetops and sailed toward the north, Koren dangling underneath.

Jason snatched up his sword and chopped down on a branch floating by in the water. "I can't believe it! What a fool I am!"

"Stop it!" Elyssa grabbed his arm and gave it a shake. "Don't punish yourself. It was a good idea."

"Not good enough. I didn't think he would—"

"It doesn't matter." She pulled him into the river and began slogging across. "Let's get moving. He has a huge head start."

Jason followed her lead to the opposite bank and then northward along the edge. "Why this side?"

Now jogging steadily, she pointed at the eastern bank. "The wolves are over there." She then pointed to the west. "Your brother's mark was over here. Maybe he'll give us more clues."

"Good thinking, as usual." Jason caught up and kept pace at her side. "There's no way we can catch up with him, and it'll be dark soon."

"I know," she said, her eyes staying fixed on the path.

Still gripping his sword tightly, Jason said nothing more, glancing between the muddy, root-infested ground underneath and the trees to his left. So far no wolf tracks, marks on trees, or human prints appeared. Since Marcelle's cart probably would have bogged down in the mud, Adrian must have traveled in the forest.

Ahead, the northbound stream would soon tumble into a chasm. They would have to cross before that point and travel to the chasm's east before finding the southbound stream and following it northward. Many miles lay between them and Koren, and not a single one would be easy, especially after nightfall.

❧

Standing in the forest clearing on Major Four, Edison shed his cloak and laid it on the ground. As he drew his sword, he let his eyes dart from one section of the forest to the other. With Solarus high in the sky, light streamed through the branches above, providing plenty of illumination. No one could sneak up without warning. Just a few steps away across the portal, the same sun hovered at a similar angle, though it should have been near evening on Starlight. For some reason, Solarus never seemed to set in the Northlands.

Orion stood next to him, wrapped in a thick, ankle-length black cloak in spite of the warmer temperature on their side of the portal. "Any sign of Marcelle? Or anyone else, for that matter?"

"We'll see." Edison sniffed the air. Although a variety of aromas entered his nostrils—oak, mold, and deer feces—no human scent blended in. Yet a relatively new odor drifted by, one recently learned. As he exhaled, he raised his sword. "I smell a dragon."

Orion swiveled toward the portal. "Should we run?"

"Not yet." Edison sniffed again. This time the odor of sweaty humans became evident, and rustling noises followed. "Soldiers are coming. I don't think Magnar will show his face yet."

Soon a line of soldiers dressed in heavy coats, double-thick trousers, and leather boots tramped through the underbrush. Their faces reflecting both nervousness and resolve, they marched around the edges of the clearing and organized themselves in concentric circles, each with a scabbard strapped at his hip and a rectangular shield at his side.

The leader, a middle-aged man with a graying beard, broad shoulders, and a slender waist, stopped in front of Edison and saluted with the traditional arm across the chest. He carried a canvas knapsack stitched with an officer's insignia. "I am Captain Reed. I assume you are Edison Masters."

"I am." Edison sheathed his sword and returned the salute. Turning his gaze back to the men, he raised an eyebrow as he took stock of the company's weapons. "No photo guns?"

"They are slow to reload and unpredictable in rapidly changing conditions. Whenever they're around, soldiers tend to rely on them too heavily. I prefer that they rely only on muscles, minds, and blades."

"Well spoken." Edison touched a sheathed dagger at his hip, then his sword at the opposite hip. "I prefer sharp metal to bursts of light anytime." He took in a long draw of the moist air. "Prepare your men for battle. There is a powerful dragon hereabouts, and he could strike with a barrage of flames at any moment."

Captain Reed glanced up, as did many of the arriving soldiers. "If you are speaking of Magnar, you may be surprised to learn that he is acting as our ally. It would seem he wishes to topple a usurper on the dragon planet." Captain Reed reached into his bag and withdrew a finger-length dragon spine. "He allowed us to carry out a mock battle with him so we could learn typical dragon maneuvers. One of my men became too aggressive and removed this spine from Magnar's tail. He was furious, and I thought he would incinerate the soldier, but he quickly cooled and congratulated my man on an excellent attack."

"Very interesting." Edison cocked his head. "How did you become friendly with him?"

"The sword maiden Marcelle established the alliance."

"Where is she now?"

Captain Reed nodded toward the sky. "Riding on Magnar's back. I assume they're flying close by and waiting to be sure the portal is open. She hasn't told me her plans. She is a very mysterious young woman."

"Yes," Orion said in a low tone, "we noticed. A chilling personality, to be sure."

Captain Reed returned the dragon spine to his bag. "Where is this portal Marcelle told me about?"

Edison swept an arm toward the space behind him. "It's invisible. Anyone who walks from here toward the other side of the clearing will find himself in another world."

"How intriguing!" The captain leaned to see around Edison. "Shall we go into this other world now? Many of us are quite ready to embark on a new adventure."

Edison scanned the troops. Standing shoulder to shoulder, at least eighty men had filled the clearing except for the center section where he and the captain stood. A long line of soldiers waited to join them, perhaps another three to four hundred. Their eyes, wide and wandering, didn't confirm Captain Reed's assertion. Many were young and scared, not nearly as hardened as their commanding officer.

"Yes," Edison said, "we can go now." He stopped himself from saying more. As a former soldier himself, he had to stifle the instinct to tell Captain Reed all. He couldn't risk diluting the effect of what Cassabrie had planned.

"I will see if Cassabrie is ready for our arrival," Orion said, turning toward the portal.

"No!" The sound of dragon wings filled the air. Magnar swooped toward the ground, Marcelle riding low on his back. "Don't let him go!" she shouted. "He'll close the portal!"

Orion leaped through and disappeared. Magnar and Marcelle darted after him. In a flash of light, they both vanished.

Three

Cassabrie hovered within Exodus ten feet above the ground and thirty feet in front of the portal. The characters and setting for her tale were ready, but how long could she keep everything in place? Edison hadn't indicated the time of his return with any certainty.

She reached into her pocket. The tube she had taken from the spear that had punctured Exodus lay at the bottom, along with its control box. The words on the tube's scorched label still pulsed in her mind—*Danger. Explosive*.

Cassabrie shuddered. The grim reality of her plan had never felt so close. Soon every man, woman, and child on Starlight would have an opportunity to get a taste of what the true purpose of a Starlighter was all about.

Shaking off the thoughts, she scanned the area. To her left, a stream flowed through a pebbles-and-sand terrain.

Bare-chested children followed the shoreline, carrying buckets filled with stones, while a dragon with a whip kept watch on her right. Red, bleeding welts striped the children's backs, dirt smudged their cheeks, and gnats swarmed around their matted hair.

When one of the smallest girls neared the dragon, she stumbled and fell. The dragon beat her mercilessly with his whip while the other children looked on, stoic, hopeless, as if they were watching the same tale they had seen a hundred times before.

Although in reality, snow lay on the ground, Cassabrie had replaced it with arid landscape in order to simulate cattle-camp conditions, but removing the snow in the air presented a far more difficult challenge. No matter how effectively she might be able to mask the falling flakes, it would be nearly impossible to keep the soldiers from noticing snow accumulating on their heads and shoulders. At the very least, they would feel the cold wetness seeping through their clothing.

Cassabrie waved her arms. The line of children retreated and began a new march from left to right, as they had done a dozen times already. She would allow the scene to replay again and again until the soldiers arrived, for any man who could witness this cruelty without feeling a passion to rescue these poor waifs didn't have the heart they needed for the upcoming battle.

After the tenth repetition, rain began mixing with the snow. Soon every flake disappeared, replaced by a cold drizzle that only served to make the destitute children seem that much more pathetic, though a close observer would notice that they did not get wet.

Without warning, Orion lunged through the portal. He gave Cassabrie a quick glance, then stooped between a boulder and the line of crystalline pegs, a hand reaching toward the center one.

"Wait!" Cassabrie shouted. "Did Edison tell you to close the portal?"

Magnar burst through in full flight, his wings snapping out to propel him skyward. Behind him, Edison and a line of soldiers materialized out of thin air — ten, then twenty, then thirty, all marching in double-time past Orion. They blinked at the rain. Some held out open palms to feel the drops.

"No more!" Orion jerked out the peg and tucked it under his cloak. The stream of soldiers ended abruptly. The arriving men, perhaps fifty in number, halted and stared at Cassabrie's slavery scene, focusing on the children as they restarted their emotionless march.

Above, Magnar flew over the treetops toward the white dragon's castle. Although no one rode on his back, a scabbard hung from one of the protruding spines near the base of his neck, as if an invisible rider might snatch a sword from it and go to battle.

As vapor rose with every drop that struck Exodus's skin, Cassabrie looked at Magnar and sighed. He wouldn't come back, not as long as she was around. She wouldn't even have a chance to calm his fears. And now that he was here, what would his entry into the North-lands spell for all of Starlight? Only time would tell.

Orion held the peg over the boulder. "I will open the portal again," he said as water dripped from his hair to his lips. "When I do, these men will go back immediately.

I have rescinded the order to come here. If you refuse, I will break the crystal."

Edison glared at him through the misty air. "Then we will all be stranded here."

"There is another way to return," Orion said, "but even if it is inaccessible, I will not allow—"

"Orion!" Cassabrie called, spreading out her arms. "Hearken unto me!"

He looked at her, blinking the water from his eyes. "Stay out of this, witch! I will not have you interfering with the affairs of the righteous."

"Do the righteous ignore the plight of tormented children?" She waved an arm toward her mirage. "They toil. They suffer. They bleed. If you send the soldiers home, who will set them free? Who will apply salve to their wounds? Who will be their liberator?"

Orion tilted his head, watching the solemn parade of children passing by. When the girl stumbled, he flinched, and when the dragon lashed her with his whip, he fell to his knees and stared, the peg now loose in his hand.

Edison and the other soldiers looked on as well, mesmerized. Finally, one man broke free from his daze and charged toward the phantom dragon with a drawn sword.

Cassabrie fanned out her cloak. Making her characters respond would be difficult, but in their confused state, the men might be convinced, especially since her hypnotizing influence would make them want to believe.

Breaking from his previous iterations, the dragon turned his scaly head and shot a blast of fire. The soldier, a young man barely past his teen years, dodged left and rushed forward, thrusting his sword into the dragon's chest, where the blade plunged in easily. The dragon lurched to the side, his tail and claws twitching in spasmodic death throes.

Stooping, the soldier held out his arms. The children ran to him, some kissing his face while others formed a circle around him, jumping and cheering.

"Edison!" Cassabrie hissed. "Shake off the effect!"

Edison gave her a boyish smile. "He saved the girl. Isn't it wonder—"

"Wake up!" Cassabrie drove Exodus forward, just enough to bump his shoulder with the outer membrane.

Edison stumbled to the side but quickly regained his balance, blinking at her while rubbing his shoulder.

"Take the peg," Cassabrie whispered. "Open the portal."

As if awakened from slumber, he staggered toward Orion. Orion scrambled to his feet and, still holding the peg, jogged toward the forest, slipping and sliding along the way.

Cassabrie twirled her cloak and sent her scene into oblivion. She had done what she could.

Keeping his stare locked on the trees, Edison stopped his pursuit and waved a hand. "Captain Reed! Come here!"

A bearded soldier shuffled his way, his legs unstable. "What's happening here? I expected snow and ice and—"

"I will try to explain in a moment. For now, we have to retrieve Orion and the peg or else the other soldiers won't be able to join us."

"He will hide the crystal," Cassabrie said. "It's the only way he can maintain control."

Captain Reed raised a shielding hand, his face pale. "What kind of creature are you?"

"I am the guiding angel of Starlight." Cassabrie offered a graceful curtsy. "As the Creator's messenger, I have been called to tell tales that will instruct mankind."

"Amazing!" After shaking his head to clear his fog, Captain Reed forked his fingers at two men. "You two, kindly retrieve the former governor."

While the soldiers marched away, Captain Reed kicked at the slush. "So why the unexpected climate change?"

"Cassabrie?" Edison turned toward her. "Can you explain?"

Pivoting in place, Cassabrie scanned the landscape. The river now ran freely, with only a few ice floes drifting in the current. Gaps in the valley's white blanket appeared, revealing boulders and bare ground. Solarus hovered near the horizon, apparently ready to set.

Cassabrie set a hand on her hip. In all her years traveling to and fro on Starlight, Solarus had never descended this low before in the Northlands. Something dramatic had happened, but neither Alaph nor Arxad had warned about this possibility. The change had begun while Edison and Orion waited for the troops to arrive, and a more sudden disruption occurred when Magnar flew out. Perhaps he was close to the portal during the times Edison opened it to check for the troops, thereby causing the earlier subtle changes.

"I think Magnar broke the curse," she said. "He wasn't supposed to come here."

Captain Reed nodded. "Marcelle spoke of this curse but knew little about it."

"I care not to tell what I know," Cassabrie said. "I see no need."

"Very well. What of the children we saw? Where are they now?"

Cassabrie pushed Exodus closer. "They were part of an illusion. I created it to infuse you with the passion you will need to march into the dragons' territory. Hearts aflame are essential if you wish to do battle with these monsters, so I hoped to inspire you with a portrait of the suffering taking place in the Southlands."

"We would not have come if our passions had not already been aroused," the captain said, "but if we are unable to open the portal again, we will need all the passion we can muster to overcome the lack of soldiers."

Breathing a sigh of white vapor into the air, Edison scanned the gathered soldiers. With drizzling rain soaking their heavy clothes, their shoulders began to sag as they stared at him expectantly. He walked toward the star, blinking at its strengthening radiance. Looking Cassabrie in the eye, he whispered, "With so few men, do you think we stand a chance?"

Cassabrie took in a deep breath. It seemed that a new stream of wisdom flowed into her mind, more than a tale—a principle, a maxim straight from the Creator. Replying in an equally soft tone, Cassabrie nodded. "A better chance than ever. The Creator prefers a few men with noble and humble hearts over ten thousand who know not how to bend the knee, and it might have been the closing of the portal that acted as the separator. The bold of heart dashed through, while the hesitant remained."

"Then so be it." Edison firmed his jaw. "We march south."

"Wait." Cassabrie waved a hand, gesturing for him to come closer. "Please. I need to speak to you and Captain Reed privately."

As she drew back, the two men followed, each one raising a hand to block the light. When they stopped out of the soldiers' earshot, she whispered, "I must tell you about a new danger that has arisen. A disease has broken out in the Southlands. It is highly contagious and always fatal. If the men come into contact with any infected slave, they are likely to contract the disease."

"We were warned about the possibility of an outbreak," Captain Reed said, "and we left behind those who didn't want to take the risk. Now that an outbreak has actually occurred, we will certainly have to be careful."

Edison nodded. "This means we can't take the slaves home. They'll infect the people on Major Four."

"Not yet," Cassabrie said. "There are promising efforts in the works to find a cure. In the meantime, you can still conquer the dragons and free the slaves from oppression."

Edison stroked his chin. "Freeing the slaves without coming near them will be a difficult task."

"Perhaps even more difficult than we know," Cassabrie said. "It's possible that the disease might still be in the air in the Southlands, and the menace would ravage the men with an invisible assault even without direct contact with the stricken."

Captain Reed glanced back at the soldiers. Some had shed their wet cloaks in the warming air. "How confident are you of this cure?"

"I have no way to measure confidence, but is my level of certainty important? Your men came here knowing they could die. Does it matter if death comes because of an unseen enemy rather than one that has wings and scales?"

Captain Reed's face reddened a shade. "A warrior would rather oppose a mortal enemy he can see rather than one he cannot. I will try to encourage them myself. They might not listen to assurances from a woman who has never faced death."

Cassabrie lowered her head and touched her pocket. "Very well," she said, taking a deep breath. "Perhaps you should encourage them, Captain. I will stay silent."

A jumble of shouts pierced the forest. The two soldiers tromped back into the clearing with Orion between them, struggling madly. Captain Reed hurried back to the gathered soldiers, followed by Edison. Cassabrie drifted slowly closer, hoping to hear from far enough away to avoid melting too much snow. The area was already too muddy.

When the soldiers stopped, one saluted. "He doesn't have the crystal. He must have hidden it somewhere."

"And there it will stay!" Orion said. "If your captain refuses to protect you from certain death, your rightful governor will."

"I will deal with him in due time." Captain Reed drew a sword and raised his voice loud enough for all to hear. "Men, I know you are not afraid to die, but I hereby warn you that the dread disease we were told about has spread through the slave population, which could bring us great peril. If this news weakens your knees, then you are free to stay here until the rest of us return."

Orion's face flushed. "Can't you fools see that this is a march into carnage? Not only for you, but for your wives and children! Even if you conquer the dragons and release the slaves, you will conduct a fatal disease back to your loved ones!"

A few of the men murmured, but with a rise of Captain Reed's hand, the voices quieted. "We will not carry a disease home. You have my sacred word. If we become infected and a cure is not found, we will die here."

"He confirms my claim," Orion said. "Stay here with me, and I will lead you safely home."

"As cowardly failures." Captain Reed scanned the soldiers. "Actually, I will need some men to stay here with Orion. I will not force him or anyone else to march into this invisible danger, but I cannot trust him to stay here alone. If he opens the portal, the disease of fear he could spread back home might be more dangerous than any other."

After surveying the men, Captain Reed found six who volunteered to stay, mostly young fathers. Once the matter had been settled, he turned back to Cassabrie. "How will you let us know if a cure has been discovered?"

Cassabrie nudged the explosive tube in her pocket. "Trust me, good captain. If I am successful, everyone will know. When the cure is ready, I will bring it to you."

"Trusting her," Orion growled, "is like trusting a fox with your chickens. She is a deceiver, a charmer. Even her truths are wrapped around lies."

"Ignore him," Edison said. "It's time to get going."

Captain Reed's eyes darted back and forth. "Where is Magnar? He was supposed to help us. Fighting without him would double our vulnerability."

Cassabrie looked again for the great red dragon, but he was nowhere in sight. His fear of retribution for killing her might be the greatest remaining obstacle to freedom for the slaves. "I know why Magnar left, but it is a private matter. He will likely join you for battle long before you get to the Southlands."

"Very well," Captain Reed said. "I will not pry into it further. Marcelle has already provided directions to Frederick's wilderness refuge, so even if Magnar joins us late, we will be able to find our way." He grasped Edison's shoulder and spoke in a low tone, though not too low for Cassabrie to hear. "With so few men, success appears to be an empty hope, and promises of a dragon ally are tenuous at best. Do you have any counsel?"

Edison whispered in return, glancing at Cassabrie. "There is another crystal that will open the portal, and I think this Starlighter knows where it is."

Both men looked at her, their brows lifted. "Do you?" Edison asked.

Cassabrie blinked. She had used that peg to unlock the device that held her body suspended in the sanctuary below the Zodiac. Might it still be wedged in the ceiling disk? If not, maybe someone picked it up. Arxad scooped a stardrop from the floor disk, but he was moving so quickly, he could have grabbed the peg without anyone noticing. "I left it in the Zodiac. Maybe Arxad knows."

"Maybe?" Edison shook his head. "We need certainty. And since Arxad isn't around, we—"

"Wait!" Cassabrie raised a hand. "Allow me to probe Starlight's tales for a moment."

While both men looked on, Cassabrie set her hands at the sides of the invisible crown that provided contact with Exodus. Images streamed in, fast and frenzied. Her time within the star had been so brief. Becoming an expert at sorting through the maze of tales probably took weeks or months. Yet, only moments remained. She had to locate the tale quickly.

Closing her eyes, she focused on the memory of Arxad's hurried flight from the sanctuary while she lay on the floor recovering from reentry into her body. The scene appeared, but not at the angle from which she had witnessed it. Her body lay motionless near the stardrop disks. Jason's tear-streaked face was visible at the side, close, as if he were holding the person viewing the sanctuary. Arxad stood with his foreclaw pinning Shrillet to the floor while she wriggled beneath his weight.

Cassabrie froze the scene and looked at Arxad's underbelly. No crystalline peg was lodged there, but one of the scales bordering his vulnerable spot reflected the light in a strange way. With a wave of her hand, she brought the image closer. When she stared at the scale, her own face looked back at her. It wasn't a scale at all; it was a circular mirror.

Keeping the image motionless, Cassabrie searched the archives of her mind for an answer. In days past, dragons sometimes exchanged belly scales with each other as a covenant, a sign of trust to seal a promise. Apparently Arxad had made such an exchange with someone who reciprocated with the only workable object he or she had.

Cassabrie waved the scene back into motion. Randall burst into the room and pushed the point of his sword against Shrillet's underbelly. "I'll watch this one," he said to Arxad. "You'd better find Deference. Fellina needs her." Arxad leaped toward the stardrop disk embedded in the floor, dipped a claw through the broken glass, and used another claw to scoop up something from a pile of shards at the side.

Cassabrie focused on the second item. It *was* the peg. Arxad *did* grab it.

Keeping her eyes closed, she lifted a hand. "Give me another moment. I have to find Arxad." She concentrated on the entry to Arxad's cave, where he was probably nursing Fellina back to health. Within seconds, an animated image came to mind, Arxad flying from the cave's opening, then soaring high over the barrier wall at the river gate. Something glinted in his underbelly scales, but it was too far away to see. A few seconds later, he entered a cloudbank and disappeared.

Cassabrie opened her eyes. "Arxad is heading north, and he has the crystal. I suggest that you begin your march now and stay out in the open where he can see you. After you ask him to open the portal for your soldiers, perhaps you can continue marching in the forest in order to approach the Southlands with stealth. Arxad is familiar with ways to breach the barrier wall, so he can provide guidance."

"With our numbers," the captain said, "stealth is essential."

Edison set the toe of his boot next to the missing crystal's hole. "Someone from our ranks will have to return to the portal and let the new arrivals know what we're doing and where to find us, and how to signal us that they have arrived." He took a step closer to Cassabrie, squinting as her radiance flooded his face. "Will you accompany the reinforcements? With your gifts, you will be able to guide them in our direction."

Cassabrie sighed. "I wish I could, Edison, but I am called to another duty. When you meet Arxad, he will provide counsel as to where you can wait, and he will inform your soldiers when he opens the portal."

"Not the best solution, but a workable one." Edison turned toward Captain Reed. "I suggest that we march south immediately and make further plans along the way."

"I agree, but for these advance troops, the mission will be extremely dangerous." Captain Reed grasped Edison's shoulder. "You have looked death in the eye more any of us have. Will you speak courage to the men?"

"Gladly." Lifting his sword, Edison faced the troops. "Men, we have arrived at a turning point in history, an opportunity to pierce evil in the heart, to grasp the throat of wickedness and cut off its breath. When we strangle this beast, we will cleanse this world of the filth of slavery and oppression. Every dragon that lashed an innocent back with a whip will feel the sting of our swords. Every dragon that forced a starving child to bear cruel loads will feel the weight of our boots on his neck. And every dragon that sent a disabled slave to the grinding mill will become food for our dogs."

As cheers erupted from the men, they whipped out their swords and clashed them together. In the midst of the chaotic noise, Cassabrie guided Exodus closer to Edison. "You are here to stop Taushin," she said. "Randall and Marcelle promised Magnar and Arxad that the army from Major Four would topple the usurper in exchange for freedom for the slaves."

"We will take care of Taushin, but we'll also exact a bit of justice. We have to make sure Magnar will never again dare to enter our world. We will spare his life and Arxad's, but we never agreed to spare them all." Edison waved his sword. "Men! Let us march!"

Led by Edison and Captain Reed, the army tromped through the mud and slush, heading due south. Soon only Orion and those guarding him remained. When the sound of sloshing footsteps died away, Orion turned toward Cassabrie, a semicircle of men hemming him in. "Now that you have sent innocent men to their doom, what do you intend to do?"

She kept her face expressionless. "If you think me a deceiver, why do you ask me a question?"

"Because I know who you are. I understand your motives. Earlier, I proved that I can repel your charms."

"Is that so?" Cassabrie crossed her arms. "Then who am I?"

Orion's face contorted. "You are the demoness who set my home ablaze when I was a child. You lured me away so that I couldn't rescue my family."

"I admit that I led you away from your home," Cassabrie said quietly, "but I did so to keep you alive."

"You are a deceiver." Orion kept his arm rigid, his finger still stabbing the air. "You would never bear witness against yourself."

Cassabrie spread her arms, fanning her cloak. "Then shall I show you the rogues from Tarkton who approached your home when you were a boy? Shall I show you how a Starlighter who didn't have a chance of opposing them awakened you with a song, hoping your family would follow you to safety?" Even as she asked the questions, the scene appeared in the forest—Orion as a boy skulking from a modest home in a rural setting. As soon as he reached the forest, Cassabrie held him entranced while eight men stole into the house, looted its contents, and set it on fire. Once the men departed, she let Orion return.

"I wept with you that night, but the evil of those events has twisted your memory."

"No." Closing his eyes, Orion clapped his hands over his ears. "You are a deceiver. You will say anything to keep control. You didn't weep. You laughed. I remember your evil grin."

"You remember your nightmares." Cassabrie guided Exodus slowly backwards. "I leave it to you men to decide who is telling the truth. Believe what you will. You have no power to stop me."

She turned and flew the star to the river and settled over it. Still flowing around islands of ice, the water gurgled and splashed, seeming to shout for joy at its new-found freedom.

Cassabrie sighed. If only everyone could find such freedom. With Orion's conspiracy exposed, Major Four had loosed its chains, and with a determined army marching south, perhaps the slaves would enjoy liberation soon. Only time would tell.

She withdrew the tube from her pocket and read the words once more—*Danger. Explosive.* Sighing again, she pushed it back in place. If everything went according to plan, only the liberator would suffer permanent loss. Now to gather courage. Only one obstacle remained to be lifted. Success wasn't guaranteed. She could sacrifice everything and not save a single life. With Magnar's curse broken, chaos would soon reign, so time was running

out. He had to come. He just had to. She was probably
the only remaining hope for the world, and only Magnar
could unleash her power.

❧

Edison led the soldiers over a rise and looked southward
into a meadow. In the midst of green grass and flowers,
a lone boy walked toward them. With shoulders low and
head down, he appeared ready to collapse.

"Halt!" Edison said, raising a hand. "Will someone with
an eagle's eyes report what he sees?"

A young man stepped up to the front and, shielding his
eyes with a hand, peered at the boy. "He is a boy of about
twelve, sir, perhaps thirteen. It appears that he has only
one eye. He carries a sword but does so clumsily. He is
not a warrior."

"One eye, you say?"

"Indeed, sir. That is quite clear."

"I have heard about this boy."

Captain Reed walked to Edison's side. "If he is an
escaped Dracon slave, he might have the disease."

"True," Edison said. "The rest of you stay back. I will
greet him."

"But the disease." The captain grabbed Edison's wrist,
but he pulled away and strode into the meadow.

When he drew close, he slowed. The boy staggered
from side to side, then fell to the ground.

Edison leaped ahead and knelt at the boy's side. "Son,
what's wrong?"

The boy's one eye blinked. He slid away, pumping his
legs. "Don't come near me. I have a disease."

"That's the least of my worries." Edison grasped the boy's wrist and hoisted him to his feet.

The boy gave him a sideways stare. "Who are you?"

"My name is Edison. Are you Wallace?"

He nodded. "How did you know?"

"My son is Jason. He and Elyssa told me about you."

"Good. I was hoping for some help." Wallace brushed off his clothes. "I was traveling with your son Adrian, his friend Marcelle, and two girls, Shellinda and Regina. Magnar came by, and Adrian flagged him down and asked for a ride to the castle. Magnar couldn't take more than three, so I volunteered to walk. Magnar said it isn't much farther."

"Marcelle was with Adrian?"

Wallace nodded. "Why?"

"Oh, nothing really. I'm just a little confused about Marcelle's whereabouts."

Wallace looked past Edison. "So where are you and those men going?"

"To the Southlands to wage war against the dragons. We have come to free the slaves."

"Why are they standing so far back?"

"They're afraid you have a disease."

"Why aren't you afraid?"

Edison laid a hand on his shoulder. "Son, I came here to fight to the death for your freedom. I'm not going to cower at an invisible enemy."

"You sound a lot like Adrian and Jason."

Edison took in a quick breath, pushing down a surge of pride in his sons. "How sick are you?"

"Not too bad. Regina died of it on the way, but she was kind of sickly already. I guess I caught it from her."

"What about Adrian and Marcelle and the other girl you mentioned?"

"Shellinda? They might all have it by now, but they weren't sick when I last saw them. That's one of the reasons I volunteered to stay behind. I didn't want them to catch it."

Edison nodded. Good news and bad news. At least Adrian and Marcelle had been spared for a while. He patted Wallace on the back. "You're a brave young man, the very sort that I want on my side."

"Then can I come with you?" Wallace raised his sword. "I can whack pretty hard with this thing."

"I'll bet you can." Edison looked at Wallace's bare feet. The poor boy had to be cold. "Will you abandon your journey to the castle?"

Wallace shrugged. "Adrian wants to take Marcelle back to his world. I'd rather stay here where the action is if I can."

"Then so be it." Edison looked to the north. Captain Reed closed in, leading the soldiers. "He has the disease," Edison called. "If you don't want to get it—"

"No need to warn us," the captain said, waving his hand. "We've already been shamed down to the soles of our shoes."

The young soldier with the eagle eyes spoke up. "I see a cart well to the south. If the boy is tired, I'll be glad to push him."

"Thanks," Wallace said. "I might need that, for a while anyway."

Eagle Eye pointed at Wallace's stomach. "What is that behind your tunic?"

Wallace lifted his tunic, revealing a small block of wood behind his trousers waistband. It had been carved into a human shape, rough but recognizable. "It's a girl named Regina who died of the disease, but it's not finished. I like to carve, but I don't usually have a knife." He withdrew a small knife from the back of his trousers. "The dragons don't like it."

"Well, come along with us." Edison waved a hand southward. "A slow march until we get to the cart. Then be ready to accelerate. We have a long way to go. "

four

Faushin sat on a boulder near the base of a mountain, his head low. With Mallerin's wing draped over his head, the cool breeze rolling down the snowcapped peak stayed clear of his face. Viewing the world through his mother's eyes had proven to be a chore. Untrained and unreliable, she rarely knew what to focus on without being told. Her years of banishment in the grinding mill basin had clearly not produced a cunning she-dragon. She knew little more than brute force and bloodshed. It was no wonder Magnar got rid of her. Having a dullard for a mate had to be taxing to the point of insanity.

Still, with so few dragons, every male needed to find a proper mate to help populate Starlight, and only one or two intelligent females remained available. One of the barrier wall guardians, Berkah, displayed high intelligence, but she was not pliable enough. Only one female displayed an excellent blend of intelligence and naïveté that allowed her to be manipulated, and soon it would be time to inform Xenith of the good news that she would become queen of the Southlands' dragons.

"Mother," Taushin whispered, "kindly look at my subjects. The time has come to address them."

"Very well, but do not think you can treat me like a slave. I am not Zena." Mallerin's vision focused on the gathered dragons, allowing him to scan them through her eyes from their elevated position. Nestled in a depression between two mountains in the southern border range, all fifty-four remaining dragons sat in various resting poses, some on their haunches and some stretched out in the stubby grass.

"I would never treat you as I did Zena, Mother. She was a foul human, a former Starlighter. She was useful for learning, but her value as a vision vessel was minimal. I used and disposed of her. You, however, I value above all others, and my loyalty to you should be unquestioned. Did we not make a thorough search until we found you?"

"Arxad's cave was an easy guess."

"True, but that does not minimize my desire to find you. In any case, one tidbit of information I learned from Zena will allow me to lure and control one of the two Starlighters. It seems that the Reflections Crystal in the Zodiac's dome room attracts Exodus with a powerful force. In fact, that crystal is the very reason Exodus found its way to the bottom of an old volcano tube in the Northlands mountains, but that is a story for another time. The point is if the dome is opened, the crystal will draw Exodus to itself, trap it, and begin absorbing its power.

Cassabrie, who now dwells within the star, will slowly die. Before we left the village, I planted a rumor that the humans' only hope is for Cassabrie to come, so I expect that the dome will open to welcome her arrival. When she becomes ensnared, I will rescue her in exchange for her loyalty to me."

"And if she refuses? I hear she is not easily influenced."

"Then she will die, but that would be only a minor loss. There is another Starlighter who has already proven vulnerable to my influence. She is not as powerful as Cassabrie, but she would serve my purposes if necessary. Without one of the Starlighters, we cannot prevail."

"Such nonsense!" Mallerin said. "Even without a Starlighter, we could conquer a thousand healthy soldiers. Why are we hiding from diseased humans?"

"We are not hiding from humans. We are in this refuge to keep us safe from another enemy." Taushin extended his neck, pushing Mallerin's wing away. "I sense that the hour has arrived. I will explain the situation to all my subjects at the same time."

He thumped his tail on the boulder. When the dragons rose and turned their attention to him, he spoke in a formal tone. "Hear me, those who are faithful to our race. As we learned earlier, Magnar and Arxad have allied themselves with humans in order to remove me from my rightful place as king over you. They have proven that their allegiances are with forces foreign to ours, so we must defend our place and position against their betrayal. You have heard that men are coming with weapons, but that is not why we are taking refuge. The humans are a pathetic lot who might perish in piles of rotting flesh before they ever arrive. We have a different enemy."

A flapping sound arose toward the forest wilderness. The other dragons' heads swayed as they searched for the source. "Mother," Taushin said, "please look to the northern skies."

Over the treetops to the northwest, three white dragons flew toward the mesa mines. No larger than normal dragons, they flew haphazardly, dipping and weaving in the gusts.

Taushin resisted the urge to shudder. The Benefile. Their appearance was expected, but not this soon. Rising to his full height, Taushin growled as he spoke. "Behold our enemy."

Berkah turned to him. "Why are we hiding from these weaklings? We could overwhelm them in mere minutes."

"Their flight difficulty is due to the length of time they spent in captivity, so do not underestimate their power. They will soon become the extraordinary flyers they once were. And they have no fear of any dragon. In fact, they are likely flying straight to our village in search of us. They mean to destroy us all."

"Why?" Mallerin asked. "What have we done to them?"

"They are the Benefile, the enforcers, misguided keepers of the Code. Like Alaph, king of the Northlands, they think the dragons of the Southlands have brutalized humans, so they have come to deliver punishment. Yet, if we position ourselves and time events perfectly, they will conquer the humans for us, and we will have a Starlighter who will, in turn, conquer them."

When the white dragons flew out of sight, Taushin straightened and held his head high. "It is time to set our bait for Koren."

"What bait might that be?" Berkah asked.

"Suffering children."

"But the children are all in the village or the grottoes. The patriarchs moved them there when they saw us leave. If the Benefile are as dangerous as you claim, the children will not be accessible to us."

"Not so, Berkah. The cattle children are in a wilderness refuge. As the most pitiful of all children, they will be the best bait possible. We need only to guide them safely to the village and see to it that they suffer along the way. Koren will see it, and she will come."

Berkah nodded. "We have searched the wilderness for that refuge before, but it has not been a high priority. Perhaps if we all search again—"

"No need, and too dangerous. If we all fly over the entire wilderness, the Benefile will certainly see us."

"Then how do you propose that we find them?"

"I will send someone on a hunting expedition." Taushin pointed a wing at a drone. "You will go."

The drone lowered his head in submission. "What must I do?"

"Since you are small, you will be able to fly with stealth. If you locate the escaped cattle children, return and report their whereabouts. Kill any adults you find. While you are hunting, we will watch from here. Even if you locate nothing, I expect that one of the traitor dragons will eventually lead us to the refuge, so watch for any member of Arxad's family."

Koren groaned. Pain in her shoulders streaked down her spine and ripped across her limbs. With every flap of his wings, the dragon's claws dug in deeper, then eased back, a rhythm of agony that gouged her senses. If only she could find the strength to speak to him, maybe he would come under her control, at least long enough to set her down and ease the pain.

As the setting Solarus bobbed in her darkening vision, cold air swept through her thin clothing. Her cloak, now dry, trailed behind, too far to reach with pain-stiffened arms. Clenching her teeth, she refused to shiver. Any movement would make the torture even worse.

Ahead, the white caps of the Northlands had come into view. Although the trees now carried far less snow than before, the mountain peaks were still buried in it. Dark clouds loomed on the northern horizon, like a gray hat sitting on an old man's hoary head.

She closed her eyes. Maybe gathering Cassabrie's messages from Exodus would bring new energy, especially if the tales carried good news.

As she concentrated, images flashed in her mind—soldiers gathering in the midst of slush and mud, then marching into fields of green grass and multicolored flowers. Farther back, a dragon flew, too distant to identify, and far enough away that the soldiers might not even know that he lurked behind them.

After a few seconds of contemplating the confusing scene, she opened her eyes. A line of men dressed in dark uniforms appeared against a backdrop of color. As in her vision, they had just passed the Northlands border and were entering the flowered meadow, but the dragon stalking them was nowhere in sight.

Koren tried to take in a deep breath, but the pain kept her respiration shallow. Only a pathetic "Beware" escaped her lips, probably not loud enough for even her carrier dragon to hear.

Soon the men began to shout. Some lifted spears and swords as well as shields, but at a command from their leader, they held back. Perhaps he was fearful they would hit the wrong target.

"This will be easier than I thought," the dragon said. "All I have to do is drop you from a height beyond the reach of their weapons and then fly away. If the fall kills you, it will be no matter. You will be freshly dead, so the contagion will be delivered."

The dragon flew higher, providing a wider view of the surrounding area. From the north, another dragon approached, beating its wings furiously. Reddish brown and snorting sparks, his powerful lines drew a familiar form.

"Magnar," Koren whispered. Forcing herself to take a deep breath, she summoned every bit of energy remaining and called out, "Dragon ... I appeal to you .... Put me down ... safely away from the humans ... and summon Magnar.... He must hear from me."

The dragon circled overtop the soldiers but stayed quiet, as if unsure what to do. Below, the men spread out under the dragon, but whether to present a less concentrated target or to be ready to catch her should it decide to drop her, Koren couldn't be sure.

Magnar closed in, shouting in the dragon tongue, "Why are you transporting this Starlighter?"

"At Taushin's bidding. She carries a disease that we wish to spread among the invading humans. Considering your disdain for the vermin, I assume that you approve."

"I do not approve," Magnar said as he joined the carrier dragon in his orbit. "Put her on my back. I have need of the human army." He lowered his voice to a quiet growl. "We can dispose of them later."

"Taushin is king now," the carrier dragon said. "Since you left our world, his coronation was legal. We must repel this attack. The vermin must die."

Magnar eyed him for a moment before replying. "You are Braynor."

"Yes."

"You are one of the Zodiac priests."

"I am."

"You heard the human's appeal. By law, you must at least listen to what she has to say. If we land well away from the humans, there will be no danger."

"Very well. I see no harm in it." Braynor flew southward, then swooped low and released his grip. Koren tumbled into a somersault, then skidded on her stomach across a stretch of flowers and feathery grass. When her momentum stopped, her cloak wafted over her, covering her head.

Groaning again, she turned and threw the cloak to the side. The dragon sat on its haunches beside her, its neck extended upward while it waited for Magnar to land. With Solarus now behind the trees to the west, twilight was nearing.

Her shoulders throbbing, Koren rose to a sitting position and looked at Braynor. Even in her blurry vision, his nervousness was obvious as his ears twitched and his body shifted from side to side.

Magnar dove toward the ground and landed in a graceful slide. When he settled, he extended his neck toward Koren. "Speak, human. Make your appeal."

Her arms shaking, Koren pulled her hood up over her head and glanced to the north. Perhaps five hundred paces away, the soldiers marched toward her at a rapid pace. She had to do this before they arrived, or they would be exposed to the disease. After taking another deep breath, she whispered, "I ... I need to ... tell you ... a tale."

"What?" Braynor's ears perked. "I cannot hear you!"

Magnar growled. "I hope you have not damaged her beyond her ability to spcak."

Braynor backed up, nearly stepping on Koren's foot before halting. "If she cannot appeal, then my vow is fulfilled."

Pushing against the grass with her feet, Koren slid away. If a fight erupted, the first casualty might be a vulnerable Starlighter. She glanced again at the men. The sound of the tromping boots drew closer, maybe three hundred paces away now.

"You are a poor excuse for a priest," Magnar said. "I will take her to safety myself."

Trembling, Braynor backed away another step. "I ... I cannot allow it. Taushin is king, not you."

"Beware, Braynor!" Magnar's growl strengthened. "I am larger than you and more powerful by far."

"Then I will have to rely on quickness and agility."

Koren slid farther away. A battle meant a delay in flying her out before the soldiers arrived. "Magnar," she said, her voice rasping. "Warn the men!"

Magnar raised his head high. "Soldiers from Darksphere! Heed my warning! If you come closer, you will be infected by a fatal disease."

"No!" Braynor leaped at Magnar, his jaws snapping at the bigger dragon's neck. Within seconds, their beating wings blocked Koren's view of the soldiers. Their tails shredded the ground as they fought, edging closer and closer to her.

Koren rolled away. A cacophony pierced her senses— the thumps of whipping tails and the grunts and growls of cursing dragons. Pushing with aching arms, she climbed to her feet, then looked back. The men had stopped within a hundred paces, perhaps worried about the disease. Yet, one man leaped toward her and ran.

Koren waved him back and staggered westward toward the river. The waist-high grass felt like whips against her aching legs, and every pounding step brought new throbs to her perforated shoulders. Blood trickled down her back, biting into lesions along the way. The consuming disease gnawed at her gut, worse than ever.

As the sounds of battle subsided, the rush of water took over. The river came into view, maybe ten paces away. She stumbled over a stone and fell to her knees. Her palms slapped the turf and sent new shock waves through her shoulders.

Koren crawled. So dizzy! Walking was impossible now. With her vision darkening by the second, the sound of water remained the only guide. Maybe the chilly current would provide a cooling wake up, at least long enough to get to the safety of the forest on the other side. With night approaching, she could blend in with the darkening shadows.

When she reached the bank, she continued a painstaking crawl into the flow. The icy water knifed through her clothes. Forearms and biceps stiffened into rigid rods. The shock sent a rush of blood to her head, snapping her awake and clearing her mind, though it also ignited a blazing headache that felt like a red-hot hammer pounding her skull.

Moving stiffly, she made her way to the center of the twenty-foot-wide river. The water buoyed her body, allowing her to stand erect and walk in the shoulder-high current. New claws, these made of icy water, dug into her skin. She gritted her teeth and drove herself onward. Now swimming, she drifted southward with the flow until her feet struck bottom again.

She pushed against the riverbed and trudged toward shore. Shivers took over. Her entire body shook violently, and her teeth chattered, making the hammer pound more furiously. With every step, her clothes and cloak grew heavier, weighing her down. But the weight didn't matter. She had to keep away from the soldiers. Maybe the man who ran after her gave up for fear of the disease, or maybe one of the dragons had stopped him.

Finally, she climbed up to the bank and continued walking, now in a weaving, stumbling stagger. When she reached the forest tree line, the desire to collapse and hide felt like a crushing boulder. She shook her head fiercely. Deeper was better, far away from the dragons

and the soldiers. Someone would eventually search for
her. She had to get away, hide in darkness, shiver alone
where the chattering of her teeth couldn't reach dragon
or human ears.

After two dozen more steps, her foot caught on her
cloak. She collapsed, more like crumbling pottery than
a falling tree. Forcing herself to crawl again, she scooted
between two bushes, lay on her stomach, and buried her
face in her arms. Spasmodic sobs shook her body. Biting
her lip, she steeled herself. Crying would reveal her hiding place. She had to stay still ... quiet.

She held her breath and peeked over her arms. The
ground-level view provided little more than a glimpse
of the forest floor—a gathering of sparsely packed tree
trunks, leaves, and needles. Soon night would be her ally.
She waited, allowing only shallow, silent breaths.

A minute or so later, a man skulked into the waning
light, a sword in his grip. With his head high and turning
from side to side, he sniffed the air every few seconds.
"Koren?" he called. "Where are you?"

Koren held her breath. The man, his gray hair askew,
stopped only five paces away and sniffed again. Blood
dripped from his forehead down to his cheek, and a
bruise painted his jaw purple. "I have excellent tracking
skills, Koren. Even in the dark, I will eventually find you.
Every minute we lose is another minute closer to death."

Koren risked another peek. The man was walking at an
angle that would miss her hiding place, but not by much.
He would probably sniff her out soon.

"I am Edison Masters, Jason's father." He slid the
sword into a hip scabbard. "Come out of hiding, and I will
help you find healing."

She cringed. *Not Jason's father! He has to stay away!*

"I will arrange for transport to the Northlands," Edison continued. "Uriel is trying to find a cure."

Koren swallowed. Trying? That wasn't good enough. It was too much of a risk.

Staring in spite of the pounding headache, she concentrated on the space in front of Edison. She had to find the energy, even if it sapped her last shred of strength.

Seconds later, an image of herself appeared at the spot, a thin vapor, barely visible in the twilight. She projected her thoughts and forced its lips to move as the thoughts transformed into spoken words.

"Edison ..." The voice was weak and frail, but it would have to do. "Please go back and let me die alone. I don't want you to get the disease."

Staring, Edison backed away a step. His eyes darted around for a moment before settling on Koren's phantom. "Dear girl, I have already been exposed. You need not fear endangering me."

Could his words be true? She shook her head, and her image did the same. Edison had just come from the Northlands with the army. He couldn't have been exposed, whatever he may want her to believe.

Tears sprang to her eyes. "You're just telling me that so I'll come out."

"Koren, how well do you know Jason?"

She made her image cock its head. The question was a surprising one. "For the short amount of time we have shared together, quite well, I think."

"Would he leave you to suffer and die alone?"

Koren's lips trembled, and those on her image did the same. "No. He wouldn't."

"Would he lie to you?"

"No."

Edison reached out and caressed her misty cheek. "Then do you expect anything less from me?"

Koren rolled up to a sitting position to better maneuver her image. Now that Edison was distracted and perhaps partially hypnotized, he wouldn't notice.

The image covered his hand with her own. "Jason has told you about me?"

"He has."

"Do you think I would accept your offer and willingly sentence you to a horrible death?"

He lowered his head and gave it a slow shake. "No, you wouldn't. But I speak the truth. I've already been exposed."

"I can't take that chance. You must leave me. If you get the disease, the other soldiers probably will as well, and then you all would either spread it to your loved ones at home or become stranded here until you die. We shouldn't imperil so many just to save one who will die anyway."

"Koren, this is the very reason we came. Every man out there is ready to sacrifice his life to break the bonds of the slaves."

"But if you and your men contract the disease, you will have no hope in defeating Taushin's forces. I saw your army. Even healthy, your numbers are small. You are no match for the dragons."

"If we are not willing to risk danger to save a dying girl, we should have stayed home. There are hundreds of stories just like yours—many Korens who would infect us if we were to come close." Edison cocked his head, as if listening for something. "Besides, we've already come into contact with a boy who has the disease, and it sounds like he just now caught up with me. He would like to speak to you."

"To me?" Koren asked. "Who is he?"

A boy walked into view, blinking his one eye. "Koren? It's me, Wallace."

"Wallace?" Koren's voice pitched higher. "It's really you!"

"It's me. And it's true, I've already been infected."

Koren's shoulders slumped. Not Wallace. Would no one escape the invisible horror of this pestilence?

"Please come out. We'll help you."

She looked at Wallace's pleading expression, then at Edison's calm, assured demeanor. They had already sacrificed their health to save others. Accepting their help wouldn't bring them further harm. "Okay. I'll try."

"No need," Edison said. "I see you now." He walked through her image, and the draft behind him dispersed it into nothingness. He pushed aside a bush and reached for her. "Don't be afraid."

She closed her eyes. Her heart beat wildly, erratically, as if ready to expire at any moment.

A shushing sound followed. "Just relax." Hands pushed behind her back and under her knees. Arms lifted her, and a walking sensation followed. Soon the sound of water reached her ears.

"Wallace?" she said. "Are you still here?"

"I'm right here, Koren. Right next to you."

"Hold my hand. Please. Just hold my hand."

A warm hand slid into hers. She exhaled. Her heart slowed to a steadier rhythm. "Thank you."

Edison let out another long shushing sound, peaceful and easy, the way Madam Orley used to shush Petra when she cried in the darkness with wordless sobs.

As the river's sounds returned, dizziness washed to and fro, casting all of Starlight into a wild spin. Sloshing followed, then men's voices. A dragon spoke unintelligible words.

Several hands lifted her higher and set her on something. She forced her eyes open for a brief glimpse. She sat upon a dragon. Someone slid in behind her and wrapped strong arms around her waist.

"Don't worry. I've got her. I won't let her go."

Men held torches with fiery tops that cast wavering light on the dragon's reddish scales.

"You're her only chance, Magnar," a man said. "Take her with all speed."

"I will return to battle with you before you reach the Southlands." Magnar's voice sounded far away, like the low gongs of a distant bell. "I hope to bring news of a cure."

The sound of beating wings filled Koren's ears. Wind whipped all around, then settled to a fresh breeze. With the arms holding her tightly, she leaned back and rested. Torturous spasms throttled her aching shoulders. Her biceps twitched uncontrollably. With every dip and weave, her backside slid an inch or two on the scales, but the strong grip always brought her back to a safe position.

"It's okay, Koren. I'm here. I won't let you go."

"Wallace?"

"Yes." His hand slid into hers again. "I'm right here."

"Good." She squeezed his hand. "But I think I'm … I'm … about to faint."

"Hang on, Koren. Just hang on."

Soon, bitterly cold wind plunged frigid icicles through her saturated clothes and deep into her skin. Every minute resurrected pain—fire in her head, twisting muscles in her shoulders, a devouring beast in her belly.

Koren let her body fall limp. Fighting to stay alive didn't help. Whether by disease or by exposure, death would come soon. It was an enemy that never gave up.

five

A rush of warm air enveloped Koren's body. Magnar landed in a run and collapsed in a heap of wings, neck, and tail. Koren spilled off his back, rolled down his scales, and sprawled across a wooden floor, her cheek pressing down and her eyes closed. She clawed at the soft wood. Her fingernails dug in rhythmically in time with her shoulder spasms.

A jumble of dragon language filtered into her ears. She tried to open her eyes, but the task was just too great. With every passing second, the dizziness grew. Although the warmth eased the muscle contractions, the pain in her lesions and the gnawing in her stomach grew worse and worse.

Something slid under her abdomen and lifted. With her limbs half-frozen, they stuck out like tree branches, unable to relax. Whatever held her in its grasp carried her in a gentle rocking motion. Whispered words replaced the guttural dragonspeak. "Hold on, child. I will get you warmed up in a moment."

It was a man's voice, a familiar voice, though it seemed impossible to place. His words dissolved to rumbling hums. As if massaged by the soothing tone, her arms and legs relaxed until it seemed that she had melted in his grasp.

As the man walked, he shifted her body, rolling her to one side, then back again. It seemed that several hands gripped and pulled, shedding her cloak and the clothing underneath. The warm air felt luxurious across her skin, like the bathing pool in Xenith's room. Was she naked? Maybe. Every sensation seemed magnified out of proportion.

Soon something soft supported her back, and a blanket of new warmth covered her legs and torso up to her neck. She forced her eyes open. She lay on a strange bed. Unlike her floor mat back at Arxad's cave, it was elevated, and wooden slats ran along each side, similar to the fences the carpenters built to keep rabbits confined. Above, a tree branch protruded over the bed, ending in a hand-shaped nub, palm pointed at the dark sky. In the dim light, it seemed old and rotting, as if it could break and crash onto the bed at any moment.

For the first time in several hours, her muscles unknotted, though the gnawing in her stomach continued to eat away her insides. Grimacing, she gave in to her heavy eyelids and let them flutter shut.

Voices returned, both the man's and the distinctive tones of a dragon. "She will not survive long enough to test the medicine," the man said. "It will take too much time to prepare the ingredients and make a new batch. I have the powder and the genetic material, but it would take an hour to energize it, and she might not last that long."

"Are you certain?" the dragon asked. "Not even an hour?"

"I have seen this disease too many times to doubt my prognosis. It has already attacked the vital organs. It's a wonder that she's still alive."

"There is a way to give her the time you need, but the task is extraordinarily difficult."

"Difficulty is not an issue, Alaph. I wish to save this poor girl, and testing the medicine might lead to a final cure that will save dozens of girls just like her."

"And your own life," Alaph said. "Surely you have been close enough to her to contract the disease."

"No doubt, but it will be quite a while before I can test the medicine on myself. The disease must take hold first."

"Then allow me to explain how to extend her life." Alaph's voice lowered. "I told you about Jason's journey into the star chamber, did I not?"

"You did. A harrowing journey, indeed."

"Exodus is here in the Northlands, so you can get the stardrop material, both for saving her life immediately and for energizing the medicine. I would collect it myself, but I am unable to touch it, and since Deference is not here to care for Koren, I will have to stay and do what I can to keep her alive."

"What of the moat and the creatures within?"

"Resolute will ferry you across, and you may take the dagger mounted next to the trophy shelf. You have seen it, have you not?"

"Yes, yes. I have seen it. It will do little good against those beasts, but I will take it all the same."

"Good. Once you reach the other side, the shining star should be easy to find in the darkness. Scoop material from the outer membrane and form a stardrop in your palms. Then bring it back here and put it in the healing tree's hand."

"Are the trees still functional? They appear to be dying."

"They still have enough power. Normally someone with Starlighter gifts must activate the tree's healing powers, but since Koren is a Starlighter, I believe it will work. When the stardrop particles rain from the hand, catch them and rub them into her cheeks, throat, and chest. Fear not that they might burn her skin. Healing often comes with pain. Yet, even with the stardrop, a tree cannot expel the disease, so we need to test the medicine."

"Very well. I will make haste."

"Wait for one moment, and I will explain something that will likely speed you along."

"If you take time to explain, she might die." The man paused. "How strange. Somehow I sense that I have spoken those very words to you before."

"You did. And I answered with these words, 'You prayed for mercy. Is it up to your discretion how that mercy is delivered or the manner or timing the deliverer chooses to employ?' The situation was the same then as it is now. Your daughter lay dying of the disease, and you were desperate to save her."

"My daughter?"

Alaph shifted to the dragon language. "Touch her head with your fingertips. Lift her eyelids and probe her orbs deeply." An icy breeze passed across the bed, filtering into her damp hair. "You remember the victims of the disease, Orson. You remember how it spreads and destroys. You picked up your research at the point you left it when you died. But has your mind blocked out the death that broke your heart? Have you erected a shield of protection?"

Koren flinched. Orson? That was her father's name. This conversation was so familiar, like a vision of the past she had conjured earlier.

"A shield," Orson murmured. "Protection."

"Look ... delve deeply ... remember."

Soft pressure ran along Koren's forehead, then on her eyelids. They lifted, revealing the face of Uriel Blackstone.

Koren tried to whisper Uriel's name but couldn't draw a deep-enough breath. Why would Alaph call him Orson?

Uriel's eyes, wide and piercing, shifted from side to side as if reading a book. After a few seconds, he drew in his lips and pressed them together. His chin trembled. "Koren," he whispered, his voice pitching higher. "My little K!"

Her lids fell closed again, darkening her vision. *My little K*, she repeated in her mind. How could Uriel know that term of endearment?

"Where is Resolute?" Uriel's tone spiked. "I must go immediately!"

"I already sent her to the moat," Alaph said. "She is waiting for you."

"Koren! Dearest one!" Fingers combed through her hair. "Stay alive! I will return soon!" The fingers lifted, and Uriel's voice faded. "Pray for me!"

Everything fell silent. Then quiet breathing drew near, and the icy breeze returned. Alaph began to hum a lilting melody that brought to mind a children's song, a lullaby about casting the stones of labor into the river and watching them sink into darkness. A scratching sound followed, and particles of some kind sprinkled over her face. They smelled like sawdust and tickled her throat, but even the sneeze reflex found no strength to activate and propel them away.

As a smooth, cold surface rubbed the particles into her skin, Alaph spoke. "You are a Starlighter, Koren. You have unique gifts from the Creator, yet you have not used them to their fullest. There have been many distractions that have interfered."

Koren forced out a weak "But," then a sighing breath. Speaking took too much energy.

"I know, dear child," Alaph said in a soothing tone. "You wish to explain yourself, and explain yourself you must, but not to me. I already know your dilemma. You have cried out that love does not need chains, yet you have been bound with chains of your own choosing."

She tried to speak again, but the dragon's shushing sound seemed to pull her breath away.

"Hush. Your dilemma was real, and I am not your judge. Rest your mind for now. You need your energy to survive until your father returns. If the Creator sees fit to allow your days to be extended, then perhaps you will have an opportunity to state your case."

Koren murmured, "Jason ... Elyssa."

"Your traveling companions. The last I heard, they were safe. You will be reunited in due time."

New pain dug into her gut. She pressed against her stomach and kneaded it with the heel of her hand, trying to push the evil beast away. The spasms returned, worse than ever. Her abdominal muscles twisted into a knot.

She rolled to her side, curled into a ball, and pressed her knees against the slats. Sweat trickled across her forehead and back, dampening the sheets. Maybe death would come soon and cast her mind into darkness. At least then the pain would finally end.

A flapping sound arrived. As it settled, a fresh wind blew across her face, drying the perspiration. The cooling sensation brought a new shiver, but instead of inciting another round of spasms, her muscles settled. Maybe the wood particles Alaph applied were helping.

Alaph's voice returned in a whisper, shifting again to the dragon language. "How could you carry her in this condition?"

"I flew here with a boy who helped me." The new voice was gruff, familiar somehow, another dragon speaking in their guttural language. "I left him at the entry." There was a pause, and a puff of hot breath swept over her. "How is she?"

"She has very little time."

"As do you."

"True," Alaph said. "My time might well be near its end."

"Thank you for allowing me to be here. I know how dangerous it is."

"The trees are weak. The limb upon which you perch might not hold you for much longer."

"I speak of the danger of my presence in the Northlands, not the fragility of this limb."

"You have broken the covenant, Magnar," Alaph said, "so the shattering of that curse has already had its effect."

"Have the Benefile been set free?"

"I have not seen them, but I have no reason to believe they have not escaped. Your bonds were the only restraint."

"For that, I am sorry. I hope we can avoid a conflict."

"Sorry?" A growl spiced Alaph's tone. "You intentionally passed through the portal. Your apology is hollow. If conflict comes, you alone will be to blame."

"That is why I came here," Magnar said. "I wish to make peace with you and your kind before the others arrive. We can share power, divide the lands. I will set the slaves free and wash away our guilt."

"If you wish to make amends, then help Orson collect a stardrop. The survival of this Starlighter will help us in the event my fellow Benefile decide to exact punishment."

Silence descended for a moment. Koren's spasms subsided further, but the gnawing beast within never relented. It continued biting and clawing from her intestines to her chest. Her heart thumped erratically, almost stopping at times before racing once again.

"If she survives," Magnar said in a low tone, "my future is bleak indeed. I will never be king again."

"Sacrifice is at the heart of repentance. Without deeds, your apology is worthless."

Magnar snorted. "We shall see how well you follow your own maxims. When Beth arrives, her fury will be terrible to behold. Your own apologies will be like acid in her ears."

"I am prepared to face the consequences of my actions. Leaving my own mate to such suffering is unforgiveable, at least in her eyes."

"Then you admit you were wrong?"

"I did what I had to do," Alaph said. "None of the other Benefile could have accomplished this end."

"Your stubbornness will be your undoing. If the human army fails to destroy Taushin, the Benefile will be our only hope against him, and a very dangerous hope, indeed. If you refuse to swallow your pride and join them, their wrath cannot be tempered, and no one will be able to stop their rampage."

"And if I acquiesce and join them, what will be left for you to rule? Even if I temper their wrath, you and your brother will be victims."

"I plan to go there now and warn him. He and our mates and his daughter will escape, and we will begin a new—"

"A fool's plan. Your own wickedness is the root of every problem, and the seeds you plant in a new society will sprout new corruption. The Benefile will pursue you forever."

"What other options do I have?"

"Help Koren. While it is true that her survival will not aid your purposes, such sacrifice is essential if true cleansing is to take place."

"I cannot go near Exodus," Magnar said. "Cassabrie hates me because of what I did to her, and now she has the power to gain revenge. If she were to see me, she would try to destroy me. At the very least, her anger at me might delay the collection of a stardrop. She is crafty and keeps her own counsel. You know this to be true."

"I know of her past unpredictability, but perhaps she will surprise you. Humans are a changeable lot, as are dragons."

The air fell silent. Only the rumbling breathing of two dragons interrupted the stillness.

Finally, Magnar spoke again. "You ask too much. I would be executing myself." The beating of wings returned, along with a whipping wind. Then the sounds subsided as quickly as they began.

Koren clenched her eyes tightly shut. It seemed that her life force was seeping out, drawn from her body by the vacuum in Magnar's wake. The healing particles were wearing off. She would die before Uriel could return, and the medicine wouldn't be tested, at least not until Uriel manifested the disease. But would that be too late? Every minute they waited was another minute Edison and his men marched farther away.

Uriel. She let the name sink into her mind. Could he really be her father? She followed with another name. *Orson.* That lovely word had comforted her through many lonely nights. Exhausted from slave labors, she had often collapsed into bed, closed her eyes, and echoed his melodic voice. *I love you, little K.* Yet no image of his face ever came to mind, only his voice, and Uriel's cry wasn't the same. The voice that followed Orson's good-night kiss was always quiet, reassuring, a blanket of comfort and protection. Uriel's tone reflected fear and desperation.

She forced out a whispered word. "Alaph?"

"Do not try to speak with your voice," Alaph said. "Use your gifts if you must communicate with me."

With pain roaring through her body, Koren bit down on her tongue. Could she conjure another image of herself?

Concentrating on the space between her bed and the one next to it, she tried to form a copy of herself. As before with Edison, her phantom form appeared as a thin fog, barely visible. She pointed the image's face toward Alaph, who now stood at the foot of her bed. His smooth white scales reflected lantern light, and thin red lines that crisscrossed his skin like a scarlet spider web seemed to pulse.

Koren cast thoughts at her foggy apparition. "Alaph, is Uriel really my father?"

"He is, child. It is a long story, but I will tell you a portion. When you died hundreds of years ago, Arxad and I preserved your spirit using the Reflections Crystal that now resides in the Zodiac. We knew Starlight would need you. Unfortunately, I no longer have the Reflections Crystal we used to capture your spirit, so if you die now, you will go to be with the Creator. In that case, we would have to battle the forces of evil without a Starlighter."

Koren's image spread out her arms, shifting her cloak. "What about Cassabrie? Her body is restored, and she is more powerful than I am. Can't she do what I would have done?"

"Cassabrie's path diverged from her calling long ago. She is independent and unpredictable, though I suspect that she is planning something that will restore her standing. She has embarked on a journey that will make her Starlighter gifts useless for the task I hoped you would accomplish."

"What task?"

"There is no need to tell you just now. I want no further stress laid upon your mind."

The biting beast within bored holes into her stomach. Koren pressed her hand hard against her abdomen, but it didn't help. Tears trickled from her eyes, and a reddish haze coated her vision. Her phantom became almost completely transparent and began shrinking. As she choked back a sob, her image's face twisted into a mournful frown. "I'm sorry," she squeaked. "I did the best I could, but I'm dying. I can feel it."

"Yes, you are, child. But do not give up hope. Though your father is likely just now reaching the far side of the moat, all is not yet lost."

"Couldn't you fly him to Exodus and bring him back? What good is keeping me alive if my father doesn't return in time?"

"Each time I approach Exodus, I risk a great deal, especially while someone is scraping its particles from the surface. If one were to blow onto me, the radiance would consume me in seconds."

"Couldn't you at least get him closer? You could stay at a safe distance." Koren drooped her head. "But I guess he would have to carry a stardrop back to you. You would still be in danger."

"Although danger to myself is a concern, there are issues that outweigh it. If I were to fly to Exodus with your father, in so doing I would destroy the opportunity to rescue an enslaved soul whose deliverance is necessary for the good of all Starlight, and even the person who holds him in bondage is in bondage herself, for her wrath is a poison that will prevent her from providing the liberation she hopes to dispense."

"I ... I don't understand."

"Forgive me for pontificating. You were not meant to understand. I was speaking about idolatry. For some, their idol is a grudge that is nursed and prepared for the day of wrath. For others it is an end to suffering, or a beloved person, or perhaps the idea of love itself. Any idol is able to turn a mind from the Creator, so they must all be purged by choice or smashed through trials, and only then will darkness turn to light." Alaph sighed. "But enough such babbling. It is a poor use of time for someone who has so little remaining."

"It's okay," Koren whispered. "I don't mind."

"Your mercy is lovely to behold, and that brings me to a comforting truth. Although your body wilts and decays, your soul is in no danger. Your death is but a stepping stone to paradise. Your chains are forever broken, and death to you has no sting. You have done well, Starlighter."

"Done well? But you said—"

"What I said is temporal. Now I speak of the eternal. Even those who do well learn temporal lessons along the way."

As the pain in her gut worsened, the image faded away. "Good-bye, Alaph," she said as she disappeared. "Thank you for trying."

Koren let out a long sigh. She closed her eyes and waited for death to come. Were the old stories true? Would a winged escort fly down from the Creator's side and carry her into paradise?

New tears leaked through. True or not, it didn't matter. She had failed. And now there wasn't anything she could do about it.

Seconds later, darkness swept her mind into oblivion.

SIX

Orson tucked Alaph's dagger into a sheath at his belt and ran toward the moat. With the snow nearly gone, the line dividing it from the darker ground was clear. Still, since night had fallen, care was essential. The slightest misstep could send him flying into the moat where he would become food for the monsters abiding in the depths. Although Exodus, hovering silently over the river beyond the moat, provided some light, it was too far away to reveal shallow ruts in the newly uncovered ground.

Ahead, Resolute waved her arms, making her visible. "Over here!" she called.

Orson hurried to the ghostly girl's side, braced his hands on his knees, and gasped for air. "Is your ... boat ready?"

She laid a hand on her invisible craft. "It's right here. You know what to do."

After she stepped inside, Orson followed and sat down, ignoring a chill crawling up his spine, and drew the dagger from the sheath. The last time he crossed this moat, clawed hands shot up from the snowy surface, though they missed their target, apparently blind to the world above their view.

While Resolute dug an invisible paddle into the whiteness, Orson cast his gaze on Exodus and the snow-speckled landscape beyond. The river underneath flowed freely, yet another sign of drastic change. A light drizzle fell, mixed with sleet. The precipitation appeared to be heavier near Exodus. Vapor rose from its membrane, partially veiling the girl within.

The boat, little more than a coracle, glided slowly along. Orson looked back at the castle. Within its stately walls, Koren, his precious daughter, lay dying. At this rate, he would never be able to return with a stardrop in time.

Gritting his teeth, he let out a growl. "Can't we go faster?"

A hurt expression crossed Resolute's face. "I dare not. Any faster and we'll awaken the moat guardians."

Regret stabbed Orson's heart. He gave her an apologetic nod. "Forgive me. I misdirected my wrath. I know you're doing your best."

"It's okay." Her eyes disappeared, leaving only tiny white sparkles. "I got yelled at a lot when I was a slave."

"I will add to your burden no more." He glared at the fake snowdrifts surrounding the boat and tried to rein in his anxiety. Resolute's name was certainly appropriate. She was bound and determined to cross the moat without disturbing the creatures below, but what good was it to survive this journey if he arrived too late to save Koren? "Can the guardians hurt you? If you fell into the moat, would they be able to catch you?"

She shook her head. "Being spirit, I can swim back to shore unharmed."

"Then allow me." He sheathed the dagger, grabbed the paddle, and thrust it into the moat. Although the "water" offered no resistance, his frantic strokes drove the boat along at double its former pace.

"Beware," Resolute whispered, her voice coming from empty air. "They will rise at any moment."

"Maybe we'll get across first."

A claw shot up from the surface and snatched the paddle from Orson's grip. Another slapped the boat, making it rock wildly. Orson toppled to the side, but just before he fell overboard, something lifted him skyward.

A great red dragon carried him above the moat. With each beat of his wings, Orson's shirt tore slightly, making him drop an inch closer to the greedy hands that swiped at him from below, each attack a narrow miss. Resolute swam back toward the castle side of the moat, pushing her boat in front.

As soon as the dragon cleared the moat, it elevated and picked up speed, heading westward toward Exodus. When it neared the river, it descended again and released Orson. He landed on his bottom and slid across the snow and mud until he came within a few paces of the brilliant star.

The dragon orbited Exodus once and landed in a skid near Orson. "Get the stardrop and climb on my back! We must hurry!"

"Magnar!" Cassabrie said. "You're here! Where is Marcelle?"

"You are a Starlighter," he growled. "Ask Exodus for an answer."

Cassabrie spread out her arms. "Magnar, I sense great hostility. If I could — "

"Hostility?" Black smoke shot from his nostrils. "Now that you have been restored to your body, you have the power to destroy me. I take great risk coming here to help this human and his daughter." Magnar's head shot out toward Orson. "Get the stardrop!"

"Yes! Of course!" Blinking at the sleet and rain, Orson fanned away the vapor and walked toward Exodus.

Cassabrie backed the star away. "Not yet."

"What?" Orson lunged toward her. "No! We can't delay. My daughter is dying as we speak."

"Koren's life is in the Creator's hands. What I must do cannot wait." From within her cloak, she withdrew a black box that appeared to be the size of a typical masonry brick. "Have you already been infected?"

Grumbling, Orson touched his stomach. "Without a doubt. I have the rash and the gnawing presence within."

"Then take your dagger and make a small slice in the star's membrane. I will give this control box to you and immediately seal the hole. Such a quick exchange shouldn't cause a problem with the contagion here in the Northlands. It is crucial that you take the box to Alaph. He will know what to do with it."

Orson glanced at Magnar. Fear in his eyes proved that he wished not to arouse Cassabrie's ire. And since she controlled the source of stardrop material, there seemed to be no option but to acquiesce. "I will do as you say."

Pulling the dagger out, he drew closer to Exodus. The huge sphere hovered less than a foot above the ground, melting any remaining snow and turning the soil into a muddy mess.

Cassabrie lowered herself to her knees at the center of the star's floor. At times she seemed to float, as if drawn upward by an invisible force. The star lifted, allowing him to walk to the point under the star where she held the box. As intense heat and bright light radiated from the outer membrane, sweat dripped from his hair and across his eyes. Cassabrie gazed down, her skin smooth and dry. A crown of light rested on her head, virtually undetectable from farther away.

Orson reached up and pushed the dagger's point against the membrane, but it felt like tough leather, too strong for an easy slice. He pushed harder and harder until the blade punctured the star.

Cassabrie grunted. Orson paused. "Did I do something wrong?"

Grimacing, she waved a hand. "No. Continue. You must hurry."

Using a sawing motion, he cut a gash that appeared to be big enough for the box to pass through.

When he withdrew the dagger and put it away, Cassabrie pushed the box into his hands, her face still contorted. As white mist seeped around her arm, she scooped sparkling radiance from the star's outer skin and pulled it inside. As if rubbing salve on a wound, she coated the gash with the radiance, her pained expression easing. A slight sizzling noise emanated, and the mist dispersed.

"Now I see how it's done." Orson pushed the box into his pocket, scooped the glowing material from the membrane, and let it rest on his palm. The glittering dust stung like a swarm of hornets.

"You have to mold it," Cassabrie said, motioning with her hands, "as if you were forming a ball of dough."

While Orson pressed his palms together and rolled the material, sweat trickled down his cheeks. "The burns will be no worse than what the disease is doing to me, I suppose."

"While you're working on that ..." Cassabrie rose and guided Exodus toward Magnar. He stood several paces away, his head turned to the side. "Magnar," she called, "look at me."

"To be hypnotized by your charms?" He snorted. "If not for your desire to help Koren, you would have slain me by now."

"I am not using my charms." She raised her hands, displaying a gap where a finger should have been on each. "And if not for the wall that separates us ..." A semitransparent copy of Cassabrie appeared next to Magnar. Wearing the same dress and cloak, she reached up, wrapped her arms around his neck, and kissed his snout. Then she backed away and vanished.

For the first time, Magnar stared directly at Exodus, his ears twitching. With every passing second, his neck sagged lower, though his eyes stayed fixed on Cassabrie. "You offer peace between us?"

Cassabrie nodded. "Peace. And forgiveness."

Orson stared. Something like joy lit Magnar's fiery eyes, but his countenance resumed its stern expression. His head lifted, and he seemed to grow even more massive. "Very well, Starlighter. Let there be peace."

Cassabrie's entire body burst into blazing light. With a smile that outshone Solarus, she guided Exodus slowly backwards. "Thank you, Magnar. You have no idea how much this means to me."

A spike of pain brought Orson's attention back to his hands. "Ouch!"

"I see that the stardrop is ready," Cassabrie said. "It must be excruciating."

As he rolled the shining sphere from palm to palm, he looked at her through the shield of fog and precipitation. "No pain is too great to endure for Koren's sake." He strode to Magnar's side. "With only one hand available for climbing, I don't think I can ... well ... scale your scales."

"Then you will return by the same mode you came." Magnar beat his wings, launched into the air, and grabbed Orson's tunic, this time with a more secure grip. As he flew a quick orbit around Exodus, his wings cleared the air. Orson looked at Cassabrie through the star's membrane. Still glowing with a brilliant aura, she stared at a tube-like object in her hands, gripping it tightly, her lips pressed firmly together.

Magnar straightened and zoomed toward the castle. Orson twisted his body to look at the river. Exodus drifted southward, then accelerated, Cassabrie veiled once again by vapor.

Orson turned back toward the castle. Whatever she intended to do was her business. He had to keep Koren

alive, buy her more time so he could test the medicine
that he hoped would ultimately cure her.

As soon as Magnar entered the castle's open doorway, he passed a boy standing in the entry room, made a
sharp left turn, and flew down a wide corridor. When they
neared the healing room, he deposited Orson on the tiled
floor, sending him into a sideways roll, and veered back
toward the entry.

Holding his clasped hands close to his chest, Orson rode
out the momentum. The final roll carried him over the roots
of the healing trees. The moment he stopped, he climbed
carefully to his feet and tiptoed across the fragile floor toward
the last bed on the right. With every step, the stardrop
sizzled in his grip, and the odor of burning flesh assaulted
his nose. The pain made him dizzy and disoriented, but he
couldn't stop to steady himself. He had to go on.

When he arrived at the bed, he paused at the rail.
Koren lay there, her red hair splayed across a white pil-
low. Her skin was ghostly white, save for the ulcers that
ravaged her cheeks, forehead, and chin. Her chest lay
motionless; no sign of breathing.

A sob tightening his throat, Orson laid his head on
her chest and listened. A tiny thump sounded in a slow,
erratic rhythm. It wasn't much, but it was enough.

Trying to slow his own heart, Orson reached up to the
healing tree's outstretched hand and rolled the stardrop
into its palm. While he waited, he blew on his own palms.
Blood oozed from deep burns, and his breath did little to
ease the pain.

The white-hot sphere sank slowly into the wood, setting the bark aglow. As sparkling particles rained down

from the hand's underside, Orson caught them. They intermingled with his blood, creating a slurry that sparkled like ruby crystals. Using both hands, he smeared the mixture across Koren's cheeks and spread it to her forehead, throat, and chest.

At each ulcer, he massaged the crystals in. Koren winced but made no sound. Soon, the smears dried and transformed into new skin, pink and healthy. Orson lifted his hands and looked at his palms. They, too, had mended. Only bloodstains and a few minor burns remained.

Koren opened her eyes. Blinking, she looked around before setting her gaze on Orson. "Are you ..." She narrowed her eyes. "Are you who I think you are?"

Tears flowing, Orson took her hand into his. With his throat tight, he had to swallow before replying. "I am your father, little K."

"It's true!" She shot up and threw her arms around his neck. "I dreamed about your voice!" As she kneaded his back, she wept. "Am I dead? Is this the Creator's paradise?"

"No, dearest one. You were at death's door, but I brought you back with a stardrop and a healing tree."

Koren drew away and looked up at the tree's hand. "The disease?"

"You still have it, so we have to find a permanent cure." He lowered the bed slats. "Come. We need to test a medicine I will make from Cassabrie's genetics."

She wrapped her body in the sheet and, with Orson's help, slid down to the floor. "Where are my clothes?"

"Resolute burned your clothes and disinfected your cloak. I'll show you where to get dressed." He set a hand on her back and guided her toward the door. Even through the sheet, her skin felt hot. Although the ulcers had cleared, fever remained.

As they tiptoed across the woody floor, Koren held her sheet together with one hand and took his with the other. "Say it again."

He looked down at her. Her head angled upward, her eyes sparkled green, and her smile shone more brightly than Trisarian's glow. "Say what again?"

"Your nickname for me." She lifted her brow. "Please?"

They stopped just past the doorway. Bending over, Orson met her gaze and reached for the passion burning deep inside. "I love you, little K."

Her eyes wide and her mouth agape, Koren seemed to absorb the words. Then, she gave him a gentle smile. "I love you, too," she whispered.

Adding a sigh, she took his hand again. "I have been wanting to say that for years, but my dreams never let me. I could never see you. You were only a voice."

He swung their clasped hands in time with their gait. "Then let's make sure we can talk to each other for a long time to come."

seven

Randall let his gaze drift from a tall evergreen tree to a moss-covered boulder to a marshy pool. The early morning sounds of the forest—cricket chirps, bird calls, and dripping dew—had diminished ... ominously so. Even the breeze had settled, and the treetops no longer rustled. In spite of the still air, leaves fell from the deciduous trees like rain, as if autumn had arrived at an accelerated rate. The loss of shelter was troubling. Soon any beast flying overhead would be able to spot them.

He propped his sword against his shoulder and whispered, "Do you hear something, Tibber?"

Standing at Randall's side, Tibalt grabbed his stringy gray hair with both hands, pulling it away from his ears. "Not a thing."

"That's what worries me."

"Yep. Noise is good. My years in the dungeon taught me that. Too much quiet means either you're dead or everyone else is. I remember once when six prisoners died on the same night. It got so quiet I started to wonder if I was dead myself, but when I heard my heart beating, I decided—"

"Shhh!" Randall craned his neck. For a moment, a flapping sound had mixed in with Tibalt's ramblings—either a huge bird or a dragon—but now silence ensued again.

"What did you hear?" Tibalt whispered.

"I'm not sure." Randall pointed his sword at a southward path, no more than a series of gaps between knee-high thorn bushes. "If Elyssa's directions are accurate, I think we should head that way."

As the two continued their single-file march, Tibalt chattered from behind. "The forest sure beats the mining area. I thought Solarus was going to pound every last drop of water out of me. But these trees are nice. And I hear water running, so there must be a stream close by." He drew in a deep breath, then coughed. "The smell could be better. Something foul is in the air, like a dead dog. It's a wonder we haven't seen vultures. Still, with no dragons around, this world of slavery and cruel oppression ain't so bad."

"True. This section of Starlight is a lot like home." After several minutes of quiet walking, Randall halted at the edge of a wide, shallow stream, one of Elyssa's landmarks. If this was the right place, the campsite she and Wallace had made should be only a hundred paces more to the south. Now it was time to listen even more carefully. If any escaped slaves were around, the two would-be rescuers might be the cause of their deaths, not by the teeth of dragons, but by the ravages of disease.

Randall scratched his chest, where a rash had erupted. Tibalt had reported the same. As old as Tibalt was, the contagion might consume him like fire through tinder wood. Yet, he seemed as spry and cheerful as ever.

"Do you still have the note?" Randall asked.

"Right here." From his belt, Tibalt withdrew a rolled-up parchment tied with a leather cord. "Should I post it on a tree?"

"Not yet. We have to make sure someone will find it." Randall listened again to the silence, waiting, but nothing reached his ears. "I suppose I should call out."

Tibalt shrugged. "At this point, what could it hurt? If a dragon hears us, we'll just die sooner rather than later. At least the disease will burn with us."

"That's not exactly an uplifting scenario."

"I tell it like I see it. As my pappy used to say, 'There's no use planting daisies around a pig sty.'"

"Wise words." Randall set a hand at the side of his mouth and called out, "Can anyone hear me?" His words echoed once, warbling, as if divided by the surrounding trees.

While they waited for an answer, Randall trained his ears skyward. The flapping returned, somewhere to the east, but no shadows interrupted the clear blue sky. The mining mesas lay two miles or so in that direction, so a dragon on patrol in that area might have ventured into the forested region.

Another flapping noise sounded, this time from the west, too far away to be the same dragon. Maybe they were birds after all, huge eagles looking for a catch at dawn, or maybe vultures that had detected the rotting flesh of two diseased humans.

"Birds?" Randall asked.

"Birds twice the size of horses, maybe. If they're hawks, I'm gonna be a scurrying rat in about ten seconds."

Randall lifted his sword and pointed it toward the eastern sky. A shadow passed across the clearing. One second later, a dragon swooped low from east to west, its reddish belly brushing the treetops. Curling its neck, it aimed its red-eyed stare at them as it passed by.

"A drone," Randall said. "Smaller than the other dragons."

"To a mouse, a hawk is a hawk. Even a small one can bite your head off."

The dragon bent into a tight circle and flew down into the clearing. As debris lifted into the air, it landed on the run straight toward them and blew fire from its gaping mouth.

Randall grabbed Tibalt's arm and dove to the leaf-covered ground. The fire shot over their bodies, igniting a swath of leaves beyond them. The dragon followed the volley, dug its claws into their backs, and flung them toward the trees one after the other.

Randall slammed into a trunk, his back bending at the impact. As he slid to the forest floor, Tibalt flew by and tumbled in reverse somersaults until his momentum eased. He rested on his back, gasping for breath. "I'm glad ... it's just a drone."

The dragon stalked toward them. More flames spewed from its nostrils. "Taushin ordered your execution. It seems that he has no fondness for invaders from Dark-sphere."

His ribs aching, Randall searched the smoldering underbrush for his sword, but it was nowhere in sight. Another dragon shadow crossed the clearing. When the first dragon looked up, Randall scrambled to Tibalt, hoisted him over his back, and ran into a cluster of densely packed trees.

He set Tibalt on his feet and peeked around a boulder. A second dragon, slimmer and of a lighter hue, landed between them and the first dragon, shadow dappling its spiny back. Both shouted in the draconic language, each retort louder than the previous one.

Wobbly and massaging his head, Tibalt looked over Randall's shoulder. "That critter slung me like a dead cat."

"Good thing you have nine lives." Randall spied his gleaming blade near a patch of burning leaves. "I need to get my sword. Otherwise, when this dragon battle is over, we might be the prize."

"Dinner for one?"

"Exactly."

"Then what are we doing here? The last I heard, the mice don't wait around to see who wins the cat fight."

"True, but I'm hoping one of the cats might be on our side."

The second dragon switched to the human tongue. "We need not kill them. I will assume responsibility and take them to Taushin myself."

"You are a betrayer, just like your mate," the drone said. "I cannot trust anyone in Arxad's family to act according to Taushin's wishes."

"She must be Fellina," Randall whispered. "Jason told me about her. She *is* on our side."

"Stay there. I'm smaller than you." Tibalt dropped to his belly and slithered toward the sword.

Fellina growled. "Leave them be, or prepare to fight."

"You think you can fight me?" The drone snorted. "You are a mere female!"

"I find it comical that a drone would make an issue of gender. You boast as if you still possess masculinity, though your whiny voice proves its absence."

"Be silent! Your mindless chatter will let them get away!" The drone flew toward Randall, but Fellina leaped in front of him. When they collided, the two bit and clawed at each other. Snapping jaws and piercing shrieks ripped through the clearing. Wings flailed, and tails swung and thumped. Fellina pushed her way on top and, like a striking adder, thrust her gaping mouth at the drone's neck again and again, but hard scales repelled every blow.

The drone slapped Fellina with his tail and rolled over her. Now on top, he clawed at her vulnerable spot.

"Help her out!" Tibalt tossed the sword. As it rotated, Randall timed the hilt's arrival, snatched it out of the air, and charged. He dove between the two dragons and plunged the blade into the drone's belly. Blood spewed over his legs and spread over Fellina's scales.

The drone snapped at Randall, but he rolled out of the way just in time. Fellina was not as fortunate; its teeth gouged her underbelly. While Fellina thrashed, Randall hacked at the drone's neck with all his might. After several blows, the neck severed, and the drone's body rolled to the side, though the head, with a foot or so of neck dangling, stayed attached to Fellina's abdomen.

"Be still!" Randall shouted. "Let me check your wounds."

"I will not!" Fellina batted the head away and rolled upright, beating both wings to balance. Scarlet blood covered her belly, but it was impossible to tell how much of it belonged to the drone. "I will not have the teeth of one of Taushin's brutes spearing me for another second."

As she heaved deep breaths, every exhale carried a shower of sparks that drizzled over the underbrush and ignited small fires.

"Well done," Randall whispered.

"Yep." Tibalt rose to his feet, brushed himself off, and called out, "You sure taught that drone a thing or two!"

Fellina's eyes flashed. "Do you think I rejoice in this conquest?" She glared at Tibalt, again spewing sparks-filled breaths. "Did I kill a dragon to rescue a pair of fools?"

Tibalt backed away, a finger raised. "Apparently at least one fool who can't keep his mouth shut when he's supposed to."

Taking a deep breath, Randall steeled his trembling legs and strode closer to her. "Please accept my sincere apologies, Fellina. My friend was in a dungeon for decades, and he sometimes doesn't think before he speaks. We are in your debt."

The fire in Fellina's eyes faded. "Perhaps one of you is not a fool after all."

While pondering what to say next, Randall smothered the closest flames with his boot. The other fires were dying on their own. "Have your earlier wounds healed already?"

"Enough so that Arxad felt that he could leave. He planned to fly toward the Northlands to see how Jason and the others are doing." Fellina wiped her wound with a foreclaw, smearing blood and revealing an oozing cut. "We must find him, and soon. The Benefile have come to the village, and they are gathering the slaves in front of the Zodiac. They intend to kill every human in order to arrest the spread of the disease. They want to allow the soldiers from Darksphere safe access to the village so they can, as one of the Benefile said, 'bring justice by the hand of the oppressed race.'"

"That makes no sense," Randall said. "They're going to kill humans to protect humans?"

"By their logic, the humans will die anyway, so putting them to death quickly is merciful and expeditious. By allowing the soldiers safe access, the Benefile hope to punish the dragons of the Southlands with a twist of irony. Xenith and I decided to sneak away to find Arxad. Since Xenith does not know the location of the refuge, she flew north while I flew south. I told her not to go far. There is no sense chasing him all the way to the Northlands."

"When do the Benefile plan to kill the slaves?"

"Xenith overheard much of their conversation, and they debated the topic to the point of absurdity, but she believes they will wait until the army from Darksphere is visible on the horizon."

Randall kicked the remaining embers. "And we don't know how long that will take."

"It will probably be a while. When Xenith left the Northlands after delivering Cassabrie's finger, she said there was no sign of soldiers. She also looked for Koren,

Jason, and Elyssa, but never saw them. It is possible that they ventured into the forest to travel under tree cover."

"Jason would do that." Randall nodded toward Tibalt. "We were hoping to find the refuge to warn the escaped slaves about the disease. Maybe you could point us in the right direction."

Fellina's head swayed as she looked Randall and Tibalt over. "You have the disease yourselves. How do you plan to warn them without risking exposure?"

Randall glanced at Tibalt again. He was brushing leaves and twigs from his hair. "We have a note we were going to post," Randall said. "We hoped people would read it without us having to come close."

"Show me the note."

"I have it!" Tibalt shuffled through the brush, unrolling a parchment along the way. Gripping the top and bottom of the page, he held the parchment in front of Fellina's snout.

While Fellina read silently, Randall read it as well, hoping the words didn't appear foolish in her eyes.

"To all humans formerly enslaved by dragons, read this warning from fellow humans who have come to rescue you. A fatal disease is spreading among those still enslaved by the dragons, so you must not venture into the village or any work colony. We will send an uninfected rescuer to you who will lead you to a place where you will be examined for symptoms of the disease. We are working on a cure, and once it is found, all slaves will be taken to a world where they will be free. Frequently return to the place you found this note, and we will contact you again with further news."

Fellina huffed a fiery stream that instantly ignited the parchment. Tibalt threw it to the ground and began stomping out the flames. "What did you do that for?"

"The paper itself is potentially infected."

Randall scooped up the charred remains, a handful of scorched scraps. "How do you know?"

"I detected human skin cells on the surface. Arxad and I have much experience with this disease, and I assure you that even the most casual contact will spread it."

"So do you have a suggestion?"

"If I fly over the slave refuge with one of you, we can warn them about the disease from a safe distance. I could deliver the warning myself, but the message would be more readily accepted if an infected human delivered it."

"You mean, show them our skin," Randall said.

Fellina's head bobbed. "I can see the rash here and there, but I am not sure how visible it will be from a distance."

"I'm probably not a good candidate for that." Randall scratched his chest through his tunic. "It hasn't progressed far enough to see. It itches quite a bit, though."

Tibalt lifted his own tunic. Red welts covered his skin from his bony ribcage to his emaciated waist. "Hoowee! I look like a beekeeper after a mutiny!"

"That looks terrible!" Randall turned toward Fellina. "Does that mean he's going to die soon?"

"There is no uniform progression for this disease," Fellina said. "Sometimes skin lesions are the first symptom, and an attack on the internal organs comes later. Other times, such lesions are a sign of the end. It is impossible to know until death comes."

"That means old Tibber gets to ride a dragon!" Tibalt clapped his hands. "I hope there's a medal for dragon riding. I've always wanted a medal."

Randall refocused on Fellina. "Are you able to carry two riders?"

Fellina looked down at her bleeding wound. "Between this injury and my previous one, too much of a load would be risky. And we must return quickly because of the Benefile threat, so it will be better if I carry only one."

Randall nodded. "I understand."

"I asked Xenith to join me if her search for Arxad proves futile. You see, it is possible that the disease was carried by the wind to the refuge, so we might have to transport sick children to the Northlands. I gave her directions, so she will likely fly over this spot eventually. If you see her, call for her to pick you up."

"I don't think I'll bother her," Randall said. "She'll probably be in a hurry, too."

"Very well." Using a wing, Fellina pushed Tibalt toward her flank. "Climb up my tail and sit on my back at the base of my neck."

After Tibalt did so, he wiggled in his seat. "How am I supposed to stay on?"

"I trust that sheer terror will keep you in place." Fellina beat her wings and launched nearly straight upward. Tibalt wrapped his arms around Fellina's neck and hung on tightly, letting out a yell that sounded both terrified and delighted. Soon dragon and rider had flown out of sight.

Randall kicked a stone, sending it hurtling into the brush. He strolled to the dead dragon. Its severed head lay atop its outstretched wing, and blood pooled next to its perforated belly. With closed eyelids and slack jaw, it seemed passive, far different from the aggressive beast that tried to kill him only moments ago. Maybe it had a family—parents or siblings that would mourn the loss.

Pressing his lips together, Randall shook his head. This dragon was one of the slavers. It tried to kill two men who hoped to rescue the oppressed. It was evil and deserved to die.

He shoved the dragon's head with his boot, knocking it off its wing. Then, setting his jaw, he turned away. Guilt gnawed at his conscience, but he brushed it back. Dragons weren't worth the trouble.

With a glance at the skies and the surrounding trees, he breathed in deeply, trying to get his bearings. The foul odor Tibalt had mentioned earlier still hung in the air, as if some hapless animal rotted nearby.

Leading with his sword, Randall followed the scent. As he plunged deeper into the forest, he stopped occasionally and used the point of his sword to etch directional marks into the bark of trees along the paths he chose. With the trees undressing so quickly, by the time he tried to return, they wouldn't look the same, and it wouldn't hurt to give Tibalt some direction, too, in case he returned soon.

The scent grew stronger and stronger, coaxing him onward. Maybe an escaped slave had breathed his last nearby. Finding the corpse and providing a decent burial would make the search worth the effort. If vultures lurked, they wouldn't get a meal of human flesh, not if Randall had his way.

Finally, he came upon a circular stand of tall trees, their trunks growing close together. Halting, Randall stared at the bizarre formation. They appeared to encompass something, maybe a glade, and the branches all grew inward and to the sides, leaving the trunks with only bare bark on their outward faces.

He let his gaze follow the trunks upward. As they narrowed, the gaps between them widened, though limbs and branches filled the gaps with woody arms and fingers. It seemed that the entire network of tree projections had been designed to protect something within the ring, or perhaps prevent something within from escaping. Only birds, small animals, and maybe a human could penetrate the web.

As he walked around the ring of trees, he searched for a wider opening, but the trees grew with little variance. After about a hundred paces, he reached the one-quarter point of the ring where a marsh stretched out to the west as far as the eye could see. Moss dangled from tree branches, nearly reaching the water, which was too calm and dark to determine its depth. Algae floated on the surface, and bugs skittered between pads that looked like the eyes of dragons—dark on the edges with hints of red at the center.

Randall shook his head. No doubt an escapee, perhaps burned or otherwise wounded, had reached the marsh and collapsed, despairing at the sight, and now his rotting corpse filled the air with its stench.

He sniffed the air again. Although the marsh emitted a moldy odor, the earlier fetid smell held sway. It definitely originated from within the ring of trees.

Again leading with the sword, he pushed between two trunks. Light from a big gap in the trunks on the opposite side illuminated a circular plot, and the sound of bubbling water filled the glade. Broken branches lay in tall piles here and there. Above, gaps marred the canopy, but not nearly enough to explain the plethora of wooden debris. The leaves seemed healthy, apparently immune to the change of seasons affecting the leaves outside the ring.

Randall walked slowly forward, weaving around the piles. As he closed in, the dirt changed to mud, then his boots splashed in shallow water, maybe an inch or two deep. At the center of the glade, air erupted from underneath in bubbling pulses that propelled the water over the ground before soaking in quickly.

On the opposite side of the depression, a humanlike form lay on its side. This had to be the source of the smell.

As Randall drew closer, it seemed that a thin white shell encased a man, keeping him motionless. Randall prodded the man's shoulder with a finger, breaking through the cold coating. The shell snapped like thin ice. Beneath, the man's skin seemed pliable, unfrozen. Maybe he hadn't been in this state for very long, but the odor told a different story.

Randall leaned closer and sniffed again. No. It seemed that the odor came from the spring, probably the erupting gas. After turning the man to his back, he brushed ice away and pressed his ear against his chest. A heartbeat pattered within, weak and erratic, and his breaths came in short, halting gasps.

Randall sheathed his sword, hoisted the man over his shoulder, and carried him to the big gap, again dodging the broken branches. A foot-high stump stood at the middle of the opening. About twenty feet above, the rest of the severed trunk dangled from the network of branches.

When he reached the outside, Randall laid the man down and brushed more ice away—from his torso, arms, and bearded face. He looked familiar, like an older version of Jason. Apparently, he had found Frederick Masters at long last.

After Randall brushed the ice away, he rubbed Frederick's chest briskly. Since his clothes were dry, it seemed that the coating of ice had protected him from the water, somehow acting as a freezing agent and an insulator at the same time.

"Come on, Frederick," Randall said out loud. "Wake up. Whatever put you in ice might come back."

After nearly a minute of constant rubbing, Frederick's eyes opened. He blinked rapidly, and his teeth began chattering, interrupting his words. "Randall ... Prescott ... the governor's son?"

"Yep." Randall grasped Frederick's wrist. "Let's see if you can walk. You need to warm up."

He hoisted Frederick to his feet and helped him pace in a tight circle. "Thank you," Frederick said, his teeth still chattering. "I thought ... I was a goner."

"Save your thanks. I'm carrying a disease that'll do you in if we can't find a cure. I just guessed that it was better to thaw you out and hope for the best."

Frederick halted, shivering. "Good choice. I have to ... warn everyone ... about the dragons ... who did this to me."

"Dragons coated you with ice?" Randall let out a whistle. "That's new."

"They are the B—Benefile. Some call them ... the Bloodless.... They're white dragons that breathe ice ... instead of fire."

"Ah! Fellina told me about them. I didn't know about their color or the temperature of their breath, but I do know that they're in the dragon village now. They're planning to kill all the slaves so—"

"Kill the slaves! Why?"

"Something about irony. They want a human army to punish those who enslaved humans, so they have to get rid of the disease first. We have soldiers marching here from our world, so it looks like the Benefile want to use them."

"Bring justice to humans by killing some and using others as a hammer." Frederick shook his head. "Madness!"

"Definitely, but what can we do about it? What are they?"

As Frederick marched in place, his chattering and shivering eased. "I get the impression that they're law enforcers of some kind. They were set free when a curse was lifted."

Randall nodded. "Magnar's curse, I'll bet. He wasn't allowed to pass his region's barrier wall. I'm guessing he went through the portal from Major Four to the Northlands."

"Magnar was on Major Four?" Frederick rubbed his biceps briskly. "There's a lot going on I don't know about."

"Well, I'll try to fill you in on what I know."

"Like the disease?"

"Right. Fellina's taking a friend of mine to your refuge, and they're hoping to warn them about the disease from the air."

"So if you're contagious, then I might have it, too. I can't risk going back."

"Right again." Randall patted Frederick's shoulder. "Let's go to the place Fellina left me. We'll get each other up to date on the way."

eight

With dawn illuminating their campsite, Jason rose from his makeshift bed of leaves and walked across the ashes of their overnight fire. Since the river to his right made enough noise to mask his approach, Elyssa, who slept on a leafy bed of her own, didn't stir.

When he knelt next to her, her eyelids twitched, maybe a sign that her probing sensors warned of his approach, but exhaustion kept her in sleep's embrace. They had jogged or marched well into the night, passing the waterfall and following the southbound stream until they couldn't travel another step. With Koren's plight torturing their minds, it seemed like betrayal to rest, but they had no choice but to give in to reality.

Jason laid a hand on her shoulder. "We'd better get going."

She woke with a start. After blinking at him with wide eyes, she let out a sigh. "Oh, good. It was just a dream."

"What did you dream about?"

"Wolves." She rose to a sitting position and pushed a hand through her hair. "They had dragon wings and chittered like squirrels, and one of them forced a flaming torch down your throat."

Jason rubbed his throat. "Thanks for the vivid imagery."

"You asked."

He helped Elyssa to her feet, gathered their supply bags, and nodded toward the river. "If you want to refresh yourself, I'll pull out some snacks we can eat along the way, then I'll take a turn."

"Sounds good," Elyssa said, "but let's hurry. I don't want to waste another second."

After only a few minutes, they finished preparations and started northward again with a relatively slow stride. Soon their legs loosened, allowing a quicker pace that eventually broke into a rapid jog. Following the river upstream, they dodged roots, ducked under low-hanging branches, and waded in shallow water to avoid prickly brambles.

About two hours passed with the same scenery drifting by — thick forest to the left and flower-filled meadows to the right. Although no dragons had come into view since Koren's kidnapper took her away, it still seemed prudent to stay under cover. It was easy to scan the sky as well as the meadow for any allies that might show up.

Finally, something new appeared in a clearing up ahead. Jason halted, blocked Elyssa with an arm, and set the supply bags on the ground. Both gasping for breath, they stared at the sight. Dead wolves littered an open space next to the stream; at least eight, maybe ten.

Walking on the balls of his feet, Jason edged closer. He prodded one of the carcasses with the point of his sword. The hide bent easily. "Pretty fresh. Whoever did this isn't far ahead."

"Adrian?" Elyssa asked, her panting now slower.

"Most likely. I haven't seen one of his marks for a while, but the tracks keep showing up." Jason pointed at a long rut in the mud. "That's probably from the cart, and there's quite a bit of blood around."

"Wolf blood or human blood?"

Jason shrugged. "Maybe both."

Elyssa dipped her finger into a red pool next to the rut and rubbed the tacky paste against her thumb. "Human. Fresh."

"So at least one of them is hurt, but it looks like the wolves got the worst of it."

Elyssa followed the rut to the stream where it abruptly disappeared about three paces away from the water. A raft constructed with saplings and vines sat halfway beached on the bank. The gently flowing stream lapped against its back edge, shifting it slightly every few seconds. As she washed her fingers in the water, she looked back at Jason. "It looks like they pushed the cart into the river."

"I see that." Jason drew closer, flapping his tunic to dry the sweat. The grass near the riverbank bent over, indicating a possible flood, which explained the missing few feet of wheel marks. Yet, the grass bent northward, upstream. "It looks like the river flowed backwards. That doesn't make sense at all."

"You told me you and Koren and Uriel rode a stream backwards," Elyssa said.

"Cassabrie made that happen, and the real Koren wasn't on the raft. She was just an image she created while the wolves dragged her away."

"I remember." Elyssa nudged the raft with her toe. "Could this be the same raft?"

Jason lifted the front and pulled it fully on shore. The way the vines bound the saplings definitely reflected Adrian's handiwork, though some connections had broken, leaving gaps. "It looks the same."

"Interesting." Elyssa pinched some sand from the narrow flood area and rubbed it between her fingers. "It's still cool and wet. If Adrian and the others rode this raft upstream, it probably wasn't long ago."

"Long enough for the stream to return to normal and push the raft back here." Jason studied the current as it swept around a slight curve in the bank. "I suppose it beaches itself here because of the bend in the stream. Adrian found it here just like we did, but we don't have a Starlighter to give us a push. If Cassabrie was around earlier, she's probably long gone by now."

Elyssa's shoulders drooped. "Another ride on a raft would've helped a lot."

"That's for sure." Jason looked Elyssa over. A sheen of perspiration made her face glow, returning her stardrop-enhanced shine. Moisture dappled her clothes, from her red vest and white sleeves down to her rust-colored trousers. Her ability to keep up in spite of her malnourishment while in the dungeon was amazing.

"Maybe we can still give the raft a try," he said.

"You mean—"

"I mean, you told me you have some Starlighter gifts."
He stooped and began retying the raft's broken vines.
"You said you could distribute Starlight's energy. Isn't that
how you healed me?"

"True, but the process drains me, and I'm already
tired."

"It's up to you. I can't judge how you feel. I'm fine with
walking."

Her gaze wandered up the river. "I suppose I could try,
but I have no idea how to reverse a river."

"If you can't, then we'll just rest a while." After finishing his repair work, he found a branch void of stems and
leaves and snatched it up. "This would make a good steering pole."

"You really think I can do this, don't you?"

"You raised Petra from the dead." Jason grinned. "This
should be easy." He picked up the supply bags, helped
her sit down on the raft, and shoved it into the flow. When
he climbed aboard, he set the bags near the front and
stopped the downstream momentum with the pole. "Now
just relax and see where your mind wants to go."

Closing her eyes, Elyssa took in a deep breath and let
it out slowly. Her pendant dangled in front of her chest,
bobbing with the raft's gentle bounces. As the seconds
passed, her brow knitted. Her glow brightened. The pendant altered from beige to orange, then to bright red.

The pressure on the steering pole eased. At the raft's
sides, the current slowed, then stopped, changing the
stream to a placid pool. Her head swaying, Elyssa let out a
quiet groan. Her eyelids clenched together, and her brow

tightened further. The pendant trembled, now almost too bright to look at.

Jason stared at the water. Although there was no breeze, ripples formed on the surface. Then the raft shifted northward, slowly at first, but after a few seconds, it sailed along at a brisk marching pace. Elyssa's face turned red, nearly matching the pendant's hue and glow. Ahead, the water rolled northward in a head-high wave.

Holding his breath, Jason dared not say a word. How long could she last? Fighting the current had to be a huge battle.

He laid the pole over his lap. The feeling of helplessness gnawed at his gut. Elyssa had wanted him to be the heroic warrior, frequently urging him to lead the way, but now he had to sit and watch her toil.

The patch of skin covering his pectoral stung. He pulled his tunic's collar down and touched the pulsing bulge made by the litmus finger—Cassabrie's finger. When he and Elyssa worked together to heal Petra, the finger pulsed then as well, and the power seemed to combine with Elyssa's to allow her to see tales within Petra's mind. Could Cassabrie somehow be lending help?

After another minute, Elyssa's face relaxed. The pendant dimmed to orange, more like glowing embers than a blazing fire. She opened her eyes and gazed at him, a look of peace in her eyes. "I think I have it under control."

Jason shifted his tunic back in place. "You never cease to amaze me."

She offered a tired smile. "Thank you. I feel the same way about you."

Jason let his gaze linger. As her aura dimmed to a more natural light, her face never looked more beautiful. Even the sinking lines of malnourishment painted a portrait of sacrifice, the loving gift of a true heroine. Her passion for the slaves had cost her freedom and health as well as blood and sweat. Yes, she was a Diviner, a gifted young woman with extraordinary power, but most important, she was Elyssa Cantor, a peasant girl who loved helpless souls bound in chains and sought no reward for her sacrifice on their behalf.

Sliding forward, he reached out a hand. As she wrapped hers around it, her smile grew. "We'll find Koren," she said. "Don't worry."

He returned the smile. "I wasn't thinking about Koren."

"You weren't?" She tilted her head. "You looked so contemplative. What were you thinking about?"

He covered the clasp with his free hand. "You."

Elyssa bit her lip. As the raft raced northward, she tightened her grip on Jason's hand and said nothing more.

During the passing minutes, they quietly ate from their provisions and drank water from the river. Lines dug deeper and deeper into Elyssa's brow, and her respiration grew increasingly labored. As if tied to her waning strength, the raft's speed diminished. Finally, after about a half hour, it slowed to a near standstill.

"I can't hold it much longer." Elyssa closed her eyes and gritted her teeth. "The force against me is too strong."

Jason glanced ahead. Not far away, the water had piled up into a mountain, running up the near side like a powerful geyser. At the top, white foam looked like a snowy cap.

If Elyssa gave in to the pressure, the mountain of water would crash over them in a mammoth wave.

"Hang on! Don't give up yet!" Jason grabbed the pole and steered the raft to the eastern bank. As soon as it struck bottom, he jumped out and pulled it to shore. Elyssa rose, her face twisting as if she were carrying a dragon on her shoulders.

"How much longer can you hold it?"

Gasping for breath, she nodded. "I'm okay. Another minute, I think."

"Then head for the meadow as fast as you can. I'll be right behind you."

As soon as Elyssa ran into the eastern field, Jason grabbed one of the loose vines and sprinted, dragging the raft and supply bags along. Seconds later, the sound of crashing water erupted. Droplets pelted his head and spray filled the air. A wave surged into his legs and swept him off his feet. He tumbled in the churning flow, seeing flashes of Elyssa splashing his way as he spun in headlong somersaults.

A hand grasped his wrist and pulled him upright. Now standing in waist-deep water, he gasped for breath, Elyssa holding his arm. As the water receded toward the river, she mopped back his hair. "Are you all right?"

"I think so." He added a quick nod. "Thanks."

After sloshing to dry ground, Jason, still dragging the raft, collapsed with Elyssa and sprawled across the grass, panting. As their breathing eased, they rolled to their backs and basked in the mid-morning sunshine. Elyssa turned to Jason and grinned. "I can't believe you brought the raft!"

"I thought we could use it on the way back." He shrugged. "No use wasting it."

"I'm not complaining. I just think you're amazing."

Jason returned the grin. "The girl who pushed a mountain of water upstream just called *me* amazing. I'll take that as a compliment."

After resting a few minutes, Jason helped Elyssa to her feet. She shifted from side to side as if still riding the raft.

"Can you walk?"

She nodded. "I think so, at least for a little while."

"Let me know if you need to rest again."

"I will." As a warm breeze blew past, she looked to the north. "How close are we?"

"It's still pretty far. Quite a few hours, I think." Jason took Elyssa's hand and walked back to the river. Water gushed southward and overran both banks.

Now on the eastern bank, they could walk through the meadow and look for signs of an approaching army in the distance. At the speed they had traveled on the raft, they hadn't been able to search for any marks Adrian had made, so it was impossible to tell how far ahead he might be.

As they walked northward, mist began to fill the air, then a light drizzle fell. Clouds to the north thickened and blew their way, like a rolling wall of gray fog that veiled the horizon. A breeze kicked up, driving the icy wetness into their faces.

Elyssa tied her hair back in a quick knot. "I'm feeling better. Let's hurry."

They jogged side by side, Elyssa to Jason's right. Ice pellets mixed into the rain, forcing them to blink, and droplets began trickling from their hair down their cheeks. Soon Jason's tunic and Elyssa's vest grew wet in front, adding to the chill, though his cloak stayed fairly warm and dry.

After a few minutes, a dark line appeared in the midst of the fog, too blurry to tell what it might be. Jason glanced sideways at Elyssa. Her furrowed brow proved that she was already probing the mystery.

"Marching men," she said, puffing vapor as she spoke. "I can't tell how many, but I think they're about three miles away."

Jason reached out and guided her to a stop. "We might as well rest. They'll get here eventually, and when they do, we'll probably have to march with them."

"Only if they found Koren. If they have her, they've already been exposed to the disease. If they don't have her, we have to keep looking for her, and we can't let them just walk into the Southlands and catch the disease."

They sat together in the midst of the tall grass and flowers, facing the oncoming soldiers. With their clothes already damp, the moist ground mattered little. The fog thickened, hiding the soldiers, but the sound of tromping feet pressed onward. They would arrive soon.

As the cool wind bent the grass blades against their shoulders, Elyssa scooted closer to Jason, touching hip to hip. "Do you know what this reminds me of?"

He turned toward her. With wet hair plastered over her forehead and down her cheeks, she posed in a familiar way. When she emerged from the dungeon, her hair was matted and her face gaunt, though her eyes sparkled with delight. At the time, her eyes had raised images of verdant meadows, the color of life. Now, with her entire face aglow and a verdant meadow providing a sheltering embrace, the moments they sat under the roots of a toppled tree came to mind. "I think so."

She rubbed her arms. "A lot has changed since then."

"I know what you mean."

Her brow lifted. As she shivered, her eyes sparkled in the same way they had that evening. "Do you really?"

Jason pulled his cloak off and spread it over her shoulders. After he had tucked it in around her, he smiled. "Yes, I do."

She lifted her index finger. He looped his with hers, then recited the chant they had shared as children. "We're hooked by these fingers together, as brother and sister forever. Like gander and goose, we'll never break loose, no dagger or dragon can sever."

As they stared at each other, Elyssa whispered, "Brother and sister forever?"

Jason switched to his ring finger and hooked it with hers. "If we both survive, we'll talk about changing the lyrics."

A tear slid down her cheek. She drew her finger gently away and leaned against his shoulder. The fog continued to thicken, and the stomps of heavy boots grew louder and closer, making the ground vibrate. The thunder of war had arrived, and one way or another, deadly battles would soon begin.

"If we both survive," she said softly. "That's a step no one can skip."

☙☙

Randall stood with Frederick in the clearing, searching the sky for Xenith or Fellina.

"My cabin is in that direction," Frederick said, pointing to the south. "Flying by dragon should take only a few minutes."

"Then Fellina and Tibalt could have returned by now." Randall scanned the forest floor. The debris appeared to be in the same chaotic mess he had left it—scorch marks, ashes, and blood—and the drone's carcass still lay in the same position. "Maybe the children already have the disease, and Fellina is arranging a way to transport them."

"Or there is trouble afoot." Frederick kicked the dead dragon's tail. "I have never seen a patrol drone this close to my cabin. If others are around, they might have noticed Fellina and followed her."

"Good point."

The beating of wings filled the forest. A dragon dropped through the canopy at a sharp angle, breaking branches as it fell. With a louder flurry, it landed in an awkward slide, its forelegs digging into the leaves and underbrush as it slowed to a stop.

Randall whipped out his sword and stepped toward it, but Frederick pulled him back. "Don't worry. It's Xenith."

Wagging her head, Xenith turned toward them, breathless. "I think I eluded them."

"Them?" Randall asked.

"My fellow dragons were hiding from the Benefile in the mountains. Three followed me, I assume to find the refuge. Of course, I led them elsewhere. I had to dive in and out of the forest, including a swim in the marshes.

They became entangled in vines, and I was able to outrace them. When I saw you, I took cover."

"That was very resourceful," Randall said. "They must be spitting mad at you."

Her eyes flashed wide open. "Get down!" Randall dove into the debris. Xenith covered him with a wing. Now in near darkness, he listened to the sounds above, trying to imagine what was going on. Wings fluttered. Dragons growled. Branches splintered. Yet the chaos occurred well over their heads.

After several more seconds, Xenith lifted her wing. "They're gone."

As Randall climbed to his feet, vine fragments filtered through the branches and fell to the ground. He picked up a four-foot section and showed it to Frederick, who was climbing out from under the drone's wing. "Evidence of Xenith's brilliant maneuvering."

"I met her only once at her cave," Frederick said. "Arxad is very proud of her flying skills. He says there is no one better in the land."

Xenith bowed her head. "Thank you for your kindness."

"So they didn't find the refuge," Randall said. "You're sure of that."

"Those three did not find it by following me, because I was still looking for it myself, but I cannot be sure whether or not other dragons have found it. Many are looking."

Frederick gazed toward the south. "Then Fellina is probably waiting there or close by, unable to leave because they're watching for her."

"Or her new injuries are more severe than she thought," Randall said.

"New injuries?" Xenith's tail whipped the ground, scattering leaves. "What happened here? Who killed that drone?"

Frederick patted her neck. "Your mother and Randall killed it. The drone bit her in the underbelly, but she was well enough to fly, so we assume she's okay. At least that's what Randall told me."

"Right now I'm not sure of anything." Randall checked his scabbard and refastened his sword belt. "Frederick, I think we need to split up. You go on foot to the refuge. If Xenith is willing, she can take me to check on the slaves in the village. Since the other dragons fear the Benefile, I don't think we'll be followed."

"But my mother might need me," Xenith said. "I can travel by land with Frederick."

Frederick reached high and laid a hand on the side of her snout. "Hear me, Xenith. Now is not the time to listen to your heart. You must listen to your brain. Where are you most needed? Whom will your speed and cunning most benefit? Will a fast dragon be needed to deliver a cure for the disease? Who else could fly Randall to the village without getting caught by the Bloodless? And don't forget, your father is out there somewhere. It's possible that only he knows how to defeat the white dragons, so you must locate him, even if it means going to the North-lands. Once you do, your speed in leading him back here or delivering his strategy might be the salvation of us all. If you decline, all could be lost."

A dour expression sagged Xenith's features. "You sound very much like my father. Mix logic with a dose of guilt, and he can get me to do anything."

"Then you'll go?" Randall asked.

Xenith let out a deep sigh. "I will go. Get on my back."

When Randall settled at the base of her neck, he touched the hilt of his sword. "You'll need a weapon."

Frederick smiled. "I stashed a few here and there. Don't worry."

"Sounds good." Randall patted Xenith's neck. "Let's go."

Xenith bent low, ready to launch. "Hold tight, human. This will be a ride you will never forget."

nine

Koren tiptoed close to a set of miniature dragon heads, the pair of brass
doorknobs that wouldn't turn the
last time she faced the great white doors. During that
visit, Alaph refused to let her in, and her only view of the
inner chamber came from a Starlighter vision while inside
Exodus. But was the expanse of pure whiteness where
she shed her black dress and boots a reflection of reality,
or just an imagined portrait of the mysterious room?

Now dressed in a simple beige V-neck tunic that fell
nearly to her knees, baggy gray trousers that would drop
right off if not for a leather cord around her waist, and the
same blue cloak she had worn throughout her journeys,
she felt so different. Although the killer disease continued
to gnaw painful holes beneath her newly healed skin, a
few hours of sleep had brought a feeling of freshness and
freedom that coursed from the top of her head down to

her bare toes. Even Resolute had noticed the attitude difference during their walk here, saying that a glow emanated from Koren's eyes. Maybe some of the power she had gained after taking a stardrop had returned.

Soon Resolute would return with Orson. After catching some rest himself, he had risen at dawn to talk to Alaph and prepare some things for making the medicine. Perhaps he felt the freshness as well. With prospects for a cure rising, it seemed that hope flooded the air.

Koren reached into her tunic's outer pocket—an accessory few tunics in Starlight had—and withdrew the box Cassabrie had given Orson. Black and rectangular, it weighed very little, no more than a meat-scraps muffin. At the center, a red button was recessed within a raised circle of black metal, apparently to prevent someone from depressing the button accidentally. She read the white letters near the edge at the heel of her hand—*DETONATE*.

She slid the box back into her pocket. This was likely the same one she had found in the room next to the star chamber, but the meaning of the word remained a mystery.

The clopping of boots sounded from behind. "Little K! I'm coming."

Koren smiled. Her father used that name every chance he could, as if trying to make up for all the years they had been separated.

He hustled to her side, Resolute guiding him, her glow brightening the corridor. "I apologize for being late," he said. "I'm glad you found it on your own."

"No one can find this place on their own." Koren winked at Resolute. "At least that's what I've been told."

Grinning, Resolute curtsied, then ran away, her feet barely touching the floor. The light in the hallway ebbed until only an odd ambient glow remained, as if particles in the air itself radiated energy.

Koren took her father's hand and looked up at him. "I've been wondering about something." She flexed her toes against the cool marble floor. "I guess I died before I could talk, and I don't remember any other father, so ... what should I call you?"

He cleared his throat and smoothed out his tunic, similarly oversized and dull of color. "I suppose, considering your age and maturity, that *Father* would be appropriate. We are both too old for Papa or Daddy, I think."

"Maybe not." She wrapped her arms around his torso and laid her head on his shoulder. "I'll call you Father, but I hope I'm never too old to call you Daddy if I need to."

He laid his hand on the back of her head. "And I hope you never outgrow Little K."

She drew away and stared into his gray eyes. "No! Never!"

"Good." He gestured toward the door. "Would you like to do the honors?"

"Thank you." Koren grasped the dragon head on the right side, letting her hand linger. Unlike before, it didn't heat up at all. She turned it and pulled the door open. Although the panel rose well over her head and the width spanned the length of a dragon wing, it felt as light as a feather.

A shaft of radiance spilled through and washed over her body. Like chalky water poured from a pail, whiteness spread across her clothes and skin until she was as white as the door itself. Her father, too, had turned white, though his eyes remained gray.

They entered together, hand in hand. As in her vision, the chamber appeared to be nothing but whiteness. "Have you been here before?" she asked.

"Only once. I brought Cassabrie's finger and the other ingredients. Alaph said the test should be performed here. He didn't say why, other than we would learn the answers we're seeking."

As they continued, Koren looked back. Even the door opening had disappeared, replaced by whiteness. "I can't see the ingredients. Everything is white."

"Your eyes will adjust in a few more seconds."

Almost imperceptibly, the whiteness dissolved. A table appeared an arm's length away. Thrice the size of Madam Orley's food-preparation table, an adult could lie down on it with room to spare. Koren touched the surface, cool and clean. As dark as marsh oak, the grains felt fine and smooth.

A scarlet box sat at the center. No bigger than her hand, it seemed to be made out of wood, but what sort of tree produced wood so red?

As the whiteness continued to melt away, a hearth took shape behind the table. Flames crackled on a stack of logs in a brick fireplace, an unusual sight in the hot Southlands village.

Orson picked up a set of tongs leaning next to the fireplace and pinched a small cup within the flames. When he drew it out, the casing pulsed orange, and thin blue smoke rose from whatever bubbled inside. The cup looked like the mortar Madam Orley used for grinding herbs, small enough to nestle in a hand and thick enough to endure the grinding.

He lowered the cup carefully and set it next to the red box. The contact raised a loud sizzle, but it seemed to do no harm to the wooden surface.

"There." Father leaned the tongs against the wall. "Now for the critical step."

Koren watched his every move. With furrowed brow and steady hands, he opened the red box and slid it closer to her. Inside, a finger lay in velvet. Stitched closed at the base, it appeared to be unchanged from the moment Zena pushed it into her hand. Without blemish or corruption, it looked like it could be reattached and used without a problem.

"Cassabrie's," she whispered.

"Yes, I have heard the story." Her father set a needle and thread on the table, then withdrew a thin blade from an inner pocket. "This is called a scalpel, a cutting tool we humans used before the disease first ravaged the world. Its main purpose is to cut with precision."

Koren bit her lip. If that meant what she thought it meant ...

"You might not want to watch."

"I think I should." Koren fixed her stare on her father's hand. He set the scalpel on the finger near the stitched base and pressed downward. With a sickening *thunk*, the blade sliced through skin and bone, separating a quarter-inch section from the rest of the finger.

As blood oozed from both parts, Father quickly stitched the open end of the finger. "Fortunately, the bone has softened over time, and with no heart pumping, blood loss is minimal. Since we need this finger to provide for many diseased souls, however, we don't want to lose any genetic material."

When he finished stitching, he laid the finger back in its place, then scooped the severed section with the scalpel and poised it over the cup. "Take a few steps back. When I drop this into the crucible, you will want a wider view."

Koren shuffled backwards. "The crucible?"

"A vessel used for melting materials at high temperatures. It's made of graphite, a substance with which you are likely unfamiliar. On Major Four we also use *crucible* to describe a severe test or trial. If Alaph's description of his expectations is correct, we will see how appropriate the word is."

With a turn of the scalpel, he dropped the bloody section and backed away, nearly stumbling as he kept his stare on the crucible. The mixture just sizzled, not much louder than before.

Blinking, Orson walked toward the table. "Perhaps it caught on the inner part—"

Phoom! A huge ball of thick blue smoke erupted. Orson stumbled backwards, but Koren caught him.

The smoke hovered in place and fanned out until it took on the size and shape of a Starlighter's cloak. As if drawn on the cloak by chalk, white shapes appeared— four dragons facing each other around a spring of upwelling water. The blue backdrop expanded until it masked the fireplace and enveloped the table. The dragons swelled and became three-dimensional, as if physically present in the room.

"The Benefile," Orson whispered. "Perhaps the answers Alaph mentioned are materializing before our eyes."

Koren edged closer to one of the dragons. In its inanimate state, it appeared to be angry or perhaps pensive, its brow low and its ears back.

She stooped and set her hand over the bubbling water. The rising gasses were warm and wet. "Is the crucible here?"

"That's my guess. According to Alaph, the mixture will activate and set the scene into motion. We'll know the reaction is complete when the vision fades away."

"Have you seen other visions while testing?"

He nodded. "The only other time I was here, I tested a smaller portion. It seems that even a single finger holds the Starlighter's gift of insight. The vision during the test showed me events from the past that I found quite interesting."

"Such as?"

"Events I will share with you at another time, Little K. For now ..." He pointed at the dragons. "Let's watch."

Koren backed away to get a better view. She stepped between two of the dragons and stood about ten paces behind one that looked like Alaph. Like gophers tunneling from below, trees pushed up through the ground. The branches filled in so quickly, it seemed that magical spiders were casting streams of brown silk from trunk to trunk to spin a web of intertwined wood. As the spindly threads hardened, they thickened into a dense matrix, blocking sunlight and dimming the area.

A shout came from outside the trees. "Alaph! Is this how you keep your promise?" The draconic words reverberated within the glade. "By hiding in the trees?"

Alaph rose to his haunches. "It is the *only* way I can keep my promise."

One of the other white dragons rose with him. "What do you intend to do, Alaph?" The voice rumbled like the purr of a predator cat, feminine and sultry.

He snaked his neck around hers. "My dear Beth, what I do now I will not be able to explain until the curse has ended." As he drew back, he spread out his wings.

"Alaph?" Beth's tone grew desperate. "Alaph, do not leave me!"

He shot up into the branches, bursting through the lowest level. In a flurry of wings, Beth followed, then the other two.

As if propelled by the motion, the entire room rose with the dragons. Koren held her breath, instinctively bending her knees to absorb the floor's upward momentum.

At level after level, Alaph splintered branches with his head and beating wings. The woody fingers immediately began growing back, the smaller ones faster than the larger. The sharp ends jabbed at Beth as she followed, but she managed to pass the lowest ones safely. Like spears cast by hunters, the branches impaled the other two dragons, one near the lowest level, the second a few layers up. They yelped, but their cries were quickly squelched.

Finally, a thick branch skewered Beth. She flailed, madly flapping as more and more branches impaled her body. With every branch she snapped, more stabbed her white skin, as if punishing her for trying. Yet, in spite of all the deep piercing, not a single drop of blood escaped the dragons' bodies.

While Beth hung suspended, she blew a blast of ice at Alaph, striking his tail as it whipped upward. The end of the tail snapped like a whip, shattering the ice into crystals that spread out in a thin layer above Beth's head. Like fog over water, the layer hovered in place, stirred by Alaph's wake.

The vision remained at Beth's level. As she struggled, the branches probed more deeply. She groaned. She wailed. Her toothy maw snapped a branch, but before she could dodge its growth, it pierced her again, raising another wail. "Alaph!" she cried. "How could you do this to me?"

After a few seconds of silence, a voice sounded from above. "I did not do this to you. I merely escaped so that I could do what must be done."

"But you cannot do it without me. The Code must have its gavel of judgment. Help me escape and—"

"I will not help you. The curse will not allow it. Until it is broken, the trees will keep you ensnared."

Beth screamed, "Then break it!" Panting as she squirmed, she stretched her neck as far as she could, penetrating the layer of icy fog. "Alaph, my mate, you cannot leave me here to suffer. The Creator will not be pleased with our separation, with my suffering."

A deep sigh drifted through the branches, stirring the thin layer of fog. "My dear Beth, I cannot break this curse. Although my suffering is minimal compared to yours, my isolation will be torture as I watch the dragons of the south carry out their plans. A day will come when all will be made right. A Starlighter will rise from the dead who will be able to destroy the schemes of all the wicked. The sacrifice presented to her will cause her to suffer more than both of us combined, and if she chooses that path, she will gain nothing for herself, only pain."

"It will never happen. You prophesy impossibilities to appease my anger. No human would acquiesce."

"Perhaps you are right. In any case, we will soon learn if a Starlighter will pass the test."

"This is a test?" she shouted. "We are being tortured because of a *test*?"

"Such tests usually have a much greater purpose. The Creator often allows us to suffer, even those who have done nothing to deserve it. Patience is called for while—"

"Patience?" Beth spat an icy ball that splattered in the branches. "Who are you to tell me to be patient? I am an Enforcer! My role has been in place ever since the beginning, and it cannot be thwarted! When I am finally released from this prison, my wrath will be great, and you will be one of my targets!"

"Very well," Alaph said in a mournful tone. "My sadness in losing your companionship will be bitter indeed."

Beth began to fade. Branches withered. The blue background rematerialized and absorbed the image until only a smoky cloak remained. As it shrank, the fireplace reappeared, then the table. The smoke shriveled and took the shape of two manacles connected by a chain lying in front of the velvet-lined box and dark crucible.

Koren took a hesitant step toward the chain and reached out, her hand shaking. When she touched one of the manacles, it dissolved. The links dispersed one by one until they and the other manacle vanished. The crucible sat alone on the table, no longer sizzling.

"A chain," she whispered. "A Starlighter will rise from the dead."

Her father picked up the crucible and dipped two fingers into it. "Lift your tunic, Little K, just enough to show your stomach."

Her mind in a daze, Koren lifted the hem. Her father smeared pink paste across an oozing rash from the bottom of her ribcage down to her navel and rubbed it in. It seemed slick and oily, like an ointment Madam Orley used on her joints, though it didn't carry the same pungent odor.

"According to my theory," Orson continued, "your skin will absorb this energized medication, then it will enter your bloodstream and destroy the disease."

The medicine felt cool at first but quickly grew hot. She kept her tunic lifted to allow air to calm the sting. "What else is in it besides Cassabrie's skin and blood?"

"Stardrop particles and a catalyst that enhances the reaction between the energy and the genetic material. The blood and skin cannot do anything by themselves, and the energy is temporary, bringing only relief from symptoms." He interlaced his fingers. "The two have to combine, adhere, become a cohesive bond in order to carry the immunity into a person's cellular structure, and that cohesion requires a violent reaction that expels a great deal of heat in an instantaneous eruption."

"Like cooking a bladder bean until it pops?"

"Similar, but much quicker, much more violent. You are not familiar with this catalyst. It existed among the humans here on Starlight back when they were the slave masters."

"Where did you get the stardrop particles?"

"I collected them in the crucible from the remains of those that saved your life earlier. It seems that only a few substances keep the particles from deteriorating, and graphite is one of them. In my earlier tests, I used expended particles from previous healings. Alaph said the old ones would be useful for testing reactions of materials but not for curing the disease. Their energy has greatly deteriorated."

Although the stinging continued, Koren lowered her tunic. The ointment had dried, feeling like prickling needles from a bad sunburn. "But if you need fresh stardrop particles to make the cure, how can you produce more? We don't have access to Exodus."

"And we likely cannot make enough from Cassabrie's finger to go around. Even if we had an unlimited supply of stardrop crystals, I doubt that I could make more than fifty doses, a hundred at most."

"Fifty won't be nearly enough. We need at least a thousand."

"Unless the disease has significantly diminished the population."

Koren winced. Thinking about how many might have died already sent a new pang knifing through her stomach. "So Cassabrie would have to donate more skin and blood."

"Assuming this test is successful, yes. Remember, Jason absorbed skin, blood, *and* bone, and even his immunity hasn't been fully tested. So if Cassabrie were to donate more genetic material, the necessity of bone would make her sacrifice great indeed."

Koren peeked under her tunic and touched one of the sores. It was still the same size, but it looked a little less inflamed than before. The gnawing in her stomach was neither better nor worse. Trying not to look disappointed, she refocused on her father. "What do you think about the vision we saw?"

"Much of it was familiar to me. The white dragons are the Benefile, a race that battled the Southlands dragons. It's a long story, but what you saw was part of a truce between the warring factions, an agreement made between Alaph and Magnar. Alaph has been confined to the Northlands and Magnar to the Southlands, while the rest of the Benefile are trapped in those trees."

Koren nodded, then, with her gaze on the crucible in her father's hand, forced herself to ask the question that had chafed at her since the vision dissipated. "And Alaph's prophecy? What do you make of that?"

Father touched her cheek, raising her face to meet his gaze. "Can there be any doubt? You are the Starlighter who has risen from the dead."

Koren swallowed hard against the lump in her throat. "So has Cassabrie. She died, but Arxad preserved her body, and now she's back in it."

"Quite true, Little K, but if it comes to a test to see who will bend her knee, Cassabrie is not a candidate. I love her dearly, but she is headstrong and unpredictable. She already failed such a test decades ago, so, although she could play an ancillary role, her time to acquiesce has passed. The Creator seems to be asking you to take her place."

"I see." Koren imagined the mysterious Starlighter, once again embodied as she spoke so boldly to Arxad. *Don't play the despondent dragon. I know you too well. You have defended justice too many times to surrender now. If you want to lament about lacking aggression, then do it while making up for your passivity.*

What courage! What audacity! Even her defiant posture painted a portrait of bravado that seemed foreign, beyond the grasp of a disease-ridden girl who feared the chains of slavery. Were all Starlighters supposed to act that way?

Koren sighed. If her body would just heal a little bit, maybe she could stoke a similar fire. Ever since taking the stardrop, something did feel different, an inner flame that begged to blossom and grow into an inferno of passionate expression, but the disease kept smothering it, like a soggy blanket cast over a struggling fire.

"What is troubling you, Little K?"

Koren looked into her father's loving eyes. It made no sense to hide from his penetrating gaze. "Did you see the chain?"

"I did."

"Do you think it means what I think it means?"

"That you have to give yourself over to Taushin?" Father picked up the crucible and stared into it for a long moment. "Let me see if I understand your thinking process. If you become his eyes, then he will release the slaves. War with the human army will be avoided as well as the spread of the disease into their ranks. Fewer will die. Fewer doses of the cure will be needed. The soldiers will be able to lead the healthy slaves home to complete liberty, because the liberator will have given herself to suffer in their place. She will die daily, suffering for all her years, but she is willing to do this in order to bring relief to the oppressed people she loves so dearly."

Koren's throat ached. The truth stood in plain sight, naked and with no place to hide. Was she really so transparent? Biting her lip, she nodded. No words seemed adequate.

"I thought so." Her father dipped his finger into the crucible and scooped out a final dab of ointment. "There is one factor that I wonder if you have fully grasped."

"And that is?"

He drew her arm close and smeared the ointment on her wrist, partially covering the abrasion from the manacle. "Are the slaves worth the suffering you will endure?"

"What do you mean?"

"I heard about your attempts to reason with them, your entreaties to rise up and fight their oppressors. Yet they rebuffed you. They chose fear. They embraced their chains rather than freedom." He gripped her wrist as if his hand were a manacle. "Are such cowards worth even one moment of your suffering?"

Koren looked into his eyes—somber and sincere. When she resurrected the scene from Darksphere, the escaped slaves splashed and played in the stream—happy, joyful, and unshackled. For a few moments, those still in chains on Starlight witnessed the ecstasy of freedom. Liberty danced before them, expressed in unbridled exuberance. It sang a melody of rapturous delight. Yet those who still stood under whips sloped their shoulders and bent their backs as they awaited another lash.

The choice was clear, obvious, without question. Yet they chose the whips. They allowed the fear of pain to smother the song. Why? They heard the lyrics about a life without chains. They saw the dance. But they couldn't feel the freedom. They didn't know what it was like to walk away from a master's cave, or a pheterone mine, or a stone-movers' raft without the burden of knowing that they had to return the next day and the next, as would their children for generations untold. Yes, the escaped children danced in the stream, but until slaves on Starlight could feel the cool water running between their own toes, the vision was no more than a dream, a tale whispered to children at bedtime to keep them from crying out in the night.

The whips were leather. Their stripes bled. Fantasy images that blew away with the wind could never overcome the brutal reality of flesh and blood.

"They're blind," Koren said. "They need to be taken by the hand."

Her father caressed her cheek, letting his fingertips linger. "You are a most introspective and contemplative young woman, and I don't deny your conclusion, but let me counter your thought with a suggestion. Freedom that is not fought for, that is not gained by personal sacrifice, is freedom that will never last, because in the heart of the one set free, it will have little value. A treasure that costs nothing is a treasure that is easily neglected and lost."

"Does that mean you think I shouldn't sacrifice for them?"

"Not at all. I just want you to think about all the factors as you contemplate. Considering Alaph's prophecy, I don't see an alternative to your sacrifice, but if there is a way to get the slaves to participate in their own emancipation ..." He let his words trail off.

"If there's no alternative to my sacrifice, then I have to submit to Taushin."

"Oh, no! Heaven forbid! I didn't say that at all."

Koren gave her head a rapid shake. "You're confusing me. If I don't submit to Taushin—"

"Koren! Haven't you learned the most basic lesson?" Orson heaved a sigh. "I'm sorry for being so harsh, dearest one, but for being as thoughtful as you are, I'm surprised that you're contemplating surrendering the greatest gift you have ever received."

"The greatest gift?"

Father pointed at her bare feet. "While I was exploring the chambers below, I saw your discarded boots. Shall I fetch them for you? Do you want to wear them again?"

Koren wiggled her toes, free and unrestricted. She had discarded those boots while within Exodus, thereby breaking away from Taushin's hold. His influence, once so powerful and burdensome, a mental chain of anguish, was now gone. She had begged to be released, and finding freedom was a gift indeed.

She lowered her head and whispered, "I understand."

"Oh, dear Little K!" Father caressed her cheek. "I believe you will have to sacrifice, but never sacrifice freedom of the soul. Be willing to suffer even unto death, but never lose your embrace of eternity. If you turn down an invitation to the Creator's heavenly abode for the sake of solving terrestrial woes, you might not receive another."

For a moment, she closed her eyes and leaned into his hand. "I'll remember." As he withdrew his hand, she looked up at him again. "Something else in the vision made me wonder. Alaph said, 'The Creator often allows us to suffer, even those who have done nothing to deserve it.'" She touched her tunic but resisted the urge to scratch the rash. "From what I heard, I died of the disease when I was just a baby. I didn't do anything wrong, but I got it anyway. Why would the Creator punish me when I didn't have anything to do with puncturing Exodus?"

"Ah! How well I know that question. Every tear you shed, every wail of pain, every labored breath ripped that question from my breast and made it fly toward the Creator in rage." He shook a fist at the air. "Why, Creator? Why must my little girl suffer so? Let the guilty suffer their own punishment. I was among those who stood idly by while the dragons were brutalized. I, too, ignored the Starlighter's warnings. Although I didn't throw the spear that pierced the star, I did nothing to counter the prideful disdain for enlightenment that led to the foolish act."

Sighing, he lowered his fist. "But it was not to be. As Alaph said, the Creator allows the innocent to suffer. Why?" He shook his head. "I never received an answer."

Koren sat quietly. With no answers available, why ask more questions?

"This much I do know," her father said, raising a finger, "although you suffered as an innocent babe, you were still in heaven's embrace. No one is born alienated from the Creator. Alienation results from a choice to serve evil. Although we both wept and wailed in the throes of

disease, this truth brought comfort: Suffering is mea-
sured by days or weeks or months, but heaven lasts for an
eternity."

Koren stared at her bare feet again. His words made
a lot of sense, but an answer to the biggest question still
lay just out of reach. If she was supposed to suffer to
rescue the slaves, how could she do so without giving in
to Taushin? Maybe that was a question she had to answer
herself.

"Well, I had better get started," she said. "I have to
begin a journey back to the Southlands. Maybe while I'm
traveling I can figure out a way to get the slaves to participate in their rescue."

"How will you get there quickly enough?"

"Since the curse has been broken, I will ask Alaph to
take us."

"Us?"

"Of course. You have to cook up the cure for as many
as possible."

"Yes. I suppose you're right, assuming it is working."

Koren lifted her tunic again. The sores had receded,
slowly but surely. "I see definite improvement."

"Your symptoms are fading, but that is not proof of a
cure." He looked at the crucible. "I wonder if a topical
ointment is sufficient. It occurred to me that swallowing it
might be an option, but consuming the flesh and blood of
another person seemed rather cannibalistic."

Koren shuddered. "I agree. I could never do that. The
Code forbids it."

"True, and absorption into the bloodstream through
your skin is safer to the medicine itself. Your stomach

acids might deteriorate the bonding between the genetic structure and the energizing crystals."

Koren sniffed her wrist. The ointment carried a familiar smell—a blend of sulfur and charcoal along with the odor of burnt flesh.

"I suspected this would happen." Her father scratched the front of his tunic. "It seems that I have contracted the disease."

She slid her arms around him and pressed close. "You're risking your life for me."

"Oh, Little K! You are more than worth the risk." He ran his fingers through her hair. "We'll both survive this somehow, and we'll rescue as many slaves as we can."

She drew back. Tears blurred her view of the man who had been, in her eyes, the eccentric Uriel Blackstone. Now Orson lived again, her father, her dreams reborn. It was amazing how things could change so quickly, in the blink of an eye. Maybe more miracles awaited on the horizon. "Then let's see if Alaph will take us south. We'll find Exodus and collect more energy. At least we can cure slaves until the finger is gone."

"And have you determined not to submit to Taushin?" His face paled. "I lost you once. I don't want to lose you again."

"Don't worry. I'll come up with some way to fulfill the prophecy. Who knows? Maybe the army from Darksphere will conquer Taushin, and we won't have to worry about it." Koren closed the velvet-lined box and slid it into her pocket. "For now, let's concentrate on stopping the disease. People are dying as we speak."

"Right, but first we have to retrieve some weapons Arxad told me about. They are in a storage area near where Exodus used to reside."

"That will take a long time," Koren said. "You've been there. You know how long that staircase is."

"Indeed. I have climbed it twice now, once with a load of books—a few research journals and histories of Starlight." He patted her on the back. "Don't worry. I hope to persuade Alaph to retrieve the weapons. Arxad said that if the curse were to be lifted, Alaph might help us in many ways."

"I think he will." Koren imagined the staircase and the globules of light that whispered fragments of tales in her ear as she descended. Although Exodus was no longer below, the depths still held tales of the past—books that revealed mysteries perhaps even Cassabrie couldn't probe. Maybe soon even those would come to light.

Ten

When the soldiers drew near, Jason rose to his feet and helped Elyssa to hers. Edison Masters and a captain led the way, both wet with rain and sweat but marching with vigor. The company seemed small, no more than fifty men.

"Your father looks strong," Elyssa said. "He's hardly limping at all."

Jason smiled, barely able to keep himself from jumping up and down like an excited toddler. "It's amazing what preparing for battle can do. He just forgets about his own pain."

"You warriors are all alike." Elyssa took in a breath and straightened her shoulders. "I'll do my best to be one."

Jason strode forward, then broke into a jog. Edison called for a halt and met him with open arms. After the two embraced, Jason nodded back at Elyssa, who walked quickly, although obviously disguising a limp.

"Are you two coming with us?" Edison asked.

"I'm not sure yet. We've been looking for Koren, so—"

"I have news about Koren, but I'll wait for Elyssa. I think you'll decide to join us."

"That's fine," Jason whispered. "I just hope she can keep up. She just expended more energy in an hour than Solarus does in a day, but I know she'll give it all she's got."

"We were hoping to have air transport." Edison looked northward and Jason's eyes followed, but the mist made it hard to see beyond a hundred paces. "Magnar said he would join us at some point. If he does, Elyssa can ride."

"Magnar will allow her to ride?" Jason whistled. "A lot has changed."

"Indeed, though our alliance is tenuous. We don't trust him, and he doesn't trust us."

When Elyssa joined them, they quickly exchanged stories, including the river's breaching of the wall, Orion's hiding of the portal crystal, the rapid snowmelt in the Northlands, and Edison and Wallace's rescue of Koren. Now that everyone had been exposed to the disease, time was short. The soldiers had marched all morning after only three hours of sleep, and no one wanted to delay the journey more than necessary. In spite of the amount of energy Elyssa expended while traveling northward, she indicated her willingness to continue, no matter what.

"We'll have to let Uriel and Alaph worry about Koren," Jason concluded. "Let's all head south."

Elyssa touched Jason's arm. "I sense a dragon approaching."

"Magnar?" Jason looked toward the north again. "It's still too foggy to see."

"Not that way." She turned him around. "He's coming from the south."

The cloudy sky appeared to be empty. "Any emotions?"

"He is melancholy, brooding." Elyssa closed her eyes tightly. "I sense no hostility, just resignation."

"Arxad," Jason and Elyssa said at the same time.

"We were hoping for his help." Edison lifted a hand and called out. "Expect a dragon to arrive in a moment. Lower your swords and bows, but keep a firm grip on them."

A few seconds later, Arxad dove below the clouds and landed several paces in front of the company. His wing beats fanned the wet grass and flowers, sending a spray of fine droplets across the gathered humans.

Jason stepped forward, intentionally keeping his hand away from his sword. "Arxad! What news do you bring?"

"Dire news." Arxad's head swayed as he scanned the soldiers. "Are these all you could muster?"

"We had more earlier, but—"

"I care not for excuses. I counted forty-eight, and an army of forty-eight men with ten thousand excuses will not conquer the menace that lies beyond the barrier wall." Arxad's head lifted, and he searched through the army again. "And where are the weapons I asked to be brought? Uriel was supposed to retrieve them for you."

Edison joined Jason at his side. "We didn't consult with Uriel before we left. With people dying of the disease, we hoped to make haste and—"

"Haste!" Arxad roared. "More excuses! I thought your world would provide wiser commanders!"

Edison took a hard step and looked Arxad in the eye. "Don't lecture me about wisdom, slave master. What were you doing while our children carried heavy stones on bent and bleeding backs? Did you rebel against Magnar? No. You enjoyed the fruits of slavery and—"

"I was plotting against my own kind!" Sparks-tinged smoke boiled from Arxad's snout. "I have waited many years for this day, and this attack would never have come about if not for *my* rebellion against *my* race. I will not be lectured by the leader of a ragtag flock of flightless bipeds who think a few dozen spears and swords are enough to conquer the most powerful dragons of Starlight. I have risked too much for too long to endure such ignorant squawking."

"You speak of ignorance, but you didn't even ask if we had reinforcements ready to—"

"Stop!" Jason stepped between them, a hand on his father's shoulder. "We could argue all day about the past, but it's gone. Everyone here has made mistakes. Let's just figure out what to do now. People are dying."

Arxad and Edison each took a deep breath, their postures becoming less aggressive. "Very well," Arxad said. "You asked for news, and I shall deliver it. The Benefile have arrived in the village, and their presence might help or hurt our cause. They will likely want to aid us in destroying Taushin's forces, but they are unpredictable. They employ a form of law and logic that often escapes me, so we will have to be wary. Still, I am highly doubtful. I flew here to give you aid, but I fear that my aid will not be enough. Your numbers are a great concern to me."

"We have more," Edison said. "Orion closed the portal before they could come through, and he hid the peg. We left a few men to guard him, thinking he might go back to our world and spread falsehoods among the soldiers still waiting to pass through."

"So you decided to march without them?" Arxad asked.

Edison nodded. "Waiting equals death. Even now my heart longs to continue the march."

"Your courage is a garland." Arxad bowed his head. "I apologize for my outburst."

"And I do as well." Edison sighed. "But our mutual apologies won't multiply our ranks."

"No, but this will." Arxad motioned with a claw toward his underbelly. "I have another peg that will open the portal. I will inform the others of your whereabouts, but with your numbers, perhaps you should wait until I return with your reinforcements."

"We want to continue on and infiltrate by stealth," Edison said. "If you would suggest a way to breach the wall and a place to hide while we see what we're up against—"

"Your stealth will be discovered. You have no hope of evading the Benefile." Arxad gazed toward the south, his ears twitching. For a moment, he seemed lost in thought. His head swayed, and the tip of his tail flicked from side to side. Then he muttered, "They probably already know you are coming. They have a seer among them."

"If evasion is impossible," Edison said, "what should we do?"

"Go forth boldly." Arxad swung his head back toward them. "They are here to punish the Southlands dragons, not to hurt humans. If you try to enter with stealth, they will perceive malice, and their response will likely be aggressive. If you go openly, they will welcome you as allies against a common enemy. Once you are safely past the barrier wall, I suggest going to the wilderness to locate Frederick. He has gathered quite a number of escaped children. From there, you can lead them to my cave. No infected humans are there, and Xenith and I burned everything Madam Orley came into contact with."

Edison nodded thoughtfully. "One moment please. Allow me to consult with the commanding officer."

"Where is Madam Orley?" Elyssa asked Arxad as Edison walked back to the soldiers.

"With the sick and dying who are gathering in the Zodiac's portico. Because the Benefile were watching the humans gather, I could risk only a glance as I peeked out of the clouds, but I assume they chose that place because it has a covering and is easy to access."

Biting her lip, Elyssa slid her hand into Jason's and squeezed it. He looked at her, reading her pensive expression. "What is it?" he whispered.

She matched his low tone. "If the Benefile want help from our soldiers, they'll do whatever they can to make it safe for them."

"What do you mean?"

"Eliminating the host of the contagion."

Jason nodded. "Pretty drastic, though."

"It's worth asking about." Elyssa gave Jason a nudge. "There's only one way to find out."

"Arxad," Jason said, taking a step toward him, "how sure are you that the Benefile know we're coming?"

"Quite sure."

Jason glanced at Elyssa, She bobbed her head forward as if to urge him to continue. "If that's true, would they kill the infected humans to clear the way for us to invade?"

Arxad eyed him for a moment, then his ears flattened. "Without a doubt. I should have considered that option. We must all make haste."

"How do we get past the barrier wall?" Jason gestured with his head toward the south. "We opened the gate, but with the river flowing, it won't be easy to get everyone through it."

Arxad's tail twitched nervously. "I have heard that there is a walkway at the base of the wall leading to the gate, but I do not know how sturdy it is. Perhaps you can walk on it. Perhaps you must swim. Do not count on any easy steps along the way."

"Especially without a dragon around to help. We thought Magnar would join us after he took Koren to the Northlands, but he hasn't shown up."

"If I see him during my flight northward," Arxad said, "I will remind him of your need for dragon aid."

"That will help." Jason bent his face into a skeptical frown. "But I'm still not sure we can trust him."

Arxad snorted a puff of smoke. "Your quandary is reasonable. I am sure we are all waiting to learn where Maganar's loyalties lie."

When Edison and Captain Reed rejoined Jason and Elyssa, Jason explained the situation, including the possible passageway at the barrier wall.

Edison lifted a water flask from his belt and gave it a shake. "We'll march double time and stop only for water until we arrive."

"What about your leg?" Jason asked.

"Ever since the healing tree, it's been fine." He pushed the flask back to its harness. "I've never felt better."

Jason touched Elyssa's back. "We know another route that won't accommodate an army, and it might be faster, so we'll meet you at the barrier wall."

"Perhaps one of you should accompany me to the portal," Arxad said. "I would not blame your men there if they mistrusted my word that I am a friend."

Captain Reed raised a hand. "I might be able to give you something they will respect."

"And that is?"

Reed lifted his thumb, revealing a pattern of thin ridges intermixed with the print lines. "I once worked as a dungeon guard, and my torch got too close to a framed medallion at the side of the entry door. When the frame caught on fire, I grabbed the medallion to keep it safe, but it was hot, and the insignia burned into my thumb. It's been there ever since. I have used it in the past to signal my men that I have given someone authority."

Arxad drew his snout close to the captain's thumb. "How so?"

"Usually with ink on a document, but since I have no ink ..." He withdrew a dagger from a belt sheath and rubbed his thumb along the blade. As blood leaked from the wound, he spread it across the insignia. "This will have to do."

Arxad lifted a foreleg. "The idea has great merit. You may apply it here."

"Very well." Captain Reed pressed his thumb against a scale on the back of Arxad's clawed hand, but the blood soaked into the dry outer layer and faded. "Hmm. This isn't clear at all."

"Perhaps this will work better." Arxad reared up, revealing his underbelly. The crystalline peg wedged between two scales glimmered, as did a circular object that replaced a scale next to his vulnerable spot.

Jason leaned closer. "A mirror?"

"A gift from Marcelle, but I have not the time to explain."

"That should do fine." Captain Reed pressed his thumb on the mirror's surface, leaving a red replica of the insignia, then backed away. "It's perfect."

"Excellent. I will take my leave now. Farewell!" Arxad leaped. His wings beat the air, lifting him into an upward spiral. Within seconds, he disappeared in the clouds.

Jason tightened his belt and checked his sword. "I suppose we should be going as well."

"Son, you know this world better than I do, so I won't question your judgment regarding the alternative route." Edison hiked up his own belt and refastened it. "May the Creator guide your way." After hugging Jason and Elyssa, he nodded at the commanding officer. "Captain Reed, if you'll give the order, we'll see if an old goat like me can keep up with your stallions."

Captain Reed waved an arm and shouted, "Double time! March!" He and Edison took off in a quick jog toward the south. The other men ran behind them, sidestepping to avoid Jason and Elyssa.

When the tromping of feet subsided, Elyssa cocked her head at Jason. "This route you mentioned. Are you just trying to keep me safe?"

"Hardly. You expended a lot of energy making the river flow backwards, so I thought you could use a rest and ride the raft back to the south."

"The current's really moving fast now. Snowmelt, I suppose."

"Exactly. It should be a ride to remember." He pulled her hand, prompting her to walk with him toward the west. "While the soldiers are marching double time, we'll take it easy."

"But it ends at a waterfall."

"I know. I told you it wasn't safe."

When they found the raft, Jason knelt beside it. The saplings had separated here and there, and several vines had snapped. Their supply bags lay torn open, and every scrap of food was gone. "Forgot about the bags," Jason said.

"So did I." Elyssa knelt on the other side of the raft and began tying vines. "Well, you promised me a ride. I guess we'd better get started."

❖

Tibalt sat in a small forest clearing next to Fellina, holding both hands against his head. In spite of the tumble from Fellina's back, no bones had broken, but his headache had to be the worst to strike any soul since the beginning of time. When three dragons converged on her at the treetops, she had to drop without warning. But a ninety-something-year-old man needs at least a hint, or else he's sure to fall. And fall he did, from at least twenty feet up. If not for the wealth of leaves cushioning the forest floor, he definitely would have been buzzard food.

Squinting to clear his vision, he looked around. Fellina sat only inches to his left, with two bigger dragons guarding her closely. Blood dripped from a gash in her belly—not a deep wound, but bad enough to keep her grounded for a while.

About fifty paces away, a small hut sat in the midst of the trees. Children filed out from the broken front door, which had been smashed by the draconic scoundrels on Taushin's order. Beside the line of waifs, the black dragon himself watched through the eyes of his psychotic mother, Mallerin. She held a thorny branch over the heads of the little slaves, poised to strike should one dare to break from the cluster gathering in front of the cabin.

Tibalt shook his head sadly. The smallest young'uns wore only a loin cloth, and they trembled and wept bitterly, while the older ones stared straight ahead. The poor little folks had probably given up on freedom. They had been so close—freed at last from the cattle-camp whips, only to have their hopeful dream turn into another nightmare.

At least a dozen other dragons stood guard at various spots. Others flew back and forth overhead, creating winged shadows that sometimes found their way through the thinning canopy.

Tibalt touched his tunic. The sores on his chest were worse than ever, making the material stick to the oozing flesh. Inside his gut it felt like two mountain bears were clawing and biting. Whether by dragon or disease, he'd be dead soon, so it didn't make any sense to just sit like a bump on a stump. He had to do something to help those kids.

He leaned toward Fellina and whispered, "Any ideas?"

"A few." She kept her voice low. "But none that we could survive."

"Not even a chance?"

"A remote chance, perhaps. We would have to count on the art of persuasion, but they are not likely to listen to me. I am considered a human-loving traitor."

"Tell me what you're thinking. I have the gift of gab, and anything's better than sitting here watching this travesty."

"I think Taushin is hoping to protect his dragons from the Benefile by using the children as a shield. The Benefile have a strong sense of justice, though it is twisted and unpredictable. Still, their justice might keep them from hurting the innocent in order to punish the wicked. Also, since the children are not infected, they will be seen as necessary for ongoing propagation of the species."

"Okay. Cowardly dragons are gonna hide behind babies. I get that, but where does the gab come in?"

"We convince Taushin that separating you from the children would keep them from catching the disease, which would be helpful to his cause. You could run back to where I picked you up, and you and Randall could find Arxad. If the soldiers are getting close, he would know—"

"Stop the chatter!" One of the dragons slapped Fellina's snout with his tail.

Fellina growled something in her language, which drew a sneer from the guard but nothing more.

Tibalt gulped. Fellina's idea made some sense, but what if the dragons decided to roast him alive instead of letting him go? A quick puff of fire and he'd be a smoking wick in no time. Disease gone. Problem solved.

Cocking his head, he pictured the scene, his body burning and smoke spreading toward the cabin ... and the children. He nodded. Convincing them that smoke carried the disease might just work.

A branch swayed to his right, more than what the wind would cause. Sitting up straighter, Tibalt blinked several times. Nearly covered by foliage, a man walked along a limb inch by inch. The foliage moved at the same rate, and a glint revealed a metal blade within the leaves.

Tibalt jerked his head back, praying the dragons hadn't noticed him watching. They had been scanning the sky for the Benefile and the forest floor for an approaching army, so they might not detect an intruder who took the middle ground. Whatever he was up to, he needed someone to create a distraction.

He coughed to hide his whisper. "Do you see the man in the tree?"

After a quick glance, Fellina nodded almost imperceptibly. With a snort, she blew out a disguised, "Frederick."

"Then here goes." Summoning his strength, Tibalt leaped up. He stripped off his tunic, ripping at the sores and exposing them for all to see. "Look at me, dragons!" he shouted, twirling his tunic. "I'm as sick as they come. If you want those young'uns to stay healthy, you'd better let me go!"

Every dragon turned toward him, some snaking their necks around tree trunks to get a better look.

"Stay back, old man," Taushin said, his eyebeams locked on his mother, "or you will burn where you stand."

Mallerin's head swayed. Her ears twitched, and smoke billowed from her nostrils.

"No, you won't!" Tibalt wagged a finger. "The smoke pouring from me will carry the disease, and then the children will surely catch it."

Taushin chuckled. "Humans from Darksphere are so easy to detect. They think dragons are like the stupid beasts that roam the fields in their world—that we are unable to unravel the simple deceptions they weave. This old man threatened the children with his disease, and then he warned me not to spread it to them. And he thinks I am too dense to see the contradiction. I think his theory that smoke will spread the disease deserves a test, Mother. What do you think?"

Mallerin curled her neck, like a serpent ready to strike. "I will gladly administer the test."

"Fellina," Tibalt said, stretching out her name, "I'm in big trouble."

"Run!" Fellina blew a blast of fire into Mallerin's eyes. Tibalt bolted toward Frederick, weaving through a maze of trunks, and hid behind Frederick's tree.

While Mallerin shook off the flames, Taushin roared, "Get him!"

Three dragons gave chase, but the closely packed trees forced them to squeeze their hefty bodies in between, slowing them down. Fellina leaped into the air. Beating her wings madly, she rose toward the treetops, breaking branches along the way.

Frederick dropped to the ground and shoved a leafy branch into Tibalt's grasp. "Take this and burn down the cabin. Make sure no children are inside."

"But the branch isn't on fire."

"It will be." Frederick gave Tibalt a shove. "Go!"

Holding the branch in front, Tibalt ran toward the cabin. The closest dragon lunged, but Tibalt shot behind a trunk, blocking the attack. He ran on, ducking and weaving from tree to tree.

To his left, Mallerin launched twin streams of fire from her nostrils. Tibalt swung the branch around, catching the flames in the leaves. He skirted the children and dashed through the doorway. Straw and leaves littered the floor. One little girl lay in the bedding, apparently asleep. An open window on the back wall let in a breeze, fanning the branch's flames.

Tibalt tossed the branch into the straw, well away from the girl. "Sorry about the disease, little tyke, but I can't let you burn." He scooped her up and took a step toward the door, but Mallerin poked her head through.

"You cannot escape now!" She blew a torrent of fire. Tibalt leaped to the side, threw the girl out the window, and dove under the dragon's head.

Crawling on his belly, he scooted past her, then jumped up and ran around the cabin. Smoke shot through the roof. From above, Fellina added blasts of fire that splashed over the debris on the forest floor; she had apparently figured out Frederick's plan to spread chaos.

When Tibalt reached the back of the cabin, he picked up the girl and cradled her in his arms. Her bare chest heaved, but she stayed silent. Sores covered her torso from her navel to her throat. "She already has it," he whispered. "It's already spread this far."

Tibalt crept to the corner and peered around to the front. Smoke filled the forest, making it impossible to see beyond the next corner. A dragon called out in its own language, and another answered in the same gibberish.

Frederick burst out from the haze, leading a line of children, a sword in his hand. He stopped and waved them toward a denser part of the forest, his arm swinging like a windmill blade. Every young mouth stayed closed, as if they had been trained to escape in silence.

When the final child plunged into the brush, Frederick signaled for Tibalt to follow.

Tibalt shook his head and mouthed, "Fellina."

Frederick ran to him. "Most of the dragons are chasing Fellina," Frederick whispered. "I heard Taushin call for his mother to help him escape, so the two of them probably took off."

"You understand that dragon talk?"

Frederick nodded. "It took a little while, but I can pick up most of it."

"So what's your plan?"

"For you to lead the rest of the dragons out into the open." Frederick dropped the sword and took the little girl from Tibalt's arms. "If Fellina is able, she will follow you. The point is to put the dragons where the Benefile can find them. Use my sword for protection."

"You don't mind giving an old man the toughest jobs, do you?"

"Take your pick. Lead the dragons on a chase, or protect forty children without a weapon."

"Well, when you put it that way." Tibalt picked up the sword. "I'll be dragon bait."

eleven

andall blinked at the blinding mist and held on to the protruding spine in front. Riding on a dragon through clouds had never been part of Marcelle's training. With the disease starting to bore a hole in his gut, it wouldn't take much to regurgitate the berries he had eaten.

Earlier, Xenith had said to be completely quiet, though her wings sounded like two soldiers beating horse blankets. She descended a few feet and lowered her head into the clear. After a few seconds, she bent her neck and brought her snout close. "We are directly above my home. Prepare for a fast dive and a sharp turn into the cave."

"Prepare? Any advice besides hold on for dear life?"

"If you fall, roll with your momentum."

"What if I fall from a hundred feet up?"

Xenith's lips bent into a grin. "Then avoid the front of my cave. We like to keep that area clean."

"Thanks a lot." Randall wrapped his arms around her spine and clutched it with both hands. "I'm ready."

Xenith folded in her wings and plunged from the sky. As they dove at a sharp angle, Randall kept his eyes open. The Zodiac's spires came into view, as well as the belfry at the Basilica. Below the spires, hundreds of people milled about near the portico, and three white dragons stood in a semicircle formation around them, as if on guard.

In the blink of an eye, the scene rose out of sight. Xenith stretched out her wings and caught the rushing air, making Randall's body press against her scales. She bent into a sharp turn and zipped into a dark hole, as if swallowed by a gaping mouth. With a blast of fire, she lit up the cave for an instant and landed in a graceful run.

When she came to a stop, Randall slid down her scales, but his wobbly legs gave way. He toppled over and rolled until he struck the side of the rocky corridor.

"An excellent roll," Xenith said. "You followed my advice quite well."

Randall climbed to his feet and massaged his ribs. "Your sense of humor is ... interesting."

Xenith blew a stream of sparks over a lantern wick. When it flashed to life, she looked him over. "Since you have the disease, I will have to scour this room with fire when you leave. Father hopes to make it a safe place for uninfected humans. Then I will search for him and let him know where my mother is."

"Do you know where the Northlands portal is?" Randall asked.

"Yes. Cassabrie showed it to me once when I was transporting her."

"Good. That's a place I'd check if I were looking for Arxad." Randall staggered to the entrance and leaned a hand against the side. "If only I could get my legs back."

"With the disease ravaging your body, you might not get your legs back."

Randall let out a short laugh. "That's what I like about you, Xenith. You're always ready with an uplifting comment." He stared at the Zodiac's spires. They weren't far away at all, maybe a five-minute walk—shorter if his legs would work properly. If he could get to the Basilica without being seen, it would be easy to sneak into the Zodiac through the tunnel, but then what? Only a dragon could fly up to the main floor, and even if he made it, what could he do once he got there?

"Are you formulating a plan?" Xenith asked.

He turned toward her. Her head tilted to one side, making her look like a curious puppy—a hideous, scaly puppy, but cute in her own way. "I'm trying. I know how to get from the Basilica to the Zodiac's lower level, but I'm not sure how to get into the Basilica."

"The front gate should be unguarded. In fact, it's probably open."

"That helps. I was thinking if I could get into the Zodiac, I could at least get close enough to listen to what's going on and maybe find some other way to help."

"Yes ... help." Xenith's face took on a faraway look.

"Do you have an idea?"

"Well, not my idea, really. I heard a suggestion through a rumor, so its validity is questionable."

Randall waved a hand. "I'll take the source into account. Let's hear it."

"We could try to draw Cassabrie here, but I am not sure if she is powerful enough to defeat the Benefile."

"She'd be a lot more than we have now," he said. "How do we draw her?"

"Do you know where the Reflections Crystal resides?"

Randall nodded. "I've seen it from the Zodiac's door. It's in a dome-like room, right?"

"Yes. If you open the dome, Solarus will activate the crystal."

"What good will that do?"

"Father has told me many stories about the crystal, how it absorbs the spirit of a human and the energy of a Starlighter. Those properties are the basis of the rumor."

"Go on."

Xenith looked upward as if studying the ceiling. "The crystal once resided underground, beneath the North-lands castle at the deep end of a shaft in a mountain. When the humans pierced Exodus with a spear, the force of the star's released gases propelled Exodus to the Northlands, where it fell into the shaft, dropped to the bottom, and hovered over the ground that concealed the crystal. The star and the Starlighter within were trapped there for centuries."

"Okay," Randall said, "I think I see where you're going. It would be practically impossible for the star to find its way through that shaft. Since the crystal absorbs Star-lighter energy, Exodus was drawn there."

"For a human, you have quite a nimble brain."

"Thanks ... I think."

She gave him a clumsy wink. "To continue my tale, Alaph, the king of the Northlands, removed the crystal and brought it to Arxad for reasons I do not know, but the removal caused a rift in the ground that allowed the star's pheterone to drip into a network of veins that supplied the planet with the gas."

"Do you think Alaph had that in mind?"

"That is likely. He considers every aspect of his plans before proceeding." Xenith shuffled to his side, and they both looked toward the Zodiac. "In its wounded state, Exodus was unable to follow the crystal, but now that the star has risen, perhaps opening the dome will draw it to the Zodiac."

"And that's the rumor," Randall said. "We don't know if Exodus will be drawn that far."

"Correct. And we also do not know how Cassabrie would react. She might consider it an affront to be called here by force."

"Not if she sees what the Benefile are doing."

"What do you mean?"

Randall formed a circle with his arms. "Did you see how they surrounded the people? I don't like the looks of it."

"What do you think they intend to do?"

"I'm not sure, but I think before you look for Arxad, you might want to investigate so you can tell him what's going on." Randall pushed away from the wall and stood upright. "So how do I open the dome?"

"There is a lever in a column that supports the outer circle of the dome. When you're at the Reflections Crystal, you will see constellations on the ceiling. Follow the stars that make the spear, and you'll find one of the control columns. A lever on that column or one next to it operates the dome mechanism. I do not remember which one."

"The spear? We must have a different name for it where I come from."

"Perhaps," Xenith said, "but it is unmistakable. It looks just like a hunter's spear."

"Got it. Now I just need to figure out how to get from the lower level of the Zodiac to the main floor."

Xenith's grin returned. "I have never seen the lower level, so I leave that to your ingenuity."

"That's what worries me." Randall straightened his sword belt and bowed to Xenith. "Noble dragon, it has been an honor."

She dipped her head in return. "The pleasure has been mine. It is clear that humans who are accustomed to freedom are able to think clearly and act courageously to secure that freedom for others."

"If only that were true of all of us." Randall bent low and skulked toward the Basilica, his legs still unsteady. It would take a while to make a wide enough circle to avoid the Benefile, but at least that would provide some time to plan a way to climb to the Zodiac's main level ... if he survived that long.

⭑⭒⭑

In the castle's foyer, Koren sat on Alaph's back, her hands on his smooth skin. With no deep recesses between his thin scales and no spines along his backbone, hanging on would be a difficult chore, especially considering the long journey ahead. Fortunately, the air outside had warmed, and the clouds had thinned, making it feel like a crisp morning in the cool season instead of the usual blistering cold.

Near the sliding wall at the back of the foyer, her father opened a leather bag and withdrew a cylinder that was about half as long as his forearm and nearly as wide. "Interesting. It reads, 'Danger. Explosive.'" He reached it up to Koren. "Take a look."

She grasped the cylinder and read the words. This was exactly the same as the tube she had found attached to the spear that pierced Exodus. "What are they for?"

"In the days when the humans were the slave masters," Alaph said, "they attached a tube to a rope and slung it around a rebellious dragon's neck. The human would then press a button on a control box that activated the weapon. The explosion destroyed the dragon, which was a loss for the slavers, but they preferred to kill rather than corral one that was prone to rebellion."

Koren grimaced. Picturing dismembered dragons didn't sit well with her queasy stomach.

Alaph touched the bag with a wing. "Arxad stored these in a chamber below. There are many down there, but I do not wish to carry more."

"Too dangerous?" Orson asked.

"According to the journals, they are safe as long as they stay cold, but when they thaw, they can become quite unstable."

"So as we journey southward, the instability will grow."

"Yes," Alaph said. "We will have to be very careful."

Orson peered into the bag. "I count ten. What do you suggest that we do with them?"

"We shall see. I want to survey the situation when we arrive." Alaph nodded at Koren. "You have a detonator that will activate the weapons. Be careful not to push the button."

Koren felt the blood drain from her face. She withdrew the detonator and studied the button. So that's what *Detonate* meant. At least pushing it accidentally wasn't likely, not with the button recessed the way it was. Still, it would be good to take some care with the control box.

Her father tied a leather cord at the top of the bag and left it on the floor. "I assume you will carry it underneath."

Alaph bobbed his head. "It will be safer there."

After putting the detonator back into her pocket, Koren grasped her father's wrist and helped him climb to a spot in front.

As soon as her father settled, she slid her arms around him and laid her cheek against his back. "I'm ready."

He patted her hands. "So am I."

"I cannot say the same." Alaph spread out his wings. "Although I am pleased to visit the Southlands again, I think my welcome there will be as frigid as the Northlands once were."

Without so much as a bump, Alaph lifted into the air and flew out the wide doorway. As they passed through, the air cooled, but not drastically. The combination of wind and Solarus shining near the horizon made Koren blink—only minor annoyances. She had her father in her grasp, and they were heading to the south to help the slaves. In spite of the new twinges in her stomach, no disease could steal this moment.

The scene below whisked by, almost unrecognizable now that most of the snow had melted. The river ran freely, driving water into the south-flowing stream and making it run more swiftly. As they continued southward, the meadow grass waved its spindly fingers, and flowers nodded their colorful heads. Every detail seemed more beautiful than ever.

Alaph rose higher and higher until the world below looked like a drawing on a scroll. A dragon passed by underneath, heading northward, too far away to identify. It appeared that Alaph didn't care to investigate. He just flew on and on, faster and faster.

After nearly an hour, a bright light came into view, a radiant sphere hovering near the ground. "Look!" she said into her father's ear. "There's Exodus."

"Ah. It seems that Cassabrie is traveling southward, though at a slower pace than we are."

"Where did you put the crucible?"

"It's safe in my pocket. I also have a wax envelope with plenty of the catalyst I told you about as well as instructions for making the medicine. If my own case of the disease progresses to the point that I am unable to make it myself, someone will have to do it in my place."

"Alaph!" Koren shouted. "We need stardrop crystals!"

He bent his neck, bringing his head close. "I will land in front of her and drop you off. Once you collect what you need, I will return to carry you the rest of the way."

"I beg your pardon," Koren said, "but why can't you stay with us?"

"Cassabrie's energy has increased dramatically, so I dare not get close while you collect the stardrop material. If just one crystal were to touch my body, it would destroy me before I am ready."

"Before you're ready?"

"The hour of my departure has not been determined. I know only that my replacement must be chosen first, and that has not yet occurred. When he or she is manifested, I will be able to surrender my life willingly."

Koren pondered his words. It seemed that Alaph was continuing his habit of speaking deep thoughts that no one else could understand. "So you could get close if we were not scraping off the crystals."

"That is correct, but I also wish to avoid Cassabrie's hypnotic power. She is much stronger now than ever before, and I am not certain of her intent. Coming under her control might be disastrous." Alaph dove toward the meadow and landed about a hundred paces in front of Cassabrie. When Koren and her father dismounted, he lifted into the air again and flew in a slow orbit well above their heads.

Less than a minute later, Exodus drew near with Cassabrie floating upright just above its floor. Although the star shone with brilliant radiance, seeing through the membrane was easy and painless. With her cloak's hood low over her eyes and her hands holding it closed in front, Cassabrie looked like a hovering blue shroud.

When Cassabrie arrived, she stopped Exodus and pushed back her hood. Her hair and eyes shone with brilliant color, and a smile lit up her face even further, genuine but weary. "If you wish to go with me to the Southlands, I would be glad to have company, but I have no way to transport you over the wall."

Koren gestured toward her father. "We need stardrop material. We have a possible cure that requires it."

Orson displayed the crucible in his palm. "I think a full container would provide enough to heal at least fifty. If it works, we could come back for more."

"You need genetic material from an immune human," Cassabrie said. "Jason isn't naturally immune, and harvesting sufficient material from Elyssa would maim her."

Koren withdrew from her pocket the velvet-lined box containing Cassabrie's finger, but left it closed. Telling Cassabrie they were using her body parts in an experiment seemed ... disturbing. After swallowing, she let out a quiet, "We have your finger."

"I see." Cassabrie opened her cloak and gazed at her hand. The gap in her fingers was evident. "How many can you cure with just one finger?"

"My guess of fifty was based on using what is left of your finger," Orson said.

"Then your plan is inadequate." Cassabrie guided Exodus closer and stopped again. "Collect what you can. Cure whom you may. But I must continue my journey as soon as possible."

"Thank you." Orson pushed the edge of the crucible into the membrane and began scooping radiant crystals. Several flew into the air and scattered in the breeze, confirming Alaph's fear. For him, being close would have been dangerous indeed.

As soon as the crystals reached the crucible's brim, Orson backed away and set a lid over the top, locking it in place with two small latches. "I will wait until we arrive to prepare the mixture. I need a fire."

"You need healing yourself," Cassabrie said. "You must hurry."

Orson laid a hand on his stomach. "Yes, I feel it, and we will hurry, but may I ask what you intend to do in the Southlands?"

181

Cassabrie gazed at the sky, her eyes following Alaph's flight. "He knows, or at least I think he does. If he sees fit to tell you, I ask only that you don't try to stop me."

"Stop you?" Koren slid the finger box back into her pocket. "Why would we want to do that?"

"I will say no more." Cassabrie guided Exodus over their heads and drifted southward, calling back, "Follow if you wish, or ride on Alaph. Either way, I am sure you will see me there. I think you will have no choice."

As soon as she traveled well out of range, Alaph flew down. After Koren and her father mounted, she patted Alaph. "What is Cassabrie planning to do?"

Alaph curled his neck and drilled a stare into her with his shining blue eyes. "Ah! She would not tell you."

Koren shook her head. "I'm worried about her."

"As you should be." Alaph turned his gaze toward the south. "Regarding her plans, I am not certain, so I will not speculate."

He rose into the air, not quite as smoothly this time, and flew lower, no more than a hundred feet above the ground. Below, Cassabrie caught up with a group of running men. Without pausing, she lifted over their heads and continued on a straight path, her face set due south. Many of the men pointed and appeared to shout, but the wind cut off their voices.

Koren touched the finger box in her pocket, frustration rising like bile. With Cassabrie being so mysterious, how could a less experienced Starlighter like herself know what to do about the prophecy? One of the two had to be the sacrificial Starlighter, and so far it didn't seem that Cassabrie was willing to reveal her choice. Based on her past, though, it seemed more likely that she hoped to overwhelm the dragons with her influence, and that wouldn't be sacrificial at all.

As she pondered her options, Koren caught sight of another dragon approaching the men from the north, flying low with a human passenger on his back. His muscular body and powerful wing strokes made his identity obvious.

"Alaph," Koren called, "Magnar is down there."

"I see him, and your friend Wallace is riding."

Koren allowed herself a smile. At least Wallace hadn't succumbed to the disease yet.

As Magnar landed gracefully in front of the running soldiers, Alaph continued. "Magnar plans to help the Darksphere soldiers, though even with his help their chance of success is minimal. They are a dedicated group, but they are far too few to hope to defeat Taushin's allies. Courage alone will not be enough to defeat so many dragons."

Koren looked back at the men as they surrounded Magnar, their whoops and hand clapping barely audible. How odd it all seemed. The dragon who had been the bane of every human on Starlight had become the hero of the Darksphere warriors. The beast who ate drugged children was now ready to fly into battle to rescue parents and siblings of those he consumed. If these soldiers were to be told of his cruelty, would they still accept him as a fellow warrior?

Alaph flew on and on. To the right, the river flowed fast and wild, bending tall grass and thin saplings in its swollen path. The snowmelt surge had traveled quickly, but its turbulent ride would end at the great waterfall.

After a few minutes, her father gave a shout and pointed ahead. Two humans sat on top of a rollicking raft, both steering with stripped branches. The water tossed them back and forth, but they managed to hang on.

"Jason and Elyssa," Alaph shouted. "It seems that everyone is converging on a common destination."

Koren shifted on Alaph's back to get a better look. "Can't we stop and help them?"

"I cannot carry another passenger. They have chosen this dangerous route, and, as you can see, they are quite capable of steering to the bank and getting out at any time."

"But the waterfall."

"They are aware of the waterfall. I know you long to ease everyone's journey, but that is not possible. Remember, your father needs healing, and your fellow humans need it as well. Allow Jason and Elyssa to complete their journey and gain the strength and wisdom their trials will add to their character. You have enough to occupy your mind with your own destination. Do not imagine that I am unaware of the battle that must be waging within you."

Koren cringed at his words. He was right, as usual. So far no sacrifice had come to mind other than giving herself to Taushin's service.

She slid an arm away from her father's waist and looked at her wrist. The earlier bout with the disease had reddened the manacle abrasions, and they were still evident. Turning herself over to Taushin would be like snapping the manacles back in place herself, whether on her wrists or on her soul.

A great weight pressed down, as if ten pails of river stones had been set on her back. The enormity of the task crashed into her mind. If she gave in, everyone else would be free, maybe even cured, and on their way to a new world while she stayed at Taushin's side, bound in chains, a Starlighter who moved and breathed but walked as a dead girl.

She lifted her tunic. The rash had receded upward, no longer visible on her stomach at all, but her chest still itched. The ointment, like the healing trees, had alleviated symptoms, but was it enough? Was Father's medicine really a cure? Maybe they did have to swallow it after all. Only time would tell.

Koren laid her head on her father's back and held him tightly. As before, he patted her hand, but this time he added words to the comforting gesture. Although the wind buffeted his voice, it seemed that the vibrations in his back penetrated her mind with every precious syllable. "Don't worry, Little K. No matter what happens, the Creator will never forsake you, and neither will I. Suffering is merely a prologue, an opening act in the Creator's tale. One way or another, whether we live or die, the story will have a happy ending."

Breathing a deep sigh, Koren closed her eyes. Was Father right? Tales in Starlight never seemed to have happy endings. Without exception, everyone was born a slave and died a slave, and whips and chains threatened every moment in between. No one ever escaped the cycle. No one.

As tears crept past her eyelids, she pushed the morbid thoughts to the side. Starlight needed a liberator, and if no one but Koren the glib-tongued girl from the cattle camp could fill that role, then so be it. At least everyone else would have a happy ending.

twelve

*J*ason thrust his branch into the river and pushed against the bed, trying to get leverage while balancing on his knees. "To the left! To the left!"

"I'm trying!" Elyssa shouted. "It's too deep! I can't get traction!"

Water flew everywhere, wave after wave sloshing from every side and splashing them in the face and body as they hurtled southward. The raft rocked like a wild bull trying to sling off a rider, and vines holding the saplings together stretched and snapped.

"Then we'll have to swim for it." He unhooked his scabbard and heaved it to shore. He then grabbed a vine and reeled it into a loop, bracing against the constant dips and rises. "We'll tie the ends to our wrists. The first one to get to shore, pulls the other one. Got it?"

"Got it." They helped each other fasten the vines to their wrists. "I hope it holds," she shouted above the tumult.

Ahead, the waterfall roared, far louder than he remembered. It would swallow them in seconds.

Jason grabbed Elyssa's wrist and forced her fingers around his tunic. "Lock on!"

"But I thought we were both going to swim."

"Never mind! Just hold on!"

She gripped his tunic tightly. Water flew from her hair as the raft bounced. "Jump now?"

"Stand first, then jump. Whatever you do, don't let go."

The roar heightened. The precipice came into view, shrouded in mist.

"Now!" They rose to their feet and leaped, but the raft slid away. They traveled less than a foot before splashing into the rapids. Still holding the steering branch, Jason kicked toward the bank and plunged the branch into the riverbed a pace ahead. Pulling against it, he drove himself forward. Elyssa's weight slowed his progress, but he battled on, jerking out the branch and resetting it again and again as he surged toward the bank. With each removal of the branch, the current swept them closer to the falls.

He dug the branch in once more and hung on, his head barely above the water. At this rate, they weren't going to make it. Pulling the branch out once more would send them over the edge.

The current swept their bodies parallel with the bank until their feet pointed toward the falls. Now only five steps from the precipice and maybe ten from the bank, he just held on. There seemed to be no other choice.

Elyssa wrapped both arms around his waist and drew her lips close to his ear. "I'm letting go! You'd make it if I weren't here dragging you back!"

"Don't you dare!" Jason coughed and spat as he shouted. "If anyone's going over, it's going to be me!"

"I'm not asking permission. This isn't suicide. I'm going to try to make it on my own." She let her arms slide away but kept one fist tight on his tunic, her eyes sad and wide. "I love you, Jason Masters."

She let go.

Jason slapped at her wrist but missed. Elyssa swam toward the bank with all her might, but the current inched her toward the falls. She wasn't going to make it.

With a flying lunge, Jason hurtled his body downstream. He caught her around the waist with both arms and, digging his feet into the riverbed, swung her toward the bank.

A surge sent him flying over the precipice, but instead of falling, he dangled in midair, his arm stretching upward as he twisted in the breeze and the river beat against his body before cascading to the rocks hundreds of feet below.

Above, the vine led from his wrist to Elyssa's two-fisted grip. With her feet planted on dry ground at the edge of the cliff and her body bending back, she pulled, grunting as she yelled. "Grab it! It's slipping off your wrist!"

Jason reached up and clutched the vine with both hands. "Got it!" Wet and slippery, it felt thin and fragile, but the roar of tumbling water kept any sound of breakage from reaching his ears. The surge from the north kept pounding at his waist and legs and knocking him into a twisting sway.

Grunting and yelping, Elyssa staggered backwards until she stepped out of sight. The vine jerked upward in pulses, rubbing against the rocky ledge. With each pulse the woody fiber making contact with the rocks splintered and frayed, then pulled up and out of sight.

Finally, the ledge drew within reach. Jason grabbed a protruding rock with one hand, swung the hand with the tied wrist to the top, and pulled himself up high enough to see the meadow. The sudden slack sent Elyssa tumbling backwards. The vine flew from her hands, and she landed on her back.

She threw herself forward and scrambled for the vine, but Jason hoisted his body onto the ledge before she could reach it.

Dripping from every extremity, he shuffled toward her on wobbly legs. She lay on her stomach, propped on her elbows, holding the vine loosely in her hands. With her head down, water formed in a pool under her nose.

Jason sat heavily in front of her. "Are you all right?" He lifted his wrist to his mouth and bit into the vine. It was so tight his hand was turning purple.

"I'm okay." Her tone was dismal, and her eyes stayed focused on the ground. "You?"

He chewed through the vine and let it drop. As he rubbed his wrist, he bent low, trying to see her expression. "I'm okay, thanks to you."

"You saved me first."

She braced her hands on the ground and pushed up. Jason leaped to his feet and helped her the rest of the way. He pinched the vine on her wrist. "Let me help you with that."

"I'll get it." She jerked away and turned her back. "You'd better find your sword."

Jason glanced upstream. The sword and scabbard lay somewhere on the bank, but they could wait. "What's wrong? Something I did?"

She shook her head but said nothing.

"Hey!" He grasped her arm and gently turned her around. Tears trickled down her cheeks, mixing with the water streaming from her hair. "Something *is* wrong. What is it?"

"It's my problem, not yours." Sniffing, she nodded toward the north. "Want me to help you find your sword?"

"Only after you tell me what's got you crying. You're too strong to break down for no reason."

She looked him in the eye, her facial muscles drawing taut. "Do you really believe that?"

"Of course." He nodded at the vine, now loose around her wrist. "Look at what you just did. You lugged a guy fifty pounds heavier than you. Dead weight. You were amazing."

"Then why didn't you believe in me before?"

He mopped water from his forehead with a wet sleeve. "What do you mean?"

"You said we would both swim, and the first one to the bank would pull the other one. But then you changed your mind and told me to hold on to you."

As he looked into her sad eyes, the reality of her words sank in. When the crisis moment came to pass, he decided to trust in himself, not her.

"I guess I shouldn't expect anything else," she continued, sniffing again. "I mean, you're a man. It's natural for you to want to protect me. Right? So I should just let you be a man and stop skipping steps, like letting go of you when you're trying to save me. In fact, I didn't trust you enough to get us to the bank, so we're really both to blame in a way."

Jason thought about her words. She was right. They both had a lapse in their trust in each other. "I can't argue with that. I don't know what to say."

Elyssa gazed into his eyes. As if entering a dark room, her pupils dilated, searching, probing. After nearly a minute, she whispered, "I guess it just takes time."

"You mean complete trust?"

"Mm-hmm." She looked to the north. "We left the soldiers pretty far behind."

"No use waiting for them. Maybe they'll catch up by the time we get to the wall."

She turned around, her eyes again probing, this time the land to the south. "It's about an hour away, right?"

"I think so. Do you sense any obstacles?"

She shook her head. "Let's find your sword and get going."

After finding the sword and belt upstream, Jason and Elyssa turned to the south and walked side by side near the chasm. Both stayed silent as the waterfall's roar dominated the soundscape.

They stepped to the edge and looked into the gorge. White water gushed from the north, flew out over the expanse, and tumbled in a free fall until it splashed over gray stones far below, some flat and some with protruding points. In response, spray flew upward in billowing towers before raining back to the stones.

The raft had broken into pieces, some lodged between stones and some floating westward in a new river that carried water to places unknown. Neither dragon nor human had mentioned any regions that lay outside the Northlands and the Southlands. It seemed that their focus stayed only on their territories, though the world of Starlight had to encompass much more than such a narrow view.

Elyssa turned and wrapped her arms around Jason. "Thank you," she whispered.

"You're welcome." He returned the embrace. There was no need for an explanation. "And thank *you* for another chance."

Elyssa took his hand and faced south. "Shall we?"

"Without a doubt."

"Then lead the way, warrior."

The two marched ahead hand in hand, leaving the roar of the waterfall behind.

※

Constance stood in front of one of the female white dragons, trying desperately to show no pain. Although her burns felt as if the flames were still raging across her skin, staying calm was the only way to prove to these beasts that she could speak on behalf of her fellow slaves. "I am telling the truth, Beth," she said through her scorched lips. "A cure to the disease is coming. There is no need to, as you say, eliminate the pestilence. We have a solution, and it is only a matter of time until it arrives."

Beth's head swayed in an arc from side to side, as if drawing a smile in the air. "I wish to take no chances. The soldiers from Darksphere could arrive at any time, and you can provide no guarantees. We will not allow dying humans to linger and suffer needlessly. Begin sorting through the sick. Have the strongest among you bring the weakest three to us."

With a sigh, Constance scanned the area. The Zodiac's portico jutted into the street from the main building, providing an elevated porch with a roof over top. From each side, stairs led to the porch, which overlooked the cobblestone thoroughfare. Not long ago, Koren stood at the front edge of the portico and addressed a gathering of slaves. So much had changed. Now the slaves gathered again, but not to listen. They came to die.

Dozens of slaves lay on the street or stairs, while others milled about, passing around water and bread. Some of the children slept, exhausted from fighting the illness. One man sat against one of the portico's support columns, his head lolling to the side. With every finger missing from one hand and with no ears, he might be dead already.

"I will do as you commanded," Constance said, "but deciding which three are the weakest will take some time."

"Then choose any three and be quick about it, or I will choose them myself."

A whisper reached Constance's ear. "I think she's an ice dragon."

Constance forced herself to keep her focus straight ahead. No matter how many times Deference spoke up, it always gave her a start. Being only spirit, Deference had stayed as motionless as possible in order to remain invisible, though she sometimes dashed to wherever she was needed when it seemed that no dragons were looking.

"So she's an ice dragon," Constance mumbled under her breath. "Why are you telling me that?"

"They'll probably breathe ice to kill the people. Tell Beth that ice might not destroy the disease. It requires intense heat."

"Do you know this to be true?"

"No, but it's a good guess. You have only a few symptoms, so maybe the heat remaining from your intense burns is keeping it from taking hold. Anyway, it's worth a try. At least it might buy us some time."

Constance turned toward Beth. "I have heard about your kind. Do you intend to freeze the sickest ones?"

"We intend to freeze everyone. There will be no exceptions. With no cure and no hope for recovery, everyone who has even the slightest symptoms will be destroyed."

"Then why should I cooperate? You'll just kill me."

"You will cooperate, because you believe doing so will give you another hour to live." Beth breathed a stream of ice at Constance's feet, chilling her toes. "I know your kind. You will obey."

With two quick kicks, Constance shook off the ice. "Freezing them will kill their bodies, but it might not destroy the disease. It is sensitive to heat, not cold."

Beth's neck whipped around, bringing her head directly in front of Constance. "Do you know this to be true?"

Constance suppressed a gulp. Spreading out her arms, she showed the burns on her skin. "I have only minor symptoms, so I assume—"

"Assumptions are unopened windows that foolish birds fly into, and their broken bodies are evidence gathered too late."

"Be that as it may, I think—"

"It matters not what you think." As Beth looked at the sky, her growl suddenly shifted to a purr. "I see that we have unexpected company."

In the southern sky, two dragons flew toward them, one black and the other the more customary reddish brown.

"Taushin and Mallerin," Deference whispered in Constance's ear.

Beth let out a series of squeaks and grunts that sounded something like normal dragon language, but the words were unfamiliar. The other two white dragons skittered toward them, flapping their wings to propel their bodies.

"What is your observation, Gamal?" Beth asked.

The larger of the two squinted at the sky. "Taushin seeks an audience," he said in a deep voice. "The dragon flying with him is his guide, his seeing eyes—a female, I believe."

"Dalath?" Beth focused on the smaller of the two. "Shall we grant this audience?"

"By all means. There are only two of them, and one is blind."

Constance glanced from Gamal to Dalath, male and female. It seemed that the only differences between the sexes were size and voice. Every other detail was identical.

"Gamal," Beth said, "fly to meet them and explain that any word or action that violates the laws of Starlight will result in death. Since the female acts as his eyes, make sure she focuses on me just before they land. I want to see his reaction when he first notices me."

Without another word, Gamal took to the air. Beth shuffled toward the man leaning against the column, latched on to him with her foreclaws, and dragged him back into the open. He groaned and twitched but little else.

Constance whispered, "Don't look, Deference. I think this is going to end badly."

"My eyes are closed."

By the time Beth stopped, Taushin and Mallerin had begun their descent, Gamal flying on Taushin's opposite side. Beth dropped the man to the cobblestones and rolled him a few feet away. With a great heave, she blasted a barrage of ice crystals over his body, instantly coating him in white.

Constance gasped. Stories of such ice abounded in legends from the Northlands, but no one here had ever seen it. And now a human lay in an icy blanket, no longer groaning or moving at all.

As the three dragons beat their wings to land, Beth looked at Constance and gestured with a foreleg. "Check him for life."

Her legs shaking, Constance walked to the man's side, knelt on her scorched knees, and touched his wrist. His arm was as stiff as the mainstay of a dragon wing, cold and lifeless, and a sheet of white ice coated his entire body.

"There is no need to check for a heartbeat," Deference whispered. "He is dead."

"Where are you?"

"I'm riding on your shoulders. It's the easiest way to move without being seen. I can't hold on to things for very long, but I can stay put without a problem."

Now on the ground, Taushin drew near, his head high as he cast blue eyebeams on Mallerin as she surveyed the portico area.

Beth extended her neck, lifting her head higher than Taushin's. "What brings you here, presumed king of the Southlands dragons?"

"I come with news that is crucial for you to hear."

"You flew into danger to deliver news that will benefit me?" Beth's purring voice seemed to glide through the air. "Taushin, from what Gamal tells me, you have no capacity for unselfish acts."

Taushin's brow bent. "Perhaps that is true, but that is the way for dragons and humans alike. No one is capable of true selfless sacrifice."

"The world has proven that time and again." Beth nodded at him. "Go on."

"Cassabrie, the greatest of all Starlighters, will come here. She resides within Exodus, the once fallen star, so you will be unable to stop her."

"Stop her from doing what?" Beth asked.

A thump sounded from the Zodiac, drawing Constance's attention. Maybe a slave had staggered in and fallen through the entryway's open floor. In any case, the dragons didn't seem to notice.

Taushin spread out his wings. "With a wave of her arms and with her mesmerizing voice, she can hypnotize any dragon who looks upon her. She plans to put you in a trance and destroy you."

"Destroy us? How?"

"Are you unaware of the legends? The star's membrane is coated with energy particles that will eat through your bodies faster than a whip can draw blood. One touch from her spherical chamber will dissolve you to a pile of white powder in mere seconds."

Beth looked at Gamal, her expression dour. "What say you?"

"It is true," Gamal said with a slight bow of his head. "The previous time we visited to bring justice, Exodus was safely stored in the Northlands mountains, so I did not warn you about it. If a powerful Starlighter is coming within the star, the danger is great indeed."

Beth focused again on Taushin. "I sense malice. You bring a solution that will benefit you and prevent our enforcement. You seek to avoid punishment and extend your rule."

"Of course." Taushin bowed his head. "I did not deny any selfish intent."

Beth's expression took on a skeptical aspect. "Go on."

"We have a device in the Zodiac that will rob Cassabrie of energy. Allow me free access here until she arrives, and I will see to it that she is rendered harmless."

"And what of our enforcement? You know we cannot leave your race unpunished."

"I will tell you where my fellow dragons are hiding. You may exact your punishment there. I ask only that you spare a few of us to continue the dragon race."

"A few?" Beth's eyes narrowed. "How few?"

"Myself, my mother and her mate, Arxad and his mate, and their daughter, Xenith."

"Six dragons to propagate the species." Beth's skeptical stare deepened. "Why these six?"

Constance raised her brow. The same question crossed her own mind. Why would Taushin want to save the dragons who weren't his allies and allow those loyal to him to be destroyed?

"I need experience and counsel from the wisest leaders," Taushin said. "And I covet Xenith as my mate. She is strong and intelligent, a fit vessel for propagation."

"A convenient answer." Beth looked at Gamal. "Do you have insight?"

"His choices are reasonable." Gamal studied Taushin. "I want to know more about the device that will drain the Starlighter. Because of our war with these dragons, we failed to complete our mission to find and restore the Reflections Crystal. This device Taushin mentions sounds as if it might have properties similar to the crystal."

Taushin cast his eyebeams on Gamal. "You have a sharp mind. The device is, indeed, the Reflections Crystal. Once I have destroyed Cassabrie, you may take it with you. I will have no further need of it. If you reject this offer, of course, I cannot do anything to protect you from her power."

"Gamal," Beth said, "is Taushin lying?"

The end of Gamal's tail twitched. "Every word he has spoken is true, though, as did you, I detect deep malice. I would not trust him."

"I rely on you for discernment, not counsel." Beth shifted toward Dalath. "What do you say?"

Dalath's blue eyes gleamed. "Kill the infected humans and lead the Darksphere army to Taushin's dragons.

Since we will be outnumbered, we might need the humans' help. If Taushin proves to be untrustworthy, his company of six will not be able to withstand our fury."

Beth nodded. "I agree. Begin killing the humans at once. Start with the oldest and most infirm."

Constance raised a hand. "No! Don't! How can you speak of justice when you kill the innocent?"

"Innocence is irrelevant," Beth said. "The disease has no cure, so we are merely shortening their suffering. At the same time, we are protecting those who are coming to rescue those who remain. In a sense, we will be dispensing showers of mercy."

"But there is *hope* for a cure. We can wait until—"

"Hope for what has never existed is a man in chains waiting to fall up into the sky. Like gravity itself, the law is unchangeable and unforgiving." Beth sprayed icy mist over Constance's face. "Attempts to delay the inevitable are simply denials of reality and a waste of time. If you continue pursuit of your so-called hope, you will learn a lesson in the law's merciful ways before the others do."

Constance brushed the ice crystals away. What could be done? If this dragon carried out her threat, hope really would die. Mallerin and Taushin whispered to each other, but they seemed unwilling to stop the plan or express an opinion.

"Mother," Deference whispered. "Take me to the Zodiac's doors. I think I saw something."

"Beth," Dalath said, "since this human heard our plans regarding Cassabrie, she is likely to try to warn her."

"An excellent point." Beth aimed her snout at Constance. "It seems that you will be first after all."

Constance stiffened. With her scorched legs, trying to run away would be futile. "Go, Deference," she whispered. "Use the ice to shield yourself from view."

"But, Mother, I—"

"Go!"

An icy spray coated Constance's vision. Frigid cold plunged through her skin and into her bones. A sense of falling took over, then perfect whiteness.

thirteen

andall jerked on the rope. The knot was good and tight, fastened securely to a lantern bracket embedded in the lower level stone wall. With the rest of the rope coiled over his shoulder, he reeled it out as he walked around the sharp stakes under the false floor of the Zodiac's entry corridor. Nearby, a dead dragon lay on the floor. Although he had no ability to interfere, his odor was bad enough to gag a vulture.

Above, the floor lay open, its two panels hanging loosely under the sides of the hall. He let the hefty rope drop to the stakes and held on to one end. Until a few minutes ago, this rope had hung from the Basilica's bell tower, but a quick stroke with his blade gave it a new job to do.

More lantern brackets lined the wall in the upper corridor, spaced apart evenly. He aimed at the bracket closest to the dome room and threw the rope. The end looped over the target, catching it perfectly, and fell back to the lower level. He grabbed the end and pulled it tight. This would do just fine.

He detached his scabbard from his belt and tossed it into the dome room on the upper level. It clanked, then settled inside. Randall flinched and waited in silence. No dragon darkened the entry door above.

With one foot on the wall, he grasped the rope with both hands and climbed. When he reached the hanging floor panel, he set both feet on it and pressed the panel against the wall, then walked across it parallel to the wall and toward the dome room, taking in rope as he traveled.

His leg muscles cramped, and his arms throbbed. The dome room was almost within reach. Just a few more steps.

When he came to the end of the corridor, he leaned against the wall to his left and studied his position. He faced the right-hand wall with both feet planted on the panel. The right edge of the threshold to the dome room lay about eight feet behind him and four feet above. A push with his legs and a lunging reach should allow him to grab the threshold, but failure could mean a nasty fall and a lot of noise.

He took in a deep breath. It was now or never.

Keeping one hand on the rope, he bent his knees, thrust away from the wall, and reached for the threshold. His fingers caught the edge but slipped away. When he swung back to the panel, his shoulder slammed against it.

As he hung on, cringing, the thud reverberated throughout the corridor. A light flickered somewhere in the passage, fleeting and fast—maybe one of the lanterns disturbed by a draft.

When the noise settled, Randall again rested, his newly aching shoulder against the back wall and his feet against the panel. So far, no one had come to investigate. Trying again might work, but it might also make things worse.

"Psst. Randall. Can I help?"

He looked up at the doorway to the dome room. Deference stood there waving her arms to stay visible. Her glow washed over him, making him feel exposed and vulnerable. "How can you help? You can't pull me up there, can you?"

"I can have an effect on physical things for a few seconds. No more."

"That might be enough."

Deference knelt close to the edge. "What do you want me to do?"

"When I push back and reach for the threshold you're standing on, grab my wrist and make sure I get a good hold. Are you strong enough to do that?"

"I hope so. I'll do my best."

"That'll have to do."

"If it's all the same to you, I think we should hurry." Deference's voice shook with emotion. "The white dragons are getting ready to kill everyone. They already killed my mother."

"They killed Madam Orley?"

As Deference nodded, a sparkle gleamed in her eye.

"Those monsters!" Randall squeezed the rope, wishing it were a dragon's throat. "I'm really sorry about your mother, but I'll do what I can to stop them from killing the others."

"Okay." The tremor in her voice eased. "I hope you can."

"I'll do my best." Randall bent his knees again. "Here I come."

With a hearty shove, he launched away from the wall. He reached for the threshold, but this time his fingers barely touched the edge. A strong grip squeezed his wrist, and he shot upward several inches. He grasped the threshold with one hand, released the rope, and thrust his other hand to the ledge. Something grabbed the back of his tunic and pulled, helping him climb the rest of the way.

Now on all fours, he looked for his phantom helper, but she was invisible again. "Thank you," he said between gasps for breath. "I wouldn't have made it without you."

She appeared on the floor well within the dark room, rising from a sitting position. "I fell when I had to let go."

"Keep moving. You're the only light in there."

While Deference waved her arms, Randall climbed to his feet, picked up his scabbard, and looked all around for any sign of dragons. Even though they were in a hurry, rushing into danger would ruin everything. "Again, I'm really sorry about your mother."

Deference faded away. "Thank you." Sparks from her voice drizzled to the floor. "I'll see her again someday."

He attached his scabbard to his belt and skulked farther into the room. "Do you know anything about this place?"

Deference walked at his side, enough movement to cast her glow several feet ahead. "I came here for my Promotion. This is where Arxad told us to write a letter to our closest loved one, and then he gave us something to drink that made me dizzy. I don't remember anything after that."

Randall touched a column that appeared to support the ceiling. If this room had a dome, the room underneath had to be a circle, but darkness hid any other columns that would have given away the location of the center. "Do you know where the Reflections Crystal is?"

She pointed. "It should be straight ahead. It was glowing when I came for my Promotion, but I think that's because the dome was open a little ways. It brightened when Arxad spoke something to it, but I don't know how it works."

"Jason told me about that. It brightens when you say something true to it and darkens when you lie."

"Then if you want more light, maybe you could tell it something true."

"I think we'll just use your glow. I don't want to alert anyone. We'll stay quiet while we're close."

As they walked, a sphere came into view atop a head-high pedestal. Twinkling dots covered the dark surface, like stars in the night sky. Deference stopped, shutting off her light and casting their surroundings in blackness. Above, more dots spread across the ceiling, curving from one edge of the room to the other. The entire chamber looked like a miniature world with stars glowing from horizon to horizon.

Randall searched for any design that looked like a spear. To his right, a line of bright stars ran from the center toward the edge of the room where two stars on each side of the end formed a point. That had to be it.

Randall walked in that direction, intentionally making enough noise with his shoes to signal his movement. Deference joined him again, and her glow illuminated their path.

When he reached the column at the end of the spear, he touched the surface, smooth and cool, probably marble. "I think we're far enough away to talk now."

"That's good." Deference waved a hand, giving light to the column. A wooden handle protruded on the side facing away from the crystal. Barely long enough to grab with one hand, it would have been nearly impossible to find in the darkness.

Randall wrapped his fingers around it and tried to push it to one side, then the other, but it wouldn't budge. When he pulled down, it moved slowly, as if attached to a chain that lifted a heavy weight. A click sounded, then a low grinding noise, but the room stayed dark.

"That's not the dome." Deference ran toward the entry corridor, her aura illuminating her wake. "Back in a minute."

As the room darkened again, Randall kept his hand on the lever. Xenith had warned that this might not be the correct one, so there was no need for alarm … yet.

A few seconds later, Deference's light appeared. She glided slowly, her finger tapping her chin. "You closed the floor back there. Maybe you should leave it that way in case you have to get out fast."

"Good idea." As they walked around the room's perimeter, Deference's glow guided their way. When they reached the next column, Randall spotted another lever, this one shorter and metallic. He grasped it and pulled down. It moved to a lower position easily, then slid completely out of its socket.

A new grinding noise erupted, this one from above. A light appeared in a hole at the apex, gradually expanding.

The Reflections Crystal brightened at the same rate, as if absorbing energy from the outside. As light filled the room, Randall looked at the lever in his hand. Notched on two sides, it looked like a long key.

"Something's wrong," Deference said. "I feel something pulling me toward the crystal."

"Can you resist?"

Her nodding head appeared. "I'd better not get any closer, though."

Randall slid the key into his pocket and scanned the area. With dragons outside, going out the front door wasn't an option. "Is there a back door, another way to get out of here?"

"I think so. Arxad led me out, but I don't remember how. I was so dizzy."

"I'm going to test this thing." Randall strode toward the crystal, but its stinging radiance kept him three paces away. Holding a hand up to shield his eyes, he searched for Deference, but she was nowhere in view. The brilliant light was probably washing out her glow.

Above, a white dragon flew over the widening hole. It glanced in without landing. Soon the opening would be big enough for it to fly through.

"Deference," Randall called, "where are you?"

"Still next to the column."

"Speak loudly enough for the crystal to hear you."

"Okay, I'll try."

"Is there an exit besides the one in front, a place a human can walk?"

"I told you," Deference shouted, "I don't remember."

The crystal dimmed, relieving some of the sting.

"You do remember," Randall said. "It's locked somewhere in your brain. Think. Where did Arxad lead you?"

The white dragon landed on the edge of the widening hole. It snapped its head back as if recoiling from the stinging radiance.

"Arxad touched something that opened a sliding door. It was wide enough for him to fit through, but just barely."

The crystal brightened, increasing the pain. The dragon on the roof called out, "I think someone is down there, but there is danger. Guard the front door. I will try to enter from here."

Randall clutched his sword's hilt. Fighting a dragon alone certainly wasn't his first choice, but it might end up being his only one. He scanned the perimeter wall. Shelves, benches, and unidentifiable wooden structures interrupted the space. Only four blank spots were of sufficient size for a dragon, and a mural had been drawn on each one—various landscapes that resembled the horizons around the Zodiac. "Did you see mountains?"

"No."

The crystal grew brighter. The dragon flew into the room and landed next to the column nearest to the main entrance. Extending his neck, he took a step closer and bellowed, "Who is there?"

Randall drew his sword but kept his focus on Deference. "Did you see a forest?"

"No."

The crystal brightened yet again.

"A river flowing into the barrier wall?"

The dragon lunged, but a new pulse of brightness made him stop just a few steps away. "Cease this activity immediately, or I will freeze you."

The grinding noise continued. As the hole above widened enough to reveal Solarus, the crystal stayed bright. The white dragon crept closer, blinking. "You were wise to stop at my command. Now tell me—"

"There *was* a river!" Deference said. "And a wall!"

"Let's go! Hurry!" Randall sheathed his sword and ran to the river mural and rubbed his hand across the design, slapping prominent parts of the drawing. "Come on! Open! There has to be a way!"

Deference ran around the perimeter wall toward Randall. "I'm coming!"

"Stop!" the dragon shouted.

A wave of ice spilled over Randall, covering him in a frosty coat. The cold stiffened his arms and numbed his fingers. Lifting a heavy hand, he slapped the wall again, but it felt as if he were swinging a sledge hammer.

"I'm here," Deference whispered. "I'll look for a switch."

The dragon shuffled closer. "That was a warning. Stay where you are, or I will kill you."

"I think I found it!" Deference said.

Gathering all his strength, Randall slammed his shoulder against the wall. It slid open, and he toppled through. Sitting with his hands propping his body, he looked back. The dragon stomped toward him, rearing his head. Another storm of ice erupted from his mouth, but as the leading edge of the storm splashed over Randall, the door slid closed, cutting off the flow.

Daggers of frigid cold plunged into Randall's body, shooting icy chills through his heart, up his spine, and out to his head, fingers, and toes.

He fell to his back. Ice crystals crunched all around. Although freezing cold drilled to his core, no shivers broke out. His muscles had locked in place.

Something thumped on the door. "Human, if you are still alive, hear me. Without help, you will surely die. The ice will slow your heart until it stops. If you are able, tell me how to open this door, and I will spare your life, at least for the time being."

Randall tried to open his mouth, but his lips had frozen together. Even drawing in breath was a chore. He couldn't tell the dragon anything, even if he wanted to.

"I assume by your silence that you are either dead or incapacitated. So be it." The sound of swishing followed, then the fading scratch and thump of a shuffling dragon.

Randall's heart pounded—once, twice, three times. Its slow cadence sounded like the rhythm of a funeral march. Soon it would all be over, but maybe the plan had worked. Maybe the dome would stay open and draw Cassabrie, and she would use her power to stop the cold-hearted dragons before they could kill too many slaves.

Closing his eyes, he imagined the process, three white dragons spewing frosty death on diseased bodies. They would become just like him, frozen mummies without hope.

He let out a sigh, maybe his last breath. Yes, hope was gone. The slaves had hoped for release but were struck down by disease instead. They had hoped for a warrior to come and break their chains, but only a bumbling kid trapped in ice and an old dungeon survivor remained. Everyone else had gone to the Northlands, much too far away to help. All was lost.

A tingling sensation brushed his face, warm and delicate. It moved to his throat, then to his chest, sending a wave of heat through his skin and into his heart and lungs.

"Are you alive?"

He snatched in a breath and forced his lips to separate. "Deference?"

"Shhh." As a glowing hand moved over his body, the warmth spread across his abdomen and into his arms and legs. "I'm melting the ice. I'm not physical, but at least I can generate some heat."

Randall's muscles loosened, sending shivers erupting along every extremity. He hugged himself and shook violently. More ice crunched, and water seeped into his clothing, worsening the biting cold.

"Those shivers are awful. I'll try to help." Now fully visible, Deference lay on top of his body, chest to chest, and wrapped her arms around him. Her body's glow strengthened. Tingling heat flowed everywhere, and Randall drew a long breath. The wetness increased, no longer icy cold, more like a warm bath.

After a minute or so, the shaking eased. Deference rose and stood at his side, a hand extended. Randall grasped it and rode her pull. The grip snapped loose, but not before he had set his feet firmly.

"How did you get in here?"

"I can slide through almost anywhere." She spread out her glowing arms. "Having no body has its advantages."

"Thank you. You saved my life."

"You're welcome." Her head dipped low. "I wish I could have done the same for my mother."

"Ten more seconds and it would've been too late for me."

She touched his hand. "If you don't mind, I think we should get going. We might have only delayed the killing."

"You're right." Randall looked around. They stood in a dim corridor, high and wide, clearly large enough for a dragon. There was only one way to go—straight ahead.

He nodded into the darkness. "Let's go."

They hustled through the passageway, a steep incline that curved slightly to the right. After several seconds, daylight came into view as the passageway ended in a huge square window with nothing beyond it except bare sky.

Randall stopped at the opening—a ledge leading to a fifty-pace gap between the Zodiac and the Basilica where a similar window opened into darkness.

Deference leaned over the edge. "I guess Arxad flew me from here to the Basilica. I do remember floating."

Randall knelt and looked down. A heather-covered lawn lay at least twenty feet below, not necessarily a fatal plunge but enough to break bones and rupture organs. A cart filled with hay sat under a tree to the left, much too far to reach with a jump.

A loud wail sounded from the front of the Zodiac.

Randall looked that way, then met Deference's glowing gaze. "They've started the killing again," she said. "We have to hurry."

His jaw tightening, Randall turned back to the ledge. He spied a branch protruding from the tree off to the side. It would take a quite a leap to grab it, especially considering his stiff, aching legs. From there, if the branch held his weight, it might be possible to work his way to the trunk and climb to the ground.

He looked toward Deference, but she was again invisible. "Can you get down?"

"Sure."

"Go ahead. I'll meet you there." Randall unhooked his scabbard and dropped it over the ledge. It fell in a slow spin and landed in the heather with a quiet thud. Taking a breath, he leaped for the branch and grabbed it with both hands. While he moved hand over hand toward the trunk, his body dangling as the branch swung, Deference slid down the Zodiac's slick exterior, feet down and her chest against the wall. Tiny sparks flew wherever her fingers, toes, or clothing touched the marble surface.

When she reached the ground, she ran underneath him and looked up, her body slowly fading. "That looks hard."

"No kidding." A crack sounded from the branch at a point between his hands and the trunk.

"Uh-oh," Deference said.

"No kidding again." Randall looked down. Still almost twenty feet away, the ground would surely break something, maybe his neck. The cart filled with hay was closer now but too far too swing to, and the branch probably wouldn't hold—

With a final crack of wood, Randall plummeted. The cart shot forward. He landed in the hay, breaking his fall. The cart collapsed under his weight, and he rolled out to the heather face down.

He pushed to all fours and shook his head. To his left, his scabbard lay just out of reach. The hilt jerked toward him, then slid sporadically until it touched his hand.

"We'd better go," Deference said. "That is, if it's all right with you."

He grabbed the hilt. "Thanks again, for everything."

A pull on his sleeve helped him rise to his feet. After reattaching his scabbard, he nodded. "Lead the way."

His calf muscles threatening to cramp, he followed the ghostly girl around the Zodiac until the portico came into view. He backed against the wall and surveyed the scene.

Ice-covered bodies lay in a straight line with a field of frost all around. One of the Benefile sprayed ice over a woman lying at one end of the row, while two Southlands dragons looked on. Beyond the white dragon, a line of slaves stood as if waiting their turn to suffer the same fate.

"Why are they just standing there like sheep?" Randall asked, his voice tight with frustration. "Why don't they run?"

"Taushin and his mother, Mallerin," Deference whispered.

Even as she spoke, one of the men dashed away from the line. Almost lazily, Mallerin took aim and blasted him with fire. Completely ablaze, he staggered aimlessly, screaming, until he collapsed next to another smoldering body.

The other slaves looked on for a moment, then turned their sad faces toward the front of the line again. The weakest ones sat or reclined. Mothers carried crying children, trying to comfort them with gentle rocking or shushes. Teenagers looked at each other expectantly, as if wondering what had happened to the hope of deliverance. Some men stood or sat with slumped shoulders, their faces downcast. Even from a distance it was apparent that they lamented their spinelessness. A few men tightened and loosened fists, giving furtive hand signals to each other, as if planning some kind of attack. Of course any unarmed venture would be suicide, but these square-shouldered men looked like the type who would risk anything to save their women and children.

Randall slowly drew out his sword. The slaves would either get deliverance, or he would die trying to provide it. "Can you create a distraction? Enough for me to sneak up on the dragon that's freezing the people?"

"I'll try." Deference ran toward the portico, becoming brighter and brighter as she accelerated. "Hey!" she shouted, waving her arms. "Try to catch me!" She ran up the stairs and hopped through the doorway to the Zodiac.

One of the white dragons shot after her. "Continue the showers of mercy. I will find her."

While the others watched the Zodiac door, Randall stalked toward the executioner dragon, grumbling, "I'll show them some showers of mercy."

fourteen

Sitting behind her father, Koren let her cloak flap as the breeze whipped it back. Although riding on Alaph had its difficulties due to no spines to grab, his wings' effortless beats made for an exhilarating ride. When she closed her eyes, it felt more like sitting still in the wind than soaring hundreds of feet in the air atop a dragon.

The few hours in flight provided plenty of time to connect with Exodus and gather tales from the past. It seemed that Cassabrie was intentionally filling the air with crucial stories, perfectly relevant for the times at hand. Some revelations proved to be astounding, including surprising tidbits about Zena and Taushin. Perhaps soon they could be told in order to help the slaves break their chains.

A new twinge of pain bit into her stomach. Every hour it was becoming clearer that the ointment wasn't enough.

Should she and the others try swallowing it when her father made the next batch? She grimaced. It would be like crunching Cassabrie's bone, chewing her flesh, and drinking her blood.

When they reached the barrier wall, Alaph landed on the north side at the river's edge. With the gate still open, the current flowed freely, raising a reminder of past thoughts. Water would eventually find a way to its destination, whether over, under, or through its obstacles. If only the slaves would strive for freedom and liberation with the same effort the river gave as it churned toward lower ground. Passion of heart could overcome anything, even a huge barrier wall.

"Dismount," Alaph said. "I placed the bag of explosives at my left flank. Take the tubes into the wall and place them in dry locations. Let us destroy the symbol of oppression that trapped those who wished to leave and repelled those who wished to enter."

Still carrying the detonator in her pocket, Koren slid down. Her cloak billowed as she dropped, and her trousers cuffs rode halfway up her calves.

Orson climbed with hands and feet, his shoes trying to find notches, but a slip sent him into a full slide. Koren caught him under his arms and helped him settle to the ground.

Gasping for breath, he held a hand against his chest. "I fear that the disease has caught full hold. Perhaps I will have to be the next to try the medicine, or else I won't be able to help administer it."

Koren checked the detonator in her pocket and picked up the bag. "You wait here and rest. I'll place the tubes."

She hurried to the base of the wall. A walkway ran from the river's edge to the gate, covered with ankle-deep water. She stepped in and tested her weight on the walkway. It seemed quite sturdy. Touching the wall to her left and extending her arm to the right while holding the bag for balance, she sloshed toward the gate.

When she reached the opening, she stopped and peered around the corner. Although Solarus shone into the space within the wall, it didn't allow a view under the river's surface. If another walkway led across to the south side, it lay hidden underwater.

She swung around the corner and crept through the gateway, sliding along to check for solid footing. The path continued, narrow and still underwater, but strong and straight.

She stopped at the heart of the barrier wall and pivoted in place, scanning the inner wall on the north side. Above, a mechanism with two wheels and a belt between them lay on a stone shelf well above her head and to the right. Whatever the device was, it had to be a remnant from the human civilization that existed long ago. No dragon could put something like that together. The shelf, perhaps three feet wide, ran parallel to the wall, over the gateway, and into the darkness on the left.

After inching her way back to the north wall, she slid her feet to the right. The underwater path continued that way, hugging the wall, a shelf similar to the one above. When she drew closer to the wheels, a ladder came into view, apparently access for anyone who needed to inspect or repair the device.

She withdrew the detonator and, standing on tiptoes and reaching high, set it gently on the shelf. Still holding the bag, she grabbed a rung with her free hand and scaled the ladder to the top. She turned and sat on the shelf, facing the south wall, a wheel to her left and the detonator and bag to her right. An odd smell emanated from the wheel, like the odor of burning pheterone.

After taking a few breaths, she lifted the bag to her lap and withdrew one of the tubes. It was warm, much warmer than the surrounding air. That couldn't be good. If the tubes were more volatile now, the slightest bump might set them off.

She rose slowly to her feet, keeping her back bent and her head low. With so little light, bumping her head would be easy to do, and that might send her tumbling. She might be blown to bits before her body ever hit the river.

Keeping her footfalls light, she walked away from the wheel and detonator. Every few steps, she stopped, withdrew a tube, and set it on the shelf. Each tube felt warmer than the one before. When she drew out the last one, its heat stung her hand. It slipped and lodged in a crack on the shelf, sizzling.

Koren spun and hurried back, careful to avoid the other tubes. She snatched up the detonator, slid down the ladder, and retraced her steps. Grabbing the corner of the north wall, she swung around it and ran toward the river's edge, shouting, "I think one of the tubes might explode!"

Kneeling next to the river, Orson spilled water from his cupped hands and looked at the top of the wall. "Alaph! Did you hear?"

Alaph flew down from his perch on the wall's northern parapet. "We must mount quickly!"

Before he could land, a long boom sounded from the wall over the center of the river. Koren stopped, still several paces from the river's edge, and held her breath. Her father dashed to her and threw her into the water. Koren flailed against the current and drifted northward. More booms erupted. Dust enveloped the wall from one side of the river to the other. Huge rocks flew in every direction. Smaller ones shot into the sky.

She swam toward the wall with all her might, screaming, "Daddy!" Her saturated cloak dragged her down. Water sloshed into her mouth, gagging her. She threw off the cloak and swam harder, but the billowing dust veiled the wall.

Another explosion ripped through the cloud. A jagged flat stone hurtled straight toward her face, but in a flash of white Alaph blocked the stone, snatched her out of the water with his back claws, and lifted into the sky.

Alaph's wings beat wildly. He bounced in erratic circles, alternately ascending and descending as he flew downstream, away from the growing cloud of dust. Finally, he dropped Koren, and they both splashed into the river. He sank for a moment before bobbing back to the surface, his wings again flailing.

Slapping the water with her arms, Koren swam toward the eastern edge until the water was shallow enough for wading.

Alaph fought the current and struggled to shore well downstream, clawing at the turf and dragging his body. Koren sloshed to the bank, ran to him, and dropped to her knees near his back leg. The flat stone protruded from his flank near his hip, penetrating several inches into his flesh, but no blood flowed.

Alaph's neck curled, bringing his head around. He clamped down on the stone with his teeth, jerked it out, and threw it over Koren's head. The stone left a deep gash, but still Alaph did not bleed.

Koren swallowed through her tight throat. "Alaph! What can I do to help you? Where is my father? Did you rescue him, too?"

"One question at a time, child." Alaph's snout drew close to the wound. He sniffed it for a moment, then turned his head toward Koren. "No vital organs have been punctured. Normally I would survive such an injury."

"Normally?" The biting demon in her belly stormed back to life. She glanced back at the wall, but the dust cloud still shielded it from view. Her father was nowhere in sight. "What do you mean by *normally*?"

"I am one of the Benefile, a species with which you are still quite unfamiliar. Unlike humans, I have the option to choose to die at any time. For me to expire at will is not suicide; it is natural."

His words registered as audible sounds but little more. She looked toward the wall once again. "Did you rescue my father?"

"No."

The word drilled into her mind, spreading numbness to her limbs. It echoed, and every reverberation felt like a stab through the heart. Her lips trembling, she repeated the awful sound. "No?"

"The rubble buried him instantly. It was all I could do to pluck you from the water to keep that stone from severing your head from your body. Your father's decision to throw you into the river surely saved your life."

A strange laugh erupted from her throat. "He's probably okay, right? Maybe he found a place to hide." Her voice sounded foreign, as if someone else were speaking. "If I can find some strong thread and sew you back together, we can go and look for him."

"No."

"Stop saying that!"

"Your father is gone, Koren, and my purpose is now complete. I will drift away satisfied."

Koren ran a shaky hand along Alaph's rear leg. "I don't know what you mean. What purpose are you talking about?"

"Each of the four Benefile has a unique purpose with regard to roles inherent in the Code. Beth is justice, Gamal is discernment, Dalath is decision, and I am mercy. When there are principles of behavior that the sons of men and dragons are commanded to follow, there must be mercy, or else no one would survive."

"Since your purpose helps people survive, then ..." Koren blinked. It still seemed that unbidden words spilled out, silly and nonsensical. "Then you made my father survive, right?"

Alaph sighed. "No, child. I am sorry." He touched her with his snout. "There will be a time to mourn Orson, but now you must gather your faculties. I hoped to transfer my role to you. As a slave who has demonstrated and experienced so much mercy, you are able to continue in my place."

"Continue in your place?" Koren laid a hand on her chest. "I could never take your place. I wouldn't know what to do."

"Ah! But you do know! You merely do not realize it yet. And as one who has been chosen by the Creator to help free the slaves, you might be the only one who can deliver the Creator's mercy."

"I can't be the one." Her thoughts straightening, Koren stood and backed away a step. "I won't let you decide to die. If I don't take your place, you have to live. And we can go and search for my father together."

"Your father is dead, Koren!" Aleph's eyes blazed blue. "He is lying beneath tons of rubble. I saw a stone snap his neck. Another severed a leg. A mountain of boulders buried his broken body, and his spirit has gone to be with the Creator. He is no longer in this world."

Koren flinched at every word. As she pictured the carnage, it came to life near the river bank. Her father stood next to the wall as he threw her into the river, his eyes wide with fear.

Just as a boulder toppled toward him, the real Koren waved her arms. "No! Go away! I don't want to see it!"

The image vanished. Koren dropped to her knees and sobbed. Pulling her hair with both hands, she screamed, "I can't stand it anymore! I just can't stand it!"

"Do not despair, Koren. The Creator's mercy will—"

"Mercy?" Koren stabbed a finger toward the demolished wall. "Do you call that mercy? My father was a hero, but what did he get for it? A painful death! A fractured skull and shattered bones! If that's mercy, I don't want any part of it!"

"You do not yet understand the substance of mercy. It is not escape from suffering; it is access to the Creator, the ability to speak to him directly as one would to a friend."

"Don't talk to me." Still on her knees, Koren bent over and laid her cheek on the ground. "Just leave me alone. Just let me die here. I don't want to live."

Alaph's cool breath wafted against her ear. "Have you decided to forsake your fellow slaves? You have been called to save them. You have been called to deliver the gift of mercy. Before this day, you have known the Creator through the words of the Code, so from that fountain alone you have sipped. Now you can drink freely from a well rising up within you, a well that never runs dry."

Koren looked up at his shining blue eyes. From that fountain alone? The image of Alaph she had conjured in the forest days ago had used almost exactly the same words.

"Your choice is simple," Alaph continued. "Take the gift I offer, and you will be able to pass it along to your fellow humans. Refuse, and no one will ever receive the gift. The other Benefile will exercise unbridled fury. It is impossible to tell where the execution of their wrath will end. Yet, with mercy in place, they will be repelled, though I know not how it will happen."

Koren tried to swallow again, but her throat was too tight. She squeaked out, "What do you want me to do?"

"Insert your hand into my wound with your palm up."

Dirt and sweat caking her cheek, Koren scooted on her knees and did as he asked. Tiny red lines that ran along his scales pulsed as if ready to burst.

"Some call us the Bloodless," Alaph said, "because we do not bleed when wounded. We have blood, however, and we shed it by choice."

Blood began to ooze from the points where the red lines met the upper edge of the wound. It dripped into Koren's palm and formed a pool. With each drop, the vessels faded from red to pink to white until they blended with his smooth scales and disappeared.

Koren stared at the pool. The blood glowed, as if infused with radiance from Exodus. "What … what do I do now?"

Alaph laid his head on his hip and stared at her. The blue in his eyes had faded to white, and the sparkle was gone. "When I have passed," he said with a wheeze in his voice, "you must drink it."

"Drink blood?" She grimaced, not caring that Alaph could see her disgust. "The Code forbids it."

"You cannot acquire the gift of mercy unless you consume it."

Koren's hand shook, creating ripples on top of the scarlet pool. "But drinking blood is barbaric." Again words flowed as if unbridled. "Can't I free the slaves some other way? I thought the prophecy said I was supposed to sacrifice myself. I could become Taushin's eyes and …" She bit her tongue. That was one idea that had to be bridled. Even considering it made her feet feel constricted, as if the boots had returned, black and tight.

"I did not say drinking my blood would free the slaves, and your interpretation of the prophecy is faulty." Alaph let out a long and loud sigh. "I presumed too much. You still lack understanding. Since you are not ready to take my place, the gift will not pass."

"Not pass?" Heat flared in Koren's cheeks. "Why are you doing this to me? First you ask me to catch your blood, and then you want me to drink it, and now you're saying not to. Are you trying to drive me insane?"

"Beware, Koren. Indeed insanity approaches, but you are unaware of the cause. It is not I who tortures your mind."

"Not you?" She clenched her teeth, spitting as she yelled. "You're the one who wanted to destroy the wall! You're the one who wanted to get rid of a symbol! And what happened? My father got crushed! He's dead! And all because of your vendetta against your curse!"

"Koren, you are torturing yourself. You are allowing the burdens of every man, woman, and child on Starlight to fall upon you, but they are not yours to bear. You must listen to me. Release the load. Drink the mercy, and you will feel the worries of the world slide off your shoulders."

"But if you're mercy, why did you leave your mate and the other two white dragons suffering in the trees? Your own mate!"

"I know this all too well, but mercy can never be the only principle in the cosmos, which is why Beth and I are mates, a balance of justice and mercy. And sometimes justice has to overrule mercy when judgment is necessary to keep the innocent from suffering."

"The innocent? Don't you keep innocent slaves in your own castle? Sure, they aren't whipped, but you still tell them what to do. They're just little ghosts who glide to and fro, serving your every whim. Doesn't that make you a tyrant, just like the other dragons?"

"If you think me a tyrant, then surely your mind is too tortured to perceive reality. You are too accustomed to burdens, and you refuse to release them. Drink the blood, and you will understand how to remove those burdens from yourself and from others. Mercy will let your mind rest."

"Oh, Alaph! I can't! I can't!" Tears broke out. A sobbing spasm shook her body as she cried, "It's forbidden! Don't you understand?"

"What the Creator has cleansed, no longer consider unclean. It is light. It is purging energy. Whoever consumes the light becomes a light."

"A light?" Koren scanned Alaph's body. He had a dragon's snout, a dragon's ears, and a dragon's scales. Dragon wings draped his back and side, dragon claws protruded from his dragon legs, and a long dragon tail extended behind him. For years dragons had brutalized and murdered her friends. Their whips raised bleeding welts, and their labors broke the bodies and spirits of every human soul on Starlight. And worst of all, they tortured tiny children in the cattle camp, literally starving them to death in order to see which ones survived. And now this dragon, a supposed dragon of mercy who left his own mate imprisoned for countless years while he ruled over slaves in his own domain, asked a human to drink his blood, a violation of the Code. Were Alaph's promises any more believable than Taushin's? How could he be light when his actions seemed to contribute to the darkness?

She shook her head. All slave masters were corrupt. Love never requires chains. Humans had to be saved by humans. "I can't." She poured the blood out on the ground and smeared the remnants on her trousers. "I can't trust any dragon. Not you, not Taushin, not Magnar."

A long exhale breezed from Alaph's snout. "What about Arxad?"

Koren bit her lip. The heat in her cheeks radiated down her neck, drawing sweat from her pores. What about Arxad? No answer came to mind.

"It seems that I have exercised poor judgment." Alaph's voice grew weaker by the second. "Perhaps, however, the Creator will use your mistake for good. There is still hope that someone who understands will come after you, someone who knows what to do with the gift you have spurned."

Koren laid a hand on her head. Confused thoughts swirled. A mistake? A gift spurned? Her reasons for rejecting the blood were good ones ... weren't they? "Someone who understands?" she said, trying to calm her voice. "With all the mysteries, who could possibly figure out what's going on?"

"You will see." Gasping, Alaph whispered, "Sprinkle grains of Exodus on me and let this tyrant pass from Starlight." With a final rasping breath, he closed his eyes and moved no more.

"Alaph!" Koren stroked his brow. "I'm sorry! I don't know what I was saying! I didn't mean to call you a tyrant. It just popped out. I was angry. I was upset. I was ..."

She let the thoughts die. Every excuse seemed foolish. Nothing could make up for her unbridled words. Maybe they were true. Maybe they weren't. But speaking them to a dying dragon didn't help matters at all.

Lifting her hand, she stared at the blood smear on her palm. Alaph's words drifted back to mind, soft and gentle. *Release the load. Drink the mercy, and you will feel the worries of the world slide off your shoulders.... Drink the blood, and you will understand how to remove those burdens from yourself and from others. Mercy will let your mind rest.... What the Creator has cleansed, no longer consider unclean. It is light. It is purging energy. Whoever consumes the light becomes a light.*

Koren nodded. She *had* taken on the burdens of Starlight. Torture had filled her mind ever since the day she decided to seek help for Natalla in the Basilica. Before that time, she was a simple slave, understanding nothing more than the labors of daily strife and the chains of oppression, but when the black egg appeared, a new realization emerged. True slavery was one of mind, not body. Although she had bent her will to Taushin's and had since been released from his chains, another war raged on.

Who was really the liberator? It couldn't be the Starlighter who read the prophecy. She could no more make a prophecy come true than she could make Solarus rise in the morning. Sure, she could choose to be the sacrifice, but even if she refused, the one who fashioned the prophetic words and rhymes would simply find someone to take her place. The real liberator was the author, not the reader.

Koren shrugged, as if trying to shed the burdens. Today, she lost the battle. Tomorrow she would fight again ... harder. But was it really possible to cast the burdens off forever?

She stared at the blood on the ground. It no longer glowed. In fact, when on the ground, it no longer carried any color at all, more like water than blood. The thought of drinking blood had nearly made her gag, but now the fear seemed foolish, a superstition expressed in the whining of a child.

She rose slowly, bent over, and again stroked Alaph's brow. Blood smeared on his scales, red on white, a stark contrast. The blood he had offered, the blood she had rejected, now lay unused on his carcass.

Letting out a wordless wail, she covered her face with her hands. What had she done? Alaph sacrificed himself, but for whom? A foolish slave girl who didn't know anything! She failed him! She failed miserably. And now maybe all was lost.

After crying for some time, she backed away, wiping her eyes and staring at Alaph's lifeless body. What should she do with it? He was far too big to bury. He asked her to sprinkle grains of Exodus on him, but her father had those in his crucible. Maybe waiting for Cassabrie was the answer. She would know what to do.

Koren turned toward the wall. The dust had settled, revealing a pile of rubble that stretched from several paces to the left of the river's edge to just before the opposite bank. Beyond those boundaries, the wall stood firm, ending abruptly at the collapse points, as if the builders had given up too early on their construction project.

Her legs shaking, she walked to the rubble where her daddy last stood. She cast an image of him there as well as one of herself and replayed her rescue. He grabbed her around the waist and threw her into the river, then, just as he made ready to leap in after her, a huge stone flew at him. She stopped the scene at that point, restarted it at the beginning, and played the loop again and again. In each repetition, although fear wrinkled his brow, his eyes shone with love. Nothing would have stopped him from saving her life.

She stepped closer. In the image, he pushed something into her tunic pocket. With his hand completely enveloping the object, there was no way to identify it.

Koren reached into her pocket. With Cassabrie's box still there, and with saturated material adding weight, nothing had seemed out of the ordinary. She drew out the crucible, its lid still tightly in place. So that was why Alaph requested Exodus crystals. He must have seen Orson transfer the crucible.

Something else lay in her pocket. She pulled out a packet of clear wax that held a handful of black powder. A wet folded parchment came along with it—her father's instructions for making the medicine. She pushed both back into her pocket. He had made sure that his work would continue.

Prying off the crucible's lid as she walked, she returned to Alaph's corpse. She stood erect and pinched a dab of crystals. Rubbing her thumb and finger together, she let them fall over Alaph's wound. A few dropped over the spot where the blood had spilled, raising tiny splashes of radiance.

As if alive, the crystals crawled along his body, sparkling, growing in size and speed. Some gnawed downward and disappeared deep in his flesh, while others raced along the surface. As they popped and sizzled, white smoke rose in sparkling plumes. They left behind nothing—no skin, flesh, or bones.

Koren backed away, flinching at every sound. Alaph had given his life hoping she would carry his gift of mercy to others, but she, like a witless slave, rejected it. She really wasn't ready to convey such a precious gift. Now his body was disintegrating along with his hope.

Soon, Alaph was gone. The blood that seeped into the ground burned, leaving a scorched circle. Whatever he had meant about the Creator using her mistake for good dissolved with him—hope lost, a death for nothing. And it was all the fault of an ignorant Starlighter.

A breeze blew through her wet tunic and trousers. She looked at the river. Her cloak was out there somewhere. Without it, would she be able to exercise her gifts with as much power? Did it matter?

She resealed the crucible and shuffled back to the collapsed wall. There was no need to wait for Cassabrie now. Alaph was gone. She had the star material and the other ingredients. If she could make the medicine herself, maybe some people could be cured.

Maybe.

She pressed a fist against her gut. The pain had subsided earlier, but her sobs brought it roaring back. The cure had either failed or was taking a long time to work. In either case, the only option was to go on. It might be hours before Cassabrie showed up, if ever.

She climbed the head-high mound of debris and descended the other side. A new battle lay ahead. The enemy awaited.

fifteen

After following the river for a while, Koren veered to the left toward the village and the grottoes. Soon the Zodiac's spires came into view, then the rear of the Zodiac itself. Moans of pain and lament filled the air along with the sounds of angry dragons. Bending low, Koren skulked to the back of the butcher's shop and crept through the narrow alley between it and the accountant's office.

When she reached the street side of the alley, she stopped and peered around the corner. To the left, the Zodiac's dome lay open. In front of the Zodiac's portico, hundreds of people stood or reclined in a haphazard line in front of a white dragon. Taushin and Mallerin sat on their haunches nearby, as did two other white dragons, apparently observing.

Behind the first Benefile dragon, several white forms lay in a row, like closely packed logs coated with flour.

Before she could get a good look at them, movement near the far corner of the Zodiac's main building caught her attention.

Koren squinted. A young man peeked around the edge of the building. He looked just like Randall. Why would he be there?

The next slave in line, a young woman, staggered to the end of the row of white logs, reeling from side to side. She lay down, as if pretending to be the next log. The dragon blew out a spray and covered her in sparkling white.

Koren gasped. Clenching her fists, she swallowed down boiling anger. Were they so hopeless that they would just lie down and wait quietly for execution? Was freedom so cheap that a few moments waiting to die were worth more than the chance of liberty?

As if echoing her thought, a man dashed from the slave line. Before he could advance ten steps, Mallerin shot a stream of fire that engulfed him in flames. Within seconds, he crumbled in a heap of bones and melting flesh.

Koren turned away. No matter how much cruelty scarred the world of Starlight, seeing a man burn was something no one could get used to. Sudden pity overwhelmed her. Faced with a choice between freezing or burning, they stood in line to await a tragic end. Someone had to show them how to fight back.

Just as she took a step to intervene, a flash of light streaked from Randall's hiding place. A glowing girl waved her arms and called out, "Hey! Try to catch me!" She dashed up the portico stairs and disappeared under the roof.

A white dragon flew in pursuit, shouting, "Continue the showers of mercy. I will find her."

Randall charged, his sword drawn, but what could he do to stop so many dragons?

Koren ran into the street, instinctively reaching for the hood that was no longer there. When she arrived near the front of the slave line, she stopped and yelled, "Listen to me!"

As if splashed in the face with cold water, every human and dragon snapped toward her. When all eyes had focused on her, Koren bent over and began stalking across the cobblestones like a cat searching for a mouse. As she made a circuit, the people and the Benefile slid backwards, creating a circular stage on the cobblestone street.

"I have come to bring a medicine that will cure the disease," Koren said in a dramatic tone, "but it will take some time to blend. While you wait, hear my tale of treachery, sorcery, and villainy." She pinched a stone from the street and lifted it to her eyes. It transformed into a blazing stardrop. With a quick glance, she spied Taushin. Although Mallerin appeared to be mesmerized, Taushin seemed unaffected, but he showed no signs of interfering. "Many years ago," she continued, "a Starlighter appeared in our midst, a girl named Zena who bore extraordinary gifts of storytelling that enthralled dragons and humans alike."

A girl appeared next to Koren. Although not fully physical, she was less transparent than any phantom Koren had yet created. Zena's red hair shone like Solarus, and her eyes sparkled like dew on a verdant meadow.

Koren spun her body. Normally her cloak would have fanned out in a wide arc. Instead, a cloak appeared on Zena, just as blue and lush as the one Koren had lost.

"She took a Starlighter's mantle, but her power bred lust for more power, so she studied the ways of the sorceress." As Koren spoke, Zena's cloak darkened. Streaks of black crawled across her hair, like ebony serpents intertwining with her tresses. She carried an open book in her arms. As she read, her features grew blacker and blacker. Even her eyes transformed from emeralds to oval lumps of coal.

"With her power becoming great enough to threaten Magnar, he took her into his service, promising her increasing authority as she proved her worth. But then Cassabrie was born, a new Starlighter whose power was greater than even Zena's. After being captured by Zena through a cunning ruse, Cassabrie cooked at the stake for days and suffered in horrific agony."

As if sprouting from soil, the cooking stake rose from the ground, and Cassabrie took shape in front of it. Wrapped in chains, she writhed as she struggled against the links.

"Yet, in her dying throes, Cassabrie foiled Zena's plans to rise in authority. Energy shot from her eyes and blinded Zena."

The scene played out Koren's words. Twin shafts of light from Cassabrie's eyes drilled into Zena's. Smoke rose from the contact points. Zena covered her eyes and ran. Yet, although her legs moved, she stayed in place, while Cassabrie and the cooking stake vanished.

"Her vision ruined, Zena resorted to a new plan. Tamminy the dragon bard had prophesied a coming prince who would hatch from a black egg. The song of hope offered relief to dragons and slaves alike."

A white cloud materialized and formed into Tamminy. The old dragon sang in the draconic tongue, low and haunting, yet lovely in tone.

An egg of ebon, black as coal,
Will bring about the dragons' goal.
The dragon rising from its shell
Will overcome a deadly knell.

Though weak and crippled at the start,
Its strength begins within its heart.
Above all others it will soar,
And dragonkind will all adore.

Its greatness, might, and crown will rest
Upon a head of promises.
Then humans far and wide will see
And hope for coming jubilee.

For paradise begins that day;
All labors cease and turn to play.
When dragons learn to see the light,
And give to men their sacred right.

A liberator comes on high
With mercy streaming from her eyes.
The slaves must take her blood and bone
And plant within this mercy sown.

In honor of this treasured hour,

We celebrate Creator's power.

The dawn of paradise will bring

An age of peace beside our king.

When Tamminy finished, the stardrop in Koren's hand sizzled and began turning dark. "Zena recognized her opportunity and consulted with Magnar. When they agreed on a plan to keep him in power, she executed it flawlessly."

Zena crossed her arms and pointed. "Bring the old bard to me. The song must be altered. I will tell him what to say."

When Tamminy approached, his eyes glazed and his legs wobbly, Koren handed the blackened stardrop to Zena. Holding it in her bony hands, she shoved it down Tamminy's throat, then backed away.

"You must alter the black egg prophecy," Zena said, "and you will sing it constantly until everyone thinks the new words were in the original."

Tamminy bobbed his head, his eyes still blank. "I will do as you say." The old dragon lifted his head and began crooning the altered song.

An egg of ebon, black as coal,

Will bring about the dragons' goal.

The dragon rising from its shell

Will overcome a deadly knell.

Though weak and crippled at the start,

Its strength begins within its heart.

Above all others it will soar,
And dragonkind will all adore.

Its virtue, might, and crown will rest
Upon a head of nobleness.
Then humans far and wide will flee
In fear of coming jubilee.

For paradise begins that day;
All labors cease and turn to play.
And slaves become like needless mites,
Unfit to stay within our sight.

So drown the vermin, cook their meat
And scatter bones upon the street.
When every human life is spent
The age of vermin truly ends.

In honor of this treasured hour,
We celebrate this dragon's power.
The dawn of paradise will bring
An age of peace beside our king.

When the last note faded, Tamminy faded with it, leaving Koren and Zena alone on the circle of cobblestones. Koren reverted to her stalking pose and added a sneer. "After Mallerin laid the black egg, Zena set about her villainy, using Cassabrie's finger to infuse poison into an embryonic dragon's heart and bring about her desired ends. To her, it seemed a fitting way to gain revenge against her hated rival."

The image of Zena sat with her arms and legs wrapped around the black egg. As she stroked the shell with a severed finger, she crooned. "The human slaves are vermin to be crushed and swept away. When you raise Exodus from its resting place, instead of sealing it, you should unleash its disease and rid the world of the human pestilence. Since Cassabrie is dead, only I remain immune to it, and we will never have to worry about anyone, either human or dragon. I will keep the dragons in line with my Starlighter gifts, and we will send one infected human to Darksphere to make sure everyone there dies as well. When we achieve these goals, even Magnar will fall to our influence. All you need is a Starlighter who will love you, and you will be king forever."

Koren waved the images away and turned toward Taushin. She let the sneer dwindle and altered to a sorrowful tone. "The prophesied prince emerged handicapped, as expected, yet no one thought blindness would be his fate. He needed eyes, a Starlighter's eyes, but he found Zena's to be inferior. He sought another Starlighter and tried to force her to love him, choosing chains as his means of influence."

Koren lifted her arms. Her loose tunic's sleeves slid down to her elbows, revealing the abrasions on her wrists. "Taushin did not understand that chains could never make someone love him, and now he stands at the crossroads of the most important decision any dragon has made in all the history of Starlight. What will he do now that he has witnessed the treachery of the one who claimed to love him? Will he understand that she forced him to wear chains of his own when she injected his heart with hatred? Will he pursue the dark path she set before him, or will he instead accept this Starlighter's reproof and travel a path illuminated by wisdom?"

Taking in a deep breath, Koren took a step closer to Taushin. As if looking through his own eyes instead of his mother's, he aimed his eyebeams directly at her chest.

"It is as if I can see into your heart, Koren." With a step of his own, Taushin closed the gap to a few paces. "I misjudged you. I thought you were like all the others, both dragons and humans, seeking her own good, pretending to serve others in order to gain something for herself. But it is not chains that keep a heart like yours close; it is the opportunity to serve others, and that is the substance of real love."

"Real love?" Koren looked at the two blue dots on her tunic. Taushin was making an emotional appeal, a desperate grab for sympathy. He knew, no matter how much power she could muster, she couldn't battle dragons of any shade without risking harm to innocent humans. Yet, with everyone locked in a state of hypnosis, was it possible to awaken the dragons one at a time to try to dispose of them? Maybe. But Taushin had to be the first victim. If he couldn't be defeated, fighting the others would be a lost cause.

Taushin's eyebeams shifted to Mallerin. "Is there a problem, Koren? Your hesitation is unsettling. Are you angry? Upset?"

"Do I appear to be upset?" Koren asked.

"My mother is not looking directly at you, so I see you only peripherally."

"I'm not upset, just contemplating." Koren concentrated on Taushin. Was it possible to generate the power she employed while trapped with Elyssa in the Basilica? Her own eyebeams blinded Zena, but it was a temporary burst. At that time, the disease had not progressed very far, but maybe the medicine brought some of her power back.

Focusing on her vision, she funneled energy from every part of her body. Weak beams emanated from her eyes and landed on Taushin's face, but they seemed to have no effect. Either he was immune, or the disease had taken too much of a toll.

After letting the beams die away, she glanced at the Benefile, then at Randall. Like everyone else, they stared in hypnotic trances. No one could help her now, not even her own Starlighter power. This battle of wit and wills was between her and Taushin alone.

"I have worn the crown of Exodus," she said, "and I have seen tales of treachery from age to age, including the deceitful way you persuaded me to raise Exodus. Don't think I will roll over and believe what slides off your forked tongue just because it is now coated with my own principles. I am no fool."

Taushin displayed a toothy smile. "On that we will agree. When I first met you, you were simplistic and naïve. You have grown in wisdom at a startling rate." He spread out a wing. "Yet, does your faith in me matter? Look around you. Your fellow humans are dying, some crumbling in the crushing hand of disease, and some lying without breath under shrouds of ice. Whether my words are true or counterfeit, you will have to find a way to secure their healing before even thinking about leading them to freedom."

She glared at him. "You have a scheme, another devious plot. Tell me what it is."

"Do I?" Taushin chuckled. "Koren, the simplest plans are the honest ones. I admit plotting to spread the disease. I believed what Zena taught me in the past. Yet what matters now is only the present moment and the potential future. If you will become my eyes, your Starlighter influence will have the same effect Zena's had on me. If you acquiesce, I will tell you the secret to curing the disease."

"Always trying to make a deal, aren't you?" Koren touched her tunic pocket, feeling the outline of the box holding Cassabrie's finger and the crucible. "I already have the secret—Cassabrie's genetics combined with energy from Exodus. Uriel and I made an ointment that seems to be working on me. I just need to make more."

"A solution that will last for hours, perhaps days, but the disease will return. You probably already feel it waking from slumber."

Koren set a hand on her stomach. How could he know? "I was thinking I could swallow the cure in a stardrop instead of applying it to my skin."

"More groping in the darkness. Where will you get enough energy material? Even if Cassabrie brought Exodus to you and allowed you to scrape its membrane until you have all you need, what of her genetics? Will she provide body parts while you conduct experiments that might or might not create a cure? She rejected her role as Starlighter before. It would be foolish to think that she will change her mind, especially when you ask her to sever another finger, or a hand, or a foot. She is overjoyed to be back in her body. She will not soon give it over to be butchered."

Koren half closed an eye and gave him a hard stare. "What exactly do you have in mind?"

"Become my eyes. You already know how persuasive I can be to a Starlighter. I will tell you how Cassabrie can be convinced to heal everyone. Already the wheels are in motion to draw her here. When she comes, she will try to overpower you with her Starlighter gifts, but I will show you how to gain complete control over her."

"And why would I want that? She's my friend."

"Friend or foe, you need her body and Exodus's energy to heal the sick. If something drastic is not done soon, they will all perish. I cannot give you power over Cassabrie unless I can see through your eyes."

Koren averted her gaze, trying not to gag at his deceit. Still, if she didn't play along, who would stop him from trying to hurt Cassabrie? If she really were coming, someone had to make sure he couldn't carry out his plan against her. "What if you fail? If the people aren't healed and sent home safely, will you release me?"

"It is too late to save some of them," Taushin said, "but if no more than half of those remaining make it safely to Darksphere, I will release you. If you are successful in saving more than half with your medicine, then you will stay in my service for as long as we both live."

Koren glanced at the Zodiac. "Will you make this covenant at the crystal?"

"Gladly, but first you should dismiss the Benefile, or else they will interfere."

She looked at the motionless white dragons. "Dismiss them?"

"Did you not see how easily you hypnotized them? They are under your control, at least for long enough to fulfill our purpose. In fact, your power has become so great, no one will come out of the trance until you directly command it. Call them by name—Beth, Dalath, and Gamal. They will listen to you."

"Where should I send them?"

"You need not send them anywhere. Make them believe all the slaves are dead, and they will leave."

Koren gave him a skeptical stare. "Where will they go?"

"They plan to go to the southern mountain range to bring wrath to the Southlands dragons for their crimes. You know from personal experience that they deserve it."

"Yes, they do." Koren kept her stare on him. *And so do you*. What was he up to? There seemed to be no downside to hiding potential victims from the Benefile. Whether this was part of his deception or not, they had to be rescued.

She waved an arm across the line of slaves. In an instant they disappeared, replaced by row after row of ice-covered bodies.

"Beth!" Koren called in a commanding voice. "Dalath! Gamal! Your work is done here! Go and bring retribution to the cruel taskmasters who broke the backs and spilled the blood of the innocent."

Beth shook her head, as if awakened from sleep. Dalath and Gamal did the same. Their blue eyes scanned the portico and the surrounding stairs and cobblestones. Beth breathed out a wispy cloud of white. "They are all dead. The disease is gone."

Koren whipped her arm southward. "Go! Justice awaits!"

"And what of you?" Beth brought her snout close to Koren's face. "If you have any trace of the disease, we must kill you first."

Koren lifted her tunic, exposing her abdomen from her waist to her lower ribs. Her skin had stayed clear.

Beth sniffed her stomach. Every exhale sent a cool puff across Koren's skin that raised goose bumps all over her body. Resisting the urge to shiver, she held her ground.

"I detect nothing. Let us go."

"I have no memory of freezing all these humans," Gamal said. "I remember ten, perhaps fifteen at the most, but certainly not hundreds. Perhaps the Starlighter has crafted an illusion."

Dalath shuffled toward one of the bodies. "I will investigate."

While the other two Benefile looked on, Koren lifted a hand discreetly.

Dalath grasped a human's leg with her foreclaw and shook it. Koren's fingers flicked, and ice crystals flew all around, glinting in the sunshine. When the Benefile dropped the leg, the image let out a thud and crunched the fallen crystals.

"All is well," Dalath said as she returned. "Perhaps the Starlighter's influence caused us to forget our merciful acts."

Koren spread out her arms. "Leave now, or you will again succumb to my influence."

"Let us go." Beth beat her wings and rose into the air, followed by Dalath.

Gamal paused in front of Koren and scowled. "If I decide that you have deceived us, I will come back with wrath."

Koren bowed her head. "So be it."

His scowl unrelenting, Gamal turned and flew away.

When the breeze of departing wings settled, Koren refocused on Taushin. Getting him to believe she was going along with his plan would be difficult. It was always hard to deceive a deceiver. "Come," Koren said, "We will test your promises at the Reflections Crystal."

"I have no doubt that my vows will be verified. I would like, however, to make one request before we begin. Release my mother from the trance. She needs to warn Arxad's family about the Benefile."

Koren thought for a moment before nodding. Even if Mallerin became aggressive, it would be easy to hypnotize her again. She waved a hand in front of the she-dragon's face. "Mallerin! Awake! I release you."

Mallerin shook her head hard, then blinked at Koren. "Has this Starlighter worked her sorcery on me?"

Taushin set his eyebeams on her. "Mother, it is not sorcery. Koren has allied herself with me, as I had hoped. Do you remember what I told you we would have to do if this covenant came about?"

"Protect Arxad's family," Mallerin said.

"Correct. Make sure they are safely hidden, then come back to me. I will be in the Zodiac."

"Were the Benefile under Koren's influence?"

Taushin nodded. "Why do you ask?"

"Why did you not awaken me so that I could kill them? It would have been easy then. They would have been unable to fight back."

"Mother ..." Taushin's eyes flared, but his voice stayed calm. "This is a new day. I have come to realize how evil our race has been, and we should delay justice no longer. If you had killed the Benefile while they were so vulnerable, the guilt upon our heads would have been worse than ever, and we would never deserve the services of a Starlighter."

"I will concede that point," Mallerin said, "but I do not wish to be a victim of Benefile wrath."

"Fear not. You heard the bargain I made with them. You and I will be excluded."

"If we can trust them," Mallerin said with a snort.

"Speaking of trust ..." Taushin's eyebeams pulsed. "Make haste in returning. If all does not go well, I will need your eyesight very soon."

"I will hurry." Mallerin took to the air and flew toward the grottoes.

When Taushin turned toward Koren, his eyebeams found their way into her eyes. The familiar probing sensation drilled in.

She jerked away and stared at the ground. "Not yet! First the vows!"

"Forgive me." Taushin bowed his head. "In my eagerness to help you, I overstepped my bounds."

"Give me a minute." Koren turned away and bent over, rubbing her burning eyes with her fists. Tears seeped over her knuckles. That was too close. This plan to pretend to go along with him was like walking through a pheterone-laced chamber with a burning torch. With his manipulative power, at any second everything could blow up in her face. She had been careful to verify every word he spoke, but as Gamal indicated, it's impossible to know that you're being influenced while under someone's influence.

She gritted her teeth. She couldn't let down her guard around this monster for one second. Yes, he might tell the truth in front of the crystal. Yes, freedom for the slaves was worth the price of giving up her own physical freedom. But nothing was as valuable as her soul.

Still, the dilemma was real. If she refused to give in, most if not all her fellow slaves would be condemned to a horrible death. But if she freely received Taushin's chains and used Cassabrie against her will, she would be condemned herself. Her black soul would be expelled to outer darkness for all eternity.

And Taushin knew full well that keeping the dilemma in mind would reignite the inner battle and bring back the burdens.

With her eyes closed, Koren focused on calming herself. She needed help, an ally, someone who would help her do battle with the dark dragon. As she concentrated, a vision replaced the blackness—Jason marched toward the barrier wall, his shoulders straight and his jaw tight. The look in his eyes told of something powerful guiding him, a hand of strength and purpose.

Taking a breath, she straightened and swiped a sleeve across her eyes. As she stood with her back to Taushin, the sensation of eyebeams brushing her clothes sent a chill up her spine. No, Taushin couldn't be trusted. And no, she couldn't forsake her beloved brethren or Cassabrie. The original plan had to remain intact. The only way to protect them was to stay with him and pretend to acquiesce, at least as long as necessary.

Yet, his power was still a problem. It seemed that the torch had been lit, and a pheterone mine lay ahead. With fire sure to come, it would take a miracle beyond all imagination to snuff the flames, but that miracle lay within reach. If the Creator was guiding Jason to the Zodiac, he might be the equalizer she needed, but the timing would have to be perfect.

She turned to Taushin, her hands folded at her waist. "I'm ready. I will lead you to the Reflections Crystal, and we shall see what will be revealed."

sixteen

rxad flew toward the portal's forest clearing. Carrying explosives in an insulated box he had packed with snow, he searched for a safe place to deposit the volatile load. In recent times, a snowdrift would have been an ideal location, but now with only a few white patches interrupting a landscape of trees and mud, it seemed impossible to know where a soft drop-off point might be.

As he approached the site, several uniformed men came into view, standing or sitting around Orion, who leaned against a boulder. When the men raised spears and shields, Arxad shouted, "Put down your weapons! I come in Captain Reed's name!"

Orion jabbed a finger at him. "He is the enemy! Pierce him now! You might not have another chance!"

"If I were an enemy," Arxad shouted as he made a loop over the glade, "I would have torched all of you already!"

One of the soldiers, eyeing him carefully, gestured to the others, speaking something too quiet for Arxad to hear. The other men lowered their weapons, though they kept a firm grip on shield and spear alike. After diving into the clearing at the southern edge, Arxad beat his wings to level out, deposited the box carefully, and slid into a muddy landing. As he slowed to a stop, he swept his tail through the mud and flung it into Orion's face. "Your foolishness is an assault on reason! You make Prescott look like a sage!"

Orion wiped mud from his eyes and slung it to the ground. "You wouldn't know a sage from a simpleton. I prevented a disease from ravaging my world." He pulled a white cloth from his pocket and cleaned the rest of his face. "History will record me as a hero."

"A coward's hero." Arxad reared up and plucked the crystalline peg from between his scales. "It is time to put your fearmongering to death. Let us bring your full army into Starlight."

"No!" Orion lunged for the crystal, but two soldiers held him back. Struggling, he shouted, "He's a dragon, you fools! The disease will slaughter your wives and children. Why are you siding with the slavers over one of your own kind?"

The man who had spoken to the others earlier stepped in front of Orion and faced Arxad, a hefty spear in his grip. "I can't say that I've ever opposed a dragon before, but what Orion says has merit. If you want to torch us, we can't stop you, but if you open the portal without us, there should be enough men to give you the fight of your life. So unless you can give us some reason to lower our defenses—"

"Cease the chatter." Arxad reared again, exposing his underbelly and the mirror, the red thumbprint still emblazoned on the surface. "I wear your captain's symbol."

The soldier leaned close and studied the mark. "That *is* his thumbprint!" He set the point of his spear against the ground, and the other men unnotched arrows, sheathed swords, and upended spears as well. "We are at your service. What can we do to help?"

"Keep Orion in your grasp. Do not let him interfere."

Two soldiers regripped Orion's arms, one at each side. Arxad shuffled toward the line of pegs. The receding snow had exposed a knee wall, and the pegs stood in a line on top. After pushing the center peg in place, he walked to the portal and poked his head through just enough to view the other side, ignoring the shout that went up as his head appeared in the Darksphere clearing. Scattered among the trees, hundreds of soldiers waited, many sleeping on the ground or leaning against trees, though a guard of sixty or so men stood at attention surrounding the portal. With sunlight passing through the trees at a nearly horizontal angle, it appeared to be early morning or late afternoon. One guard, apparently the one who had shouted, pointed at Arxad while nudging the guard next to him.

Arxad drew his head back to Starlight and waved a wing. "Come. All of you. I will give everyone instructions at the same time."

"Go back to our world?" Orion said. "Are you actually coming to your senses?"

Turning his snout toward Orion, Arxad breathed hot air over him until perspiration trickled from his brow, "If you continue to insult me," Arxad said, "you will learn what most dragons do when a human speaks with such arrogance." Arxad again waved a wing. "You guards go first and explain my presence. I will speak to Orion alone."

The soldiers walked single file through the portal, each one disappearing in a spray of sparks. When the last one vanished, Arxad focused on Orion. The Darksphere governor stood with his shoulders square, but his trembling legs belied his confident posture.

Arxad removed the peg from the center hole. "Where did you hide the other crystal?"

Orion gestured with his head. "In the forest. Somewhere back there."

"Show me. I want it."

"And if I refuse?" Orion blinked rapidly. "If you kill me, you will never find it."

Arxad bared his teeth. "Do you realize that I closed the portal so the others could not hear our conversation?"

"I guessed as much." Orion maintained a calm tone in spite of his knocking knees. "You plan to kill me, hide my body, and claim that I ran away. But you cannot lie to the Starlighters. This world will know the truth, and the tale will eventually trickle to mine."

"Since you have lost control of your region, martyrdom is the only hope you have remaining for your legacy. I will not participate in your elevation to that status."

Orion wiped his forehead. "I care only for the people of my world, not for my status."

"I had hoped for your cooperation. You could have contributed in a truly heroic way."

Orion looked to the side, smoothing out his cloak as if feigning disinterest. "And how might that be?"

"Adrian and Marcelle are at the castle, and they will be coming here soon. I need to make sure the portal is open for them to return to your world. If I could trust you, I would leave you here to act in that capacity."

"I don't see why a dragon would trust me," Orion said. "I certainly wouldn't trust a dragon."

"And lack of trust is the core of our conflict, is it not?"

Orion nodded. "We are finally in agreement."

"Then hear me, Orion. I will be the first to take a risk. Watch my trust in you and then decide if you will act heroically or not."

Arxad reinserted the peg and walked through the portal. On the other side, the soldiers stood at attention in an array of straight rows and columns, all eyes on him.

Arxad glanced back. A cool breeze blew through the portal. Orion had not closed it yet.

An officer stood in front of the closest line and gave Arxad a chest-thump salute. "We almost gave up hope. We very nearly decided to go home, but now we are ready to march and join the others."

"March you must, and you will join the others, but our plans have changed. We brought you to this portal because we knew it to be safe. At this time, no one is guarding the Southlands portal, so you will save much time and energy if you go there. I will open the portal from our side and allow your passage."

The officer gave a shallow bow. "Begging your pardon, but we don't know where it is on our side."

Arxad stared at the officer, a youngish man as humans go. It seemed that his question rolled a boulder in front of the new plan. It would take too long to guide the soldiers to the other portal and then return. Orion might be trusted for a few moments to keep the portal open, but for an hour? That was far less likely. "I suppose, then, we will have to go the long route and—"

"Father!"

The call in the dragon tongue came from Starlight. Arxad whipped his neck around and pushed his head through the portal.

Xenith landed in a muddy skid. When she stopped, she wheezed as she spoke. "Father, the Benefile are planning to kill the slaves!" As she caught her breath, her voice settled. "They are going to freeze them to destroy the disease so the army can safely invade."

Arxad caught a glimpse of Orion watching from behind the boulder.

"Repeat your concern in the human tongue so the human warriors on Darksphere can understand you." Arxad nodded toward the portal. "That way."

Xenith extended her neck toward the portal. "The Benefile are planning to kill the slaves. They hope to destroy the disease by freezing them all."

"And why have you come so far to tell me this?"

Xenith drew her head back, confusion touching her fiery eyes. "Because what they plan to do is wrong, Father. Humans have a right to live."

Nodding his approval, Arxad met her perplexed stare. Even after her long flight, her eyes stayed sharp, clear, filled with purpose, ready to do whatever else she could to help the slaves. He extended his neck and nuzzled her cheek to cheek, whispering, "You have done well."

"Thank you, but what do we—"

"Excuse me for a moment." He swung back around to Darksphere and addressed the officer. "If you will wait another minute, I think I have a solution."

The officer bowed again. "Excellent. We will await your instructions."

Arxad walked fully back into Starlight. "I feared that the Benefile might do this. Sometimes they are unpredictable, but I have never underestimated their cruelty."

"So what do we do?" Xenith asked.

"How is your stamina? Can you fly to the Southlands again?"

She drew in a long breath. "I can."

"Have you heard about the portal at the mining mesa?"

She bobbed her head. "I have heard talk of it, and I know where both mesas are, but I do not know exactly where the portal is."

"It is at the mine closer to the village. If you go through the secondary entry, you will see a line of crystals similar to the one here, only embedded in the ground instead of on top of a low wall. The center peg is missing." Arxad touched the center crystal with his tail. "When I return to Darksphere, take this peg to the mesa portal and place it in the open hole. If all goes well, I will already be on the other side of the portal with many more soldiers. Perhaps with your speed, you will open it in time to stop the Benefile."

"I appreciate your faith in me." Xenith wrapped a clawed hand around the peg. "I am ready."

Arxad curled his neck around hers. "Do you have news from your mother?"

"Only that she is at the wilderness refuge. Randall said she has a minor wound, but my concern is that she will not take care of herself. That wound or her earlier one could easily worsen."

"Your concern is valid. Your mother is not one to pamper herself. She and I are both ready to sacrifice everything to protect our race." He pulled back and looked Xenith in the eye. "You are not required to do the same. You have a choice."

"Do I really?" Xenith nodded toward the portal. "Go, Father. I will see you in the Southlands."

Arxad looked at the boulder. Orion was gone. Would he retrieve the other crystal and open the portal for Adrian and Marcelle? Maybe. He was an unpredictable human indeed.

"When I disappear," Arxad said, "fly with all speed. If you see your mother, tell her ..." He shook his head. "I will tell her myself when I return." With a powerful wing beat, he burst into the air. After circling the glade once, he snatched up the weapons box and zoomed through the portal.

❧·❧

With Elyssa and Edison at his side, Jason stood atop a ridge of rubble that had once been the great barrier wall. Who could have destroyed such a massive structure? It seemed impenetrable, a symbol of dragon dominance, but now a one-hundred-foot section lay in a head-high, east-to-west line of boulders with a gentle slope on the north and south, easy to climb.

The river flowed over the rubble's midsection, stripping sand and grit from the top and creating a slurry that slowly clarified as the water drifted northward. The soldiers rested on the south side of the ridge at the river's edge, some taking long drinks straight from the current and others just catching their breath and eating from their rations. Drenched with sweat, river water, or both, they needed a break to cool down and dry off. Wallace sat among them, telling stories about being a slave. If nothing else, the tales would infuse passion in the weary men. With the battle against dragons still to come, they might need it.

Magnar perched atop the wall's remains on the east side, searching the area. He had volunteered to act as a watchman, so they could relax without worry.

"Any ideas?" Jason asked.

Edison shook his head. "My imagination isn't big enough to grasp the power needed to do what has been done here. It's as if the Creator himself punched the wall with a mighty fist."

Elyssa lifted a scorched scrap of paper and sniffed it. Wrinkling her nose, she handed it to Edison. "What do you think?"

He sniffed it as well. "Sulfur?"

"Yes." Elyssa crouched and laid a hand on top of the pile. "The rocks are warm, but they're even warmer underneath. With Solarus shining, the opposite should be true."

"So the ones on top are cooling off," Jason said. "Something generated a lot of heat."

Edison looked at the river. "What's this?" He jogged down the heap and waded into the shallows. Bending over, he began pulling something from under the pile.

Blue and saturated, it looked like a blanket, but when he straightened it out, a hem and a hood took shape.

"It's a cloak," Elyssa said.

Jason ran to his father and took the cloak. Although the wetness made it darker than usual, the size and shape were all too familiar. "I think it's Koren's."

Elyssa joined him and rubbed her fingers along the hood's lining. "Definitely."

"She wouldn't have left it here unless ..." Jason couldn't finish the thought. It was too awful.

Elyssa dropped to her knees in the water and laid both hands on the ridge. "I'll start probing!"

Jason grabbed a stone from the pile and heaved it into the river, raising a huge splash.

"No!" Elyssa shouted. "I need to concentrate, and you have no idea where to look."

While Elyssa probed, scooting slowly toward the river's edge, Jason sat heavily on the pile and closed his eyes. Koren's image crept into his thoughts. What did her cloak's presence mean? Did she find healing? According to his father, she was near death when he found her. It would have taken a miracle for her to survive.

He leaned back and focused skyward. Didn't Koren deserve a miracle? She was so loving, so sacrificial, so passionately dedicated to her fellow slaves. Maybe the Creator had a special miracle just for her, something amazing, something that would prove to her how much everyone loved her. But ... she would never leave her cloak behind.

"I found something!" Elyssa began grabbing stones and throwing them to the side. Jason and Edison leaped up and joined her, one at each side, pulling, throwing, and rolling stones away from the heap.

"Can you tell if it's a body?" Jason asked, gasping as he rolled a boulder.

Sweat rolled down her reddened cheeks as she nodded. "A human. That's all I know."

They continued the desperate digging, grunting in three distinct tones. Finally, Jason unearthed a hand. "Here!" he shouted.

The three joined together at the site and soon uncovered an arm connected to a male torso. A bit more digging revealed his gray-haired head, wobbling loosely attached to the torso, his neck obviously broken.

Edison turned the man's face upward and brushed dirt away from his cheeks and eyes. With a deep sigh, he whispered, "It's Uriel."

Jason swallowed through a lump. Half of his mind shouted in relief, *It's not Koren!* But the other half wailed for his friend.

"Poor Uriel!" Elyssa dropped to her knees and wept. "It's so awful!"

His stomach churning, Jason picked up a stone and slung it away. Uriel Blackstone had survived for all these years, seemingly handpicked by the Creator to live long enough to find a cure for the disease, only to be buried in a heap of boulders before the job could be finished. It was all so senseless. Such a waste.

Edison touched Elyssa's shoulder. "Could there be another body?" he asked.

"I ..." She sniffed back a sob. "I don't think so, but I'll keep looking."

"No need." Edison climbed to the top of the ridge and shouted at the men, "I want everyone here, on the double!"

Soon dozens of hands joined the search. Stones flew everywhere, and even the biggest boulders were no match for the strong and practiced arms that rolled them aside. Wallace joined in and dug ferociously.

Magnar watched from his perch on the wall, apparently aware that he wouldn't be much help. After a while, the ridge flattened to a field of scattered debris, but no other bodies turned up.

Jason, Edison, and two other men buried Uriel under a pile of rocks. When they finished, Edison knelt at the side of the pile while everyone gathered around. "We will not have a funeral here. We erected this to protect Uriel's body from scavengers. When we return, we will take him home. I swear it."

Jason draped Koren's cloak over his arm and took Elyssa's hand. Tear tracks stained her cheeks, but they seemed dry now. "I wonder if she ever found out that Uriel was her father," Jason said.

"Impossible to know." She touched the cloak. "It's still wet."

"The material's thick," Jason said. "It holds water."

"No matter." She took the cloak, whipped it around her back, making it flare out, and settled it around her shoulders. With a new tear trickling from her eye, she raised the hood. "In Koren's honor."

"It's appropriate." He looked her over. Elyssa's eyes sparkled green from within the hood's shadow, sad but vibrant. "Very appropriate."

After everyone gathered on the south side of the field of rubble, Jason surveyed the crew—forty-seven men, a boy, one woman, and a dragon. The men had swords in scabbards at their hips, many clutched spears, some had quivers on their backs, and the woman wore a blue cloak and a pendant on a chain. Yet the woman without a weapon might prove to be the most powerful of them all.

Jason gestured for his father, Elyssa, Wallace, Captain Reed, and Magnar to gather around. When they formed a close circle, Jason spoke in a low tone. "I once heard Taushin speaking about his plans, and if I understood him correctly, he and the other dragons will be holed up somewhere to hide from an attack. They won't be in the village."

"Taushin is crafty." Magnar's eyes pulsed. "He is not hiding like a cowardly child. He is merely waiting for all the pieces to fall into place while he is away. He wants a Starlighter, and his absence will make everyone feel safe enough to come to the village, including either Koren or Cassabrie."

"An interesting theory," Edison said. "I had planned to march straight for Frederick's refuge in the wilderness before launching a search for the dragons, but if a Starlighter comes to the village, shouldn't we be there to protect her? When we saw Koren fly overhead with Alaph, I thought she might be heading there, but finding the cloak made me think otherwise. Now I'm not sure either way."

Magnar wagged his head. "It is folly to try to protect a Starlighter. The stubborn girls choose their own course, and there is nothing you can do to stop them. Since Cassabrie is within Exodus, and Koren is with Alaph, they are not vulnerable to Taushin. I suggest following your original plan."

"Even though the soldiers are probably contagious?" Elyssa asked.

Captain Reed scratched his chest through his tunic. "Not merely contagious, I'm afraid. We will keep our distance and see if we can lead the children to safety."

Jason scanned the soldiers. Many were scratching here and there, and some grimaced as they paced. "Elyssa and I will sneak into the village and look for Koren and Cassabrie. I'd feel a lot better if we knew they were all right. When you collect the children, we can meet in the forest just past the grottoes, and we'll let you know what's going on."

Edison nodded. "The men will make signs here telling the second company to go to the meeting place as well. When they arrive, we can all invade the village at the same time."

"What about me?" Wallace asked. "I know this place better than any of you."

Jason grasped Wallace's shoulder. "Stay with us until we get near the village, then you can mingle with the other slaves and find out what's going on while we search the Zodiac or the Basilica. If we can't find each other, we'll meet in Arxad's cave before we go to the forest."

Wallace nodded. "Sneaking around is my specialty."

After saying their good-byes, Jason, Elyssa, and Wallace marched toward the forest. "I'm impressed," she said as they strode over rocks and old cart ruts.

Jason kept his focus on the rough path. "Why?"

"What we're doing is probably more dangerous than going to the wilderness. I mean, if the Benefile are killing humans, it's like walking into a death trap."

"I suppose it is." He gave her a quick glance. "What's your point?"

Smiling, she faced straight ahead and marched on. "Just an observation. Lead the way, warrior."

"If you say so." Jason broke into a medium-pace run, Elyssa at one side and Wallace at the other. When they entered the forest, Jason slowed and hacked at brambles and vines with his sword.

Soon they broke into an open span of flat, arid ground, some parts covered with sparse heather and some parts completely lifeless. The grinding mill basin lay in the center of the expanse. As they skirted it, Jason peered over the edge. Neither Mallerin nor Julaz stalked the floor, and the cage embedded in the wall was still open, its gate charred and broken.

They jogged to the village from behind the Zodiac, a safer route than the street out in front, and slowed to a walk. Without a word, Wallace broke away and strolled boldly into the street. Seconds later, he was out of sight.

As Jason and Elyssa skulked around the Zodiac's left side, keeping close to the wall, they passed a broken cart partially covered with hay. Human boot tracks led to the front of the building.

Jason stopped at the corner and peered around. Elyssa pressed close, her arm against his. Hundreds of people stood, sat, or lay in various positions under and around the Zodiac's portico, all motionless except for hair or clothes flapping in the light breeze. Closer to the corner, several ice-covered objects lay in a row, and Randall stood like a statue between the corner and the portico, his sword clutched at the end of his stiff arm.

"Psst! Jason!" Something tugged his sleeve.

Jason froze. A tingling sensation rode up his arm.

"Over here! It's me. Deference."

Shaking off the shock, he turned. The shining girl waved a hand. "Follow me," she said. "I think Koren's in trouble."

"Koren's here?" Jason followed Deference into the open, Elyssa close behind. When they passed Randall, Jason gave him a quick scan. Although bruises and cuts marred his chin and cheeks, he appeared to be relatively unharmed. He had the look of a hypnosis victim, so it seemed that a Starlighter had been here. But why would he be in a trance if the Starlighter was no longer present?

Still following Deference, Jason and Elyssa ran up the portico stairs and stopped at the Zodiac's entry corridor. At the far end, a light flashed on and stayed bright for several seconds before slowly dimming.

Deference dashed into the corridor, hissing, "Come on!"

Jason whispered to Elyssa, "Quietly now," then walked in on tiptoes. Once well inside, his heavy exhales echoed. He held his breath, stifling the noise, but his trousers, dampened by sweat, swished with every step.

When they reached the dome room's doorway, they flattened themselves against the wall to its right. Jason leaned and peeked inside. Elyssa laid her hands on his shoulders and watched from behind.

At the Reflections Crystal, Koren and Taushin stood facing each other, Koren to the left of the crystal and

Taushin to the right. Deference glided in, stood behind a column, and peered around it. With the dome wide open, Solarus's rays filled the chamber with light.

Koren locked her gaze on Taushin, her green eyes glowing. "If fewer than half of the remaining slaves fail to go Darksphere alive and healthy," she said, "you will release me from your service."

"Under those conditions, I will release you." Taushin's blue eyebeams danced across Koren's chest. "Immediately."

The crystal brightened, almost too radiant to behold.

Jason's face stung as if tiny needles pricked his skin— irritating but not too painful.

As the sphere slowly dimmed, Koren glanced at it before continuing. "All the released slaves and the humans from Darksphere will be allowed to leave without resistance from you of any kind."

Taushin nodded. "That is correct."

Again the crystal flashed, verifying the dragon's words.

Koren walked around the sphere and stood in front of Taushin, her back to the doorway. "What do I do now?"

"Let me look into your eyes. Allow me to connect more fully than I ever have before. In the past, you have successfully resisted. Now it is finally time for our union to be complete. No chains. Only trust. You will walk freely in my service."

The crystal flashed brightly yet again.

"I understand." Heaving a sigh, Koren bowed her head. "Allow me one moment to search for news of my friends from Darksphere. Before I seal our covenant with a final vow, I want to know that they're safe. If they are all dead, then the slaves' rescue will be impossible."

"Very well. I, too, will be interested in a report on their well-being."

Koren closed her eyes. "I will decide whether or not to let you know."

Elyssa grabbed Jason's arm and shook it, whispering, "We have to put a stop to this!"

"Right." Jason drew his sword. "Never make a deal with the devil."

"Are you going to attack Taushin?"

"That was my plan."

Elyssa raised the cloak's hood. "If he's using Koren's eyes, he'll see you coming."

"Only if she's looking this way." Jason bent over and padded in. While near the perimeter of the room, the partial roof shaded his progress, so he stayed close to the wall and circled to the right side. Now able to see Koren's profile, he halted. Any farther and he would walk into her field of vision.

He crouched and took in the scene. Why would Koren do something so foolish? It didn't make any sense. Might it be better to wait and see whose side she was really on before attacking? But waiting too long might be just as dangerous. Once Taushin had her in his grasp, it might be too late.

Koren lifted her head. "I am ready."

"Did you see the Darksphere humans?"

She nodded. "An army has breached the barrier wall, and they are approaching the wilderness refuge. It seems that a rescue is at hand, as we both had hoped. All we need now is to find a cure."

The Reflections Crystal brightened once more.

"Excellent. Now open your eyes fully. I am coming in."
Taushin's beams flashed brighter. The blue shafts struck
Koren's chest and began shifting upward. She trembled.
With a look of panic, she rotated her head as if searching for something. When the beams rose to her chin, her
stare locked on Jason's. She mouthed the words, "Help
me!"

Jason leaped up and charged with his sword. Just as he
made ready to swing at Taushin's neck, Koren thrust out
her arms. "No!"

A wave of bright light flew from her hands and
slammed into Jason's face, sending him flying backwards.
He landed on his bottom and slid until his head smacked
against the wall.

Elyssa grabbed his sword, fire in her eyes as the cloak
fanned around her. Jason reached to stop her but pulled
back. With his world fuzzy and twirling, he wouldn't be
able to stand, much less fight.

As Elyssa stalked toward Koren and Taushin, the
sword quivered in her grip. "How dare you! Jason has
done so much for you! He would die for you!"

The Reflections Crystal pulsed with brilliance. Needle-
like radiance flowed across Jason's face, again stinging
his cheeks, worse than before. He blinked to keep the
needles at bay. It had to be far more intense where Elyssa
stood.

Taushin shook his wings and roared, "What is happening? Koren, give me a report."

"In a moment." Koren extended her hand and spoke in
a soft tone. "Give me the cloak, Elyssa."

Elyssa touched the clasp in front. "Why?"

"Because it's mine." Koren gave her a pleading look, an expression that didn't match her demanding tone.

After eyeing her for a moment, Elyssa took the cloak off and tossed it to her. Koren caught it and threw it over the crystal.

"Taushin!" Mallerin flew into the open dome and landed next to him.

Jason cringed. More trouble. But with his head swimming, he could do nothing but watch.

Taushin slapped his tail against the floor. "Finally. Now I will be able to see."

"I returned as quickly as I could," Mallerin said. "I saw Magnar helping the invaders from Darksphere, but I saw neither Fellina nor Xenith. I told a drone to bring a report to you if he saw either of them."

Taushin growled, "Did you tell him to come to the dome room?"

"No." Mallerin's wings drooped. "I apologize for my lack of foresight."

"Well, your foresight is lacking, but your timing is convenient." He cast his eyebeams on her. "We have intruders who have interrupted the establishment of a covenant between Koren and myself. If not for them, I would be seeing through Koren's eyes by now."

"Koren's eyes?" Mallerin drew her head back. "Are mine insufficient?"

"Your eyes are perfectly suited for one task and Koren's for another."

Koren spread out her arms. "There is no need for concern, Mallerin. If you will listen to me, I will explain everything."

"Please do." Mallerin stared at her, her head swaying.

Jason tried to scoot to a higher sitting position against the wall. What was Koren up to? It seemed that everyone needed an explanation.

"Mallerin," Koren said, "you might not be aware of this, but one of these intruders, Elyssa by name, saved your life. When you were at the grinding mill, one of the Darksphere warriors was about to strike you, but Elyssa had pity on you and blocked his blow."

Mallerin said nothing more. She just stared directly at Koren, her back to the crystal.

"Congratulations, Koren," Taushin said, "You have again neutralized my defenses."

"Yes, but you can see me through Mallerin, and now it's safe for us to talk without risk."

"Talk?" Her face reddening, Elyssa pointed the sword at Koren. "There's nothing to talk about! You can't make a covenant with that monster. You can't turn away from the people who are sacrificing everything to rescue you. We trusted you. We were all in this together."

Koren spread out her arms. "We're still all in this together, but I couldn't let Jason kill Taushin. He's going to help us."

"Help us?" Elyssa let the sword droop. "You can't trust Taushin!"

Koren's eyes glowed. "But he says he's changed."

"He says? Have you gone out of your mind?"

"She is in her right mind," Taushin said. "She has decided to give herself to my service, and now she protects me. Since Jason attacked without warning, Koren had to respond instinctively. There was no time for explanation."

"We're still friends," Koren said, extending her hand toward Elyssa. "Give me the sword as a sign that you trust me, and you will be free to go out and help our cause."

Elyssa looked Koren over, as if probing. "And Jason?"

Taushin shook his head. "Jason attacked me. Until he has an opportunity to prove his trust in our new alliance, he will stay here."

Jason gazed at Elyssa. With her hand clutching the sword's hilt tightly and her feet set apart, she appeared ready to fight both Taushin and Mallerin, but her contorting face expressed worry.

"Elyssa," Koren said as she withdrew a small, capped bowl from her pocket, "you can be a lot of help right now. I'll look after Jason while you try to make the cure for the disease at Arxad's cave." She lifted the bowl. "This is a crucible filled with stardrop material, and I have the other ingredients and instructions as well. When you make the medicine, you can distribute it to the people. Since you're immune, you're the best one to do it."

Elyssa edged closer and looked at the bowl.

Taushin's eyebeams brightened, still resting on Mallerin. "We cannot risk that," Taushin said. "If Arxad is there, he will learn about your covenant with me and will interfere."

"Not as long as you're holding Jason." Koren nodded toward Elyssa. "If she trusts us, she'll do exactly what we ask. If she doesn't, she'll be worried that you'll hurt Jason if Arxad tries to interfere. Of course, we won't hurt him, but until she decides to trust us, she won't believe it."

Elyssa fumed. "How dare you negotiate about me like I'm a—"

"Excellent logic." Taushin waved a wing toward the dome room's perimeter. "Zena told me there are chains and manacles in a box near a wall, the ones they use to bind victims to the crystal. Put Jason in irons, and we will let Elyssa go."

Koren nodded. "That sounds like a good idea."

Rolling her eyes, Elyssa let out an exasperated sigh but said nothing.

"Before you do ..." Taushin's ears flattened. "Have you tried to locate Cassabrie? You should be able to conjure an image of her recent past."

"No." Koren looked up at the sky. "I think I'm too weak to extend very far right now."

Jason studied Koren's expression. What was that look? Misdirection? Deception? Was she intentionally keeping her eyes pointed away from Mallerin to hide her aspect?

"She will eventually arrive," Taushin said. "It would be good, however, to have some warning. Perhaps Elyssa's talents can find her."

"You want me to find Cassabrie for you?" Elyssa laughed. "Even if I did stoop to that level, why would you want her to come? She would never help you, and she's more powerful than Koren could ever hope to be."

While Elyssa talked, Jason rolled to all fours and began a slow crawl toward the door. It was time to escape while they were distracted.

"You continue to think of me as your enemy," Taushin said. "I am now your ally. We need Cassabrie to help us with producing a cure. The paltry amount of raw materials in Koren's crucible will never produce enough medicine for hundreds of sick humans. When Cassabrie realizes this, she will become our ally as well."

"Is that so?" Elyssa began to pace in a short circuit in front of Taushin, gesturing with her hands. "Not if she knew you were holding a hostage to get her to comply."

Jason passed a column. Only two more before the door. But with Mallerin's eyes aimed this way, these last two would be the most dangerous.

"A hostage?" Taushin said. "Your terminology is so dramatic. Jason is simply surety, a pledge of cooperation. I will provide his freedom in exchange for Cassabrie's help. Since I need him for this purpose, you can be assured of his safety."

"Surety? Pledge?" Elyssa stopped pacing and growled under her breath. "Blackmail is another word that comes to mind."

"Blackmail is designed to take something for selfish purposes. We are trying to heal the slaves and send them to freedom."

Jason crawled over the threshold to the corridor leading out. *Keep talking, Elyssa. If I can make it to Randall, maybe—*

"Stop!" Taushin shouted.

Jason looked back. Taushin flew toward him. Elyssa swiped at Taushin with the sword but missed.

His claws extended, Taushin swooped, grabbed Jason by the seat of his trousers, and sailed into the corridor. He made a sharp turn and flew back into the dome room. With a heave, he tossed Jason into Elyssa. He rolled into her legs, making her topple over and drop the sword.

His head pounding, Jason watched as Koren picked up the sword and helped Elyssa rise. While they stood close together, Koren pushed the crucible into Elyssa's hand as well as a couple of other items, whispering as she made the transfer.

Taushin landed next to Mallerin, smoke puffing from both nostrils. "You are fortunate that I am your ally. Otherwise, I would have killed you."

Elyssa offered Jason a hand, but he shook his head. "Just go."

"What do I do?" Elyssa asked. "Make the medicine? Find Cassabrie? Tell Arxad about you being held hostage?"

"I don't know. My head's pounding so hard, I can't figure anything out."

She knelt and ran gentle fingers across his scalp. "We're a team. I don't want to do this without you."

"I wish I could go." He covered her hand with his. "Just do what you think is best. I trust you."

"Go," Koren said, pointing at the door again. "I'll take good care of him."

Elyssa glared at her. "As long as you're in service to that devil, your words are worthless."

Koren backed up to Taushin and set a hand on his neck. "If you think him a devil, then what will you do?"

"I'll keep my own counsel." Elyssa shot to her feet and stormed out of the room.

"Find the chains," Taushin said as the clopping of Elyssa's shoes faded away. "We cannot afford to give him time to recover. He is too strong, and his hatred of me will feed his aggression. Then we can complete our covenant, and I will be able to use your eyes instead of my mother's."

Jason rolled from his back to his side. With Solarus still shining into the room, everything should have been clear, but the scene blurred at times, and dark spots danced around in random places.

At the perimeter wall, Koren laid the sword behind a trunk and threw a loose lid off the top. She fished out a set of chains and manacles and dropped them on the floor. "I saw iron rings embedded in the tiles next to a column. That will be a good place. It's in the shade."

"Of course," Taushin said. "Since we want no harm to come to him, his comfort is paramount."

She scooped up the chains and dragged them to a column. "I couldn't find the key to the manacles."

"Will they lock without the key?" Taushin asked.

She nodded. "I think they just snap into place."

"That will do for now. You can keep looking for the key once he is securely anchored to the floor."

Still in range of Mallerin's vision, Koren helped Jason crawl to the column. She fastened the chains to rings near the base and set a pair of manacles on his wrists. All along the way, she whispered repeatedly, "It's going to be all right. We're going to get through this."

When the second manacle snapped into place, he grasped her wrist and ran a finger along an abrasion. "I came … to set you free."

"I know. It's not over yet. Just try to trust me." She backed away slowly, staring at him while biting her lip. "I'm finished."

"Good," Taushin said. "Now while we wait for Cassabrie, we can complete our agreement."

"Maybe I should go out and release everyone from the trance first. If Elyssa decides to work on the medicine, I can send someone to guard her. It's dangerous out there."

"That is a minor issue. We can send someone after your vow."

"But I said I had to know if my friends from Darksphere are safe before I would complete the vow, and you agreed. If you renege and refuse to let me see to Elyssa's safety, you are not trustworthy, and I won't continue."

"You were talking about the approaching soldiers," Taushin said, "not Elyssa."

"I am more concerned about Elyssa's safety. They are well-armed. Elyssa is not."

"Very well. I am wary of your stalling tactics, but I will not have my integrity impeached by such a minor point." Taushin waved a wing. "Restore my mother and climb on my back. I will take you."

Koren waved a hand at Mallerin. "Awaken! You need to guide your son outside."

Blinking, Mallerin shook her head. "You hypnotized me again."

"I did." Koren took her cloak from the Reflections Crystal and put it on. "I was concerned that in your passion to protect Taushin, you might kill one of the humans."

Mallerin growled. "If you do it again, you will be the next human I kill."

"I will be careful to honor your wishes."

While Koren mounted Taushin, Jason rubbed his eyes, making the chains clink. His vision was improving, and the pounding had eased, though the numbness in his back and legs made walking doubtful, even if he could escape the chains.

Now on Taushin's back, Koren looked at Jason. Tears sparkling, she mouthed, "You can trust me."

She patted Taushin's scales. "Let's go." He and Mallerin flew out the corridor and disappeared. Their wings provided a brief draft, but the air quickly stilled.

Jason stared at the floor. The image of Koren's face stayed in his mind's eye, earnest and passionate. Her lips formed *You can trust me* again and again.

The image warped. Koren's face remained visible, but it now resided within a black oval, the portal viewer in the chamber next to the underground river. Their first meeting seemed so long ago, but the memory was still fresh. The overflowing river had risen to his chest, but if he had taken his fingers from the wall holes the river would have changed course and drowned Elyssa.

Jason read Koren's lips. *If only I could pull you out.* She extended a hand, pain streaking her face as a manacle tore her skin. *I ... can't ... reach ... any farther!*

He lifted a hand and looked at one of the manacles. So much had changed, yet so much remained the same. Elyssa was gone, again seeking help. He was alone, unable to help himself. Koren again spoke to him with silent lips, this time from atop a dragon instead of from within a reflection of the egg that hatched him.

He let the chain fall noisily to the floor. And now *he* wore the manacles—no worse really than the holes in the wall. There was no choice but to wait. The situation was out of his control.

Another vision came to mind, his last view of Koren as he succumbed to the flood. She buried her face in her hands. Blood streamed from her wrists to her fingers as she wept. She was Taushin's prisoner. And now she remained his prisoner, and she still had no way to escape from his grasp.

"Jason?" A glimmer of light appeared, taking the form of a swaying girl.

"Deference?" Jason kept the chains motionless. "Am I glad you're here!"

"What can I do to help?"

Jason lifted a manacle, dragging a chain with it. "See if you can find the key. The chains came from a trunk next to the wall, so it might be in there."

"I'm on my way." In a flash of light, Deference zipped toward the wall.

Jason leaned back against the column and allowed himself to smile. Hope remained. Between the efforts of a valiant girl from home and a glimmering girl from Starlight, maybe there was a chance to get out of this mess after all.

seventeen

dison, Captain Reed, and the other soldiers stayed close to the forest's north-flowing river. Earlier, it had split into two streams, one of which exited the forest to the east, while the one they now followed flowed from the south. Not far to the west, the barrier wall ran parallel to this stream and provided a guiding boundary. At least they wouldn't stray too far to that side.

Trees towered over them all around, and thick brambles hugged the trunks and spread out in between. No obvious path appeared anywhere, so they had to forge a path of their own. Listening to the persistent chopping of blades against wood, Edison shook his head. They had opted to stay deeper in the woods to avoid detection, but at this rate they should have traveled closer to the eastern edge of the forest, where the undergrowth was thinner.

Edison hacked with his sword at a low-hanging vine. When it dropped, a hefty snake fell with it and flopped to the ground. After lying stunned for a moment, it slithered into a cluster of low bushes.

"I am not familiar with the varieties of serpents here," Edison said, "but I think we should assume they are all venomous."

"Agreed." The captain nodded toward a clearer area about twenty paces ahead. "Magnar landed. Let's see if he has a report."

They hacked their way through the brambles and broke into a brighter section of the forest, where Magnar sat looking up through a thin network of branches. Fewer trees and bushes grew here but enough to make maneuvering difficult for a dragon.

"Is there trouble?" Captain Reed asked.

"A great deal of trouble." Magnar kept his focus on the sky. "Fellina and a rider are coming. I guided them to this spot. They should arrive at any moment. To the east, the Benefile are battling those of my race. It is an air battle, but it is difficult to see through the smoke."

Edison sniffed. "I smell it."

"The section of forest under the battle is ablaze." Magnar backed out of the center of the clearing, crushing brambles and small trees in a cacophony of crackling branches. "They are coming."

The beating of wings filled the air. Fellina plummeted through the trees, breaking branches along the way. With a desperate flurry, she slowed enough to avoid smashing into the ground, but her momentum threw her into a tumble.

A man flew off her back and hurtled into a bramble bush, sending it into a violent shake. When it settled, a weak "Ouch" rose from the thicket, then a sigh.

While Magnar shuffled toward Fellina, Edison ran to the bush. An old man crawled out, his clothes and gray hair filled with thorns. "My mother didn't raise me to be a pin cushion," he muttered.

"Well," Captain Reed said, "if it isn't my old friend, Tibalt. Back in my days as a dungeon guard, we had quite a few long talks."

Tibalt plucked a thorn from his nose. "We did, but you never believed a word I said."

"Believe Tibber the Fibber? Why back then I'd just as soon—"

"Cease the foolish chatter," Magnar growled. "Do you care nothing about an injured dragon? Fellina is Arxad's mate, one of the few who thought of your kind as something more than vermin."

Edison helped Tibalt walk to the fallen dragon. She lay with her neck curled back toward her body and a trickle of blood oozing from her mouth. Tibalt knelt at her side and stroked her neck. "Fellina's been flying all around those mountains to the south, and a bunch of dragons have been chasing her. Then they saw Frederick herding the children this way, so they took off after him."

"Frederick?" Edison steeled himself. "My son?"

"The same. Those white dragons flew in from the north and attacked, and then it was like someone opened a jar of chaos. Flames and ice shot everywhere, and the trees caught on fire. I guess those kids are somewhere in that blaze. When Fellina saw Magnar, she headed this way, hoping he could help."

"Where are the children now?"

Tibalt pointed over his shoulder with his thumb. "That way, near the forest edge, due west of one of the mesas."

"We can follow the smoke." Edison grabbed the hilt of his sword. "Captain, another double-time march! Magnar, lead the way!"

"What about Fellina?" Tibalt asked. "We can't just leave her here."

Magnar let out a growl. "Does only one human have compassion for our kind? Will you leave Fellina to the birds of the air?"

"I have to rescue children." Edison whipped out his sword. "When it comes to a choice between Fellina and—"

"Do not say it!" Magnar glared at Edison. "This is madness. I go to fight against my own kind for the sake of those who care nothing for the condition of the grandest of all she-dragons. If only Arxad were here so he could see what his beloved humans are really like."

"We can't do anything for Fellina," Edison said, "but we have to protect the children from fire-breathing slavers. If you want your kingdom back, we'll need your help."

Tibalt stripped off his tunic and pushed it against a wound in Fellina's belly. "I'll stay with her. No buzzards can get her while I'm around. They'd probably eat me first. I'm easier to tear apart."

Magnar snorted. "At least one of you has sense." He beat his wings, raising a debris-filled breeze, and lifted into the air. As he circled over the treetops, he called out,

"The children are not far. March in the direction I go, and you will arrive in moments." Then, he flew away.

"March!" Edison shouted, pointing his sword in that direction.

He ran through the forest, clearer here than in the earlier section. Still, the terrain stayed rough as he dodged trees and leaped over roots and logs. From ahead, a low murmur reached his ears and quickly grew to a tumult—dragons roaring, children screaming, and flames crackling. With every step, smoke thickened. The noise spiked. The soldiers coughed but kept the pace.

Soon, children came into view, huddled in the midst of the densest smoke, coughing and choking. A man swung his sword at a dragon snaking its head toward them between two trees. From each side, a few of the bigger boys hacked at its neck with broken branches. Flames leapt all around, engulfing trees and underbrush. Dragons flew above, darting this way and that as streams of orange and white filled the sky.

Edison ran past the children, leaped in front of the man, and jammed his sword into the dragon's snout. Screaming, the dragon's head shot back and disappeared. Captain Reed and the other soldiers formed a line between the children and the retreating dragon, their swords, spears, and shields raised.

The man grabbed Edison from behind, spun him around, and pulled him into a tight embrace. "Father!"

"Frederick?" Edison drew back and caressed Frederick's face, scruffy and covered with cuts and bruises. "Is it really you?"

Frederick nodded, then coughed several times. "No more time," he said, his voice pinched. "These dragons want the children."

Edison blinked at the stinging smoke. "Why?"

"To protect themselves." Frederick pointed in the direction the dragon had gone. "They're fighting the Benefile out in the open and flushing us out with fire, hoping to gather the children around them. They think the Benefile won't hurt the children."

Edison coughed through his reply. "If we don't move ... the children will suffocate.... Some of the men ... will engage the dragons.... The rest will lead the children to safety."

Frederick waved at the thickening smoke. "If you know where *safety* is, I'm all for going there."

Edison lifted his tunic and covered his mouth and nose, muffling his voice. "The way I came isn't clear, so you'll have to stay close to the forest edge. Lead the children toward the village. We'll keep a line of men between you and the dragons."

"I'm on my way." Frederick limped toward the children and began herding them out of the smoke.

Amidst a clamor of screaming dragons and crackling flames, Edison ran to Captain Reed. The men's eyes aimed toward the sky, their heads swiveling as they followed the dragons in flight. More fire shot into the branches, then rivers of white. Crystals rained on their heads.

Captain Reed caught some in his palm. "Snow?"

"Ice." Edison brushed crystals from his shoulder. "Let's see what's going on out there."

As he led the way toward the forest boundary, the men followed. The screams intensified. Flashes of orange looked like lightning, and the falling crystals grew into a virtual hailstorm.

When they reached the edge, Edison walked out into the open. At least ten frozen dragons littered the plateau, some sitting on their haunches with their necks curled as if ready to strike at a target above, and some lying on their bellies with wings spread as if fallen from the sky.

He touched the closest dragon. Coated in frosty ice, it looked like a snow sculpture.

Above, thirty dragons or more flew in all directions, swerving and diving, all beating their wings furiously. Three white dragons flew among them, each one faster and more agile than their Southlands counterparts. One of the white dragons blasted a geyser of ice that slammed into a reddish dragon. Like a slithering white blanket, the ice wrapped around him, freezing him in flight. He dropped to the ground with a thud. Although crystals splattered, the ice held fast.

A new barrage of fire poured into the trees. One of the Southlands dragons dove at Edison, spewing flames. Magnar swooped in between and blocked the volley. "Hide yourself!" Magnar yelled. "Unseen is safe for now!"

He swerved and flew directly at the attacker. Edison ran back to the soldiers and waved toward the north. "Stay in the woods, but keep moving. The dragons are too busy with each other now to be concerned about us."

As the men marched, their feet pointing north and their weapons and shields pointing east toward the open area, Edison kept a watchful eye toward the west. Deeper in the woods, the tail end of the line of children came into view. An older boy carried a tiny girl, his head low.

Above, the circles of dragons widened, and the entire field of wings, scales, and claws drifted southward.

"They're moving with us," Captain Reed said as he marched next to Edison. "Any idea why?"

"The village is that way. Maybe the Benefile want everyone to go there."

A frozen dragon dropped through the trees. Branches cracked and fell, and the stiff body slammed into a bush, flattening it. A white dragon swooped low, gave the men a quick look, then flew back to the battle.

Edison kept a steady pace. "They are clearly the superior fighters, so they might be intentionally guiding the other dragons."

"Why not destroy them out here?" the captain asked. "Why the delay? Why would they follow us?"

"I think they want *us* to follow *them*. Maybe they intend for us to deliver the final blow in a symbolic setting, such as the Zodiac. Remember what Arxad said. They have strange ways, and they will see us as allies in their cause."

"Unless they find out that we already have the disease among us," Captain Reed said. "Then we might transform from the protected to the targets."

Edison nodded. "We will have to keep that secret as long as we can."

⤛·⤜

As soon as Taushin landed in front of the Zodiac's exterior doors, Koren dismounted and ran to the portico's front edge between the two main support columns. From this point, every entranced person was in view—Randall to the left, and the ragged line of slaves stretching from near where he stood to a point well down the road toward the grottoes on the right. She waved her cloak, pivoting in place as she shouted, "Awake! All of you!"

Randall staggered forward to keep from toppling. He looked around, squinting. "Where are the white dragons?"

Moans erupted from the sea of diseased slaves. A few of those standing crumpled to the ground. Some who had been sitting keeled over and lay motionless.

"He's dead!" a woman cried out. As she continued her lament, new moans and wails drowned her voice.

His sword bared, Randall marched up the portico's side stairway. "Koren! What's going on? Why are you with Taushin?"

Koren held up a hand. "Stop!"

He halted, blinking. "Are you using your Starlighter power on me?"

"Only to give you information." She pointed toward the grottoes. "Go to Arxad's cave and help Elyssa. She will provide all the information you need."

Rubbing his eyes, he backed down the stairs. "Elyssa?"

"Yes. She needs your help."

When Randall reached the bottom of the stairs, he turned toward the grottoes and began an unsteady march. As he weaved through the crowd of slaves, he stumbled at times but caught himself.

When he was out of earshot, Taushin set his snout near Koren's ear. "I said I would allow protection for Elyssa, but this one is dangerous. I do not want the two Darksphere visitors to conspire against us."

Koren turned. Mallerin sat behind Taushin, scanning the area. "Were you able to see the look in his eyes?" Koren asked. "He wanted to kill you."

"He is far too ill to do me any harm, but I want to avoid encouraging Elyssa with his presence and his knowledge. Bring him back."

Koren nodded. This could work out perfectly. "Randall!" she shouted.

Nearly falling as he spun, Randall gave her a confused stare. "What now?"

She raised her hood and locked gazes with him. "Rest, my friend. Think of the forests and creeks on your world. Think of shade and cool water." As she spoke, the circle of cobblestones around him transformed into lush grass with a bubbling stream passing next to his feet. "Enjoy the refreshment. I will bring you back here at the proper time."

"Excellent," Taushin said. "As ill as he is, this is the best situation for him. If Elyssa has already made it safely to Arxad's dwelling, she needs no guard, and she is quite capable of working alone."

A boy skulked past Randall and headed toward Arxad's cave. Koren focused on him. From the back he looked like Wallace.

A man called from the crowd. "Koren! What are we to do? Where is the medicine?"

"It's coming very soon." She spotted the man, a young miner from the looks of his dirty, calloused hands. He sat only a few steps away, holding a motionless little girl in his arms. Her dark, stringy hair draped his muscular forearm. "One of the Darksphere visitors is preparing it."

"Are you sure it works?"

She lifted her tunic, once again revealing her stomach from her navel to her lowest ribs. Her skin had stayed clear, but the miner couldn't see the pain growing within. "This is what it did for me. I'm not sure if it's a complete cure, but it helps."

"It's a lot better than nothing." He stroked the girl's head and ran his fingers through her hair. "Reesa doesn't have much time."

Pressing her lips together, Koren nodded. "I know. None of us do. Just try to be patient. The medicine will be here soon."

Taushin set a wing on Koren's back. "Let us go now to complete—"

"Wait!" Koren blinked. A vision from Exodus flowed into her mind, a dragon with fear in his eyes flying this way from the south. "I see a messenger dragon, one of yours. I think he bears bad news. He will be here soon."

"Mother," Taushin said, "guide me to a better viewing place."

He and Mallerin flew down to the street, while Koren navigated the stairs. After avoiding several slaves, she reached the bottom and stood next to Taushin. Koren and Mallerin both looked up. Clouds drifted across Solarus, forcing it to peek through intermittent gaps.

After a minute or so, Taushin murmured, "Koren, have you been able to see Cassabrie?"

"Not yet. I've been scanning as far as I can to find her."

"Either you are telling the truth, or you are a skillful liar." Taushin settled to his haunches and said no more.

A few moments later, a drone flew toward them from the south. When it landed, it gasped for breath. "I found Fellina!"

"Where?" Taushin asked.

"She is down. Magnar has joined the battle against the Benefile near the closer mining mesa. Fellina is in the forest near that area, but I could not tell if she is dead. An old man is sitting with her, and they are out of the battle zone."

"How are our dragons faring against the Benefile?"

"Not well. They have to battle the ice and the spears of the human army. They hoped to use the slave children as a shield, but the humans have thwarted that plan."

A look of worry bent Taushin's features. "Did you see Xenith?"

"Not in flight," the drone said. "Several have fallen victim to the ice, but when covered in white, they are not recognizable."

Taushin spread out his wings. "We must join them. Mother, you will be my eyes once again, but first, take the sword from the Darksphere human."

While Mallerin shuffled toward Randall, Taushin touched Koren's abdomen with a tip of his wing. "I hear churning within."

Koren slid her hand under his wing and pressed her stomach. The pain was definitely getting worse.

"Your alliance with me will be tested now. Do not let me down." Taushin waved a wing toward the dying slaves and set his eyebeams on her cheek. "It would be tragic if you lost these people after all you have gone through."

"I know." Koren looked away, dodging the beams. "Maybe you'd better hurry. Fellina needs you."

Taushin waved a wing at the messenger. "Guide us to Fellina." The messenger took off, followed immediately by Mallerin and Taushin.

The breeze from the three sets of beating wings blew back her hair and flapped her cloak. While she waited for them to fly out of sight, moans and cries rose all around. The miner called, "What will you do now, Koren?"

Koren took a step toward him. He sat in the same place with Reesa in his lap. With her face covered with sores and her hair falling out, she looked more dead than alive. "How is she?"

"She's breathing. That's all I can say."

Letting out a sigh, Koren looked toward Arxad's cave, then at the Zodiac's entry doors. Taushin probably wouldn't be gone long, and there was so much to do.

"Hold on. I will be back as soon as I can." She ran to Randall and grabbed his arm. "Wake up! I need you!"

Randall shook his head hard. "Where am I?"

"I'll explain later. Just come with me." Tugging him along, she hurried up the portico's stairs and marched through the Zodiac's entry corridor. Randall staggered now and then, but his eyes seemed to grow clearer and clearer. As they neared the entry to the dome room, she spotted two ropes pinched between the floor panels and leading to one of the wall lanterns. She hadn't noticed them while flying in and out with Taushin. Maybe he hadn't seen them either.

When they arrived in the dome room, she stopped at the interior threshold and let go of Randall. "Follow if you can. I'm in a hurry." She ran to Jason and slid on her knees, stopping in front of him. She grabbed his hand in both of hers. "Oh, Jason! I'm so sorry about everything. I prayed that you'd come and rescue me from Taushin. I saw you in my vision, so I knew you were near. That's why I let him get so close. I hoped you'd interfere before he took complete control, but at the last second, I saw Mallerin coming, and I didn't want her to kill you. If she had seen you attacking Taushin, she might have burned you alive before I could stop her."

She took a deep breath. "Do you understand?"

Jason stared at her, obviously focusing on her eyes. "Is Taushin looking at me?"

"No. No! He never got in." She yanked at a manacle, but it held fast. "I have to get you out of here."

Jason glanced toward the doorway. "Randall's coming, but he looks dazed. Did you hypnotize him?"

"I did, but he's shaking it off." She jumped up and ran to the trunk. The lid still lay at the side, allowing easy access.

"Deference has been looking for the key," Jason said. "She searched through that trunk three times."

Koren picked up the sword she had laid behind the trunk. Fortunately she had remembered to block Mallerin's view of it from the moment she picked it up until the moment she hid it. "If Deference is here, where is Madam Orley? It would be odd for them to be apart."

"I have no idea. She didn't mention Madam Orley."

"Where is Deference now?"

"I don't know. I think she's still looking for the key, but I haven't seen her in a while."

"That's Deference. She'll do anything for you, but you don't always know when she's around." Koren set the lid back on the trunk and scooted to Jason. Stooping, she laid a hand on the back of his head. "I'm really sorry about this."

He pulled away. "Why were you making a covenant with him? If he has control over you, why should I trust you?"

"First of all, I didn't make a covenant with him. He recited his part of the agreement, but I never said I'd do anything for him. I'm pretending to be on his side because he has a plan to hurt Cassabrie. He thinks I'm going to help him, but I'm really going to stop him."

"And you can't be sure you can stop him unless you stick by his side."

"Exactly." She raised the sword. "Let's see if I can break one of the chains."

Jason slid to the side and pulled on a manacle, stretching a chain across the floor. "The links look too thick."

"I have to try." Koren chopped down. The blade clanked against the chain and recoiled, vibrating painfully in her grip.

Randall shuffled up to them and crouched. "You just nicked the blade. You'll never cut those links with a sword." He mussed Jason's hair. "Don't worry. We'll get you out of this."

"I'm glad *you're* confident." Jason's voice took on a skeptical tone. "Koren, do you have an alternate plan?"

"Just to get the key." Still holding the sword, she patted Randall's arm. "I'll need your help." As she and Randall headed for the entry corridor, she called back. "Jason, I don't blame you at all for not trusting me. I'm not even sure I can trust myself, and I know what Taushin's up to. He's crafty, and his influence has overwhelmed me before. I just have to be careful to keep my boots off."

"Keep your boots off?"

"Never mind."

"Where are you going?" Jason called, his voice muffled by the Zodiac's walls.

"When I gave Elyssa the medicine ingredients, she told me where a copy of the master key is. It's hard to get to, so I wanted to check the trunk again first." She stopped at the middle of the corridor and looked up at the wall mural. A redheaded, green-eyed girl stood in the midst of Exodus. Wearing a Starlighter's vestments—a white dress and blue cloak—she gazed toward the sky, her mouth open as if telling one of Starlight's tales.

"The key's up there, Randall." Koren reached with the sword and touched one of the Starlighter's hands. "In that little hole in her palm."

Randall nodded. "I see it. Can you get it out with the tip of the blade?"

"I don't think so. Even if I could, it's not a good idea. Elyssa said the floor would open if we take it, and you already know what's down there."

"Sharp stakes and a stinky dead dragon." Randall turned toward the dome room. "I found a lever that closes the floor, but I'm not sure it would work without the key in place. Too risky without a test."

Koren rested the blade on her shoulder. "And we can't test it without removing the key."

"I have an idea." Randall jogged to the rope's pinch point near the interior door and began pulling one section upward. It rubbed against the point, forcing Randall to pull harder. He gasped and paused, pressing a hand against his stomach, then set to work again. With light from the dome room framing him, he looked like a miner standing on top of a mesa hauling a bucket to the top. After several seconds, the rope snagged.

"Do you want me to cut it?"

"You'd better. I think we have enough."

While Randall leaned to tighten the rope, Koren crouched and chopped at it horizontally. The sharp blade cut it cleanly.

Randall staggered to the wall and braced himself there. Wagging his head, he loosened the rope from the lantern post and fed it around the door's highest hinge. As he walked backwards toward Koren, he pulled the rope, checking the new attachment's strength. "It looks secure."

"What are you planning?"

"I thought I'd boost you to the key while I hold the rope. When you get it out, I'll swing with you to the doorway."

"Over sharp stakes?"

"And a stinky dragon." Randall shrugged. "Unless you have another idea."

A new voice piped up. "I have one." Deference crawled along the wall like a spider until she settled next to the Starlighter's palm. "I'll drop the key to you. All you have to do is catch it and swing on the rope. It'll be a lot easier than carrying Koren."

Koren looked at Randall. His eyes were alert but blood-shot. "Let me swing," she said. "You go to the door and catch me. I'm lighter, and you're sicker than I am."

"Are you sure?" He looked like a slave trying to choose between working while sick or taking a beating for claiming sickness.

"I'm sure." She handed the sword to him. "I don't think I could catch you if something goes wrong."

Randall backed toward the dome room, letting the rope slide through his hand. "I appreciate the excuse."

When he arrived at the doorway, he laid the sword down and set his feet. "Ready."

Koren wrapped the rope around her waist, hung on with one hand, and extended her other toward Deference. "Let it drop."

eighteen

Elyssa smoothed out the note on the table in Arxad's kitchen and squinted at the messy script. As she read, her pendant dangled at the end of its chain, twirling one way and then the other over Uriel's instructions.

Wallace stood beside her. He appeared to be his usual self, if a bit tired. He set a wood carving on the table, an exquisite representation of a girl with a feather cap, though only the top portion was finished.

"Who is that?" she asked.

"A girl named Regina. It's a long story. We'd better get started."

"Well, she's beautiful." Elyssa pointed at a lantern on the floor. "I'll need more light."

Wallace picked up the lantern and held it close to the table, illuminating their makeshift surgical surface. A butcher's knife lay next to Elyssa's hand as well as the finger box, the wax envelope, and a needle and thick black thread. The crucible, now unsealed, sat in a roasting pan over a fire in a brick oven embedded in a wall.

"It says to combine the gunpowder with the energy crystals by grinding them together in the crucible." Elyssa touched the wax envelope. "Do you see anything to grind this with?"

"I'll look." Wallace rummaged through a basket of instruments. "Something hard with a rounded end?" Clinks and thunks echoed in the chamber.

"Yes." Elyssa picked up the box from the table and opened it, revealing Cassabrie's finger. From the tip to the second knuckle, it was intact, but tight stitches bound one end, obviously truncated.

Elyssa removed the finger from its velvet bed and set it next to the knife. Chopping off a section would be the hardest part of the procedure. The instructions called for using half the finger in hopes of saving some for another time, but if the mixture produced no blue smoke, they would have to use the rest immediately.

"This should work." Wallace set a gray pestle on the table. "Right?"

"That's perfect, exactly what I need." Elyssa frowned at the note. "This is confusing. I think I was supposed to grind the crystals and the powder together before I put it over the fire."

"That can't be helped now." Wallace grabbed a set of tongs and carried the crucible from the fire to the table. The particles within radiated brilliant light, too bright to stare at for more than a second.

Wallace set the lantern on the floor near the cave wall. "I don't think we'll be needing this."

"Probably not." Elyssa tore open the wax envelope and sprinkled half of the powder into the crucible. Yellow sparks sprayed in long arcs, and white smoke spewed toward the ceiling. She jumped back, batting sparks from her hands. After several seconds of spitting and popping, the reaction settled.

Wallace picked up the pestle and laid it in Elyssa's hand. "Do you need gloves?"

"I don't think so. The sparks didn't hurt. They just startled me." She pushed the pestle into the crystals and pressed down, twisting as she applied pressure. More sparks jumped. Heat from the crucible rose into her fingers and face, but not enough to cause pain.

"Does it say how long to do it?" Wallace asked.

Elyssa shook her head. "I just have to guess." After nearly a minute, she lifted the pestle and laid it next to the finger. "Now the hard part."

"I can cut it for you," Wallace said. "I know how to handle a knife. I can stitch it up, too. I cut my foot once really deep. I sewed it up with fiber from a vine."

Elyssa winced. "That must've hurt."

"Not as much as a dragon's whip. I had to get back to work."

"Well, then you're just the man for the job." Elyssa smoothed out the note again. "According to this, we should stand back when we add the genetic material, so I'll do that part."

"That's when I'll do the stitching." Wallace picked up the knife. "But first the cutting. Don't look."

Elyssa turned toward the cave entrance. Outside, a clamor of odd voices grew. A thunk sounded over the other noise. Elyssa cringed. She turned back to the table, but Wallace had already moved away to the other side of the cave, his back turned. "I'm stitching. Better get to it."

Elyssa stared at the table. Half the finger, from the tip to the slice, lay next to the crucible, dark blood oozing. Sucking in a breath, she scooped it up and dropped it into the crucible in one motion.

A sizzle erupted. It lasted for several seconds, then died away.

"Did you see any blue smoke?" Elyssa asked.

Wallace turned and shook his head. "I wasn't looking."

"Give me the rest." Elyssa held her hand out but didn't bother to look. As soon as the finger touched her palm, she dropped it into the crucible.

This time a loud whoosh sounded. Blue smoke shot into the air and spread out like a vertically hovering blanket. An image of Fellina appeared, lying motionless on her side in a forest. Tibalt lay nestled against her, his eyes closed and a hand pressed against her belly. A large bird hopped toward them and leaped up to Fellina's wing. With another hop, it landed on Tibalt's back. One of Fellina's wings twitched, and Tibalt's brow furrowed, but they offered no resistance.

The sizzling faded, and the smoke shrank toward the table. It took the shape of a pendant on a chain, then dispersed.

Elyssa touched her pendant. "Fellina and Tibalt need me."

"I saw that, but do you know how to get there?"

"No. Did you recognize the area?"

Wallace nodded. "I hid there a couple of times trying to get away from a beating."

"How do I find it?"

Wallace drew in the air with his finger. "The stream comes from the mining mesa, flows through the forest, and into the main river. Just follow the stream from the point it enters the forest."

"I know where the stream is." Elyssa touched the rim of the crucible, now merely warm. The crystals inside had congealed into pink salve. Using her finger, she scooped out a large dollop and began rolling it into a ball between her palms. Whether or not it would be enough for a human and a dragon was anyone's guess.

Wallace dipped his finger in and lifted a dab. "It's hot, and it's getting hotter."

"It's the stardrop energy."

"Ow!" Wallace smeared the dab on the edge of the table, then gave Elyssa an apologetic look. "I'm sorry."

"Don't worry about it. Just take the rest to your people. Maybe at least it will keep some from dying."

Wallace picked up the crucible. "I'll deliver it, but maybe I should show you that spot."

"I can't afford to wait, but if you can catch up to me, that'll be fine." Now clutching the ball of salve, Elyssa ran out of the cave. To her left, the Zodiac sat at the top of a rise beyond a low wall, blocking the dying slaves from view. Jason likely still sat in chains inside, but that couldn't be helped. At least he was alive. By the time she reached Fellina and Tibalt, they might not be.

She turned to the right and ran. The plateau lay before her, the closer mining mesa in view. About two hundred paces ahead and to the right, dragons flew over the edge of the forest, three white and the rest of them darker. They battled in the sky with blasts of orange and white. The stream lay beyond the battle scene, so finding Fellina would require getting past the storm of fire and ice.

Slowing her pace, she tried to steady her rapid breaths. How could anyone run through such a gauntlet without getting fried or frozen? Yet, she had no choice. Fellina would die without help.

A man dashed out of the forest and threw a spear at one of the Southlands dragons. It wedged between two scales but didn't penetrate deeply. The dragon grabbed the shaft in its teeth and crunched it into splinters. During those few seconds, a line of children dashed out behind the man and ran toward the path to the village.

A white dragon sprayed the speared dragon with ice, freezing him in mid-flight. He fell like a stone and smacked the ground near the line of children.

They ran on, the spearman now running alongside, coaxing them with shouts of "Hurry!" and "We're almost there!"

Elyssa stopped and waved her arms. "This way!"

Several seconds later, the man arrived, gasping for breath, while the children gathered around, panting and groaning. "Elyssa! I didn't think I'd see you here."

Elyssa cocked her head. Even though a beard and dozens of abrasions disguised his face, there was no mistaking a son of Edison Masters. "Frederick!"

"Greetings later. Help me get these kids to Arxad's cave while I fend off the dragons."

"But I have to—" She shook her head. "Never mind." She laid a hand on one of the bigger girls. "Everyone follow me!"

She ran while looking back over her shoulder. Wearing barely any clothes, the children pumped their skinny arms and legs, puffing as they struggled against the incline. Frederick trailed at the end of the line, his sword raised. Farther back, at least forty soldiers ran out of the forest and began ascending the hill at a rate that would soon overtake the line of panting children.

From the plateau, dragons swooped over the soldiers, shooting fireballs and knocking the men down with their massive bodies. The soldiers, some with sleeves or trousers aflame, jabbed with their spears and swords while still on the run.

One of the dragons dove at the rear of the line of children, blasting fire across the stragglers and igniting their hair. Amidst the children's high-pitched screams, Frederick leaped and grabbed one of the dragon's back legs.

Elyssa held her breath. The furious dragon thrashed his legs and snapped at Frederick, only to be beaten back by his slashing sword. Rising higher into the air, the dragon sailed toward the front of the line, as the children helped each other swat away the flames left by his attack.

Frederick swung his sword and chopped off the dragon's hind foot. As he dropped, his legs pumping as his momentum carried him forward, he threw the sword down at Elyssa's feet. He hit the ground running well up the rise but fell into a tumble.

The crippled dragon landed next to Frederick and stomped him with his truncated leg, pinning him to the ground.

Elyssa sprinted that way. "Let him go!"

The dragon shot fire at her. She leaped to the side and rolled back down the hill until the children stopped her. A white dragon sailed only inches over their heads and blew a stream of ice over both the crippled dragon and Frederick, instantly freezing them.

The white dragon landed next to Elyssa and spoke in a smooth, sultry tone. "Your passage to safety is now assured. Take these innocent ones where you must."

Elyssa waved the children on. "You have to help Frederick!" she shouted. "Thaw him out!"

"The human?" The white dragon glanced Frederick's way. "He was infected with the disease. Any who are infected must be eliminated. We will protect the human species from the contagion."

Elyssa pointed up the rise and called to the children. "Do any of you know where Arxad's cave is?"

An older girl near the front of the line raised her hand. "I do. I'll take them."

As they hurried along, Elyssa eyed the young escapees. Those without shirts bore the telltale signs of early disease on their torsos—sores from their navels upward. Stripes of various length and age crisscrossed some backs, especially those of the thinnest children.

Holding the medicine in one hand and the sword in the other, Elyssa stormed toward the white dragon. Maybe a distraction would keep it from guarding the children too closely, at least for a while. "Get back! I have to save Frederick!"

The white dragon blinked at her. "You are risking contagion. You must have the disease as well."

"I don't. I'm immune." Elyssa stopped within a sword's length of the dragon's snout and lifted her tunic in front enough to show her stomach. When the dragon lowered its head to look, she swung the sword at its neck.

Just as the blade neared its pasty skin, something grabbed her wrist and bowled her over to the side. Still clutching both the medicine and the sword, she leaped to her feet. Edison Masters stood between her and the white dragon, holding one hand up and supporting himself with the other on his knee. "You don't understand!" he said, gasping. "It's helping us!"

Elyssa pointed at the white dragon. "But that thing just froze your son!"

"I know. I know." While he braced himself, coughing, the other soldiers breezed past and began escorting the children up the hill, some men scooping up the slower ones along the way. A few men shook their scorched arms or batted residual sparks, but they marched on with powerful leg strokes.

The white dragon lifted into the air effortlessly, smiling as if unaware of Elyssa's attack.

Edison waved a hand. "Come. We'll see about Frederick."

Above, the dragon battle raged directly overhead. Ice intermixing with sparks rained down on Elyssa and Edison as they ran past the frozen dragon and knelt at Frederick's side. Frosty ice covered his body from head to toe. Edison brushed away the frost from Frederick's face. With his cheeks slack and his lips blue, he appeared to be dead.

As roars and shrieks pierced the air, Elyssa shouted, "Do we just break it?"

"No choice." Edison drew a dagger from a hip sheath and rammed the butt end against the ice over Frederick's chin. A chip flew from the contact point, but the ice stayed intact. He switched to using the point of the blade and jabbed with it again and again, mumbling, "We need some heat!"

Elyssa opened her hand and looked at the little ball of medicine. Putting part of it into Frederick's mouth would probably provide a lot of heat, especially if she were to straddle him and use her manna wood pendant to try to heal him. If Edison could punch a hole, maybe it would work. Still, the medicine was meant for Fellina and Tibalt. This small amount might not be enough for them already, much less if she shared it with Frederick.

"Heat," she whispered. "I know how to get it." She leaped up and waved her sword. "Dragons! Let's see how much fire you can send down here."

A Southlands dragon broke away from the battle and flew toward her. She shoved Edison out of the way and spread her body over Frederick, her face to the sky. Fire gushed from the dragon's mouth. Elyssa lunged to the side and into Edison's arms. The flames splashed over Frederick's body, raising a plume of white vapor.

The dragon swerved toward Elyssa and Edison, its mouth wide. A ball of fire appeared at the back of its throat. Another dragon collided with it and knocked it into a spinning crash.

The second dragon landed in front of Elyssa. Scorch marks smudged many of his scales, and ice crystals hung on to his drooping ears. "I heard you are a healer. Fellina needs your help."

"Magnar?" Elyssa shot to her feet. "Can you take me to her?"

"At once."

Elyssa looked at Frederick. The shield of ice had melted away from his face down to his waist, but his cheeks and lips were still blue. He needed internal heat.

"I have to heal Frederick first, then I'll get more medicine and—"

"Always the humans first!" Magnar bellowed. "Fellina is near death!"

"So is Frederick!"

"Since you care so much for humans, let it be known that there is an elderly human with Fellina, and he, too, is close to death. Any delay could cost both their lives."

"But Frederick is—"

"He is no more valuable than your elderly friend and certainly no more valuable than Fellina." Magnar knocked her sword away with his tail and jumped into the air. As he shot upward, he grabbed the back of Elyssa's vest with his claws. "You are coming with me."

She kicked and squirmed, but when he gained too much altitude, she settled down. Getting loose and falling from this high up would be stupid.

Below, Edison knelt over Frederick, rubbing his arm, but there seemed to be no response. The dragon battle had shifted to the Zodiac, where white and dark dragons clashed in spectacular fury. Only about twenty-five of the darker dragons remained. The bodies of the others littered the path between the village and the plateau region, frozen in battle poses. All three Benefile seemed healthy and unharmed. In fact, their aerial acrobatics appeared to be a game as they dodged the fiery volleys and responded with icy blasts.

At the Zodiac, Wallace gave the crucible to an elderly woman. He then spun and ran back toward Arxad's cave, his form small in the distance.

From the Zodiac's direction, a black dragon flew toward Edison, its blue eyebeams focused on a larger dragon at its side.

Elyssa grimaced. Taushin and Mallerin. What trouble might they cause?

She opened her hand and looked at the sphere in her palm. She had to put everything else out of her mind and leave the rest to Edison, the soldiers, Wallace, and ...

And Jason. She pulled in her lip. Blinking away tears, she rolled her fingers around the medicine and focused on the forest. The stream entered the eastern edge and flowed into the river not far to the west. Somewhere in between, Fellina and Tibalt lay as food for the birds. Right now, for the healer, nothing else really mattered.

❖

Edison grabbed Elyssa's sword and shot to his feet. Taushin and Mallerin landed just out of reach, Taushin with his eyebeams focused on his mother.

"Where is Magnar going?" Taushin asked.

Edison glanced toward the Zodiac. With the battle now raging over there, it seemed no surprise that this cowardly usurper decided to vacate his holy house. "Why should I tell you?"

"Because I know how to revive your son. He is not dead but is hibernating. Yet, if he does not receive help soon, he will die."

Edison gazed at Frederick's blue-tinted face. Giving in to this monster felt like swallowing broken glass, but it couldn't be helped. Taushin could chase Magnar and find out for himself anyway. "Magnar is taking Elyssa to Fellina and Tibalt so she can heal them."

"Excellent. We located Fellina but decided to return to secure Elyssa's help. When we saw Magnar, however, we had to proceed more cautiously. He would kill me on sight."

A storm of sarcastic replies pelted Edison's mind, begging to be uttered, but Frederick's life was more important than a satisfying barb. "That seems likely."

Taushin's scaly head bobbed at the end of his black neck. "Have you seen Arxad or Xenith in your travels? I fear for their safety."

"How many questions will you ask before you help my son?"

"Just tell me if they are among the Benefile's victims. That will be enough."

"Let me think." Edison recalled the menagerie of frozen dragons littering the plateau. Although it was impossible to distinguish one dragon from another, Xenith couldn't have been among them. She had been flying missions for Arxad and wouldn't have had the time or a reason for joining in the battle. "She's not among the victims."

"That is a relief. I have learned to admire Arxad—"

"Spare me the pretense!" Edison strangled the sword's hilt. "You waste time, dragon. I told you what you wanted to know."

Taushin chuckled. "It is so comical when humans try to get uppity around their superiors." Adding a growl to his voice, he continued. "I am not one to break a covenant. The medicine is being distributed among the slaves. We will take Frederick to them. Once he receives a dose, it will shake him out of hibernation. But I will keep him close to us to ensure that your soldiers do not attack my mother or me."

Edison waved the sword. "Go. I will be there as soon as I can."

Mallerin snatched Frederick up by his tunic and flew toward the Zodiac. Taushin followed close behind, like a second tail swaying in flight.

Edison ran up the rise and passed a dragon cave entrance where a dozen soldiers stood guard. After giving them a nod, he ran on. The Zodiac drew closer and closer. Above, dragons continued screaming. Fire and ice drizzled everywhere. A dragon swooped. Edison swung his sword and hacked off a claw, sending the beast back into the sky.

After dodging a dozen or so motionless human bodies, he climbed the portico stairs. A sea of broken humanity lay at the top, where most of the slaves had taken cover under the roof. Men, women, and children, all bearing ulcerated faces and arms, followed him with their gazes as he slowed to a stop.

An old woman knelt next to an unconscious little girl. With a gnarled hand, she rubbed pink slave across bloody sores on the girl's chest and stomach. Dozens of others gathered around, some barely able to stand. Sad but hopeful, most looked on intently, their whispers growing in volume and excitement. One woman knelt nearby with her hands clasped tightly and her face nearly touching the floor.

Taushin and Mallerin sat close to the Zodiac's main doorway with Frederick lying in front of them. "We will wait here," Taushin said. "Verify that the medicine is effective and let us know when to bring him."

Edison sheathed his sword and glanced between the dragons and the sick girl. Soon her sores began fading. Stifled gasps rose. The girl opened her eyes and looked around. Her gaze locked on the kneeling woman, and she cried out, "Mama!"

Sobbing and shaking, the mother crawled over and lifted the girl into her arms. As they wept together, sharp voices rang out.

"Me next!"

"No! My son!"

"My sister!"

Like a swarm of locusts, the crowd converged on the old woman. She stood and held a small bowl high. "Cast lots!" one man shouted.

"Youngest first!" another called.

"No, the sickest!"

"Who will decide that?"

Fingers jabbed forward. Hands slapped at the old woman's arm. The bowl flew from her grasp and fell to the portico floor with a crack. The crowd knocked her toward Edison and swarmed around the bowl, kicking and clawing.

Edison caught her, keeping her from tumbling down the stairs. When he steadied her, he drew his sword and stepped into the fray. "Stop fighting!"

Everyone froze in place, staring at him. A woman holding the bowl thrust it toward him. "Take it. Tell us what to do."

"No!" someone else called. "Who made him our leader?"

"Don't be a fool!" yet another shouted. "Just let him decide."

Several others murmured, "Yes," and a wave of nodding heads passed across the desperate sea.

"Your son is dying," Taushin called. "Shall I bring him now?"

"Wait." Edison cast his gaze from man to woman to child, sick and tormented souls who had been told what to do all their lives, and now at the cusp of a cure to a disease worse than any whip, they had no capacity to break their invisible chains long enough to save their own lives.

"The sickest children first," Edison said. "Bring those under ten years of age who are unconscious, then those who cannot walk. We'll start from there."

While the people shifted to allow adults with incapacitated children to come forward, the woman who had been distributing the medicine caught Edison's sleeve and pulled him close. "My name's Isabelle," she whispered.

"Edison. Edison Masters."

"Well, Edison, there isn't enough to go around. Wallace told me we have to make more. He knows how, but he needs more ingredients."

Edison looked toward Frederick. He would probably have to wait for the next batch. Swallowing hard, he turned back to Isabelle. "What ingredients?"

"I'm not sure. He said something about having enough black powder, but he needs a finger, which I didn't understand at all, and some energy from Exodus. He said a girl named Elyssa knows how to get it."

"Elyssa?" Edison shook his head. "I don't think she's coming back anytime soon."

"Then what should we do?"

"I'm not sure. Everything's falling apart. We came to rescue you, but if the white dragons win, they'll kill you before the disease does. If the other dragons win, my small number of soldiers won't stand much of a chance against them. We have more coming, but I don't think they can get here in time."

"You need your son. We all do. One more fighter on our side can't hurt." Isabelle's whisper dropped further. "Wallace left a little bit of medicine in Arxad's cave. I will get it for your son."

"It's too dangerous," Edison said. "I should go."

"Nonsense. I'm already dying. Besides, the dragons will ignore me. And you're in charge of distributing the medicine. This lot is sure to fight over it again if you leave."

"I guess I trapped myself into this job." He heaved a sigh. "When you get to the cave, tell Captain Reed to send every man he can spare."

"Will he trust my word?" Isabelle asked.

"Tell him if I had an insignia on my thumb, I would give it to him in blood. That should do it."

Isabelle shook her head. "You Darksphere folk are a strange lot."

Edison smiled. "Don't worry. The captain will understand."

Taushin spoke up again. "With your soldiers present, I will have to keep Frederick with me. He is my insurance."

Edison gritted his teeth. "I understand."

As the battle screams continued above, Edison surveyed the portico area. A man stood at the front of a line with a girl in his arms. As limp as a rag doll, she appeared to be four or five years old. The man pulled up her tattered shirt, revealing stomach and chest ulcers.

Edison copied Isabelle's application procedure, dipping his finger into the bowl and spreading the ointment on the girl's skin, starting with as little as he dared. Her skin was hot to the touch, the sores sticky.

"What's her name?"

"Reesa." The man's voice was weak, deadened.

"And yours?"

"Dorman."

Still rubbing in the ointment, Edison gave him a smile. "I'm Edison Masters."

Dorman nodded. "One of the soldiers from Darksphere. I know."

"Not all has gone well," Edison said, "but there is still hope."

"Hope? Really?" Dorman sighed. "Are you a father?"

"Three boys." Edison gestured with his head toward Frederick. "My eldest lies there cold and stiff. He might not make it."

"Then you understand better than I do. Reesa is a breeder child, but I love her all the same. I stole her from the cattle camp and hid her for months. When the disease struck, I had to bring her out. I heard people talking about a cure."

After a final rub at the edge of a sore, Edison pulled Reesa's shirt down. "I have no idea if it'll work, but I'm going to hang on to hope, maybe enough hope for both of us."

Dorman finally smiled, though it was a weak effort. "You're a good man, Edison Masters. I will go to your son and watch over him while you finish here. I don't trust those dragons."

"Thank you."

As soon as Dorman walked away, a woman stepped up, her face haggard and ulcerated. She carried a little boy about the same age as Reesa. She said nothing, but her pleading eyes made words unnecessary.

Edison dipped his finger in the medicine. As he looked down the line of worried faces, it seemed that his heart might tear apart. This duty had to be done, and if it took a warrior to deliver a healing salve, then so be it.

nineteen

Koren focused on the Starlighter in the wall mural. Deference's phantom fingers reappeared and swept the key from the crevice. The moment it hit Koren's palm, the catch holding the floor in place clanked, and the panels swung open. She fell, nearly dropping the key. As she sailed on the rope, she turned toward the door and set her feet in front. They struck the wall below the door, keeping her from slamming into it. She pushed away once before settling again.

"Hang on." Randall hoisted her up and wrapped his arms around her, strong yet shaking. "You made it! Great swing!"

"It's about time I did something right." Koren raised her hood and stalked toward Jason.

"What do you mean?" Randall's stomping boots thudded behind her. "You're amazing!"

She spun back to him. "I'm a … a pariah."

"A pariah?" Randall squinted with one eye. "What do you mean?"

"I glow like a moon, but I'm the weakest reflection around. No matter how hard I try, I never do anything right. I'll always be an outcast, the least of the heavenly lights."

"That's not true. You're—"

"There's no time to argue about it." Koren knelt in front of Jason and shoved the key into the manacle's lock. "How are you feeling?"

"A lot better." As soon as the first manacle clicked, he shook it loose and rubbed the back of his head. "No permanent damage."

She threw off the other manacle and helped him rise. Jason stretched his back and neck. "So now that I'm free, how are you going to convince Taushin you're still on his side? He won't believe that I got loose myself."

Deference glided in, her aura making a sparkling trail. "Lock Koren in the chains. Hide the key and tell me where you put it."

"That won't work." Koren picked up a manacle and showed them the mechanism. "Taushin knows I can put these on myself. And when he asks me if I let Jason go, the crystal will tell him if I'm lying."

Deference swung a radiant fist. "Then hit her on the head with the chains. A big purple knot on her forehead will keep Taushin from asking."

"Deference!" Jason said. "We couldn't do that!"

She crossed her arms tightly. "If you love Koren and the other slaves, you could."

Jason and Randall looked at each other for a moment, then shook their heads at the same time. "We'll just take Koren with us," Jason said. "We'll find Elyssa and figure this out together."

"Sounds good to me." Randall took Koren's hand. "We'll work on the medicine together."

Koren jerked loose and shuffled away. "Let me think a minute." She stopped at the interior threshold and looked at the exit doorway at the end of the long corridor. The miner stood at the opening, carrying Reesa. Her head and arms hung limply, as if someone had poured her liquid body over his arms. Was she dead already? If not, someone had to get the medicine to her as soon as possible.

Yet, what about Cassabrie? Where was she? Another someone had to stay and ask for more Exodus energy. Maybe Cassabrie had a solution that would provide genetic material as well. Not only that, someone had to foil Taushin's evil plans against her. He said she would come. How did he know?

A sharp pang knifed through Koren's stomach. She dug a fist into her abdomen and took deep breaths. Did she have enough strength to learn Cassabrie's location? When she told Taushin she was too weak to search very far, it wasn't a lie. She just wasn't sure, but if the Reflections Crystal hadn't been covered by her cloak, Taushin might have noticed her uncertainty in the crystal's dimming.

She fanned out her cloak and gave it a spin. "Starlight, tell me where your star resides. Focus on the recent past—as recent as possible."

A brilliant sphere of light appeared in the corridor, floating slowly toward the dome room. Cassabrie stood inside, her face brighter than ever before and her eyes focused on the threshold. Only a step or two in front of Koren's feet, a white flower sprouted and grew knee high. Bearing four velvety petals with thin red veins, it swayed in an undetectable breeze.

Exodus stopped and floated a few inches over the flower. Cassabrie lowered herself to all fours and studied it, her brow deeply creased. She pushed her hand against the inner wall and grasped the flower, as if forming a glove with the star's membrane. Exodus lifted, uprooting the flower, but no dirt came with it, only sparkling green roots.

Cassabrie straightened and pulled the entire plant through the star's skin. Tilting her head, she touched a petal. She jerked her finger back, flinching. Then she touched a second and a third without reacting. When she touched the fourth, she smiled, plucked it from the flower, and put it into her mouth. As she chewed, her eyes glowed brighter and brighter, until light streamed from them like Taushin's eyebeams, only completely white with sparkling dots swimming within that looked like the whisperers from the star chamber.

She dropped the remainder of the flower and rose to her feet. When the plant touched the star's floor, it burst into flames, but the fire quickly died away, leaving sizzling ashes.

Exodus drifted onward. It entered the dome room and passed right through Koren. The river appeared next to it, and the broken barrier wall and the long pile of rubble took shape near the Reflections Crystal's pedestal. The moment Cassabrie and the star floated overtop the pile, the image vanished.

Koren walked toward the pedestal, her legs heavy. "She's coming this way."

"Are you sure?" Jason asked. "She might be planning to join our army in the wilderness."

Randall shook his head. "She's coming here. That's why I opened the dome. Xenith told me the crystal would attract her, and I thought we could use her help."

Jason looked up. "Can you close the dome again?"

"I think so." Randall slid a slender metal rod from his pocket. "I have a key to the mechanism."

Koren grabbed the key. "We need her to come. She's the only one who knows how to cure the disease. The medicine we have alleviates the symptoms only temporarily." She pointed at the doorway, her words coming faster and faster as the vision became clear in her mind. "You saw her eat the flower petal. She's fulfilling the prophecy! *A liberator comes on high with mercy streaming from her eyes. The slaves must take her blood and bone and plant within this mercy sown.* Alaph was the mercy portion of the Bloodless, and the plant grew from his blood, so somehow Cassabrie has to activate the medicine made from her blood and bone. Our medicine doesn't work completely because she hasn't done that yet. But Taushin has some kind of plot that I think will hurt Cassabrie, so someone has to stay here and make sure he can't follow through. We need to make sure Cassabrie does it her way, not Taushin's."

Taking a breath, Koren lifted her brow and forced a weak smile. "Understand?"

Jason shoved a hand into his pocket and looked at Randall. "Did you understand?"

"Only the part about eating the flower. I saw that. How the Bloodless can have blood threw me."

"They have blood! It's just that—" Koren stamped her foot. "I'll just have to do it myself." She stormed to the column, sat heavily, and fastened the manacles around her wrists. When they clicked in place, she scanned the room for a wisp of light. "Deference? Are you here?"

"I'm coming." The glowing phantom glided from behind one of the columns and stood in front of Koren. "What do you want me to do?"

Koren lifted one of her chains. "Hit me on the forehead—a good, strong whack."

"No!" Jason shouted. "Wait!"

Before either he or Randall could stop her, Deference grabbed the chain and whipped it at Koren.

Sharp pain ripped across Koren's forehead and down her spine. Dark spots invaded her vision, worse than the time she fell from a tree after collecting eggs from a nest.

As the spots diminished, Koren rubbed the wound. A knot had already formed, and warm liquid trickled over her fingers. "That really was a strong whack."

"Sorry," Deference said, "but it's the only way to convince Taushin."

Randall shook his head, staggering for a moment before righting himself. "He'll never believe Jason would hit you that hard. He'll just ask you, and the crystal will give you away."

"Maybe he won't ask," Koren said. "Maybe I'm far enough from the crystal that it won't detect a lie."

Jason pointed at the crystal. "But just a minute ago you were worried about it giving you away. Now you're ignoring the risk."

"I know. I know." Koren cupped a hand over the wound. "Just leave and find Elyssa. Get the medicine and save some people from succumbing to the disease before Taushin and Mallerin come back. I'm only one person. I'm not worth the trouble."

"I can't let you do this." Jason extended his hand. "Give me the key to your manacles, or I'll have to take it from you."

Koren gave him a glare, trying her best to show anger. "Go now, or I'll force you to go. You know I can."

"Then just give me the key, and I'll let you stay. If Taushin finds it on you, he'll know you faked my escape. Like Deference said, we can hide it, and she can bring it to you when you need it."

"No tricks." Koren raised the fist that held the key. "Say it to the crystal, that you won't try to force me to leave."

Jason's fingers rolled up. "Do you think I would lie to you?"

"I …" Koren swallowed. "No, it's just that—"

"It's just that you're forgetting who to trust." Jason drew his hand back. "I'm not talking to the crystal. Either believe me, or don't believe me. It's up to you."

Koren clenched her fists, trying to keep them from trembling. Heat surged into her cheeks and ears. Her body shaking uncontrollably, she rose to her knees and hugged herself to stop the tremors. "Oh, Jason, I'm so confused!"

He knelt and wrapped his arms around her. As he held her close, she slid her arms around him and wept on his shoulder, making his body shake with her sobs. "I found out my father was alive, and now he's dead. I practically killed Alaph because I was too stubborn and stupid to trust him. And now I almost lost faith in you." She took a quick breath. "I want to do what's right, but like you said, I can't figure out who to trust. I try to make sure no one else gets hurt, but then they get hurt anyway."

Jason patted her on the back. "You did the best you could. You always do. You can't control everything."

"But I'm even messing up the things I *can* control. When I saw what Alaph did to his mate, I couldn't trust him anymore, so I wouldn't drink the mercy blood."

"The mercy blood?"

"Right. I should have taken it. So now I feel the burden of all of Starlight, and I can't just shrug it off. Like I said, I have to stop Taushin from hurting Cassabrie, but even when I know he's trying to influence me, I think I can outsmart him—"

"Koren," Jason whispered. "Slow down. Your mind's running too fast. Take some deep breaths and relax a minute."

Nodding, she breathed deeply for several moments, then drew back and wiped her tears. "Thank you."

Jason swept a tear from her chin with his finger. "Do you want to tell me about Alaph and the mercy blood? Is Alaph dead?"

Tears welled again. "Yes. And, no, I don't really want to talk about it. I shouldn't have mentioned the blood. There's nothing that can be done about it anyway."

Though she kept her gaze on the ground, Koren could feel him watching her. After a long pause, he said, "Okay. That's fine. I trust you."

Koren let the words melt into her mind, soothing, strengthening. *I trust you.* How could she hold back the same gift?

Koren grasped his hand. "Thank you, Jason. I trust you, too. I know you won't force me to leave." She set the manacles' key in his palm but kept the dome key. "I'm so glad you understand."

"Understand?" Jason laughed under his breath. "Not really, but I said I'd trust you, so that's the way it's going to be."

Koren gazed into his sincere eyes. No, he didn't really understand. He was trying, but it was simply out of his reach. He had never been a slave. He had never felt the futility, the despair. And he wasn't a Starlighter. He wasn't called to carry the burdens of Starlight. He was a man of the sword, not an angel of mercy. He couldn't fathom the absolute necessity of protecting Cassabrie at all costs. He had to do his part, and she had to do hers.

"I think you should go," she said, turning away. "Thank you for all the help you're giving us."

"I'm not ready to go." Jason laid his hand on her cheek and gently turned her toward him. "Listen to me, Koren. I know you want to protect everyone and be the only one who gets hurt, but Elyssa and Randall and Tibber and I didn't come here to sit around and let any slave offer herself at an altar. When I saw you chained to the black egg, I made a vow never to allow a slave to toil in misery while I lived at ease. I'm not about to let that happen now. I'll leave you here for a little while, but one way or another, we're going to get out of this together."

She grasped his hand and kissed his knuckles. "I believe you, Jason Masters. When I see you again, I hope the burdens will all be lifted."

Jason rose slowly. "Come on, Randall. I hate leaving her here, but we don't have any choice. Let's hide the key where only Deference can get it, and we'll find Elyssa."

"Wait." Randall pulled Jason a little distance away and passed him his sword. He ripped open his tunic at the neck, revealing the top of his chest. Oozing sores covered his skin, deep ulcers that exposed muscle tissue and ribs. Their conversation dropped to a whisper.

Koren craned her neck and listened, but they were obviously making secret plans. And who could blame them? They probably thought the strange Starlighter had gone mad.

Randall backed away from Jason.

"Are you sure?" Jason asked.

"I'd only slow you down." Randall sat on the floor, moaning as he clutched his stomach.

Jason helped him slide to the column next to Koren. "Wait here. I'll see if the medicine's ready."

His eyes tightly closed, Randall nodded but said nothing.

Jason scanned the room. "Deference, could you come with me for a moment? I need you to watch where I hide the key, then come back and take care of these two while I'm gone."

"Sure." She rose from her knees at Koren's side. "If you're going to close the floor with the lever so you can get out, I think you have to put the key back first."

"Can you do that?"

She shook her head. "I can carry something small that far, but I have to keep dropping it and picking it up again. With the floor gone, it wouldn't work very well."

"Is there another way out of here?"

She slid her ghostly hand into his. "I'll show you. It's not an easy exit, but Randall made it. And it's also a perfect place to hide the key. I can slide it back to Koren without much trouble."

"Lead the way."

As Jason and Deference left, her voice continued, fading as they neared the back of the dome room. "We have to walk close to the wall, because the crystal draws me toward it. I don't want to get pulled ..." Soon they disappeared through a hidden door in the wall.

Now alone with Randall, Koren gave him a nudge. "I really appreciate you wanting to watch over me, but you don't have to pretend."

Randall fell to the side. His head settled in her lap, hot and dry. "Randall?" She pushed up an eyelid, but only the white of his eye was visible. Sores ravaged his cheek and jaw. He wheezed and gasped for breath, as if suffocating.

She pushed him upright and felt his wrist for a pulse. His heart beat erratically, sometimes nearly stopping before racing again.

Koren bit her lip hard. No one could fake that. Even if he had been pretending earlier, he wasn't pretending now.

She looked toward the hidden door, lost again in the mural of the barrier wall. "Deference! Are you there?"

No one answered, and no glimmer of light appeared anywhere.

Koren pulled Randall close and combed her fingers through his hair. Her manacle brushed his neck but not enough to hurt him. "Thank you for not leaving me, dear friend. Deference will be back soon, and when I convince Taushin that I'm still on his side, maybe we can get out of this mess I made."

⇥·⇤

As Magnar descended toward the forest, Elyssa, still dangling from his claws, pumped her legs. She had to hit the ground running. With Tibalt and Fellina lying motionless on the ground, there was no time to lose.

A vulture stood on Fellina's head, pecking at her eye. Magnar shot a thin line of flames. Just as the huge black bird leaped to fly away, the fire blasted into it and ignited its feathers.

Elyssa's feet touched down. While Magnar swung around to land, she ran to the site, knocked the flaming vulture to the side, and knelt next to Fellina and Tibalt. Tibalt, shirtless and reddened by Solarus, lay face down, his hand still pressed against Fellina's underbelly, while Fellina lay with her neck curled toward him as if she had positioned herself to speak to him privately.

Elyssa set her fingers on Tibalt's throat, unable to avoid deep ulcers that exposed raw neck muscles. A pulse thrummed—weak and erratic. She placed her hand in front of Fellina's nostrils. A bare wisp of breath spread warmth across her skin.

Elyssa exhaled in relief.

"Healer!" Magnar said as he skittered to a stop beside her. "What do you detect?"

"They are alive, but barely." She opened her hand and looked at the medicine sphere in her palm. Next to Fellina's massive body it looked so small, but it would have to do. *Now how to divide it. Seventy percent for the dragon? Eighty?* This wasn't science; it was pure guesswork. And this medicine was designed to cure the disease, not a dying dragon. Still, it had stardrop material, so swallowing it should help.

She tore the sphere. "Magnar, please open Fellina's mouth."

Magnar shuffled into position and used his foreclaws to pry her mouth open. "She is resisting. I suggest you hurry."

Elyssa shoved the medicine fragment toward the back of Fellina's throat and jerked her arm out. "See if you can get her to swallow it while I work on Tibalt."

"Do you have a suggestion on how to accomplish that?"

"I don't know much about dragon anatomy. Maybe massage her jaws or stroke her neck muscles."

He puffed a blast of smoke, then shuffled closer and began to massage Fellina's throat clumsily with his foreclaws.

Elyssa turned Tibalt face up. His skin, hot to the touch, was dry and leathery. When his body shifted, his hand pulled away from a blood-soaked tunic and Fellina's wound. Blood still trickled from a six-inch gash, but not too badly.

She mashed the remaining medicine and rubbed it into Tibalt's chest, not much more than a mass of connected lesions. The ointment warmed, then grew hot. Tibalt flinched. Spasms ran across his bare arms, locking his wiry biceps.

"I think she swallowed it," Magnar said.

"Perfect. Thank you. We'll give it a little time to work."

Magnar touched Elyssa with a wing. "Let me know when I may assist you again."

"I will." She grasped his wing's mainstay and gazed into his eyes, not nearly as fiery as they were the first time they met. "We've come a long way, haven't we?"

Magnar bobbed his head. "Indeed. Perhaps an ancient rift can be mended."

After releasing Magnar's wing, Elyssa patted Tibalt's cheek. "Tibber? Can you hear me?"

Tibalt licked his parched lips. "I'm dreaming that a pretty girl is building a fire on my chest."

"It's me, Tibber. Elyssa."

He opened his eyes. They looked weak and dry. "Well, I was right about the pretty girl part."

Elyssa grinned. "You old charmer."

"I thought I was a goner. What did you do?"

She showed him the ointment residue on her fingers. "It's the medicine that supposedly cures the disease. It looks like it's working."

"What about Fellina?" He sat up a little and looked at the dragon's face. "Did you give her medicine?"

"By mouth. I'm only guessing that it'll help."

Tibalt dabbed the blood leaking from Fellina's wound. "Is there anything else we can do?"

"One more thing." Elyssa looked at Magnar. "Can you turn her on her back? I need access to her heart."

"I can. Help me by spreading her wings so they are not damaged when I turn her."

Elyssa jumped up and pulled one wing to the side. Tibalt slid to the other and held it in place. Using his tail and back legs, Magnar shoved her body until she shifted to her back.

"Now the hard part." Elyssa climbed onto Fellina's chest and straddled her. "I tried this on her once before. I think I did some good, but since she's so big, I don't know if I have enough energy."

Tibalt climbed to his feet and stood close to Elyssa. "Healing drains your energy?" he asked.

"Yes." Elyssa lifted her chain and showed him the pendant. "This manna wood channels my energy to Fellina, which activates the stardrop material inside her. The more energy she gets, the more she heals."

"I get it." Tibalt laid a hand on his stomach. "Does it work in reverse?"

"What do you mean?"

"I have that stardrop stuff on my skin. Can that pendant use that energy and send it into Fellina?"

"I suppose it could. Once I get the process started, whatever the pendant can absorb on the outside will be sent into Fellina." She gave him a quizzical look. "Why do you ask?"

"Just thinking. I'm not sure the medicine's going to heal me. It feels like a rabid porcupine is stirring my guts into a stew with a pitchfork."

"I didn't give you much. I'll try to save some energy for you."

He smiled and patted her cheek. "Don't worry about me. Heal Fellina. She deserves better than to let those human haters knock her out of the sky."

"Too much chatter," Magnar said, thrusting his head between them. "Proceed with the healing."

Elyssa ignored him. "Let me try first."

She turned and laid her hand on Fellina's chest. Her scales were thick and hard, making them difficult to penetrate, but after several seconds, the stardrop came into focus. "I've got it. Now to give it a boost."

As she concentrated on the channel, the pendant began to glow. Energy drained from her body. Her arms ached, and dizziness swam through her head. Inside Fellina, unseen except to her probing senses, the medicine sphere expanded, and thin lines of radiance shot out in all directions, as if sending healing power throughout Fellina's body.

"Elyssa," Tibalt said, "you look like you're losing a fight with a battering ram."

Gasping for breath, she nodded. "It's draining me. I think it's working, but I don't know how long I can hold out."

"Well, let me ride that pony. I'll help you lasso that fireball." Tibalt climbed onto Fellina's chest in front of Elyssa and scooted as close as he could, face to face. He grabbed the pendant and pressed it against his chest. "Let's see what happens now."

"Tibalt!" She tried to snatch the pendant back, but he held on. "You're too weak. If it drains you —"

He returned her gaze squarely. "I know. Just keep channeling, or whatever it is you do." Tibalt's voice weakened. "Like I said, she deserves it. Besides, those slaves need a warrior dragon on their side more than an old coot like me."

"Magnar," Elyssa said, trying to calm her breathing, "try to wake her up. Once we know she's not going to die, we can stop."

"Yes, of course." Magnar nudged her head with his snout. "Fellina. You must awaken. These humans are trying to help you, and their efforts are endangering them."

Fellina lifted her head. "Magnar?"

"There!" Elyssa said, pointing. "She's up. She's going to be all right."

Tibalt released the pendant. His shoulders slumped, and his head drooped.

"Tibalt?" She prodded his arm. "You did it! Without you I could never have—"

He fell to the side and toppled to the ground.

"Tibber!" Elyssa leaped down and pulled him into her arms. "Tibber, are you all right?"

Fellina scrambled to right herself and snaked her neck to bring her head close to Tibalt's face. "He is breathing, but he carries a death rattle in his chest."

"Oh, Tibber!" Elyssa drew his emaciated body close and rocked him as she wept. "You didn't have to do that. Healing is my job."

Magnar brought his head close as well. "His heroism is astonishing. I have never seen such a sacrifice among the slaves here—and for a dragon no less."

"I'm a hero?" Tibalt murmured.

"Tibber?" Elyssa lowered him to her lap. "Yes, you're a hero, one of the greatest."

His eyelids fluttered. "Don't heroes get a medal?"

"Absolutely." Elyssa looked at Magnar. "Isn't that right?"

"If my recommendation carries any weight," Magnar said, "he will receive the highest honors possible."

"I always wanted a medal, but they don't give those out in the dungeon." Tibalt's eyelids settled closed, and his head lolled to the side.

"Tibber?" Elyssa kneaded his scalp. "Tibber! Say something!"

"He is gone," Fellina said. "Flown to be with the Creator."

"Nooo!" Elyssa wailed. "It can't be! He's not a soldier! He's not a warrior! He's ... he's ..." She pulled him close and rocked him again. "He's my friend."

Fellina touched Magnar with a wing. "What are we to do?"

"We must join the battle against the Benefile and Taushin's forces. It goes poorly for us. We are desperately needed."

"But we cannot leave Elyssa here alone."

"Go, Fellina," Elyssa said through a narrowed throat. "I'll find my way back."

"You cannot carry Tibalt's body that far. You are too weak, and you cannot leave a hero's body to the vultures."

"I will carry him," Magnar said. "It will be an honor."

A new voice sounded from the forest. "I'll take care of him."

Wallace ran into the clearing and knelt at Tibalt's side. "I've been watching for a while. I didn't want to poke my nose where it doesn't belong."

Elyssa laid a hand on Wallace's shoulder. "You'll keep the vultures away until we come back?"

"I'll do better than that." Wallace lifted the wooden figure from his trousers. "While I'm waiting, I'll make a carving just like this one. A hero deserves that, right?"

"A permanent image of Tibalt." Elyssa slid Tibalt's body to the ground. "Thank you. I'm sure he'd appreciate that."

Fellina bobbed her head. "We will be sure to honor this courageous human after the battle is won."

"And I," Magnar said as he stretched out his powerful wings, "will fight like I never have before. The humans will be set free. I swear it."

Elyssa rose and touched Magnar's wing. "Shall I ride on you?"

"It will be an honor." Magnar lowered his head, allowing Elyssa to climb to his back. When she settled, he and Fellina took to the air. As they ascended, Wallace picked up a stray branch, sat next to Tibalt, and began whittling the bark.

Elyssa straightened and looked ahead. New tears for Tibalt tried to emerge, but she shook the sadness away. Too many battles lay ahead, along with too many healings. Conserving energy was paramount.

She clutched the pendant and pressed it against her chest. This symbol of hope had drained the life of a dear friend. It brought joy and sorrow at the same moment. The rejoicing over a healed dragon was drowned in laments.

Closing her eyes, Elyssa breathed a quick prayer. "Creator, may this instrument of healing never be a cause for weeping again. And may I be as courageous as the hero from the dungeon. Let me take up his sword and fight in his name."

twenty

*J*ason rolled out of the broken hay cart and stood upright. His back sore from the tumble, he stretched it out. Deference's "other way out" wasn't exactly what he had in mind. "Okay, Deference, that worked."

"Good." She appeared at his side, waving a hand at the ground. "Don't forget your sword."

He picked up the scabbard and looked toward the front of the Zodiac. "Are you going back to Koren now?"

"I'll come with you. If I can see what's going on, I can report it to Koren. It's easy for me to go through the main corridor even without a floor. If you let me ride on your back, I'll stay invisible."

"Okay. Go ahead."

Gripping with her sparkling hands, she shimmied up his back, raising a sea of tingling goose bumps. She wrapped her arms around his neck, whispered, "I'm ready," and faded from sight.

Jason attached the scabbard to his belt. "Let's go."

He drew his sword, jogged to the corner, and peeked around. Above the portico roof, dragons battled in the air, screaming and spitting fire and ice. Three white dragons zipped up, down, and around as if able to turn without regard to momentum. The Southlands dragons seemed slow and lethargic by comparison, perhaps exhausted by combat. Even though they outnumbered the white dragons ten to one, they were clearly outmatched.

Soldiers from Major Four stood around the portico, weapons and shields ready. At the top of the stairs, many slaves had gathered in a tightly packed group, most sitting and some standing in a short line. Jason's father stood at the front of the line, facing the others, his body and head bent.

Keeping his head and sword low, Jason ran toward the portico. He dodged a frozen dragon and came upon a human body curled on its side about ten paces before the bottom of the stairs. With long hair covering her face and curves drawing a post-adolescent figure, she appeared to be about fifteen or sixteen. Wearing the short trousers of a labor slave, her legs were bare, save for deep sores from ankles to knees.

Jason pushed her hair back, revealing her ravaged face. Although marred by sores, she looked a little like Elyssa.

"She's dead," a man leaning on a staff called from the top of the stairs.

"Are you sure?" Jason pressed his fingers against the girl's neck and checked for a pulse. Nothing. He set a hand in front of her mouth and nose but felt no air. After turning her to her back, he laid his ear against her chest and listened, holding a hand over his other ear to shut out the screaming dragons.

"Should I go now?" Deference whispered.

"Can you check this girl for a heartbeat first?"

"Sure." She climbed down from Jason's back and sank into the girl's body. A few seconds later, her head protruded from the girl's chest. "It's beating. Just a flutter, but she's alive."

As soon as Deference fully emerged, Jason sheathed his sword and scooped the girl into his arms. A quick scan of the street revealed at least thirty more bodies, some frozen and some likely victims of the disease. "Can you check all the rest? If you find anyone alive, come and tell me."

Deference curtsied. "I beg your pardon, Jason, but what about Koren? She's waiting for me."

"She's all right for now. Finding survivors is more urgent."

"I understand." Deference glanced at the portico, then rushed to the closest body and sank into it.

Jason hurried up the stairs, where the man with a wooden staff met him and used it to walk at his side. With a few strands of gray in otherwise dark hair, he appeared to be in his forties. "My name's Benjamin. Is there any way I can help you?"

"Don't you have the disease?"

"Sure. It hurts like a hundred whips, but I can't let that stop me from helping."

Jason hiked the girl higher in his arms. "Then stay close. Maybe we can figure out what to do."

Benjamin nodded at her. "She's a breeder, and a daughter of a breeder. She never knew her parents, and she's had maybe three children already, but the breeding forewomen took them from her right away."

"Does she have a name?"

"I heard someone call her Bantur, the dragon word for ugly, but I think her real name is Kenna."

"Kenna. Such a pretty name." Stepping around the seated and prone bodies, Jason made his way to his father and presented Kenna. "She's barely alive."

"As are many here." Edison swept his finger around the inner wall of a little bowl, scooping up a pink salve. "There's enough medicine left for only one more. Even your brother isn't getting any."

A wave of murmurs rose and quickly settled.

Jason looked around. "Is Adrian here?"

"Not Adrian." Edison point toward the Zodiac's doorway. "Frederick."

A body lay near the door, guarded by Taushin and Mallerin. The two dragons sat and watched, as if waiting for something. A man carrying a limp little girl stood nearby, peeking into the Zodiac's entry corridor.

Jason shifted his gaze to a man standing at the front of the medicine waiting line. In his arms he held an infant who lay just as motionless as the girl Jason carried.

"Can we get more medicine?" Jason asked.

Edison smeared the remaining ointment on the infant's chest. "We need some ingredients—stardrop material and Cassabrie's genetics."

"I heard that Cassabrie's coming this way. I know how to get stardrop material."

"And her genetics?"

"I have some. It's probably not enough to cure everyone, and from what Koren told me it won't make a permanent cure, but it should help." Jason laid Kenna down and
ripped his tunic open in front, exposing the litmus finger
embedded in his chest. "Cut it out of my skin."

Edison's brow shot up. "Cut it out? Son, are you sure?"

"It's not very deep. Just a small cut should do it. You
should be able to reach in and pull it out."

"That's not what I mean. I know you're not afraid of pain.
But won't that take away your immunity to the disease?"

"I'm willing to risk facing what you, my brothers, and
all these other people are already suffering. If we can't all
get the medicine, then I won't get it either. At least we can
ease some suffering for a little while."

"Very well." Edison touched a sheath at his hip. "I have
a dagger, but I blunted it trying to get Frederick out of the
ice."

Jason glanced back at Benjamin, who now stood watching intently from a few paces away. "Can you help?"

Benjamin lowered his staff and limped to Jason's side.
"Name it."

"Are you able to stand well enough to steady my sword
while my father cuts with the tip?"

"Without a doubt." Benjamin drew the sword from
Jason's scabbard and held it firmly.

Edison pinched the blade and set the tip against the
outline of the litmus finger. "Are you ready?"

Jason closed his eyes and nodded. "Do it."

A sharp pain jabbed his chest. As gasps rose from
the crowd, warm liquid dripped down Jason's torso and

spilled over his trousers waistband. He peeked at his chest. Edison pushed against Jason's skin until the finger protruded from the cut.

Benjamin lowered the sword. "You're braver than I am, young man."

Jason pinched the litmus finger and dropped it to his palm. It glowed bright blue through a smear of blood, warm to the touch. It seemed smaller than before, probably due to his body absorbing part of it.

A woman hobbled to him and dabbed his wound with a cloth. "Don't worry. It's clean."

Jason flinched, not only from pain but also because the disease likely swarmed all over this "clean" cloth. Still, the infection would come anyway. It was only a matter of time.

He took the cloth and pressed it over the wound, whispering, "Thank you."

"If you get stardrop material ..." Edison displayed a small bowl in his palm. "This is what they put the medicine in."

Jason took the bowl and shoved it into his trousers pocket.

"An impressive sacrifice, Jason Masters." Taushin shuffled toward them, Mallerin at his side, cradling Frederick in her forelegs. "I suspect that your escape was equally impressive."

Jason glared at him. No use giving away any information, especially if it meant trouble for Koren.

As the dragons drew near, Benjamin and the other slaves shifted to give them room, some on their own power and the others helped along. Mallerin laid Frederick gently on the floor, then drew back several steps.

"I know you lack trust in me," Taushin continued, "so I offer your loved one freely with no conditions. He still lives. When you make the new medicine, I hope it heals him and everyone else."

Jason looked at Frederick. The bluish tint to his lips and skin raised a chill. "You're right about one thing. I don't trust you. What's in it for you?"

"As I said, there are no conditions. Of course, I do hope that my gesture will soften your heart toward me. As I am sure you noticed, the battle is going poorly for my side, and if the Benefile are victorious, you will find that their version of slavery makes ours compassionate by comparison."

"So you want me to do something to help you in the battle."

"Not in battle. I am ready to signal a retreat before I lose all my dragons. I will send them to a refuge the Benefile cannot enter. They might give chase, but they might also stay here to finish their destruction of the slaves. In either case, they will eventually destroy the remaining humans. It will not matter that some are on the mend, and they will not listen to claims of a cure while the disease is still ravaging so many. They know about Darksphere, so they will try to repopulate this world by taking some from your world after the disease is gone." Taushin cast his eyebeams on Jason's chest. "What I need is for you to keep the Benefile here until Cassabrie comes. When they see her, they will be overcome by her presence, and she will have an opportunity to hypnotize them. They will then be vulnerable to an attack."

"I see. You want us to kill the Benefile for you while Cassabrie has them hypnotized."

"You are a gifted thinker, as I expected."

"A surprise attack while they can't defend themselves." Jason smiled, but the twist in his face felt wrong. Why would satisfaction sprout from such an attack, a cowardly ambush? The Benefile were dangerous, yes, but to slaughter them in their sleep? Who could find pleasure in that?

"Give me a minute to think." He looked at Taushin, then at the finger in his hand. The devil of a dragon had bided his time until the litmus finger was removed. With Cassabrie's influence gone, he moved in and plied his deceptive trade.

Jason closed his fist around the finger. So this was how Koren felt while dressed in black. Taushin infected her mind and injected influences she didn't know how to deal with. Being a slave all her life, she always had to say yes to whatever she was told. And now that Koren had been set free, Taushin was looking for new victims.

"And I nearly gave in, too." Jason laughed under his breath. "You plan to attack us after we've done your dirty work."

"Not at all. We—"

"Just stop it, Taushin. I'm not buying it. I've seen enough of what you did to Koren to know not to listen to you. I shouldn't have let you get two words out of your mouth." Jason grabbed the sword from Benjamin. Clutching it tightly, he glared at Taushin, then at Mallerin. Her head swayed like a snake ready to strike, and sparks fell from her nostrils. One false move, and hundreds of slaves would die. No wonder Father allowed Taushin and his mother to stay here. Even though they probably had enough soldiers to defeat two dragons, they couldn't risk innocent lives.

"Just get out of my sight," Jason said as he lowered his sword. "We can take care of ourselves."

"We will leave, but perhaps you will tell me how you escaped from the chains Koren put you in. Did she find the key and release you, or do you have talents of which I am not aware?"

"I'm not going to tell you anything. Just leave."

"Then I will ask Koren when I next see her. She is more pliable than you are." Taushin and Mallerin lifted into the air as one and flew down to the street. When they landed, Mallerin looked up while Taushin kept his eye-beams on her, both apparently watching for Cassabrie.

Jason knelt between Frederick and Kenna and touched each with a hand, his fist still closed around Cassabrie's finger. They both seemed lifeless. He laid his ear on Kenna's chest again. Although it was quieter under the roof, the cries of battling dragons still flooded his ears.

"I'm here," Deference whispered from his back. "You wouldn't believe how hard it was to get past everyone without being seen by Mallerin."

"I believe it." With Mallerin's evil eyes always trained on him, Jason kept his whisper as quiet as possible. "Can you check Kenna again?"

"Sure. By the way, I couldn't find any living slaves out there. They're all dead, including the frozen ones."

"Okay. Try to hurry."

Deference zipped from Jason's back and into Kenna's chest. Jason raised his head and set a hand in front of

Kenna's lips. Not a puff of breath touched his fingers. After a few seconds, Deference's eyes appeared on Kenna's tunic, blinking. "I'm sorry, Jason. She's dead."

"That's what I was afraid of." He gestured with his head. "When you get a clear path, go back to Koren."

"Okay." She sank back down.

Jason shifted his hand to Kenna's cheek. The poor girl was left out on the street like a pile of trash. No parents to mourn her. No one to carry her up the stairs to get out of the rain of fire and ice. She surely died alone.

"She's dead."

Edison knelt beside him. "At least you tried."

"Yeah, but it wasn't enough." Jason slid over to Frederick and grasped his clammy hand. "Now we just have to wait for Cassabrie."

"Edison?" A little girl walked toward them from the Zodiac's entry, a man following.

Edison looked up. "Reesa! I'm so glad you're feeling better!"

"Me, too." She lifted her shirt and rubbed her finger across some leftover ointment. "I have a little extra for your son and that girl. I hope it's enough."

The man with the infant stooped with them. The little boy wiggled in his arms, his sores mostly faded. "We can find some, too," the man said.

"I'm afraid it's too late for Kenna," Jason said, "but I appreciate whatever you can do for my brother."

Benjamin pointed at Jason with his staff and called out, "Everyone who has some extra medicine, put it on this young man's brother. We need warriors like him to go out and fight." Spreading his arms widely, he shouted, "Look at us! We've been sitting here like defeated donkeys, our backs slack and our tails between our legs. I don't care how sick you are; we can't let these men fight alone. There aren't enough of them. If they die, we die. That's no worse than living like cowards."

A few weak cheers rose from the crowd, but they quickly faded. At least ten children pressed close, each one with a finger raised. One after another, they smeared ointment across Frederick's face and rubbed it in.

Jason had to bite his lip to keep it from trembling. These slave children were giving all they could, and it might turn out to be the greatest treasure they could imagine.

By the time they finished, Frederick's lips had turned from blue to pink. His cheeks flushed red. Then he blinked, looked around, and smiled. "Well, this is a pretty sight. Look at all these beautiful children."

The children clapped their hands and bounced on their toes. Jason grasped Frederick's wrist and hoisted him to his feet. Edison joined them and wrapped both his sons in a powerful hug.

Jason punched Frederick's arm. "Are you ready to go back to battle?"

"Ready, little brother." Frederick touched the sword at his hip. "What's the word?"

"The Southlands dragons might retreat soon, so I say we battle them now and try to keep them here. It's the best way to get help from the Benefile."

"Won't we add to their desire to retreat?" Edison asked.

Jason shook his head. "Not if we capture Taushin."

"Good point, but what about Mallerin?"

"I'll handle Mallerin." Benjamin limped closer, his staff resting against his shoulder. "Just provide a distraction."

"Any particular kind of distraction?" Jason asked.

Benjamin leaned to the side and peered at the sky. "I see Magnar is back in battle. If you could call him down, I think that will be the only distraction Mallerin will need. He's her mate, and they have an unsettled feud."

"A dragon spat as a distraction," Edison said, nodding. "Will she attack Magnar?"

Benjamin smacked his staff with his palm. "Not if you get the Benefile to attack him first. One strange thing about dragons and their mates. They might scratch and claw each other, but if someone else threatens one, the other comes to its defense."

Edison nodded again. "I have seen that in humans as well. It could work."

"Father," Jason said, "remember the war story you told us about the Piedmont Campaign?"

"Feigning dissension?"

"Right." Jason sheathed his sword. "Just follow my lead."

"Whatever you decide to do," Benjamin said, "wait for me to get into position, then call Magnar down to join you. I'll do the rest. When Mallerin leaves Taushin by himself, be ready to take him." He hobbled down the stairs on the grottoes side, ducking to avoid the fiery rain.

Frederick drew his sword. "Let's do it."

"I'm ready." Jason wrapped the litmus finger in the cloth the woman gave him and pushed it into his pocket. "Since Magnar is back, maybe Elyssa is, too. We'll go to Arxad's cave next."

Jason, Frederick, and Edison hurried down the stairs. At the bottom, they summoned Captain Reed and the other soldiers. Ten stayed to guard the portico while the rest gathered at the bottom of the stairway. Above, the dragons continued their aerial battle. With only twenty or so Southlands dragons remaining, it wouldn't last much longer, especially with Magnar fighting against both species, shooting and clawing any dragon within range. He seemed to be the most powerful force in the sky, larger than any other dragon, though not as fast and agile as the Benefile.

Edison cupped a hand around his mouth and shouted, "Magnar! Come to us!"

After slapping a drone with his tail, the mighty dragon flew down and landed on the run. When he stopped in front of the soldiers, he panted showers of sparks. "Have you finally decided to join the battle, as you promised?"

"We cannot fly," Edison said, "and our spears are ineffective from this distance. If you have a way to bring the battle to us, we will gladly join it."

Magnar pointed at the sky with a wing. "The key is to lure the Benefile down. We need to do something that would require punishment. Beth is their leader. If she comes, the others will follow."

Jason glanced at Benjamin. Standing next to Mallerin about thirty paces down the street, Benjamin pointed toward the portico. Mallerin rose from her haunches. Even from this distance, the fire in her eyes was obvious.

"Will you be the bait?" Jason asked.

Magnar bobbed his head. "I am willing, but I expect you to be my allies and fight with me."

"To the death," Edison said, "but be ready for surprises. This deception will take perfect coordination."

"I'll be right back." Jason hustled up the stairs, scooped up Kenna, and carried her down to the street. After laying her in front of Magnar, he called out, "Beth! Look at this dead girl!"

Above, Beth descended several feet and flew in an orbit over them. "Why have you summoned me? There are many dead girls."

"This girl was a breeder, forced into the worst kind of slavery by a savage, uncaring dragon." Jason pointed at Magnar. "And here is the culprit. Justice demands that he be punished, but he has eluded you. I demand that you come and execute justice. If you refuse, then justice itself will cry out against your apathy."

Beth dove and landed in front of Jason. "Stand back, human, and we will focus our wrath on this evil son of corruption."

Magnar's eyes flared. For the first time, he appeared frightened.

"Back off!" Edison stepped in front of Magnar and waved his sword. "I will not allow anyone to hurt my ally!" Captain Reed and ten other soldiers joined him and blocked Beth's way.

Beth let out a high-pitched whistle. The other two Benefile broke off from the battle and landed behind her, while the Southlands dragons flew to the edge of the grottoes and settled in a group, panting and gasping.

"Now you have too few allies, Magnar." Beth's eyes shone bright blue, and her voice rumbled like distant thunder. "It is finally time to face justice."

Jason checked his sword in his scabbard and grabbed Frederick's sleeve. "Let's go!" They ran side by side toward Taushin. Mallerin passed them going in the opposite direction. Blind and alone, Taushin shouted something in the dragon language, but his mother continued her flying charge toward Magnar.

"I'll get the neck," Jason said. "You go after the belly."

"I hear you, fiends!" Taushin shouted in the human tongue as he reared back his head. "Do not approach or—"

"Or what?" Jason leaped up his tail and ran across his spiny ridge. When he reached the top of Taushin's back, he grabbed the black neck and pulled back as hard as he could.

When Taushin reared up, Frederick pricked the vulnerable spot with his blade. "Don't move a muscle!"

Taushin froze, his head high and Jason riding his neck eight feet in the air. "Imbeciles! I am your only hope against the Benefile! My plan was proceeding perfectly, but you are ruining it. You are blinder than I am."

"You're not fooling anyone," Jason growled. "The day of dragon deception is over. Just be quiet and still, or you're dead."

Back at the portico, Mallerin landed on Beth's back and began clawing and biting. The other two Benefile sprayed her with ice. Edison, Captain Reed, and the other soldiers charged into the fray. Magnar joined them. Swinging blades gleamed. Wings and tails thrashed. Flames splashed against shields. Spears cracked and splintered. The other Southlands dragons launched toward the chaos. In seconds, the battle would turn into a bloodbath.

"Jason!" Frederick called. "Let's go!"

"What about Taushin?"

"We brought the battle to the ground. It's time for us to join it." Frederick flexed his arm, as if ready to plunge the blade. Taushin beat his wings, shot backwards, and whipped his neck, flinging Jason off.

Jason rolled and sat up. Frederick grabbed Jason's wrist and hoisted him to his feet. As they ran, Taushin flew toward the battle. Just as he slammed into the turmoil, the other dragons crashed in as well.

A light flashed in the sky, and a loud cry sounded. "Stop! Cease your fighting!"

Every swinging arm, beating wing, and snapping jaw fell limp. Heads angled toward the light, eyes wide. Exodus floated toward them from the direction of the barrier wall, still high but descending. Cassabrie stood within on the curved floor, her arms and cloak spread. Streams of light flowed from her eyes, though her face seemed strained, labored.

As she drew nearer to the crowd, she slowed. Jason jogged alongside, his scabbard whipping his leg. Humans and dragons alike squinted, some lifting arms or wings to block the brilliant glow. Blood flowed from cuts and gashes, but no one seemed to notice.

Jason slowed his pace to stay abreast of the decelerating star. "Is something wrong?"

"Something is pulling me, drawing me away." Cassabrie's voice was strained, as if she were carrying a heavy load. "The force is almost irresistible."

"Can I help?"

"I don't know. I'm not sure what's causing it."

"I might know. Maybe I should try—"

"Oh! I think I have it under control now." Exodus stopped a few paces from the edge of the battleground. Cassabrie lowered her arms, her face pain-streaked. Sighing, she looked at Jason. "So it has come to this? All-out war?"

"Unfortunately." Jason let his gaze pass across the scene. Dragons sat in various positions in a haphazard line from the bottom of the portico's western stairway westward about a hundred paces. Soldiers stood in their midst. With swords and spears drawn and clutched stiffly, they looked like life-sized toys. Edison and Frederick stood back to back. Although blood trickled from a cut on Frederick's cheek, they both seemed healthy. Some dead slaves lay here and there, while most of the living stayed under the portico roof. They, including Benjamin, stared without moving.

"Why am I not hypnotized?" Jason asked.

"You were. I released you immediately."

Taushin shuffled out from the crowd, his body teetering. "I see you, Starlighter. My mother has her gaze fixed on you." He stopped next to Jason and settled on his haunches. "What do you intend to do?"

"I am the liberator." Cassabrie grimaced, and a grunt blended with her words. "I assume you know what that means."

"I do, and I also know what is causing your struggle. If you will release my mother so that I will have mobile eyes, I will tell you so that you may fight it more effectively."

"So you can escape the battle like a coward," Jason said. "You plan to fly to a hiding place."

"The human who attacks a blind enemy speaks against cowardice. Your hypocrisy astounds me." Taushin cast his eyebeams on Cassabrie. "I need you to release my mother."

Cassabrie batted through the beams. "You have no influence over me. I renounced my alliance with darkness long ago."

"Then hear my appeal. I need my mother's vision and power so that we can destroy the Benefile while they are entranced. It is our only hope of survival. They will destroy me and all the other Southlands dragons, and when they learn that all the humans are infected, they will destroy them as well."

"Now who is the hypocrite?" Cassabrie asked. "Would you slaughter the Benefile while they are unable to defend themselves?"

Taushin dipped his head. "I grant your point, but I will choose hypocrisy over annihilation."

"Cassabrie"—Jason pulled the wrapped finger from his pocket—"there's a cure to the disease. If we can make more, the Benefile won't kill us. All we need is star-drop material. We have the immune genetics."

She drew Exodus closer and looked at his hand. "You have immune genetics in that cloth?"

Jason opened it over his palm, revealing the blood-smeared finger. "Yes."

Cassabrie lifted her hand and looked at the gap in her fingers. "Your search for a cure is misguided. You are masking the symptoms but not killing the disease. It will return."

"But it could buy us some time. Fewer people will die, and maybe the Benefile won't know the difference."

"Fear neither death nor the Benefile. Mercy will triumph over both."

Exodus began drawing away. Cassabrie pushed against the forward wall, slowing its motion, but it continued backing up.

"Release Mallerin!" Taushin shouted. "We must destroy the Benefile or we all will perish!"

Jason pushed the finger back into his pocket. "If you release her, I'll need protection! Give me Magnar and my father and brother!"

Her eyes wide, Cassabrie waved her arms. "I release you all!" Then she lifted higher.

Jason leaped and grasped for Exodus. His fingers dug into the membrane but quickly slipped away, leaving his hands filled with scalding radiance.

As he molded the particles into a big ball, the battlers shook their heads as if waking from a deep sleep.

Taushin shouted, "Mother! We must take Jason to Arxad's cave!"

Mallerin leaped into the air, grabbed Jason's tunic with her back claws, and lifted him into the air. Taushin joined them and flew at Jason's side.

Still molding the ball, Jason glared at him. "What are you up to now?"

"Saving your people and foiling the Benefile."

"For what purpose? There must be something in it for you."

"There is, but I need not tell you. Just be assured that I will help you make and deliver the medicine. As you told Cassabrie, at least this will buy you some time."

His hands burning terribly, Jason twisted and looked back. The battle continued, but the low angle allowed only a view from the side. Above the portico, Cassabrie pushed Exodus toward the north, but the Reflections Crystal pulled her back toward the dome room.

Jason gritted his teeth. If only he could help Cassabrie break free. Yet, that was impossible. She would have to fight that battle herself. Fortunately, she had the power to do so.

As Mallerin flew close to Arxad's cave, she dropped Jason off in front of the entrance, then swerved to avoid it. Hitting the ground running, Jason let his momentum carry him inside. A lantern sat on a tabletop, creating a pair of silhouettes on the table's surface in the shape of a human and a dragon.

Jason dashed to the table and held out his hands. The radiance lit up the surrounding faces—Elyssa and Fellina. "Quick!" Jason shouted. "There's a container in my trousers pocket. Get it out!"

"The crucible?" Elyssa yanked it from his pocket and set it on the table. Jason balanced the ball on top.

"Stories later!" Jason blew on one hand while pulling the cloth from his tunic pocket. He laid it out on the table and peeled the sticky material from the finger. "Now you should have all the ingredients. When you make the medicine, bring it to the Zodiac. My father and brother are in mortal combat, so I have to go."

When he turned to leave, Elyssa grabbed his wrist. "Tibber is dead."

Jason stared at her. A huge lump swelled in his throat. "Tibber? Dead?"

Her lips trembling, she nodded. "He died a hero." Her voice pitched higher. "He saved Fellina's life."

Jason looked at Fellina. With his throat so tight, he couldn't squeeze out a word.

"It is true," Fellina said. "Magnar would not let me join the battle because of my open wound, but Elyssa has stitched me quite well, so I will now fight in Tibalt's name."

Jason swallowed, loosening his throat. "So where is his body?"

"Don't worry. We have someone guarding him." Elyssa pulled Jason into her arms and whispered into his ear. "Don't forget our promise. We all go home together, dead or alive. And you know what to do with the medallion."

Heat from her medallion radiated across his skin and into the recent incision. Warmth flowed, similar to the warmth Cassabrie brought when she dwelt within. Yet this sensation was fuller, more luxuriant, a message of love and healing. Every ache and pain in his body eased.

He pulled back, keeping a hold on her hand. "I will honor the promise, and that medallion will be around your neck when I walk down the wedding aisle."

Tears welling, Elyssa kissed him on the cheek and stepped back. "Go get 'em, warrior!"

Jason spun in place and ran from the cave, his sword again slapping his leg. The sounds of battle rolled down the rise — grunts, growls, screams, and clashing of metal on scales. In a matter of moments, he would be battling for his life and for the lives of his family and newfound friends.

Drawing his sword, he continued running. *And that's exactly what I came here to do.*

twenty-one

Koren stared at the open ceiling. Surely Taushin would show up soon. Even if Fellina was badly hurt, what could Taushin and Mallerin do to help her? Bring her to the Zodiac? She looked at Randall, still unconscious at her side. If only he would wake up and show some sign that he wasn't near death. At least she wouldn't worry about him so much.

She shifted her gaze to the hidden door Jason and Deference had gone through. Deference should have returned by now. Only she could bring the key, but she had to wait for Taushin to arrive first. Once he was convinced that Jason had escaped on his own, Deference could slip the key to her. But when would everyone show up? With all the terrible noises outside, maybe it would take a long time.

A light glimmered above. High in the sky, Exodus descended.

Koren rose to her knees. Taushin wasn't here yet to hatch his plan. Maybe she could secretly warn Cassabrie before he arrived.

Her heart pounding, she looked again at Exodus. The star flew straight toward the dome room. Inside, Cassabrie shoved frantically against the wall to her right, as if trying to redirect its course.

As Exodus continued downward, the Reflections Crystal pulsed wildly. A shaft of light shot out from the sphere and attached to the star, like a radiant spear stabbing a flying dragon. As if pulled by the beam, Exodus drew closer and closer. Cassabrie pounded on the star's back wall but to no avail. Finally, Exodus rested on top of the crystal, wobbling for a moment before settling in a perfectly balanced position, a large sphere atop a smaller one.

The Reflections Crystal slowly grew brighter, while Exodus dimmed at the same rate. Cassabrie fell to her knees and covered the connection point with her hands, white radiance streaming from her eyes. "Don't drain the star!" she shouted. "I need its energy!"

Koren lunged, but the chains held fast. "Cassabrie! Is there any way I can help?"

"Koren?" Cassabrie stared at her. "Are you all right?"

She jerked at a chain. "I'm trapped."

Cassabrie's eyebeams penetrated the star's membrane and washed across Koren's face. "Who put you in chains?"

"I did it myself to fool Taushin, but I have access to a key." Koren shouted toward the hidden door. "Deference! Where are you?"

"Deference is here?" Cassabrie shook her head and refocused on the connection point between the two spheres. "Never mind. I need some kind of plug to stop Exodus from draining into the Reflections Crystal. Long ago, the crystal was beneath the floor of the star chamber in the Northlands, so there were rocks between it and Exodus. That barrier made the energy drainage too slow to notice."

"What do you need? A rock? A board?"

"Almost anything solid." Cassabrie jumped up and threw herself against the inner wall. Exodus vibrated slightly but didn't budge. Cassabrie slid on her back down to the star's floor and sighed. "If you have any ideas, I'm listening. Once Exodus is drained, it will die, and I will die with it."

Koren jerked both chains as hard as she could. The links rang, but the manacles just tore at her wrists. The hooks embedded in the floor creaked but wouldn't give way. The granite tiles were too strong. "I'm so sorry, Cassabrie. I did this so Jason could get away. I thought I would have access to the key, but Deference isn't here to get it for me."

"How strange that I didn't know this." Cassabrie knelt again at the connection point and touched the inner membrane. "Maybe the Reflections Crystal is not allowing the events in here to reach me. It seems to absorb various kinds of energy, so the tales are not exiting this room."

Koren rose to her knees and leaned as close as she could. With Exodus taking up half of the dome room, the outer wall was only a few paces away. "Taushin probably knows you can't see what he's been plotting here. He wants to trap you and use you to heal the slaves. I think he wants to influence you to give him parts of your body."

Cassabrie furrowed her brow. "Parts of my body? What makes you think Taushin wants that?"

"To make more medicine to heal the slaves. He thinks I will give myself over to him if more than half the slaves are healed. He wants me to be his eyes."

Cassabrie shoved the wall with her hands to no avail. "Well, it seems that the trap has already been sprung, but don't fool yourself. He has no desire to use my body parts to help the slaves. He simply wants vision and power, and he is skillfully filling your ears with lies and guiding events in hopes that one of us will be persuaded to give in."

"His schemes will fail. I won't be persuaded."

Cassabrie's pained expression returned. "Are you listening to yourself? You put your own wrists in manacles! Koren, how many more times are you going to enslave yourself? You think you won't be persuaded to join the darkness, but your bonds say otherwise."

Koren jerked a chain again, but the effort brought only more pain. "I provided for a key. It's just not here yet. My reason for locking myself in this room was to explain Jason's escape and to be sure I could warn you about Taushin's plot."

"I appreciate your loving motivations, but don't expect to outwit a master deceiver by playing his game." Cassabrie nodded toward the exit doorway. "Taushin knows Jason is free, and he has not come here to see how or why he escaped. He has thrown a net over you by giving you the idea that he wants to hurt me. Even if you were not in chains, he knows you would not leave. He is using your love against you. Such is his devilry."

Koren shook her chains. "Then all of this was a waste!"

"Not necessarily." Cassabrie's voice weakened to a whisper. "Your confinement might be just what I need."

"What *you* need? How?"

Cassabrie laid herself down in a curl, her eyes still on Koren. "When mercy is offered to the many, and the one who is supposed to deliver it fails to act, we never know when or if another offer will come. Invitations are precious." She closed her eyes and said no more.

"Cassabrie!" Koren lunged, but the chains again held her in place. "What do you mean? Am I supposed to deliver the mercy? How can I do it while in chains?"

Koren closed her eyes and slapped her hand against the floor. How much more frustrating could it get? She locked herself here to warn and protect Cassabrie, and now Cassabrie was dying and the chains and manacles kept her from helping at all.

"Koren?"

Koren looked toward the voice. "Yes?"

Deference appeared at the doorway to the main entry corridor. "I'm here. Sorry about the delay. Jason needed me, and it took longer to crawl along the wall than I thought it would."

"Do you have the key?"

As Deference approached, she pointed at the hidden door. "It's still where Jason hid it. I'll get it now."

"No. Wait." Koren nodded toward at the trunk. "The lid to that trunk is loose. Can you move it?"

Deference glided to the trunk and set her fingers under the lid. "A little at a time, I think. It has to be lighter than Randall."

"We don't have much time. Cassabrie is dying. Someone has to push the lid between Exodus and the Reflections Crystal, or maybe even knock Exodus away."

"I'll try," Deference said, "but the crystal draws me toward it. I think it might swallow me if I get too close." As she stood in place, she slowly faded away.

"No! I don't want it to swallow you."

"But if Cassabrie is dying—"

"Randall!" Koren elbowed him in the ribs. "If you can hear me, we need you now!"

He fell to the side again. This time Koren caught him and bit his ear as hard as she could.

"Augh!" Randall shot up and banged his head against Koren's chin. He climbed to his feet and swayed in place while rubbing his ear. "What's going on?"

Koren pointed at the trunk. "Get the lid and shove it between Exodus and the crystal!"

Randall looked at the trunk then at Cassabrie. "Why is she—"

"Don't ask questions! Just do it!"

Randall lumbered over to the trunk, grabbed the lid with both hands, then, looking like he might tip over at any second, shuffled toward Exodus. Just before he reached it, he toppled forward. The lid flew from his grasp. His face smacked the floor, and the lid leaned against the Reflection's Crystal. Exodus vibrated, rousing Cassabrie.

"Randall!" Koren screamed. "Are you all right?"

Randall lay quiet and motionless.

Groaning, Cassabrie pushed up to all fours. "So weak! I can barely breathe."

"Cassabrie!" Koren shouted. "Hurry and tell me what to do. You said something about me delivering mercy."

"There is something." Cassabrie climbed slowly to her feet. Teetering while standing, she looked at Koren. "Do you have the control box I asked Magnar to give you?"

Koren touched her pocket where the box lay. "Yes."

"Good." Her cloak streaming behind her as if blown by the winds, Cassabrie withdrew a tube from an inner pocket and clutched it against her chest. "I am ready. Push the button."

"Push the button?" Koren jerked the control box from her pocket and laid it on the floor next to her hip. "That tube will destroy you! I've seen what it can do."

"It's the only way, Koren. I am the mercy cure. I know you heard the prophecy:

"A liberator comes on high
With mercy streaming from her eyes.
The slaves must take her blood and bone
And plant within this mercy sown."

Koren rubbed her thumb and finger together. "But I thought we could just take stardrop material and combine it with your—"

"My blood and bone. I know." Cassabrie's voice grew weaker again. "But it won't work. First, the medicine must be swallowed. Second, mercy is the missing ingredient. I ingested that, and now all the components are in place."

"The flower petal?"

Cassabrie nodded. "Now push the button and release the cure before the crystal once again drains my energy."

Her throat cramping terribly, Koren picked up the box and laid it in her lap. How could she—

"No! Don't kill her!" A flash of light streaked toward the center of the dome room. Deference picked up the trunk lid and shoved it between Exodus and the Reflections Crystal. The lid wedged in place, but before Deference could turn, her radiant body stretched out. Like a slurping beast, the crystal sucked her in, and she disappeared.

"Deference!" Koren lunged once more, but the manacles bit her wrists hard and held her fast. Her wrists now bleeding, Koren covered her face and wept. "Oh, Deference! Poor Deference! It's all my fault!"

"She has given us more time," Cassabrie said.

Koren looked between her fingers. Cassabrie knelt, again touching the connection point. "It's draining very slowly now. Almost imperceptible."

A shadow passed across the floor, then another. Two dragons flew in—Mallerin followed by Taushin. Blood dripped from Mallerin's cheek and from Taushin's underbelly, though neither wound looked life threatening.

Koren grabbed the control box, slid it behind her, and covered it with her cloak, careful to avoid the button. Cassabrie rose to her feet and looked on, her arms crossed loosely, apparently unalarmed at Taushin's presence.

The two dragons landed on the run between the crystal and Koren, both stomping on Randall as they slowed. "Scan the room," Taushin ordered, his eyebeams set on Mallerin.

The she-dragon cast her gaze around the perimeter. When her eyes met Koren's, Taushin shouted, "Stop!"

"I'm glad to see you." Koren gave him a painful smile. "Did you rescue Fellina?"

"You tell your tale first." Taushin shuffled closer. "I see much has happened since I departed."

"Well ..." The pain in Koren's gut suddenly spiked, and her cheeks flushed hot. "Cassabrie came. I think the Reflections Crystal drew her here."

"Yes, I know that. Even a blind dragon can solve simple puzzles." Taushin's eyebeams flashed bright blue. "When you answer my questions, speak directly to the Reflections Crystal."

"Okay." Koren nodded.

He flared a wing toward Randall. "Did that Darksphere warrior hit you?"

"No," Koren said, projecting her voice toward the center of the room. "Someone who was with him hit me. Randall is the only one who stayed. The disease kept him from leaving."

The crystal flashed brighter than ever, then continued pulsing as it slowly drained Exodus. Taushin's smile made it clear that he saw the flash through Mallerin's eyes. "Where is the key to your bonds?"

"I don't know. He took it with him."

Again the crystal flashed briefly.

"He? Jason?"

"Yes."

The crystal brightened again.

"How remarkable." Taushin smiled, baring several teeth. "The one you took a fancy to has bloodied your

head, enchained your wrists, and left you behind. It seems
that you have become a pariah in his sight."

Koren hid a gulp. That was the exact word she had
used to describe herself. How could Taushin know?

He turned his beams on Koren's chest. "Mother, leave
before these Starlighters hypnotize you, and take the
Darksphere human with you."

Mallerin growled. "Leave you again? But—"

"Just do as I say. I need you to keep Fellina and Xenith
out of the battle. I can find my way to the top of the portico, so if you see me there, come to my aid."

Her brow bending, Mallerin launched into the air,
snatching up Randall with her back claws as she rose.
Seconds later, she flew over the Zodiac's wall and disappeared. Cassabrie watched her leave, apparently making
no effort to use her gifts to rescue Randall.

"Now you will submit to me." Taushin shifted his
beams to Koren's eyes.

She clenched them shut and swung her head away.
"No! You can't! I won't let you!"

"You will if you love your fellow slaves." His voice was
soft and smooth. "The battle goes poorly for the Southlands dragons, and it has encroached upon the sick and
dying slaves. Soldiers from Darksphere have joined
in, and they are fighting against both races of dragons.
They are few in number and will not last long. With fire
and ice flying all around, many slaves will die, so we
must deliver the medicine immediately. The only way
for me to convince Cassabrie to help is for me to look
through your—"

"Never!" Koren's heart thumped. "Spew your venom somewhere else, you lying monster! I don't believe a word you say!"

"So the Starlighter in chains thinks she is free from my control. Have you forgotten so soon the shocks you experienced when you resisted me before? These chains are similar, and I will do what I must to save your friends."

Koren gritted her teeth and peeked out through a slit. His beams had shifted to her chest again. "I haven't forgotten." She focused on her bare feet. "Do your worst. I'll never give in again."

"I regret this action, but you leave me no choice." The beams drifted toward one of the manacles. "I trust that this form of persuasion will remind you of your duty toward your friends."

The second the beams touched the manacle, pain bit into her wrist and crawled up her arm, like a swarm of bees stinging savagely as they wrapped around her elbow and bicep. The fiery torture flew up and down her back and plunged into her spine and skull. Every muscle cramped. Daggers stabbed her brain. Whips lashed chest and legs, one flaming hot lash after another.

Gasping for breath, Koren writhed in place. With pain stiffening her jaw, she cried out, "Cassabrie! Help me!"

But no help came.

Koren glanced at Cassabrie. She stood in the same position as before, weeping. She couldn't hypnotize Taushin. He was immune to a Starlighter's charms.

Finally, Koren looked toward the sky. "Mercy! Creator, please have mercy!"

The pain eased. Her muscles unlocked. The stinging sensation receded to her wrist and faded away.

Her body feeling like a knotted rope, Koren sat up and leaned against the column. She glared at Taushin but stayed quiet.

"It seems that we are repeating the previous episode," Taushin said. "You have received mercy. Will you now acquiesce as you did before?"

Koren focused again on her bare feet. "I will never be your slave again. Kill me if you want. My body is in chains, but my mind is free."

"Taushin!" Cassabrie shouted. "Hearken to me!"

He kept his back toward Cassabrie. "What do you want, Starlighter?"

Cassabrie spread out her cloak. Radiance sparkled throughout the material, making it crackle with every movement. "Release Koren! She has made her decision."

Taushin chuckled as he turned toward her. "Although I am immune to your charms, you have the power to stymie my efforts. Why did you not?"

"The trial was necessary. For Koren's sake."

"Ah! A test of strength and resolve. I understand. Perhaps a similar test is in order for you. You know what I want."

"I do," Cassabrie said. "And it's not genetic material to heal the slaves. That was a ruse to weaken Koren, and now that she has rejected your advances, you will turn your lust for Starlighter power on me."

Taushin growled. "You have always been the one I wanted. You are more powerful than Koren."

"I see." Cassabrie lowered herself to her knees, again revealing her weakness. "That is no longer true, I'm afraid."

"I can release you." Taushin's beams struck Exodus's membrane and passed through to Cassabrie's chest. "Give in to me, and you will live."

"Begone, deceiver," Cassabrie said. "Threats of death mean nothing to me."

"Perhaps not toward you." Taushin faced Koren again and spread out a wing. "But since Koren is no longer useful to me, perhaps a threat against her will change your mind. Since she will not give me her eyes, they will be my first target."

Cassabrie raised her hood. "Guard your eyes, Koren! I will chase this monster from our presence."

Koren clenched her eyes shut just as a slap of leather and claw tore into her cheek. Crying out, she ducked, but not before another claw slid across her forehead wound, digging deeper into the gash.

"I am blind," Taushin shouted, "but I know where she is. I will claw her to death."

"Taushin!" Cassabrie's voice boomed, making the floor vibrate. "Listen to me! Give up this mad obsession and join your mother in battle. She has willing eyes. She and the others fight for you while you pursue selfish goals."

The slapping stopped. Koren dared not open her eyes. Once more Taushin's hot breath huffed over her face, raising new stings. Shuffling noises followed, fading slowly. Taushin was moving toward Cassabrie. "You have one final chance to give in to me, Starlighter. If you do not, I will incinerate Koren."

"Hold on, Koren! Help is on its way."

"It is too late," Taushin said. "There is no one here to save her."

A tail swished somewhere close to Cassabrie. Koren cringed. He was coming back. Any moment the flames would strike.

"Taushin?" The beating of dragon wings sounded. Koren risked a peek at the sky. Mallerin flew in and settled close to Taushin. "You never came out," she said. "I thought you might need help."

"Your timing is exquisite again. Look at Koren. I want to burn her eyes out first so she will know the pain of blindness."

"Look at Koren? Which one?"

Koren glanced around the room. A perfect replica of herself sat chained to each column. The entry door and trunk were gone, eliminating any marker that would give her real position away.

"A Starlighter's trick!" Taushin snorted. "I will soon put an end to this nonsense."

"Koren," Cassabrie said. "Hold your breath and stay completely still."

Koren held her breath and stiffened her muscles. One clink of a chain could mean death.

Silence descended. Koren ached to breathe, but even that might give her position away. This couldn't work for long. He would eventually find her by sense of smell.

Taushin charged one of the Koren replicas and blew a torrent of flames, instantly vaporizing it.

Trying not to gasp, Koren steeled her muscles. Why was Cassabrie doing this? Taushin would never give up. He would blast every last image. She should know that.

"Mallerin!" Cassabrie called. "Look at the sky!"

Mallerin turned and looked up. Cassabrie waved an arm and fanned out her cloak. "You will keep your eyes focused on the sky until I give you leave to do otherwise."

"Focused on the sky." Mallerin's head swayed. "Until you give leave."

"A temporary solution," Taushin said. "A vision of this room is still in my mind. I will eventually find her." He launched another firestorm, striking the second image, only four images to Koren's left. It, too, vaporized.

Koren stared at Cassabrie. Why was she creating images that vaporized? If one of them would burst into flames, Taushin might be convinced that he found the right Koren.

The next two images vaporized, then another. The next target was made of flesh and blood.

Cassabrie draped her cloak over her body, then repeated the motion.

Koren touched a corner of her cloak. It was still damp. She jerked the cloak around and covered her head and body. The chains jingled loudly. Instantly flames roared over her. Heat radiated through the cloak — as did the smell of smoke. Now the vaporizing images made sense. Cassabrie couldn't fake the odors.

Keeping her eyes closed, Koren let out a heart-stopping scream and shook her chains.

As the barrage of flames continued, the cloak sizzled, growing hotter and raising a stench, but would that be enough? When Taushin took a breath, he would expect the odor of burning flesh.

Cringing, Koren slid a hand over the cloak. Fire splashed against it, and she screamed again, this time without faking pain. She jerked her hand back in and sucked her fingers, silencing her voice.

The crackling eased. Koren shrugged the flaming cloak off and held her breath. The fingers of her left hand were splayed, the tips blackened and smoking. To her side, her cloak lay in a smoldering heap. Careful to keep the chain quiet, she slowly lifted her scorched hand close to Taushin's snout.

Taushin drew in a deep breath, then sighed. "It is unfortunate to lose this valuable Starlighter, but her rebellion and your refusal forced my actions."

Cassabrie sobbed. "You wicked monster!"

"As I said, it was your—"

"Get out of my sight!" Cassabrie waved an arm. "Mallerin, fly away immediately and lead this devil of a son out of here."

Mallerin lifted into the air and circled above. "Son! Our dragons need your guidance. Come! Hurry!"

Taushin shifted toward Cassabrie and felt his way to the crystal. He set a clawed hand on the trunk lid and shoved it to the side. "Good night, Starlighter. The last of your breed will finally perish."

Exodus rocked but stayed in place. Cassabrie gasped and dropped to a sitting position.

Smiling, Taushin lifted into the air. When he flew out of earshot, Koren rose to her knees. Pain throbbed in her fingers. Every beat of her heart sent a new shock wave from her fingertips through her arm and into her skull where sharp spikes jabbed from ear to ear. "Can you see

Deference? Is she inside the crystal? We need someone to move the lid again."

Cassabrie bowed her head low, muffling her voice. "I already tried to look. I can't tell."

"So what do we do now?"

"We?" Cassabrie looked up. "I can do nothing. I am trapped here, and I am dying. You are the only one who can set us all free."

"You mean ..." Koren reached back for the control box and laid it on her lap.

"Yes. Even if Elyssa managed to concoct more medicine, it will ultimately fail, as you well know. There is only one cure possible, and when the real cure is made manifest, the false cure will become worse than the disease itself. Those who choose the pretender and refuse the authentic will perish within moments. And like rain from the sky, the real cure will purge the very air of the disease, so that its scourge will inflict no one else." Cassabrie sat up straight and withdrew the explosive tube from her cloak. "Push the button, Koren. You have proven that your mind is free from Taushin's influence. Do what you must before it's too late."

Koren cupped her hand over the box's detonate button. "But I can't kill you. That would be murder."

"My life is an offering, Koren. Yes, my death will come by your hand, but that is all part of the plan."

"But why? You could have kept the box and destroyed yourself. Why did you send it to me?"

"Because those who need liberation must make a decision to value freedom. You are the last Starlighter, and as such, you will begin the process. Your decision will set off a chain of decisions among your fellow slaves, whether for good or for evil. If I made the decision myself, if freedom were to be given without the sacrifice of heart and mind, it would be cheap. It would be of no value to the ones whose chains have been loosed. They would soon return to their bondage."

A dragon shriek shot through the corridor. A woman screamed, "No! Don't kill my baby!" A tumult of sound followed—more screams and shouts, along with the grunts and bellows of angry men. Metal rang against stone, and flames crackled.

Furrows of pain dug into Cassabrie's brow. "The battle has come to our very doorstep, Koren. What will the last Starlighter do?"

Koren held the box in her shaking hands. She stared at the button, then at Exodus as it dimmed further while the Reflections Crystal brightened.

Cassabrie rose to her knees and clasped her hands, the tube tight within. "Koren, I beg you. You must push the button. I am weakening. The battle is raging outside. Your fellow slaves are dying. We have only seconds before ultimate disaster can no longer be avoided."

"But Jason and Elyssa might come and—"

"This is *our* world, Koren! Our friends from Darksphere are here to help, but time has run out, and they cannot be the guiding light the people need. Only you have enough knowledge and wisdom to see this through. Only you will be able to apply the prophetic words, the true meaning of 'The slaves must take her blood and bone.' When you push the button, you will understand."

Koren closed her eyes. The image of the barrier wall's destruction flashed to her mind. Huge boulders had flown in every direction. Only an impossibly powerful force could break apart and fling weights like those. Such an explosion would rip Cassabrie to tiny pieces and scatter her remains hundreds of feet away. How could she brutally destroy someone so wonderful, so beautiful, so loving? In a very real way, she would be the one butchering Cassabrie, only worse.

"Push the button, Koren."

"I can't."

"You have to."

"I won't."

"You must."

"There has to be another way."

"There isn't. See for yourself."

Slaves filled the room in a semitransparent copy of the portico floor. As they sat in haphazard array, Elyssa rushed from one to the other, passing around finger dabs of ointment from a little bowl. The slaves helped each other rub it in to their abdomens. Soldiers stood at the perimeter of the floor, swinging swords and spears at attacking dragons, staving them off.

"Taushin has given the order to kill all the humans," Cassabrie said. "He thinks you are dead, so he has no reason to keep them alive."

The scene pulled back, providing a perspective from the air. Flames spewed from the Basilica's bell tower. Dragons blew fire on the roof of the Zodiac's portico, setting it ablaze. As it burned, screams pierced the dome room from the real-life corridor. Smoke passed in front of Koren in thin streams, like the fingers of a ghost.

A shout erupted. "Get out! Everyone! Down the stairs!"

The scene returned to ground level. Jason appeared, carrying two children down the portico stairs. A dragon swooped at him, but Magnar dove in and blocked it with his body. When the two collided, Jason ducked under both. The dragons crashed to the steps and battled, wings and tails thrashing.

Elyssa followed Jason. With an infant in her arms and an old woman on her back, she bent low and hobbled past the fighting dragons before joining Jason at the bottom of the stairs.

White dragons blew ice at the escaping slaves while the Southlands dragons blew fire. One slave after another either froze in place or erupted in flames. Although several hundred slaves remained, they wouldn't last long.

Jason stood next to Elyssa, each still carrying a child. A smoky breeze blew back their hair. Bloody soot streamed down their faces. With their free hands, they interlocked their fingers and leaned their heads together.

The vision evaporated, but screams and dragon roars continued to rush in from the entrance.

Cassabrie sighed. "The valiant warriors from Darksphere cannot come to our aid, Koren, and they cannot win. They hoped for more allies from their world, but they did not come, so you must be their ally. Unless you do as I ask, all will be lost. I am the liberator, and you must send me out to the battle so I can set the slaves free."

Koren stared at the control box. It vibrated in her trembling hands. As she slid her thumb toward the button, sobs erupted. "Cassabrie ..." Her voice cracked. "Cassabrie, I love you.... You said ... you said we'd have a nice talk someday ... I need to know how to be a better Starlighter ... a better Starlighter like you."

"Shh, dear Koren. Fear not. We will talk again someday at the Creator's hearth where fires bring only comfort. You are a wonderful Starlighter, and I love you with all my heart."

Cassabrie folded her arms around the tube, knelt, and closed her eyes. After taking in a deep breath, she sighed and said no more.

Koren held her thumb over the button. How could she kill this beautiful angel? Might it be possible for the Creator to decide? There was still one other option. The explosive tube could detonate on its own, like the one at the barrier wall did. If the Creator wanted Cassabrie to sacrifice herself, maybe he could detonate the tube. Or maybe the Creator could keep Cassabrie alive and destroy all the dragons another way.

Koren looked up at the sky. *Creator, do I push it? Or will you take care of everything in some way I can't see?*

Another scream shot into the room. "Oh, dear Creator help us! They're dying! They're all dying!"

Her hand shaking violently, Koren set her thumb directly over the button. *I need an answer, and I need it now.*

twenty-two

Holding Reesa in one arm, Jason locked fingers with Elyssa and leaned his head against hers. Smoke billowed from the portico roof. Dragons whipped it into tight swirls as they flew around and under the covering. The protective line of soldiers had been breached. At least twenty had fallen to either fire or ice, and now a mass of slaves ran, shuffled, or limped down the stairs, escaping the inferno. Those who had received the medicine carried, pushed, or dragged those who had selflessly declined treatment in deference to others. Now with the ointment gone, more than half of the slaves were near death, including Reesa's father, Dorman, who lay somewhere in the battle zone, a place too dangerous for Reesa to venture.

Although Fellina had joined Magnar, they were no match for the combination of the Benefile and Taushin's forces. Even now, they fought valiantly, but two dragons against more than twenty amounted to impossible odds. Randall lay in the butcher's shop where two women worked on his wounds, but whether or not he would live was uncertain. Tibalt's corpse lay there as well. Wallace had carried him all the way from the forest, and now, with the disease ravaging his body and his energy almost drained, he rested outside the shop, carving a hunk of wood.

Taushin sat on the roof of the Zodiac, well away from the flames, while Mallerin battled ferociously. Hefty in girth, the she-dragon did a lot of damage by colliding with Magnar and deflecting him from battle. At least her activity kept Taushin from seeing well. He had to sit and wait.

"Are you giving up?" Elyssa asked.

"Never." Jason transferred Reesa to Elyssa's free arm. "First I have to get Koren out of there, and maybe Deference. Unless something went wrong, she should have given Koren the key by now."

"Watch out!" Reesa said, pointing upward. "Here comes another dragon!"

From the north, a dragon zoomed across the sky, faster than any taking part in the battle. Elyssa set the children down and followed the path of flight with her stare, as if probing from afar. "It's Xenith."

Xenith passed by with barely a look and rushed toward the plateau. Within seconds, she faded into the smoky air.

"Is she too scared to fight?" Reesa asked.

Jason shook his head. "Not Xenith. I don't know what she's up to, but she looks like she's on a mission." He drew his sword and ran toward the stairs. Even if the floor of the corridor lay open, he'd get inside somehow. Maybe he could flag down Fellina and ride her to —

A loud explosion rocked the ground. Jason and everyone else toppled over, and the impulse tossed the dragons' flight paths away from the Zodiac.

Jason rolled up to his seat. From the Zodiac, a plume of blue smoke and shimmering sparks shot into the air. The portico roof fell, but few if any slaves remained under it. Then the rest of the building collapsed in a billowing cloud of dust. Taushin leapt from his perch just in time and fluttered to the street, too blind to go anywhere else.

The sparks rained all around, tiny pink spheres no bigger than stardrops. They bounced before settling to the cobblestones, sizzling and slowly shrinking. A few pelted Jason, but they bounced off without doing harm. The slaves brushed the spheres away and stared at them.

Shrieks sounded from above. Beth crashed to the ground, her wings covered in flames. As more spheres rained on her, new flames erupted. Fire engulfed her entire body. The other two white dragons fell nearby, each one ablaze.

Mallerin retrieved Taushin, and they flew with the other Southlands dragons out of the rain of scalding spheres. They landed a few hundred paces away and watched the sparkling shower.

Magnar and Fellina settled between the other dragons and the humans, gasping for breath. The surviving soldiers, including Edison, Frederick, and Captain Reed, formed a line near the two dragon allies and faced the enemy dragons.

Jason jumped up and ran toward the Zodiac's rubble. He stopped at the edge and stared. "Koren?" he called. "Deference?"

A mop of dirty red hair rose from the debris, then a head, shoulders, and a torso. Crumbling stones fell at her side until she fully straightened. It seemed that a vaporous crown of light rested on her head, though it faded in and out of visibility.

Jason tried to call her name again, but only a whisper emerged. "Koren."

She slogged through the rubble. Chains weighed down her wrists, each one dragging a floor tile. Tears streaming down her dirty face, she pointed at the street. "Everyone—" She coughed out a cloud of dust, then continued in a choked voice. "Everyone has to swallow one of the stardrops! It's the only way you can be healed!"

Jason ran to her and helped her out to the street. "Swallow a stardrop? Are you sure? Most of them got some medicine, maybe only the ones who didn't get any should—"

"No!" Koren bent over and scooped up a stardrop. "Tell everyone to hurry! The stardrops won't last long!" She laid it on her tongue and swallowed. As it went down, she closed her eyes and sighed. "Cassabrie," she whispered as she lowered herself to her knees. "Thank you."

Jason swallowed with her, imagining the torturous heat passing through her esophagus. How could she stand the pain?

Koren's eyes shot wide open. She clutched her stomach and bent over, wailing, "Oh! Oh! Dear Creator! What are you doing?" Her face turned redder than her hair, and white smoke poured from her mouth.

"Elyssa!" Jason shouted. "Hurry!"

Elyssa sprinted to Koren's side, her pendant swaying in front. While Jason helped Koren lie on her back, Elyssa pressed a hand on Koren's chest.

"I found the stardrop," Elyssa said. "It's burning inside, like a fiery cyclone attacking everything it touches."

While Koren continued writhing and moaning, hundreds of slaves gathered around, some with worried expressions, others with skeptical frowns. Reesa pushed through the crowd and knelt next to Koren, saying nothing.

A middle-aged man picked up a stardrop, then let it fall. "It's as hot as a burning coal. You'd have to be crazy to swallow one of those."

"They have a point," Jason whispered to Elyssa. "I know how hot those things are, and if it's burning Koren, who would want to swallow one?"

Elyssa shook her head hard. "That's not what I meant. The fire is burning the *disease* inside her, not her organs. It has to burn away the infection, or she can't be healed."

The older man lifted his shirt, showing healthy skin. "I don't need one. I'm already healed."

Others echoed his claim, while still others pushed closer, their ulcerated faces reflecting their desperation.

Jason touched a stardrop sitting on the ground, already slightly smaller than when they had first fallen. As it sizzled, a thousand thoughts tumbled into each other. What happened in the Zodiac? Where was Cassabrie?

Why did Koren make sure she stayed in the dome room? How could she have survived the explosion?

Then, as if a Starlighter had fanned out a cloak in his mind, the entire tale came to life—a tale that began at the dawn of Starlight, a tale of noble sacrifice, a tale of selfless love—all personified in the hearts of a pair of green-eyed redheads.

He picked up the shining little sphere and gazed into its pink radiance. "Cassabrie!"

Elyssa squinted at him. "What?"

"I'll explain later! We have to get people to swallow these stardrops!" He opened his mouth and tossed the sphere in, then swallowed it as quickly as he could. The heat going down wasn't as bad as expected. Even when it dropped into his stomach, it didn't burn much at all.

Koren gasped for breath, her eyes still closed as she cried out, "Oh, it burns! It burns!"

Jason touched the wound where the litmus finger had been cut out. Unlike in Koren, the disease in him hadn't had time to spread much at all.

He jumped to his feet and pointed at a stardrop. "They're dwindling!" he called out. "Don't lose your chance! Swallow one before they're gone!"

"Not me," a man said. "I'm fine, and I sure don't want to go through what Koren's going through."

Elyssa grabbed as many stardrops as she could carry in her cupped hands. "Jason. No time to argue with anyone. Just spread the word and feed the children. Don't let any stubborn adults stop you."

"Right." Jason nodded toward the butcher's shop. "Give one to Randall. He'll help us once he's healed."

"On my way." Elyssa took off in a dead run.

Jason clutched a stardrop, ignoring the pain, and scooped Koren into his arms—chains, tiles, and all. He pushed through the crowd and climbed to the top of the Zodiac's remains. Koren squirmed, still moaning loudly enough to draw attention. Her face glowed with a pink hue but likely not brightly enough for others to notice. Although she lay horizontally, the crown stayed on her head, just a ring of glowing glitter that adhered to her scalp.

When everyone looked Jason's way, he shouted at the top of his lungs. "Hear me! Everyone must swallow a stardrop! Yes, it will hurt. Yes, you will suffer, maybe as much or more than Koren did, but if you don't take one, you will die. Cassabrie herself—her flesh, blood, and bone—is within these stardrops. She gave everything so you could be healed. Don't waste it. Time is running out."

A buzz passed across the crowd. Some scrambled for the stardrops and began swallowing them and passing them around, while others looked on, unmoved. Grumbles filtered into the hum, expressions of disgust at consuming someone's body.

"Father!" Jason called. "Bring the men! Distribute the stardrops to those who want them and can't get them, and make sure the children swallow them."

Led by Edison and Frederick, the men marched into the crowd, collecting stardrops along the way. Soon they were dispensing them as ordered, though many slaves still refused to take them.

Seconds after swallowing stardrops, slaves began writhing in pain. Cries of anguish rose all around. It seemed that with each new cry, more people declined taking the stardrops, no matter how passionately the soldiers tried to persuade them

Finally, the soldiers each swallowed a stardrop and waited silently for the reaction. Some knelt and looked toward the sky. In the distance, the Southlands dragons arrayed themselves in a line, facing the remains of the Zodiac while Mallerin and Taushin stood in front of them. Smoke shot from their nostrils, and their ears flared. Apparently Taushin was getting them riled up for the next battle.

Still cradling Koren, Jason surveyed the crowd. Reesa knelt near Dorman, combing through his hair as he shook violently, his face flushed. Many of the soldiers clutched their stomachs, including Edison and the captain, though they and the younger children didn't appear to be suffering as badly as most.

Soon all the remaining stardrops dwindled to nothing, but it seemed that everyone who wanted the new cure had been able to receive it. Yet, who could tell when the cure would take effect? Although Koren had become quiet, she still hadn't recovered. Others who had been in pain also settled, and they emanated a similar pinkish glow from their skin. Time would tell if true healing was taking place.

Jason looked at the Southlands dragons again. As he watched, they spread out their wings and beat them against the still air, not launching themselves into the sky yet, but as if limbering themselves up in preparation for another attack. With nearly everyone incapacitated and vulnerable, they would meet very little resistance.

Whether the cure would work or not, the slaves might soon succumb to another plague, one of teeth, claws, and flames.

"Jason?" Koren blinked at him, her face tear-stained and dirty, though no longer glowing.

"Are you all right?" he asked, leaning over her once more.

"I think so. Let me try to stand."

He set her gently on her feet. The chains jingled, and the tiles clanked on the debris. She wobbled for a moment but quickly steadied herself. "I think I'm fine."

"Is the disease gone?"

She laid a hand over her stomach. "For good this time. I'm sure of it."

"That's great!" He grasped her shoulders, but when her eyes showed no sign of joy, he slid back. "What's wrong?"

New tears trickled. "She's gone, Jason. Cassabrie is gone. I watched her explode into thousands of pieces. Deference is gone, too. The Reflections Crystal swallowed her, and the explosion smashed it."

Jason scanned the debris. No sign of the glimmering girl appeared across the collection of rocks, glass, and toppled columns. "They're not gone forever. It's impossible. Their spirits have to exist somewhere."

"I wish we could find out for sure." From the rubble, Koren grabbed a corner of a piece of blue fabric. As she pulled, rocks peeled away, revealing her cloak—scorched, tattered, and dirty, but fairly intact. Within the folds, a rectangular box with a red button on one side came up with it. She slid the box into her trousers pocket, her chains still weighing her hands down.

"Wait." Jason grabbed a fist-sized stone. "Set your wrists on the tiles."

Koren complied. Jason pounded her manacles with the stone until they broke away. "That should be a lot better."

Rubbing her wrist, Koren smiled. "Let's go. Taushin is ready to attack. I am able to hear his plans when the tales come to me. In fact, I can see every recent event in all of Starlight."

"Even without Exodus?"

Her crown glittering, Koren whipped the cloak around her neck, fastened the clasp in front, and raised the hood over her head. "I *am* Exodus."

As they climbed down the ruins, Jason looked over the battlefield. The Southlands dragons took to the sky with Mallerin and Taushin trailing. Edison and Captain Reed shouted for their men to fall into line. Most ran to obey, while a few limped into place, using a sword or a spear as a crutch.

Elyssa ran from the butcher's shop. Her face glowed pink, and her pendant blazed orange.

When Jason and Koren reached ground level, Koren fanned out her cloak. "Go, Jason. Fight for us. I will do what I can from here."

Just as he drew his sword, Elyssa grabbed his arm. "I swallowed one of the stardrops, and I've never felt so powerful. Send all the wounded to me."

"Will do." Jason charged toward the line of soldiers. He, too, felt stronger than he could ever recall, his legs and arms filled with energy.

The enemy dragons approached, fire already blazing. Magnar and Fellina launched to meet them, but they suddenly multiplied from two dragons to four, then to eight, then sixteen. Soon the sky was filled with images of Magnar and Fellina. When the original pair blew fire, the others copied their assault perfectly.

On the ground, the soldiers also multiplied until it seemed that a thousand armed men crowded the street. They ran into the field, cheering and waving their weapons and shields. As Jason ran, he glanced back. Koren stood with her arms spread out wide and her face glowing almost as brightly as Exodus itself.

The enemy dragons swerved to avoid the onslaught. Taushin shouted, "Fools! They are decoys! Insubstantial copies!" He and Mallerin shot out fireballs, incinerating duplicates of Magnar and Fellina, then flew right through several more.

The real Magnar and Fellina took advantage of the distractions and attacked unsuspecting dragons, although some regrouped and broke through their defense to rain fire on the soldiers. Although they raised their shields as one, hundreds of duplicates disintegrated. At least five dragons landed and began sweeping their tails through the false ranks, destroying many fake soldiers and toppling several real ones.

Jason jumped over a tail, narrowly avoiding a sharp spine. When he landed, he ran straight to the dragon, slid feet first under its belly, and rammed his sword into the vulnerable spot. When he yanked out the blade, fluids gushed over his chest. The dragon's legs gave way, and his huge body came crashing down.

Thrusting his legs, Jason tried to slide, but his feet slipped in the fluids. Something grabbed his arm and jerked him out of the way just in time, then hoisted him to his feet. "Didn't you learn better dragon-combat methods in warrior school?"

Jason turned in place. "Randall! How did you—"

"Best doctor in Starlight energized me." Randall pointed with his sword. "Let's go. More dragons to kill."

As Jason and Randall advanced on the field, the enemy dragons continued burning away the copies and bowling over more real soldiers.

Jason hacked at a dragon's neck and drove the blade in deeply. Randall sliced a wing in half. Shrieking, the dragons launched fire and slashed with their tails, but with so many duplicate soldiers, they had no idea whom to attack.

Just as Jason pulled his sword back to strike another scaly neck, a great shadow swooped over him and jerked him off his feet. Above, Mallerin carried him over the battlefield and back toward the Zodiac. Taushin followed behind, his blue beams pulsing.

Jason hacked at Mallerin's legs, but a crushing pinch from her claws paralyzed his arm, forcing him to drop his sword. Below, his father and brother lay near each other on the battlefield, both with bloody leg wounds and scorched clothes.

Mallerin deposited him in front of Koren and pinned him face down with her massive tail. When Taushin landed next to his mother, he shouted, "Koren! Dissolve the copies immediately, or I will kill Jason!"

Koren lowered her arms and glared at Taushin. "Haven't you yet learned that you have no control over me?"

"I do as long as I hold Jason captive. Your love for him is the only chain I need."

"No, Koren," Jason grunted. "Don't give in. This is war. You can't give up the battle just to save one warrior."

Close by, the mass of slaves parted, and Elyssa walked out from their midst, Wallace and Dorman at her side. With her arms crossed and her face glowing, she looked ready to take on Mallerin herself.

Koren looked at Elyssa. "What do you think?"

"The warrior has led the way. It's time to follow his lead." Elyssa waved her arm. "Now!"

Elyssa, Wallace, and Dorman charged, followed by dozens of slaves. They jumped on Mallerin, scratching and punching. Elyssa climbed Mallerin's neck and clawed at her eyes. Taushin blew fire aimlessly, keeping the slaves at bay.

Seconds later, Mallerin toppled over. Jason squirmed out and leaped to his feet as Mallerin began slinging people left and right. Dorman flew one way, Wallace another, but Elyssa hung on ferociously. Finally, Mallerin shook like a wet dog, flung everyone off, and launched into the air.

Elyssa fell on top of a slave and rolled over two more before coming to a stop. Shaking her head, she took Jason's hand and rose.

"Thanks for the rescue," he said.

"You're welcome."

"I have to stay here and protect Koren."

"I know." She released his hand, but let her fingers brush his arm. "And I have a lot of healing to do."

Jason caught her hand and interlocked their fingers. "I'll see you again. I promise."

"And I'll hold you to that promise." As soon as Elyssa slid her finger away, she ran into the battlefield and found

Wallace helping Randall climb to his feet next to a dead dragon.

Jason scanned the ground and spotted his sword only a few steps away. He ran to it and and snatched it up. Now he had something to protect Koren with.

Taushin leaped into the air and joined Mallerin in a slow orbit just out of the reach of swords and spears. A drone entered the orbit with them. "The field is clear," the drone announced. "Magnar and Fellina have fallen. All the soldiers are either dead or disabled, and the duplicates are gone."

"Have everyone land. They will not dare attack us again." Turning his beams on Koren as he circled, Taushin laughed. "It seems that you are not as free from me as you would like to believe."

Staring at him, Koren crossed her arms over her chest. Dirty and bloodied, she looked defeated but defiant.

Jason ran to her side. "Are you all right?"

"I'm fine. Just watching the tales of Starlight, recent tales."

"Good ones?"

"Trust me." She spoke through clenched teeth. "It's not over yet."

twenty-three

When the fifteen or so remaining dragons, including Mallerin, had landed, Taushin skittered to the ground in front of them, while the messenger drone kept watch from above. Taushin cast his beams into Koren's eyes again. Without a flinch, she kept her defiant pose.

"Be my vision, Koren," Taushin said, his head swaying hypnotically, "and I will let your loved ones live."

"Soldiers are coming from the mining mesa!" the drone called. "And more dragons."

Taushin snorted. "Another Starlighter trick. The real enemies are defeated. Come and help me with a final task that will ensure our dominion here."

"Very well." The drone landed and joined the line.

Taushin kept his beams aimed at Koren's eyes. "Cease this nonsense. You and your duplicates are defeated. If you refuse to let me in, we will begin setting your friends ablaze, beginning with a child among the slaves."

Clutching the hilt of his sword tightly, Jason stayed quiet. Koren's entreaty kept repeating in his mind. *Trust me.*

He looked beyond the dragons. Hundreds of soldiers ran toward them from the direction of the mesa, getting closer and closer, while two dragons flew above the leading line. Why was Koren bringing these duplicates? They couldn't be the reinforcements. Even running full speed, they couldn't have traveled here from the Northlands in such a short time. Besides, they were coming from the south, not the north.

On the battlefield, Magnar struggled to his haunches, but he teetered, and his head swayed. He couldn't possibly help now. Fellina lay nearby, motionless.

Koren lifted a hand and lowered her hood. Her dirty red hair spread across her shoulders, and her green eyes sparkled. "I am the last Starlighter," she said with a boom in her voice. "You have no power over me. Begone, before I cast you from my sight. You saw what I did to Jason when I protected you. You will soon experience a force far greater."

Jason glanced again. The soldiers continued running, their footfalls sounding like thunder. They would arrive in seconds, but what would a bunch of phantoms be able to do?

"You are becoming tedious." Taushin waved a wing at Mallerin. "Make a torch out of a child and bring her here to show Koren the light."

Just as Mallerin turned, a chorus of whistles sailed in. Ropes slung around each dragon's neck including Taushin's and Mallerin's. With weights tied at both ends and a metal tube embedded in each one, the ropes whipped around and around until they slapped the dragons' scales. The tubes pressed against the dragons' throats with layers of rope holding them in place.

As the dragons reeled back, hundreds of soldiers flew into the line with swords and spears slashing, Adrian and Marcelle leading the way. Adrian plunged his sword deep into a dragon's belly. Marcelle grabbed a dragon's spine, swung up to its neck, and gouged its eyes with her sword.

Jason tried to leap at Taushin, but Koren grabbed his wrist and held him back. "Wait!"

Taushin and most of the dragons beat their wings and lifted over the fray. Six dragons fell victim to the onslaught and writhed under the pummeling swords, spears, and fists. Adrian stood atop a fallen dragon's flank and shouted, "Arxad! Xenith! Let them fly but keep them close! We want to account for them all."

Arxad and Xenith flew around the escaping dragons and kept them hemmed in with their flames, claws, and whipping tails. Magnar broke into the orbit, bit through Mallerin's ropes, and forced her to the ground.

When the other dragons rose about fifty feet, Koren withdrew the box from her pocket and pointed it at Taushin. "It is time for the hatchling from the black egg to meet the Creator."

"What?" Taushin shouted. "No! Have mercy!"

"Sometimes justice triumphs over mercy." Then, Koren whispered, "For Cassabrie."

She pushed the button. Explosions rocked the ground. Soldiers fell like toys, toppling into each other in a chain reaction that swept across the field.

Jason caught Koren and fell with her. As they sat on the street, pieces of dragon rained all around—necks, wings, midsections, and tails. Finally, Taushin's neck and attached head dropped next to them, writhing like a dying serpent. A hint of blue still radiated from his eyes. As the head's movement slowed, a pair of weak beams found their way to Koren's chest. The light pulsed brighter, then the eyes closed.

Jason helped Koren rise. They walked hand in hand toward the battlefield. With so many men climbing to their feet, it seemed that someone had blown a wake-up call on a bugle. In the midst of the field, Adrian and Marcelle were helping others rise, soldiers and slaves alike, while Elyssa, her face and pendant glowing, hurried here and there, checking for injuries.

Mallerin threw off Magnar and bolted into the air. With her wings beating madly, she flew away. Magnar rose slowly to his haunches and watched her shrink in the distance.

Jason and Koren walked into the throng, helping people to their feet. When Jason reached Edison and Frederick, they were already sitting with their trousers cuffs rolled up to their knees. Bloody gashes striped their legs, but smiles dressed their faces.

Jason crouched next to them. "Are you two okay?"

"I've had worse," Edison said. "It'll take more than a few licks from dragon fire to keep me down."

Frederick laughed. "I think I'll stay down till Elyssa comes. This ground is feeling pretty comfortable right now."

Jason rose. All around the field, former slaves checked each other's arms and torsos for signs of the disease. The ones who had taken stardrops appeared to be disease free, while others, even those who claimed no need for Cassabrie's cure, now lay motionless with sores on their arms and faces.

"Jason!" Adrian ran up from the side and embraced him in his powerful arms. "It's about time you showed up here!"

"Me? I've been here for ages!" Jason shoved Adrian away and punched his arm. "Where did you come from?"

"To make a long story short, the portal at the mining mesa." Adrian mussed Jason's hair. "The rest will have to wait. There's a lot to tell."

"That's an understatement," Marcelle said as she jogged to their side. After giving her sword an expert twirl, she slid it into its scabbard. "Probably more than you'd ever want to hear."

"Soon we'll have time to tell everything." Jason grasped Adrian's forearm. "For now, though, there's still a lot to be done."

Marcelle looped her arm through Adrian's. "He's right. Let's go help the wounded."

As soon as they left, Dorman and Benjamin limped up to Jason, Dorman now carrying a beaming Reesa in his arms. "What's the word?" Dorman asked. "Are we going to your world? Or should we stay here and make a new world for ourselves?"

"That's a good question." Jason looked ahead. Arxad and Xenith had landed and joined a huddle with Magnar and Fellina. Although the latter two hung their heads low, and their wings sagged, they appeared to be recovering from their wounds. "Why don't you talk about it among yourselves, and I'll see what the dragons say."

"What about those who wouldn't take the stardrops?" Dorman asked. "Should they have any say in the matter?"

"I don't think they'll feel like saying much, but I'll leave it up to you."

Jason and Koren continued on, hand in hand. When they met Elyssa, she gave Koren a warm hug, then took Jason's hand on the other side and walked with them. "We lost twenty-seven of the original soldiers," she said, a tremor in her voice. "I'm guessing about two hundred slaves died, either from dragon fire or ice or from the disease."

"What happened to those who didn't take a stardrop?" Jason asked.

"They're all dead. Every one of them, as far as I can tell. It looks like the disease sped up, almost like the presence of the stardrops made it stronger."

Koren nodded. "Cassabrie said this would happen. She said those who refused the real cure would die right away and that the air would be purged by the falling stardrops."

"Then the disease is gone," Jason said. "Forever. The soldiers who came from the mesa portal won't catch it."

Elyssa picked up a shredded piece of blue fabric. "Good thing, since we have no cure. No stardrops. No Exodus material." She pushed the fabric into her pocket. "And no Cassabrie."

"Right. No Cassabrie." Jason dragged his shoe along the ground. What more could he say? Losing her was a tragedy, and no words could describe the loss. "So ... how are things at the butcher's shop?"

Elyssa lifted her pendant, still glowing orange. "I treated those with the worst injuries. Wallace, Randall,

Adrian, and Marcelle are carrying others who need treatment to the shop. Captain Reed is there with a broken arm and ribs, but he's not complaining. I'll be joining them after I get a few minutes to rest. They've all swallowed stardrops, so they'll be fine."

When they reached the gathering, the four dragons greeted them with tired nods. With dragon blood and mismatched scales coating their bodies, they looked like a child had put them together with the wrong puzzle pieces.

Jason nodded in return. "The slaves are wondering about what's going to happen to them."

"Yes," Arxad said. "We were just discussing that. Although it is tragic, it seems that we will have to wait for the infected slaves to die before you can safely transport anyone to Major Four. For them to watch while their fellow slaves march to freedom would be the ultimate torture."

"Is there no hope for them at all?" Fellina asked.

"They're already dead," Jason said quietly. "The disease accelerated after the stardrops fell." For a moment, silence ensued. Jason glanced at each sad face. It seemed that no one wanted to state the obvious. The cure had been available to all, and those who refused it had paid the price.

Jason looked around at the carnage of fallen dragons surrounding them. "Arxad, how are you handling these deaths? They were your friends, your neighbors."

Arxad lowered his head and looked at the humans at their eye level. "It seems," he said, tears sparkling in his eyes, "that justice has come to Starlight. Although many of our dragon friends have died, we will learn to cope with the tragedy. It is my hope that mercy will now reign among dragons and humans alike."

Koren threw her arms around Arxad's neck and pulled him close. As they nuzzled, steaming tears dripped from Arxad's eyes. When she drew back, she laid a hand on his cheek. "Although I lived as a slave in your abode, Arxad, high priest of Starlight, I served you as a daughter who had lost her father. I was lonely and afraid, yet trusting in you as a wise counselor. Now loosed from my chains, I will again look to you for advice, because my father has sacrificed his life for mine and has left this world."

"Orson is dead?" Arxad asked.

Koren's chin trembled. "He would want his little K to be well cared for, don't you think?"

Arxad wrapped a wing around her and held her close again. "You are the first human I ever truly loved, and that love will never falter. You will always be welcome in my home."

"And we will gather our own honey," Xenith said, smiling. "No more bee adventures for you."

After Arxad, Fellina, Xenith, and Koren laughed together for a moment, Arxad spread out his wings and gestured for attention. "We have spoken of love and mercy, so with those blessings in mind, may I suggest that the king of this land should make a proclamation regarding the slaves? It seems to me that since the army from Major Four has triumphed and dragons have been conquered, capitulation is in order."

Magnar, who had been quietly scanning his devastated domain, turned toward the group. "Are you asking for a formal surrender?"

Arxad nodded. "It seems appropriate, considering the circumstances."

"Agreed, but I will do even more." Magnar extended his neck toward Koren and lowered his head to the ground. "Starlighter, if you would give me the honor, I will take you to the Zodiac's remains, where we will address the people together."

Koren spread out her cloak and bent her knee. "The honor is mine, good dragon." She climbed up his neck and settled on his back, her scorched cloak flowing behind her.

"Follow us, my friends." Magnar spread out his wings and flew over the battlefield toward the pile of rubble.

Xenith nudged Jason with a wing. "You and Elyssa look like you need a ride, too."

"That won't be necessary." Smiling at Elyssa, he curled his ring finger around hers. "We'll walk."

"Very well." Xenith flew toward the Zodiac.

"If you do not mind," Arxad said, "Fellina and I would like to walk with you. It will take some time for Magnar and Koren to gather such a large crowd."

"Please do." Jason and Elyssa set out at a slow pace, Arxad and Fellina to their right. Arxad bent his neck toward Jason and Elyssa as they walked. "When the difficulties in your world are settled, will you return to us? We hope to establish peaceful relations between our worlds. The two of you would make excellent ambassadors."

"Thank you," Jason said. "I don't know about being an ambassador, but I hope we return someday."

By the time they neared the remains of the Zodiac, Magnar and Koren were standing side by side on the

debris with hundreds of slaves and soldiers looking on.
Koren shifted her weight from foot to foot, her eyes darting. Her face radiated her familiar glow, but her clothes
and cloak were torn and dirty. With the glittering crown
of light on her head, she looked like a shining angel disguised as a peasant.

The street was now clear of casualties. The original
soldiers had moved the dead human bodies and smaller
dragon parts away, perhaps to the Basilica. The fire there
still burned, a good place to incinerate the dead.

At Magnar's request, the crowd made room for Jason
and the others to come to the front. As Jason passed, he
glanced from face to face, each one clear of symptoms. He
didn't bother to try to count them to verify Elyssa's number. At this point, it didn't really matter.

When everyone settled again, Magnar waved a wing
and spoke with a loud voice. "I will be brief. This is a day
of new beginnings, and it behooves us all to move on. It
is impossible to express my regret for all the evil I have
committed, and it is equally impossible for me to amend
every wrong, but I will do all that is in my power. My
mate and I will retire in peace to a place where we will no
longer be a scourge to anyone."

Magnar bowed his head. "I hereby formally surrender
to the liberators from Major Four. I release all claims to
ownership of any humans, and I abdicate my rule and
hand it over to Koren the Starlighter."

Koren jerked her head toward him. "What?"

The crowd erupted in cheers, drowning out Magnar's
reply. When the noise subsided, Magnar shuffled close to

Koren and cupped a wing around her. "As the new queen of Starlight do you have anything to say?"

Koren stood stiffly for a moment. After scanning the crowd, she cleared her throat. "Well, the first thing that comes to mind is whether or not I will have any humans with me."

"You have at least one." Wallace pushed to the front, climbed the mound, and joined Koren. "I hear the barrier wall is gone. We're free to live anywhere we want."

Excited chatter erupted until Magnar gestured with his wings for quiet. "I beg your pardon. I forgot to mention an important detail or two. Alaph, the king of the Northlands, has passed away." He waited through another surge of chatter. "Before he died, he told me that the great castle is to be given to Koren if she chooses to remain as the sovereign of this world."

Wallace raised a hand. "All hail Queen Koren!"

The crowd echoed, "All hail Queen Koren!" After two repetitions, each one louder than the previous, they settled down.

Koren's face glowed red. "I ..." She licked her lips. "I don't know what to say."

"Accept!" Wallace shouted. "Be our queen!"

After dozens of yeses rose from the crowd, silence ensued. Everyone stared at Koren while Magnar and Wallace drew back. She walked down from the debris and stood at street level only a few paces from the closest onlooker.

Spreading out her cloak, she dipped into a low curtsy. When she rose, she shifted her gaze from face to face. "I accept on one condition—that you will be my friends and not my subjects. We will learn how to be free together under a new kind of rule. Remember the prophesy. 'In honor of this treasured hour, we celebrate Creator's power. The dawn of paradise will bring an age of peace beside our king.' And our king is not a dragon or a human. Our king is the Creator himself." Cheers erupted. While Koren waited for the noise to settle, she continued scanning the crowd. When her gaze locked on Jason's, she smiled. "And in this newfound freedom, I hope to get a lot of help from our friends from another world who have sacrificed so much to bring us liberty."

She ran to Jason and wrapped him in her arms. As warmth spread across his skin, he slid his arms around her and held her close.

When she pulled back, she looked up into his eyes, tears magnifying her emerald irises. "I can't stand the thought of you leaving, Jason. From the moment I saw you through the black egg, I knew somehow you would set us free, that you would break my chains. And now ..." Her face twisted in grief. "And now you're leaving."

"Only for a while." Jason gestured for Elyssa to join them. As the three embraced, Jason whispered, "I will cherish the day we met, Koren. Anytime you need help, we're just a portal hop away. Don't ever forget that."

"We're closer than sisters now," Elyssa said. "Don't be surprised when I stop by the castle uninvited."

A new voice chimed in. "And I'll make sure the castle is spotless for your visit." A glimmering girl appeared at Koren's side, her fists on her hips. "When that crystal exploded, it sent me flying almost to the mountains! I thought I'd never make it back here!"

"Deference!" all three said at once.

Smiling broadly, she curtsied. "I heard you need help with the wounded, but I thought I'd let you know I'm here." She spun toward the butcher's shop and hurried away.

Arxad joined the three and touched Jason's shoulder with a wing tip. "The portal is open, and the path is clear. Those who wish to go with you to your world will follow. I have already discussed the situation with your captain, and he will conduct the soldiers home when all is settled here and the dead and wounded are ready to be transported."

"Including Tibalt and Uriel?" Jason asked.

"Yes, they will not leave any resident of your world behind."

"Then I'm ready," Jason said. "We need to go."

"Good-bye." Koren kissed Elyssa on the cheek, then Jason, and backed away slowly. She mouthed the words, "I love you, Jason Masters. You will always have a special place in my heart."

Jason laid his hand on his chest and formed a silent response on his lips. "And you are in mine forever. I love you, Koren … my Starlighter."

Smiling, Koren climbed back to the debris mound and spread out her cloak. "Our friends are leaving. Whoever wishes to go with them is free to follow." As tears flowed, she shouted, "Did you hear that? You are free!"

The loudest cheer yet erupted from the crowd. Men shook hands and embraced, women hugged and wept together, and children squealed for joy.

While those wanting to go to Major Four collected their few belongings, Elyssa treated those with the most serious wounds. Later, Arxad and the other surviving dragons flew her and several of the Major Four warriors, including Jason and his father and brothers, to the river to get cleaned up and refreshed.

The former slaves gathered food from the homes of the dead dragons and distributed it freely to the survivors. While eating, Edison and Captain Reed decided that that the soldiers who arrived from the mesa portal should stay in the Southlands for a while to make sure they were free of disease symptoms. Since they had no opportunity to take a stardrop, it seemed prudent to make sure they didn't carry the disease back to Major Four.

As a crowd of excited men, women, and children gathered between the ruins of the Basilica and the Zodiac, Jason called together his father, Elyssa, Koren, Adrian, Frederick, Randall, and Marcelle on the south side of the crowd and faced the mesa.

Jason laid a hand on his father's back. "We have a lot to be thankful for. Will you do the honors?"

"Gladly." Edison lifted his face toward the sky. "Creator," he said, his voice streaked with emotion, "you have brought us this far. There are many broken bodies and broken hearts, and we ask that you mend each one. We will look forward to seeing our lost loved ones again in our heavenly home, and we trust that slavery in both worlds has come to an end. Thank you for guidance, protection, and most of all, for freedom."

Edison knelt and plunged his dagger into the ground. "The battles are over. Let the suffering be forgotten, and let the rejoicing begin."

After a moment of silence, Jason hugged Koren, Adrian, and Marcelle. Elyssa did the same. When all the good-byes were said, Koren led Adrian and Marcelle toward Arxad's cave, where the two planned to wait until they were sure they were disease-free.

Jason took Elyssa's hand. "I think we're ready."

"You're right. We're ready." She grinned. "Should I say it?"

"If you don't," Jason said, "I'm not going."

Elyssa pointed toward the portal. "Lead the way, warrior!"

twenty-four

Koren stood on a stage three steps up from the main floor in Meso-lantrum's Cathedral, holding a bouquet of yellow and purple flowers. Dressed in a sky-blue gown that covered her in silk from neck to ankles, she stared down at the hundreds of onlookers sitting on cushioned benches and absorbed the wonder. Only five years ago, she lay on a thin mat after a grueling evening of collecting honey from angry bees and hauling it to Arxad's cave. At that time, she wore ratty short trousers and a hole-infested tunic, and home was little more than an opening in the side of a rocky hill. Now she stood in the midst of abundance, waiting to celebrate a coming union, a marriage of choice rather than one of necessity.

Jason stood on the same stage a few steps away. As she glanced at him, he smiled and winked. Wearing a perfectly pressed military uniform, white gloves, and polished black shoes, he was handsome indeed. Earlier, he had said that his father wore that uniform decades ago on his wedding day, Adrian wore it when he married Marcelle shortly after the liberation of Starlight, and now it was Jason's turn.

He flashed Koren a smile and mouthed, "Thank you for coming."

She dipped her head and silently formed, "I wouldn't miss your wedding for the world."

While they waited for the bride's entry, Koren looked around. Edison stood at Jason's side as best man. Frederick and Adrian were stationed at the rear door as "heralds," a Mesolantrum custom. When the bride was ready, they would perform their duties.

A few steps behind Jason and Koren, a dark blue curtain veiled the rest of the stage floor. Hundreds of flower arrangements stood in front of it near the sides of the stage, giving the wedding party only a small area on which to stand. Carrying baskets of flower petals, Natalla and Solace stood quietly at each side of the curtain, their grins wide.

A quick scan of the crowd revealed Wallace, Randall, Marcelle, and several former cattle children, including the two boys Jason rescued—Basil and Oliver. Everyone was dressed in finery, reflecting the Masters family's generosity in sharing the great reward the kingdom had bestowed on them for liberating the slaves.

"Ladies and gentlemen," Adrian called from the door. "It is my honor and pleasure to introduce to you, Elyssa Cantor, daughter of Meredith Cantor."

At the other side of the door, Frederick added, "Because Elyssa's father has gone on to be with the Creator, she will be escorted by another, someone whom you all will recognize."

Adrian lifted a hand. "All rise!"

Everyone stood and angled toward the rear. Frederick's cryptic announcement hung in the air like a prize no one could quite grasp.

In unison, Adrian and Frederick pulled the doors. Elyssa stood at the center of the opening. Her bridal gown, dazzling white and covered with silky lace, draped her body from just below her neck down to the floor. A thin veil covered her face, but it couldn't hide her glowing smile. A train of white stretched out behind her, shimmering like Solarus on still water.

Jason gasped, then gulped. As he looked on his bride, his lips trembled.

A man walked up to Elyssa's side and took her arm in his. Amid gasps from the crowd, an organ began playing a lovely march that set the processional's slow pace.

Koren grinned. It seemed that no one could believe that Counselor Orion would escort this young woman, the very girl he once accused of being an evil Diviner. After five years of seclusion in which he walked the slave trails on Starlight—tramping the tear-stained path of the cattle camp children, sleeping on the mats in the grottoes, and eating only what he could find in the forest or in the dragons' garbage—he emerged a changed man.

Her gaze firmly set on Jason, Elyssa strode along a red carpet through a scattering of white petals, her body erect and her shoulders back. Her pendant rested in the middle of her chest with the closed hands on the front. As if activated by a recent healing, the pendant shone with an orange glow.

Jason stared back at Elyssa, now composed. It seemed that they communicated silently, a heart-to-heart connection that needed no words.

When Elyssa and Orion arrived at the front, they stopped and waited, facing the stage. Jason and Elyssa smiled at each other, then at Koren and Edison. The crowd murmured. So far, no one had come to the stage to officiate.

A rumbling voice boomed from behind the curtain. "Who gives this woman to be married to this man?"

Orion bowed his head. "Her mother, Meredith Cantor, and I do."

Still grinning, Natalla and Solace ran to the middle of the curtain and pulled the panels to the sides. Arxad stood on the stage. His freshly polished scales glimmered in the Cathedral's gas-powered lights.

As new murmurs passed across the crowd, a hint of a smile bent Arxad's lips. "Let us begin."

Jason descended the steps, took Elyssa's hand, and guided her up to the stage, while Koren made sure the dress's train didn't catch on anything. They faced Arxad, their index fingers hooked together.

Still on the main floor, Orion turned to the audience. "As a counselor of Mesolantrum, by law I am vested with the privilege of sanctioning marriages until I die. Although a dragon priest from Starlight is officiating, I am overseeing the ceremony, so the uniting of these two will be legal and binding." He then took a seat on the front row.

The rest of the ceremony seemed a blur. Natalla sang a lovely hymn. Frederick played a melody on a wooden reed-like instrument, and the audience joined in with the lyrics. Edison read from the Code. Jason and Elyssa exchanged rings of gold. Arxad led them in reciting their vows of mutual love and fidelity, of life-long service to one another.

Koren drank in the words. Such beautiful poetry! And knowing Jason and Elyssa, they would never fail to live up to the promises.

Finally, Arxad said, "After hearing their sacred vows and witnessing the binding symbol of rings, I declare that these two are husband and wife."

Arxad nodded at Jason. "You may now kiss your bride."

Jason raised Elyssa's pendant and turned it to the other side, revealing the open hands and the liberated dove. He then lifted her veil and hooked their ring fingers together. Jason and Elyssa kissed, a long, tender kiss that seemed to stop time.

A knock sounded at the door.

Koren stepped back from the stage and waved at the scene. Jason and Elyssa, the Cathedral, Arxad, and all the people melted away, leaving a room of white.

"Come in," she called.

One of the tall white doors opened, and Wallace strolled in. With each step, the whiteness gave way to dark wood floors, ivory colored walls and ceiling, and Koren's desk and high-backed chair. Flames crackled in the nearby fireplace, and several wooden figurines stood on the mantel.

"I finally finished it." Wallace held up a box big enough to hold one of his sandals.

Koren clapped her hands. "Wonderful!"

"Once I found a big enough hunk of ivory, it took only a few weeks." He pulled the lid off the box and withdrew a sculpture of a dragon. White and void of scales, it looked exactly like Alaph. From the tip of his tail to his magnificent wings to his noble face, every detail was perfect.

His single eye scanning his masterpiece, Wallace pointed at the thin red lines coursing across the figurine's surface. "It took hours to paint these. I had to use a single hair for my brush."

"Oh, Wallace, it's beautiful!" She kissed his cheek. "Thank you so much!"

He laid it in her hands. "That's the last one. Is there anything else you want me to do?"

Smiling, she looked him over. Dressed in gray work tunic and trousers, he was his usual self—humble and unassuming, but now eighteen years old, he had grown into a strong young man. "Not at the moment, Wallace. You've been a jewel."

"Oh! I forgot!" Wallace pulled a small box from his pocket. "The portal messenger brought this. The label says it's from the Mesolantrum army."

Koren bounced on her toes. "It's finally here!"

"What's here?"

"Follow me. I'll show you." Koren walked to the fireplace and set the sculpture of Alaph in the spot near the center of the mantel she had long reserved. Madam Orley's figurine stood next to it, holding a cooking pot. Petra sat in a chair reading a book, and Tibalt watched over her with a drawn sword. Lattimer held a Starlighter cloak by its shoulders, as if ready to drape it over someone. Tamminy stood with his head held held high and his eyes toward the heavens, singing a prophetic song. At the very center, Cassabrie, wearing a white dress and blue cloak, stood with her arms outstretched as if offering something to the entire world.

Koren took the box, opened it, and withdrew a ribbon with an attached medal. Silver and shining, it read, "Medal of Valor, Tibalt Blackstone, Hero from the Dungeon."

Fighting tears, she pressed it close to her chest. "It's perfect! Just perfect!" She turned to Wallace. "It took forever for them to get it right. I had to send it back three times."

"What are you going to do with it?"

"This." She draped the ribbon around Tibalt's figurine and let the medal rest at his feet. After aligning it, she whispered, "I wish I could have given this to you in person."

"Well," Wallace said, "I'd better get going. Frederick is coming to check on our crops. He's going to teach us something new about getting rid of bugs."

"That's great. I'll be down to see him soon."

When Wallace left, Koren slid into her desk chair and waved an arm at the wall. The whiteness cleared, replaced by a stunning view of the Northlands scenery. Now covered with green grass and plowed fields, the countryside looked nothing like a frozen wasteland. Lush crops flourished, flowers bloomed everywhere, and the river sparkled as it ran freely through the fertile meadow. Men, women, and children darted from place to place, either working the farm or splashing in the river.

Koren smiled. It was all a dream come true.

She slid a figurine on her desk closer — Orson holding up a crucible — and stroked his cheek with a finger. "It was your dream, Daddy. If it wasn't for you, we'd all still be slaves."

Koren pulled a parchment from a drawer and set it on the desk. As she dipped a quill in an inkwell, memories of each sacrificial death flowed through her mind. For as long as she lived, the people of Starlight would never forget their love.

Writing with the quill and dipping for more ink frequently, she poured out her thoughts.

Dear Jason and Elyssa,

I watched your wedding again today, and I look forward to your visit next week.

I received the medal for Tibalt. It was worth waiting so long to get it personalized correctly. I think he wouldn't have minded his name being spelled wrong, but I wanted it to be perfect for him. I'm sure he's happy.

I enjoyed reading your recent letter and the news about peace in your land. Randall's installation as governor will be an exciting celebration. Randall already sent me an invitation to be his personal dinner guest at the affair, and I accepted. I know what you're thinking, and I will not disguise my impression that he is a courageous and sacrificial gentleman. May the Creator guide us as we learn more about each other.

If it isn't too much trouble, please bring the video tube

of Orion. Wallace is ready to carve his likeness. Orion's tragic death after the wedding was a shock to us all. Since he became such a model of the power of mercy, I want to honor him with a figurine.

When you come, I'll make sure Myrrid is here in the Northlands. He is a handsome young dragon, the image of Magnar with just a hint of Mallerin's eyes. Xenith is wary and staying aloof for now, but I think she'll warm up to him when he is of age.

We are all looking forward to your arrival, especially Deference and Resolute. Resolute wants to show you the moat and how she tamed the creatures therein. Deference started a hospital and is training two doctors and a nurse. She's hoping Elyssa will explain what she knows about stardrop therapy. Although we no longer have stardrop material, just last week she discovered a way to infuse light energy into a body that might have the same effect.

That's all for now. I love you both with all my heart. I know someday we will be together at the Creator's fireside, and we will never leave each other's company again. Until then, you will be in my daily thoughts.

With great affection,
Koren

She rolled up the parchment and tied a ribbon around it. "Yes," she whispered, "with great affection."

"Koren?" Deference peeked into the room. "Will you go for a walk with me?"

"Gladly." Koren slid away from the desk and joined Deference at the door. "I have to take a letter to the portal courier."

"I love walking there, and I saw Arxad and Fellina and Xenith flying over that way."

"Excellent." Koren took her hand, walked out of the room, and closed the door behind her. "Let's see what our dragon friends are up to today."

Warrior

When the black egg hatches, unleashing a new dragon prince, Koren and Jason work to find the one person who can help them free the human slaves. Little do they realize the secrets of Starlight go deeper than anyone imagined, and they may soon snare Koren in a deadly deceit.

Diviner

Koren begins to doubt the path she has chosen, and seeks for a way to use her gifts for a nobler purpose. Meanwhile, Jason and his friend Elyssa attempt to rescue loved ones from the dragons' jaws, and Elyssa uncovers gifts of her own that could be a powerful weapon in the coming war.

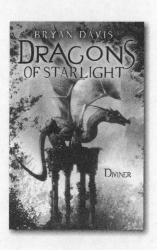

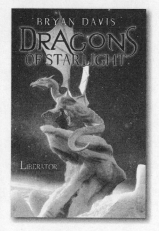

Liberator

Jason, Koren, and Elyssa struggle to alert the soldiers about a deadly illness that has been released, one that already has Koren in its grip. Meanwhile, Cassabrie works to counter Taushin's latest maneuverings, but no one knows the details of her risky plan. Will love, faith, and courage be enough? Is Cassabrie the human's last hope?

Eternity's Edge (Book Two)

With the secrets behind the mirrors unlocked, Nathan and Kelly set out to save three colliding Earths from certain destruction. But they are not the only ones on a mission: an intergalactic stalker is fighting for control, forcing Nathan and his friends to journey through mystifying realities.

Nightmare's Edge (Book Three)

The destruction of the three Earths is imminent, and only Nathan's father knows the secret to saving billions of people. Nathan is tasked with freeing his very-much-alive parents from a dream world, while Kelly sacrifices herself to rescue Nathan. Time is running out, with the universe and Kelly's life hanging in the balance.

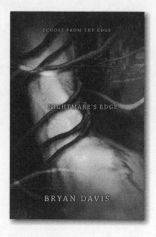

Talk It Up!

Want free books?
First looks at the best new fiction?
Awesome exclusive merchandise?

We want to hear from you!

Give us your opinions on titles, covers, and stories.
Join the Z Street Team.

Visit zstreetteam.zondervan.com/joinnow
to sign up today!

Also—Friend us on Facebook!

www.facebook.com/goodteenreads

- Video Trailers
- Connect with your favorite authors
- Sneak peeks at new releases
- Giveaways
- Fun discussions
- And much more!

ZONDERVAN®
.com